The

Ruby
Tear Catcher

An Iranian Woman's Story of Intolerance

A Novel

Nahid Sewell

Published by Summerhill Press
www.therubytearcatcher.com
Copyright © 2010 by Summerhill Press

This is a work of fiction. Names, characters, places, and events are either the product of the author's imagination or are used fictionally. While the story is based on historical events and every effort has been made to ensure the accuracy of the timeline, some dates and events may not be exact. Neither the author nor the publisher assumes any responsibility for such errors. Any resemblance to actual persons, living or dead, business establishments, events, or locales is entirely coincidental. The publisher does not have any control over and does not assume any responsibility for author or third-party websites or their content.

Edited by: Kathy Nelson
Cover Artwork and Imaging by: Daniel Peters
Book Design by: Julie Green

Library of Congress Cataloging-in-Publication Data
Sewell, Nahid

The Ruby Tear Catcher / An Iranian Woman's Story of Intolerance / Nahid Sewell

Library of Congress Control Number: 2010903083

ISBN 978-0-9826763-3-2

Printed in the United States of America

Dedicated to my brave sisters
in the Middle East.

Acknowledgments

First and foremost, I must express my deepest gratitude to my husband, Gerry, for your unwavering support and for the dozens of times you read, re-read, and edited each draft of this book with painstaking care. As in our life together, you've transformed my black and white into a beautiful, colorful masterpiece of art. Thank you.

I am eternally grateful to the book clubs, from Illinois to Colorado, who read my early drafts and provided invaluable, honest feedback. I couldn't have seen the things you saw, and you've helped me more than you realize. I am also very thankful to many friends, colleagues, and agents for their candid opinions and advice throughout this journey, including Bob Tipton, for sharing your knowledge and wisdom, and my first editor, Debra Ginsberg, whose direction led me to a story with a great beginning and beautiful ending. Thank you, Helen, Lorraine, Ken, Randy, Sherri, Ray, and Claire. Many thanks to my sister, whose honesty helped make the story relevant and interesting.

Special thanks to my editor, Kathy Nelson, for your exquisite work, your advice, and for exposing me to words I never knew existed. Thanks to Dan Peters for the beautiful images and for your boundless creativity. Many thanks to Alexa for your generosity; you are beautiful. And Julie Green for wanting to be a part of this project . . . just because. My deep and ongoing gratitude to Julie Umnus for your world-class marketing. And thank you, Brian Tucker, for your creative support.

Last, I must thank my family. My sons, for the time I took away from you to work on this project; my father, the inspiration for all of the wonderful things in *Baba*, and for searching the bazaars to find me a beautiful, antique tear catcher; and my mother, for recounting details of traditions I'd long forgotten, and for giving up her own dreams to raise her children.

My name is Leila, and my story begins in the hills north of Tehran where I was born thirty years ago. Except for my years in college, Tehran has been my home. The Tehran of my youth bustled late into the night, with children in the park enjoying the taste and texture of blue and pink cotton candy on their tongues while their parents cracked pumpkin seeds and gossiped with neighbors. Clandestine lovers met hand in hand at twilight, dreaming of romance and of the day they would marry. Here I learned to savor life in its multitude of colors and tastes. I embraced the scorching heat and dust of summer, knowing winter's fresh snow would cleanse the air, blanket trees, and scatter glistening ice palaces atop the Alborz Mountains. Back then, I lived in the safety of my family, my community, my beautiful city.

Today it's a different Tehran. Life is a monochromatic gray canvas desperate for brushstrokes of color. Children are secluded in the safety of homes. Lovers, if discovered, are arrested, even stoned to death. Soldiers' heavy boots stamp bas-relief footprints in the powdery white snow.

Aside from my memories, a ruby tear catcher is all I have left from the Tehran of my youth.

ONE

It was a gray morning in 1988, the air rich with a loamy dampness after a rare rain the night before. I looked out the kitchen window at the swallow bathing in a shallow puddle on the brick patio. His fluttering wings sprayed raindrops across his back as he flew away. I took two aspirin from the cabinet and swallowed them dry to ease my headache. Forcing a good-bye to my husband, Farhad, I prepared to make the trip to my grandmother's. Yes, by this time I was married, with another childhood dream tottering on the verge of extinction. Like other men in Iran, Farhad expected his wife to cater to his desires and respond only with deference, even in the face of a sour mood or a beating. He spent years attending university in the U.S., but if he'd ever held Western notions of respect for women, they'd been tossed aside long ago. Small deviations in daily routines caused him to seethe with anger, yet he blithely ignored obscene atrocities right before his eyes. If dinner wasn't ready when he came home, even if he was hours earlier than expected or if he was late and the rice had dried, I was to blame. But humans slaughtered in the name of religion raised in him less empathy than a beggar on the street.

As I got ready to leave that morning, I saw reflected in the mirror the image of a stranger, face drawn with anguish, a flaring purple bruise on her cheek, eyes swollen and bloodshot from weeping. I gently touched the cheek Farhad had slapped the night before and shivered in pain, an outward sign of my soul's growing despair. The blow came when I confronted him about his mistress. By morning, he was remorseful, with yet another promise to end his physical violence. But his abusive streak, concealed earlier in our relationship, now pushed me deeper into darkened isolation. How did I arrive at this place, and how much longer could I tolerate this life?

For weeks now I'd been visiting my grandmother every day. She lived alone, and her health was steadily declining. Maman Rouhi, as we called her, clung to her Iranian traditions, never comfortable removing her head scarf. Approaching eighty, she stood barely five feet tall, her hands tanned by the sun and gnarled with arthritis. She was wiry and emaciated yet possessed a hidden endurance that belied her frail appearance. Black kohl decorating her dark brown eyes, she was every bit the classic Persian grandmother.

When my parents fled Iran, she lost the home she'd shared with us for years, but she retained our cook, Fatemeh, and Mahmood, our chauffeur. It broke her heart to think of letting them go; they'd loyally served our family for nearly thirty years. Plus, the extra help and companionship were welcome. As a child, Fatemeh spoiled me, sneaking after-dinner treats my mother denied me. And Mahmood, involuntary eavesdropper on my conversations with girlfriends as he drove us here and there, was like a surrogate parent. With a Hercule Poirot mustache gracing his gaunt tan face, he cared for me as a father for his daughter.

Now outside my house, Mahmood stood curbside in his dark jacket and cap holding open the back door of the old Range Rover. He'd retired his Western ties but took great pride in his chauffeur's cap, a relic of kinder days. The battered green car with its cracked and faded black leather seats held memories of my childhood, all girlish giggles and whispered confidences.

"Good morning, Leila *khanoom*," he said, smiling broadly.

"Good morning, Mahmood *agha*." The agha salutation showed my respect despite his societal ranking. Ashamed to be seen as yet another abused Iranian wife, I pulled my head scarf closer around my face, hoping he wouldn't notice the bruise. I put on oversized dark sunglasses to hide my swollen eyes. Whatever he may have noticed, he said nothing.

He closed the door behind me and began the short journey to Grandmother's. The narrow streets overflowed with cars and trucks. Thick smoke billowed from rattling mufflers, swelling the opaque brown cloud that blanketed the city. In a mad dash, drivers jockeyed for position with blatant disregard for lane markings and traffic signals, competing with bicycles, motorbikes, and pedestrians who, against all odds, were rarely the victims of this chaos.

Glancing in the mirror, Mahmood said, "Your grandmother believes this to be an ominous day. This morning, while she was having breakfast, a little bird hit the kitchen window and died. She took it as a bad sign and is quite upset."

"Being alone isn't good for her, and she really misses my parents."

"How are your father and mother? Have you heard from them?" Mahmood's love and respect for my father was unwavering, and the guilty pronouncements by the Governing Council would not sway his opinion. He would never be convinced that my father was anything but a blessing from Allah.

"They're well, Mahmood, and send greetings. Maman's not happy to be away from home, but they're starting to make a new life in Paris. And they live close to Uncle Mohsen. Of course, Maman still complains of her aches and pains."

"With all due respect, her aches and pains have their source in her head," he said with a hearty laugh.

"You're so right." Since my brother and I were old enough to notice, my mother was constant victim to new maladies and afflictions. Even Grandmother laughed as Maman bartered for sympathy down the wandering paths of hypochondria.

We turned onto Negar Alley, now called Shaheed Salimi, presumably honoring some martyr. Following the revolution, streets were renamed for martyrs and religious figures, but whether it was due to rebellion or just difficulty remembering, most of us privately used the old names. Mahmood was out of the car holding the door before I could move.

"You spoil me. Farhad would disapprove."

"Then he's a fool, little one. Kindness is a blessing always returned," he said, with a short bow. While he would never admit it, Mahmood disapproved of my husband.

Climbing the concrete steps to the house, I opened the polished dark mahogany door, glistening from its new coat of varnish. Inside, I heard Maman Rouhi. "*Azizam*, I'm upstairs." I loved it when she used that endearing term.

I saw the beaming face of the world's best cook, besides my mother. "*Salam*, Fatemeh *khanoom*. How are you today?" I handed her my *roopoosh*, the black cloak covering my body, a "gift" of the Islamic government to Iranian women. For now, I kept on my head scarf.

"As well as can be expected for one so old," she said, fishing for a compliment.

"Don't be silly. You look younger than me, and you're twice as healthy," I replied, playing my role. "You still have no wrinkles."

She noticed the bruise on my cheek, but in deference turned her head. With a gentle smile, she scurried back to the kitchen to make fresh tea on the electric samovar. The Russian brass samovar that used burning coals to heat the water had long ago been placed in storage. The stairs creaked as I climbed to the second floor, holding the smooth wooden banister.

"*Salam*, Maman Rouhi."

"Come here," she said, holding out her arms. I took off my sunglasses and slipped them in my purse. With her failing eyesight, she'd never notice the bruise.

A bright rose-printed bedspread covered her spindly legs as she leaned against the pillows. Sunlight streamed through the nearby window and glistened off the polished wood floors, highlighting a corner of the Tabriz carpet my grandfather had bought for her many years ago. It was an antique, its dense orange and beige floral motif adding dazzling colors to the otherwise bare room. A small mahogany table stood next to her bed, a much-loved picture of my grandfather and another of my parents displayed beside a worn copy of the Koran. There was a picture of my brother, Amir, in his navy cap and gown, the white tassel dangling to the right, his broad smile showing the dazzle of naturally perfect teeth. I'd taken the picture in the U.S. at his college graduation, a ceremony only I could attend. Maman Rouhi held my hand as I sat on the corner of her bed. A wide strand of straight brown hair wandered haphazardly across her wrinkled forehead like a curtain drawn at the theater, tucked behind an ear. I smiled as I caught a glimpse of the birthmark on her neck, the one she'd passed on to my mother and me. Her other hand clutched her amber prayer beads, clicking each bead as they slipped through her trembling fingers. I knew she was worried when the beads, a pilgrimage gift my grandfather brought back from Mecca, were in her hand. She held me for several minutes, mumbling prayers in Arabic.

Fatemeh walked in carrying a silver tray with small glass teacups on

delicate gold inlaid saucers flanked by sugar cubes and *nabat* rock candy.
I loved letting the tea slowly melt the sweetness of *nabat* in my mouth.

"I gave your grandmother some aspirin this morning," Fatemeh
said, averting her eyes from my bruised cheek. "She was a bit feverish,
so I called Dr. Soleimani and asked him to stop by later."

I handed Grandmother her teacup as she popped a piece of *nabat* in
her mouth. She slipped it under her tongue, a trick she'd taught me to
prolong the pleasure, and began sipping the strong dark liquid while
warming her hands with the cup. Like a flower braced against winter,
Maman Rouhi looked shriveled and drawn with concern. I brushed
back her hair, feeling tiny beads of a worry sweat lining the furrows
along her forehead.

Suddenly from downstairs there was a loud commotion, angry
shouts, and stomping feet. Grandmother grasped my hand tightly as I
stood up and wouldn't let go. Without notice, three uniformed men
barged into the room, rifles in hand, while Fatemeh and Mahmood
trailed behind, yelling they must wait to be escorted.

"Why do you barge into an old woman's house?" I asked the uniformed man in the lead.

"*Allah o Akbar*. In the name of God Almighty, you are under arrest
for crimes against the Islamic Republic." His eyes glinted with an unfor-
giving light.

"What crimes? I've committed no crimes." I tried to sound confident
and defiant, aware my hands were trembling.

"You are accountable for crimes committed by your family. You are
coming with us."

"Where is the warrant for my arrest?" I demanded, knowing full
well they wouldn't leave empty-handed.

As the soldier grabbed me from behind and shoved me toward the
door, my grandmother shot from bed with a vitality that surprised everyone. She grasped my arm and began pulling me away. With the back of
his hand, the soldier struck her, knocking her down, prayer beads bouncing noisily like amber pearls across the wood floor, resting only as they
bumped the edge of the Tabriz rug. I watched in horror as another soldier
pointed his rifle at Mahmood and Fatemeh as they rushed to help her. I
felt something strike the back of my head, and then everything went dark.

TWO

I awoke sprawled on the cold floor of a dark cell. Still dazed, I struggled to stand. Reaching behind, I gently probed the lump on the back of my head and surveyed my surroundings. It was a low-ceilinged room, perhaps three-by-three meters, damp and rank with the stench of former tenants. A dangling bare bulb cast a dim light through a barred window in the cell door. In its pale glow, I could almost make out the space that enclosed me like a sarcophagus. One stained concrete wall bore vertical scratches, perhaps a prior occupant's attempt to calendar the days. In one corner of the floor, spotted brown with water marks and dried blood, was a hole—the toilet. In another corner, there was a platform with cracked wooden slats nailed to a rickety frame. The planks that might once have held a scent of pine now stank of urine and sweat. Atop the frame was a thin gray mattress with a threadbare blanket haphazardly tossed at one end. It had been bright yellow but now was faded, randomly splashed with shapes of gray and brown and equally infused with the smell of decay. I sat on this bed and hugged the worn blanket to my chest, trying to quiet the chaotic thoughts running through my mind. I had no idea how long I'd been here. Was my grandmother hurt? Was she alive?

Fear gripped me at the sound of approaching footsteps. A tall, brawny uniformed guard, his black beard untrimmed and matted, unlocked the heavy metal door and swung it open. Tossing a bundle on the floor in front of me, he spat "Put it on!" and left without another word. The sound of his footsteps vanished with a loud clang as the outer cell door slammed shut.

Inside the bundle were a rough gray gown and black head scarf. With a glimmer of rebellion, I thought to ignore his order. My anger was rising but so was fear, and it seemed wiser to do as I was told. I changed into the sackcloth robe and tried to clear my head. With no windows, I could see nothing of the outside world, and the only sounds to penetrate my solitude were echoing footsteps or an occasional distant moan from a fellow prisoner down the hall. I sat on the bed, wondering when Farhad would angrily storm in and take me home.

My arrest had nothing to do with my political views or any crime I'd committed. My father's anti-government sentiments had reached the wrong ears. My first reaction was righteous indignation; I wouldn't take this lying down. Still a bit queasy, I stumbled to the cell door, pounded it with my fist, and screamed into the empty hallway, "Let me out of here. You have no right to hold me. I've done nothing wrong."

My cries echoed off the bare walls as I protested the injustice with what little strength I had. At first, there was no response, and I continued, "You have no right to hold me. I demand to be released." I felt throbbing in my hand but kept pounding.

The outer metal door creaked opened as three soldiers marched to my cell. Finally, some answers. Perhaps Farhad had come. The cell door swung open, and a soldier, the leader, stepped into the room. The other two stayed behind him, rifles pointed at my chest.

"Why am I being held?" I demanded. My legs were shaking, but I steadied myself and prepared for the face-off.

He made no reply, but without breaking stride or looking me in the eye, he swung and hit me viciously with the back of his hand, knocking me hard against the wall. "Silence, whore!" he screamed. "Any more noise from you and I'll put a bullet in your head."

I struggled to stand, as his blow left me dazed, but I faced him, holding back tears, and drew on the strength my father had instilled in me. Arms stiff at my side, I stared in the face of his angry shouts. He pulled his pistol and shoved the muzzle to my forehead.

"Lucky for you the Interrogator wants you, or I'd shoot you here and now like a dog, you traitor."

For several seconds I returned his stare, feeling the cold steel of the pistol. Fear rose like bile, but I fought it back. Finally, he holstered his weapon and motioned the guards to collect my things. The door shut with a clang, and I crumbled to my knees as tears came unbidden. There would be no quick intervention, no immediate release. The madness consuming my country had now swallowed me. I was in the belly of the beast.

THREE

Sometime after the guards left, my shaking subsided. I collapsed on the bed, pulling the rough blanket over me for comfort and within minutes drifted into a dream.

My dream was awash with echoes of raindrops. Rain is infrequent in Tehran, but when it comes, it's welcomed joyously like a long-awaited guest. Raindrops dancing off the trees in our courtyard played like Rachmaninoff in my ears, freckling the flagstone patio. I'd spend hours staring out my bedroom window as summer showers washed the dust from vibrant rose petals and left spider webs gleaming like dazzling diamond strands on the fence around the pool. My carefree childhood blossomed and flourished in that house, a two-story stone and stucco structure in a posh neighborhood north of Tehran. Our backyard was expansive. Tuscan pines guarded an eight-foot red brick wall like sentries surrounding the estate. The garden was filled with fruit trees; my favorite was a solitary pomegranate tree tucked near the back amidst tall bushes. It was my haven when sadness gripped me. In spring, its reddish orange flowers perfumed the air and painted the branches like sunset. In fall, the fruit ripened and hung like round ruby jewels in the leafy shadows. And in winter, tinkles of icy light cavorted on the few dead leaves still hanging on bare branches. My dog, Rostam, a black and white German Shepherd, would prance about the yard, head uplifted, tongue out-stretched as rainwater caressed his face. When my parents gave him to me as a birthday gift, I chose his name from stories my father read from the Shahnameh. Rostam was an epic hero of ancient Persia, a warrior king who defeated a dragon in defense of Iran. Every little girl longed for just such a protector. Rostam became my friend and confidante, prowling the yard and guarding my flank as I sneaked my first cigarette in the farthest corner of the yard. And he'd sit patiently by me with sad eyes as I cried under the pomegranate tree over lost friendships or love.

My dream of carefree days was suddenly shattered. I jolted from sleep, sat up in bed, and rubbed my eyes. How long had I been out? Where was I? I looked around the cell wondering if this were another dream. But soon the stench in the room confirmed it was all too real. My feelings fluctuated as I paced the confine, trying to understand why I'd been detained. They wanted to arrest my father, but why take me now, so many months after he and Maman had fled the country? And where was Farhad? What was he going through? Was he sick with worry, searching for me desperately?

My prison routine began, filled with uncertainty, confusion, and anger. Occasionally a guard approached and shoved a plate of food beneath a cut in the door. I quickly learned to return the plate through the same rough-hewn cut or I wouldn't soon eat again. For water, they delivered a plastic pitcher every few days. If it ran out, I drank from the short hose that served to flush the hole-in-the-floor latrine. The lingering stench of my excrement and the collected waste of the prison was a constant reminder of my situation.

In time I grew accustomed to the hard plank bed, but I couldn't get used to the ever-present darkness. I was permitted no sense of time. No dazzling sun marked the morning; no transient moon tracked the night. The only source of light was a bare bulb outside the cell, its changing mood reflected with intermittent flickering. As days and nights passed in solitude, nightmares became a regular occurrence.

One day, after so long alone, they came to take me. The door swung open, and my nemesis from the first day entered.

"Stand and put your hands in front of you," he demanded.

I did as I was told, and the second soldier roughly cuffed my hands and pulled a burlap bag over my head. Dragging me out, they led me down the hallway. The blindfold created the chilling effect of powerlessness and terror.

In the interrogation room, they pulled the bag off my head and forcibly thrust me down onto a small chair. My eyes squinted to adjust to the bright light from the bare fluorescent bulbs in the ceiling. Handcuffs stayed. Four armed, uniformed men stood about the room. They were the Pasdaran, the Iranian revolutionary army. The windowless room smelled damp and stale; I guessed we were underground. The man I came to know as "the Interrogator," Lieutenant Mehraban, was anything but kind, denying his surname. He entered the room dressed in army fatigues and mirrored sunglasses, which he kept on during our sessions. In all the times I was dragged before him, I never saw the man's eyes. He was slightly taller than I, perhaps five-foot-eight, and thin to the point of emaciation. He bore the stereotypical Muslim look, his salt-and-pepper hair cropped short, his beard long and untrimmed. Unlike the other guards, his khaki uniform was neatly pressed, silver braids on each shoulder. He carried a riding crop, which he'd slap against the battered table, to spice up interrogations and intimidate the prisoner. Lt. Mehraban methodically began his barrage of questions.

"Where is your father?" Pausing for emphasis, he paced behind me, his boots clicking across the concrete floor. "By the time we arrived at the house, no one was there. Who alerted him? Who helped him escape?" He paused and stood next to me. As he leaned down, I felt his breath against my face and smelled his day-old sweat. "If you don't tell me where he is, perhaps your grandmother will. How well do you think she might stand up to interrogation?"

He probed my weakness. For all I knew, my grandmother was already dead, though I immediately pushed that thought from my head. I noticed a short, stout soldier intently following the proceedings. He looked away as I caught his eye. The Interrogator stepped in front of me, arms folded across his chest. "You hold her," he commanded, nodding to a soldier who stepped behind me. With another nod, a second soldier moved in front. As though choreographed, the man in front hit me while the other held me to the chair. His blows were not designed to bring the relief of unconsciousness but to prolong pain. Each stinging strike felt as though it were shattering my face.

"Why have I been arrested?' I pleaded. "I've done nothing wrong. Please, contact my husband. He'll tell you I'm innocent." But in a flash, my defiance took over. "My husband is from a rich, well-known family. He will have you all executed if you don't let me go immediately." This time he hit me even harder. The sting brought a pool of tears to my eyes and hot swelling to my cheek. This dance continued to the grunts of my assailant and my whimpering cries, interrupted only by another round of questions. It was an eternity before they were done. My face was bruised and battered, one eye swollen shut, and blood was flowing from my mouth and nose. But I had nothing to say. Their condemnation of my father was ludicrous. He despised the new régime for destroying Iran's economy and the people's spirit. They accused him of treason for his anti-war statements. What father wouldn't rail against violence as he grieved the sons of Iran slaughtered in the senseless war with Iraq? Regardless of threats and accusations, I'd embrace death before I'd speak.

Lt. Mehraban sat behind a table, studying a scribbled notepad. Without looking up, he waved a dismissive hand and calmly said, "This is useless. Kill her."

Taking out his pistol, the guard pushed its cold muzzle against my forehead and pulled the trigger before I could even close my eyes. "Click."

Lt. Mehraban looked up with a sneering grin, "Ah, lucky this time. Get her out of here."

Two soldiers dragged me to my cell after pulling the bag over my head. One lingered outside as the other walked me to the bed. As I collapsed, the short, stout soldier who'd watched intently bent down and picked up the blanket. He looked over at his colleague, whose back was to us, quickly placed the blanket over me, and left. I lay for hours, shaking quietly, listening for a sound, a smell, anything to comfort me. The light outside flickered, then went out completely. In the pitch dark, gripped by terror and hopelessness, I sought memories, my only source of comfort and sanity. My thoughts wandered to days when life was a joy, back to my beautiful Tehran.

FOUR

Tehran, 1963

It was the night of *yalda*, the winter solstice. My brother, Amir, and I sat under the *korsi* in the family room, listening intently as my mother told stories. I'd helped Maman set up the korsi earlier. Together, we lifted the corners of the oversized, multicolored quilt and laid it over a low wooden table. Amir, who was two years older, carried a round copper container filled with smoldering coals into the room. I wanted to do it, but Maman insisted it was a task better suited for boys. The coals glowed brightly in the hot dish, but Amir, at age seven, understood the danger and carried it with heavy kitchen gloves. Maman lifted one end of the quilt as Amir slid the coals under the table and gently pushed it to the center. Together, we laid checkered woolen blankets of green, red, and yellow around the *korsi* for seats and oversized cushions for backrests.

The night of *yalda* was exciting. We were allowed to stay up past bedtime and indulge in late-harvest pomegranates, ending the evening with hot tea and nabat. Seated on the scratchy blankets and resting against the pillows, Amir and I reached for the clay fruit bowl in the center of the korsi. We raced to be first to take the biggest pomegranate. I grabbed my first and began to knead it with my thumbs, being careful not to split open the pliant scarlet skin. Amir followed, moving his fingers faster to beat me to the finish. Maman kept reminding us to slow down so as not to crack the skin and get red juice on our clothes; the stains would never come out. When satisfied that every seed inside had been bruised to bleed, we'd lift the fruit to our lips and squeeze the skin together with our teeth until we punctured a hole, all the while massaging the round fruit until the first burst of the tangy juices flooded our mouths. Deftly, we sucked the nectar from our pomegranates and, when satisfied that there was nothing left but pulp, tossed the remains in another bowl and went after the next. With Baba working late, Maman sat with us under the korsi, stretching her legs to the side to avoid the hot coals.

"Ready for stories?" she asked, a contented smile on her round plump face as she watched us savor the sweet juice. Her raven dark hair was pulled back in a bun, a few rebellious curls poking free on the sides. Her translucent ivory skin bore none of the wrinkles that would later mark the pain of passing years. To me at age five, she was the prettiest maman on earth. My eyes fell upon the small teardrop-shaped birthmark on her neck, just below her right ear, and I touched my own replica, as though to make sure it was still there. She was still in her house dress, with white flower petals cast against a pale blue background, and a rich wine-colored shawl pulled about her shoulders to ward off the cool evening air. The glow of the coals seemed to embrace me in gentle waves, warm and comforting. Their smoldering scent rose from under the blanket and tickled my nose. Amir remained focused on draining his pomegranate, while I gave Maman my rapt attention.

"Maman, tell us 'bout when I was born," I begged for my favorite story.

"Not again," moaned Amir in feigned disgust. My hurt look quickly brought a teasing smile. While we were two years apart and competitive, I loved Amir fiercely, just as he loved me. We bickered as brothers and sisters will but in truth were inseparable. Even at this young age, Amir was devilishly handsome. His face already displayed sharp lines and a strong chin like Baba, tempered with the fullness of Maman's glowing cheeks. His jet black hair wasn't curly like mine, but parted neatly on the left, falling just over his ears. When he laughed, his dark eyes danced with glee, and thick eyebrows rose and fell like gull's wings. A yawn escaped his lips; it had been a long day, and we were both a little sleepy, the warmth of the *korsi* enhancing our drowsy stupor.

"Leila, you were born in a tent in the mountains of Sohanak, just north of Tehran. Back then, each summer our entire family would go to Sohanak for a holiday. That particular summer, we packed our things and headed for the mountains."

"But Maman, weren't you soooo big?" I extended my arms in a huge circle before my little belly, puffing out my cheeks.

She laughed, "Yes, I was so big. But we wanted Amir to spend time with his cousins, and your father needed the vacation."

Amir and I slumped into pillows on either side of Maman, drawing closer to the radiant heat as the outside temperature dipped. We listened as she told us in great detail about the day I was born in their camping tent.

Sohanak is a quaint village, a short drive north of Tehran. Its Main Street consisted of a barbershop, small general store, funeral home, and bakery specializing in *lavash* bread. Just off Main Street on a winding side road sat the town mosque, boasting a century-old tree in its center courtyard. To the north, rolling farms nestled among the hills. We stayed at a farm owned by family friends, over thirty acres but lacking permanent buildings or animals. Tall unruly trees, overgrown shrubs, and colorful wildflowers spotted the hills. A furrowed field baked by the summer sun resembling a brown, threadbare carpet sloped down one hillside. Nearby, an unspoiled mountain stream provided water, shallow enough to be no threat to children, but deep enough for a bracing dip on hot summer afternoons.

The camping tradition had begun once grandchildren arrived in an effort to maintain family ties. The families arranged their tents in the shade in close proximity. Each day the women prepared meals over gas burners or charcoal grills. Cooking was not a chore, rather an occasion for passionate discourse about husbands, children, and neighbors, interspersed with idle gossip. For the men, this was a much-needed family vacation, away from the hubbub of work and the pollution in Tehran. The kids loved being immersed in nature, free to roam the nearby hills, pick flowers, or skip rocks in the stream.

"Can we have our tea now?" I interrupted, excited at the idea of tea at such a late hour.

Maman poured the tea that had been brewing atop the brass samovar in the corner of the family room. She pushed the silver bowl of *nabat* and sugar closer, reminding us to take only one. Sitting up, I felt the chilly night air on my shoulders, but the hot coals by my toes and the warm tea slowly melting *nabat* under my tongue were enough to keep me toasty. Maman continued with her story.

Evenings were cool, mountain breezes chasing away the daytime heat. The family gathered outside the tents by the flickering light of kerosene lamps, enjoying the clear night sky and bright moon. The uncles, smoking their Marlboros, by turns enthralled the children with ghostly tales, always right before bedtime. The women, ultimately tasked with getting kids to bed, reprimanded the storytellers for the timing of their yarns. But relaxation was the rule, days filled with sunshine and simple pleasures, life peaceful and uneventful for the two weeks.

"And that's when you decided to join the family," Maman smiled sweetly.

It was a scorching day, the mountain breeze offering little solace, everyone contentedly lounging. The men were engrossed in Iropoly, Monopoly retrofitted for Iran, when my mother felt the early pangs of labor. At first no one took her seriously, but when her contractions grew stronger and more frequent, panic set in. There was no time for a drive to a hospital in Tehran, so they sent for the village midwife. The elders kept shooing the kids away from the birth tent. They honored their parents' request, only to return by stealth and sneak a peek through tiny holes in the rear of the tent until discovered again.

"And then out you came to greet the whole family," Maman said. "You had dark curly hair, big brown eyes, ten fingers and ten toes." Amir giggled at the mention of my fingers and toes. I was getting sleepy, having slid down, my head on the pillow, eyes fixed on Maman, struggling to stay at half-mast.

Each time Maman told this story, she filled in different gaps. She recounted aunts and uncles rushing to boil water on the gas stove; cousins watching in horror as sheets bloodied in the process were carried from the tent. Although they were thoroughly washed, my cousin Neda, who was four at the time, refused to ever sleep on the sheets again. And finally, Maman always concluded with my favorite part of the story: "We paid the midwife with a loaf of bread and a dozen eggs."

With my head in her lap, I drifted off to sleep.

FIVE

The first home I can remember was a quaint ranch in the south of Tehran with a small yard and a persimmon tree teeming with orange fruit. The house had a *hose*, a small shallow pool of water in the middle of the yard. We used it for play, but before the days of indoor plumbing, the hose was used to wash dishes and laundry. It was also for the pre-*namaz* cleansing of the body. I remember visiting relatives carrying out the ritual washing before facing Mecca for prayers.

Like all women I knew, my mother was a homemaker, a skilled seamstress who enjoyed knitting and crocheting. I was the recipient of many handmade sweaters and scarves. My favorite was the long scarf she made when I was seven. I had to wrap the scarf around my neck several times to keep it from touching the floor. It was brightly colored with stripes of orange, red, blue, and yellow, just like my crayon rainbow creation that sat framed on Baba's desk.

Maman had also crocheted a lavish bedspread, creamy in color, with intertwined patterns of daisies and flower petals bound together by soft, twisting vines. It took her a full year to make. I remember being scolded after I jumped on my parents' bed and unraveled a flower in the middle. I was in tears, but she consoled me, saying she scolded me only because the bedspread was an heirloom that she would one day give to me when I had a family of my own.

Maman was a marvelous cook, too, an expert at rice dishes and Persian *khoresht* stews. My favorite was her *abghoost*, a rich simmered stew of lamb, beans, tomatoes, and potatoes. Though we had a house-keeper, Maman insisted I help with household chores. One day she handed me a broom and told me to sweep the second-floor hallway. "Why can't the servants do it?" I asked.

"Because you need to learn to do these things for yourself."

"How come Amir doesn't have to?"

"Amir is a boy; it's different for boys. You must learn to cook, clean, and sew so that you can take care of your own family someday."

"Amir will have to take care of his own family too. He always pretends he's reading and gets off the hook. It's not fair, Maman."

"Be quiet now, and do as you're told. And leave Amir out of this," she said, wagging a finger. I knew it was a no-win situation.

I didn't understand why things were different for Amir. He got to take swimming lessons while I practiced stitching. Amir went off to Uncle Mortezah's stationery shop, while I stayed home to clean herbs and make flowers out of radishes. When he returned from his apprentice trips, Maman excitedly inquired about his day, then asked *me* to bring him tea so he could "unwind." Later, Amir would tell me about the fun he'd had, making me even more jealous that I didn't get to do the things he did. At times like these I wished I were a boy.

In Iran, weekends begin on Friday, so Thursday nights the family often gathered at Maman Rouhi's house. Adults would discuss the week's events while children played. Neda, my favorite cousin, and I often wandered away from others, finding a quiet spot to chat. We talked about parents, annoying siblings, school friends. One evening, together we approached our parents in a united cause.

"Baba, can Neda and I sleep at Maman Rouhi's tonight?"

"Me too, Baba," echoed Amir.

"Please?" Neda begged her mother.

"I'd love to have the children's company," Maman Rouhi chimed in, and the matter was resolved.

Sleepovers with Maman Rouhi meant a night of exquisite entertainment. My grandparents lived in a grand old house with an expansive flat-top roof that offered a view of the entire estate, the pool, and the colorful gardens. Daytime on the roof was stifling, with the sun beating on its surface till it burnt our bare feet. But as evening fell, cool breezes transformed the sizzling rooftop into a welcome open plaza, just right for gazing at the moon and stars dotting the night sky.

When permission was granted for a sleepover, my cousins and I anticipated a night of stories, dreamy moonlight, and chocolate fish beneath our pillows. Maman Rouhi helped roll out homemade mattresses on the roof floor. We each grabbed a pillow and blanket for when cool evening breezes arrived. Then we sat in a semi-circle around Grandmother for the real entertainment. Maman Rouhi had a knack for telling enchanting stories. My grandfather sat with us, as mesmerized as we children by his wife's fables. I loved it when she told stories of my parents' wedding.

"Your father is from Esfahan," she began, "the ancient Persian city filled with beautiful blue-tiled mosques. Old kings of Persia and their royal families lived in Esfahan in magnificent palaces overlooking a polo field and watched teams on horseback play the game of kings."

"So is Baba royalty?" I asked, bursting with pride.

"In our eyes, yes, *azizam*," she replied. "I remember the first time he came to our house," Maman Rouhi said, her smile exposing the gap in her front teeth. "He was a tall, handsome man, his dark hair curling behind his ears, just like yours, Leila. Your mother was just fifteen, but already she had captured his heart."

Things progressed quickly, and following a lavish society wedding, my parents settled in a small house. The only child from a family of eight to attend college, my father taught Persian literature at Tehran University while my mother became a homemaker.

"It wasn't long before Amir was born, and then two years later, Leila came along," she concluded.

As it grew late, Grandmother passed around a glass of cold water and told us to lie down for sleep. While her stories transported us to a dream world, we anxiously anticipated the end. As we lay down, we each slid a hand under our pillows and found a chocolate fish. Though by now it was tradition, each time felt like the first discovery of this magical treasure. Lying on the mattress in the glow of the moonlight, I studied my fish for a few moments, which was enclosed in a multi-hued aluminum wrapper with a fish-scale design, eyes, and fins. Neda and I huddled closer, comparing and exchanging, although beneath the colorful wrappings, all were identical. Once share and compare concluded, I slowly unveiled my fish and slipped the sweet candy into my mouth. I took my time, letting it gradually melt me away to sleep.

SIX

Tehran, 1988

I awoke in a cold sweat, holding my knees to my chest, trembling in terror. Somewhere during my dreams of childhood, the nightmare of prison and torture had returned. There was no pillow, no chocolate fish, and no grandmother telling tales. I hugged the frayed blanket closer and tried to steady my emotions. I wasn't sure if it was morning or night. The light bulb that had flickered out of existence before now shone brightly. Had someone replaced it, or did the old bulb find new life? I tried to lift my head and sit up, but sharp pain shot down my back. On the second attempt, I gave up; the agony was too great.

I could still feel the cold metal of the gun pressed to my forehead, see contempt blazing in the young soldier's eyes. Why? What had I done to him, to any of them? In that instant, fear had paralyzed me. My senseless death would devastate my parents. The click of the hammer on an empty chamber brought little relief. Clearly, I was nothing to them. My life could be tossed aside on a whim like a useless rag.

My meandering thoughts came to a halt at the sound of heavy footsteps. In a moment of panic, I ignored the pain and sat up in bed. Perhaps Farhad and his father were here to gain my release. My hopes were dashed as the short, stout soldier appeared outside my cell. He paused briefly by the barred window without looking in and continued his walk. Perhaps he wanted to say something but changed his mind. I pulled myself out of bed as quickly as my battered body allowed and moved to the cell door. I pressed my cheek against the window bars to see him, but he had passed from sight. Counting on his return, I listened for his footsteps, and the moment he was in sight, I reached between the bars and said, "*Agha*, can you help me, please?" He continued walking. "*Agha*, please. May I ask you something, please?" I begged. No answer. "*Agha*, just an aspirin, something for the pain," my voice trailed to a whisper as he disappeared. When I returned to the bed, lifting the worn blanket, I saw blood stains on the mattress. I searched my arms and legs for a sign of bleeding but found nothing. I touched my face and held up my hands searching for signs of blood.

Despite my body's demands, I'd been reluctant to use the toilet. The thought of getting close to the noxious-smelling hole made me nauseous. But I had to. I walked over, holding my breath. Crouching, I positioned my legs on either side of the hole in the ground, leaning against the wall for support. I wasn't used to traditional Iranian toilets, having grown up with the Western variety. My battered body could barely tolerate the squatting position. Half-crouched over the stinking hole, I noticed the blood dripping down my inner thigh. How was I going to deal with this?

I walked to the cell door and scanned for a sign of life, but there was none. I beat my fist on the door to draw attention, but all I managed was a dull thump. I looked around for something to make noise and saw the soup spoon under the bed; it must have fallen off my food tray. I rattled the spoon against the cell window bars. It felt good, my momentary act of rebellion. Within minutes, the short guard approached, holding his rifle. "What's all this noise?" he demanded angrily.

"*Agha*, I'm sorry, but I need something." I was trying to determine how to broach the subject. I hadn't even dared discuss my period with my mother when at thirteen I experienced my rite of passage to woman-hood. I'd quietly gone with Neda to a store where I wouldn't be recognized and bought sanitary napkins. Now, I stood in front of my jailor, a man no less, facing the same gripping fear.

"You all need something. What else is new? Give me that and stop the noise," he demanded as he grabbed the spoon and turned to walk away.

"*Agha*, please. Please, it's important. Is there a female guard you can send?"

He ignored me and continued walking.

"*To ra Khodah*, I beg you. I need female things. Please . . ."

The metal door slammed shut. I went back to the bed but didn't want to sit. How would I deal with my monthly cycle?

At least I knew I'd been here almost a month. In the distance, I heard footsteps, not as pronounced as before. I froze, holding my breath and listening. Fear arose again as memories of the last beating engulfed me. Please, not again. But these footsteps were quiet, unlike the pounding of military boots. I watched the slowly moving shadow of the approaching figure. It was a woman in Islamic *hijab*, holding a rifle, the first woman I'd seen since my arrest. She bent down and slipped a small brown bag through the opening in the door and, without a word, disappeared back down the long hallway. There was silence again.

Inside the bag were several sanitary napkins bound with a thin blue rubber band and a pair of fresh new underwear. I lay in bed a short while later, hopes revived. In the heart of these atrocities, I'd stumbled onto a small glimmer of humanity. Grateful for a way to deal with my period, I began to doze. Soon I was dreaming of another time, when the humanity and dignity of life were unquestioned realities.

SEVEN

Esfahan, 1960s

A bright summer morning, and I was almost six years old. We'd departed Tehran early for the six-hour car ride to Esfahan, bouncing along desert roads in sweltering heat. As we drove past the *kavir e namak*, Baba pointed out this was no regular desert. It was a salt desert, "where the salt we eat is mined. The water here is so heavy in salt, you couldn't drown if you tried," he'd add, though I never understood why anyone would try.

Just outside Esfahan, we spied a farmer on the side of the road selling muskmelons from the back of his beat-up old pickup. Baba pulled over and parked behind his truck. Maman and I stayed in the car and watched as Baba taught Amir to tap the middle and sniff the ends of the fruit. If it smelled sweet, it was ripe. And if the tapping didn't return an echo, it was too old. Amir imitated Baba as they tested melon after melon, sniffing and tapping until finally Amir announced he'd found a winner. Baba gave it his blessing, and Amir proudly carried the chosen melon to the car. Maman said, "*Bari kala*—bravo."

The streets of Esfahan were different from Tehran's. Old pickup trucks of all colors, faded with age and covered in dust, roamed the tree-lined streets, transporting workers in the back. Their dark skin glistened with perspiration, faces tanned like leather from hours working in the scorching summer sun. Residential streets were narrower, offering an occasional glimpse of a yard over brick walls, where laundry hung on clotheslines, flapping in the breeze. The air in Esfahan was dry and dusty, and Amir would get a bloody nose each time we made the trip. Esfahan is closer to the equator than Tehran, Baba explained. It's hotter, and rain is less frequent.

We arrived in the early evening as the sun set against a backdrop of rose-painted hills and crimson hibiscus. We always stayed at the house where Baba had grown up, now home to his younger brother, Morad; his wife; two daughters, Khorsheed and Noor; and a son, Mojtabah. Baba parked in front of the single-story white stucco house. Uncle Morad came out to greet us, his face practically buried behind his thick dark beard.

"*Salam alaykum*. Welcome, welcome," he cried, embracing my father, three kisses on alternating cheeks. Maman stood back, smiling, but not moving to greet her brother-in-law. Uncle Morad turned to her. "Welcome, Soraya *khanoom*," he said with a nod, and then came over to Amir and me. Patting us both on the head, he said, "My, how big you've grown. Ali, you're feeding them far too well."

We followed Uncle Morad into a house virtually devoid of furniture. Empty rooms with white-washed walls stood bare, lacking decoration. Persian carpets of intricate design graced the floors. In the main room, there were a few sparse shelves with mirrors and Persian *khatam* artwork. On the wall facing the entrance was a framed image of the prophet Mohammed. There were no chairs or tables. In a central room, huge stuffed pillows were cast casually around a large *Bakhtiar geleem* rug. The pillows rested on top of folded wool blankets, offering little cushioning but more comfort than the hard floor. The smell of baking bread and a charcoal fire filled the air, mingled with the scent of spices and flowers. In the back corner of the room, a dark colorful sheet hung from the wall, ruffling like waves each time the tall floor fan blew a breeze in its direction. I ran over to explore and peeked inside to find a small storage room. This, I guessed, was the closet.

"Maman, there's no place to hang my clothes. Where are the hangers?" I whispered in surprise. Didn't all closets have a rod and hangers?

"Quiet now. I'll help you in a bit," she said, with a look which meant I'd crossed a line. "Take your clothes out and put them here on the floor for now." She was busy emptying Amir's suitcase, refolding his clothes and stacking them. Had I insulted my uncle with my comment about the closet? I dutifully knelt beside Maman and took out my things, piling them next to Amir's.

"Come, let's have tea," said my uncle, waving us out of the room.

We stepped out to the middle courtyard. A stone porch evenly spaced with wooden doors leading to the several rooms jutted into the rectangular enclosure. In the center of the backyard stood the *hose* water reservoir, a necessity in this house without central plumbing. Uncle Morad led us to the far corner where the family was gathered, sitting atop blankets on the floor. The samovar was steaming, hot tea brewing. Small pieces of pistachio *gaz* nougat, a specialty of Esfahan, rested on a small plate, ready to be served with tea. I eyed a bowl of pistachios but decided it was impolite to take any right away. Uncle Morad served the finest pistachios from Rafsanjan, roasted with salt and lime juice. Uncle Rajab was engulfed in a cloud of thick aromatic smoke from his hookah, while his wife sipped black tea and cleaned herbs for dinner on a newspaper spread before her on the floor.

"Where is Sepideh *khanoom*?" asked Maman, referring to Uncle Morad's wife.

"She's making *egerdek* cookies for the children. She'll be along soon. Sit down, relax, have some tea. You've had a long trip."

With so many relatives, we had to be re-introduced each visit, names floating over my head like butterflies never to be captured. While my mother was dressed in a knee-length floral dress and stockings, the women here all wore the dark *chador*, covering themselves to their ankles, and head scarves pulled below their chins to completely hide their hair. Frankly, I had to control giggles as they scurried about, serious and foreboding as a gaggle of crows. The only one in the bunch who drew my attention was my cousin Mojtabah. A few years older than I, he was taller than Amir and at his young age already quite handsome with straight black hair and hazel eyes. He was the sole cousin closest to our age and a ready playmate. We spent hours chasing each other around the *hose* in the yard, searching after insects. It was Mojtabah who invented the outlandish sport of pin the tail on the fly.

"You have to sneak up on them," he said, gingerly approaching a fat black fly with his hand inches apart. "Then cup your hands a few inches above it and clap. It'll try to fly up, and you can catch it."

He sneaked up slowly on a lazy fly crawling along the concrete edge of the *hose* to demonstrate his technique. He missed the first time, but on his second attempt, he captured the slightly dazed fly. "Now for the fun part," he said. Holding the fly by a wing, he picked up a thin broom bristle from the ground. Like a skilled surgeon, he impaled the

fly with this makeshift lance. Setting it down, we watched gleefully as
it struggled to take flight, dragging its artificial tail. Mojtabah usually
squashed it in a minute, ending its misery.

Mojtabah made visits to Esfahan tolerable, with his knack for
inventing games and drawing amusement out of tedium. I found the
rest of my Esfahani relatives far too austere, different from family or
friends in Tehran. Time spent in Esfahan felt unnatural. I had to sit on
the hard ground, carefully watch my words, and use an outhouse. Over
the years, I came to dread family reunions in Esfahan. Had it not been
for Mojtabah, they would have been unbearable. My female cousins
never interested me much. They scurried behind their mothers, helping
with dinner or dishes, and never played. Mojtabah was different. But
despite his welcome diversion, as I grew older and more aware of the
cultural divisions, trips to Esfahan became agonizing.

Years passed, and as school closed each year for summer, it was
time for yet another visit to Esfahan.

"Do we have to go, Maman? It's boring, and they're all so weird."

"They're different from us, *azizam*, because they follow the rules of
Islam more strictly, but they're still family."

"I know, but I feel out of place."

"Don't say such things. You'll hurt your father's feelings. They're
his family, after all."

"Why can't I stay here with Maman Rouhi?" I pleaded, imagining
rooftop starry nights.

"Leila, go pack now. It won't hurt you to learn about your culture."
I hated when she talked like that. I wanted nothing to do with this
other culture and their differences. But I had no choice. My only consolation was that Amir, despite his usual privileges as a boy, had to go too.

We made the long journey to Esfahan, passing the *kavir* and stopping for melons. While I dreaded the time spent with my aunts and
uncles, I looked forward to seeing Mojtabah and the games we'd play.
By now, Amir was almost twelve, and I'd turned nine a few months
earlier. We were a bit old for spearing flies, but there had to be other
adventures in this odd place.

Uncle Morad welcomed us. Once Amir and I said our greetings,
we searched for Mojtabah in the family crowd. Spotting him, we ran

over to greet our favorite cousin. He readily embraced Amir, but he ignored me and walked away to stand with the men roasting corn on the cob on hot charcoal. His aloofness confused me. I walked to him and attempted a conversation.

"*Salam*, Mojtabah. How are you?"

"Hello," he replied, never looking at me.

"I'm in fourth grade now," I began. "What grade are you?"

"Seventh, and you know, it's improper for a Muslim woman to address a Muslim man in this manner," he added rather gravely.

I was hurt by his rebuke. "Now that you're in seventh grade, we can't play anymore?"

"No, you're no longer *mahram*. You're not even covered as you should be."

"But I'm just nine years old," I replied indignantly, the sting of tears filling my eyes. I stood there, hoping my aunts weren't preparing to swoop down and instantly enshroud me in black.

"At nine you're a woman according to Islam. It's no longer proper for us to be friends and certainly not to play."

He walked away, leaving me in a state of confusion and hurt. My sole distraction from the staid and stolid world of my father's family in Esfahan had vanished. I watched as Amir joked with Mojtabah, and they wandered off to ride my uncle's motor scooter. A year had passed, and suddenly I was an outcast.

Baba and Uncle Morad were chatting by the garden as I approached in a huff over my cousin's affront. Standing beside Baba, I interrupted, "Baba, Mojtabah says I can't play with him because he's a Muslim man and now I'm a woman."

Uncle Morad interjected, "Ah, Leila *khanoom*, don't be upset. Mojtabah takes himself too seriously, but also he's right. This year, you're nine years old, no?" I nodded. "The Koran says that a young Muslim woman like you must not be casual with men."

"Is this true, Baba?" I hoped he'd say I was exempt, that the rule didn't apply to me.

"We'll discuss it later. Now go help your mother unpack till dinner's ready."

In the room where dinner was served, a long white tablecloth lay on the floor with fifteen place settings. Seated on cushions, we passed around kabob, rice, and *sabzee*. Aside from sitting on the floor, this was a meal just like we'd have at home, except the women kept to one side of the room, the men to the other. I leaned to whisper to Maman, "How come we don't sit with Baba and Amir?"

"Shush." She looked around as though to see if anyone had overheard my silly question.

As dinner proceeded, my legs cramped more than once, not being used to sitting cross-legged so long on the floor. At meal's end, Uncle Morad, seated at the head of the tablecloth, let out a ponderous belch and said, "*Alhamdolillah*—praise be to Allah." Here in the hinterland, Uncle Morad's belch was an expression of pleasure with the meal. In Tehran, it would have been considered rude.

After dinner, the women went about the business of cleaning up, while the men returned to the patio, lounging on cushions around a hookah. Maman and I were exempt from cleanup since we were guests. The pungent, sweet odor of tobacco floated in the cool night air, accompanied by the soft murmur of voices and sounds of laughter. We joined the men on the patio, though again off to one side, sitting on padded cushions on the floor. Amir, quite the opportunist, asked my uncle if he could try the hookah.

"Why certainly," said Uncle Morad, handing Amir the spiral hose. The hookah was tall with many parts. I'd watched my uncle assemble it, much like putting together a puzzle. The glass bottom filled with water was a deep-blue crystal etched with flowers. Heat was visibly rising from the smoldering coal on top. Amir took the end of the pipe and placed it between his lips. He blew into it, causing the water in the base to bubble and boil, drawing chuckles. Following my uncle's instructions, Amir then took a deep draw and began coughing violently, leading to uproarious laughter from everyone. I laughed too. Amir looked funny as the heavy tobacco smoke hit his lungs, his eyes watering with a bemused look on his face as he glanced at the other men. I got up and walked over to where Amir and Baba were sitting.

"Can I try?"

"No," Baba replied curtly, with a frown. "Go sit with your mother."

Feeling crushed, I took my seat next to Maman. Once again Amir

got to do something I couldn't. I wasn't sure what disappointed me
more, that I was excluded or that this distinction between the sexes was
again thrust in my face.

Far from the city, the night was clear and bright with abundant
stars dotting the pristine sky. Amir and I were soon nodding from the
long day of travel. Aunt Sepideh led us to our room, where homemade
mattresses and pillows were laid out on the floor. Even at this time of
year, evenings were cool, so blankets were provided. It felt like a night
at Maman Rouhi's, camping on the rooftop on thin stuffed mattresses.
But there was no clear sky above, no stories, and no magical chocolate
fish under my pillow.

The next morning we drove into Esfahan to visit the blue-tiled
mosques, the ancient palace of the kings, and the bazaar. During the
excursion, I took the opportunity to question Baba. "Why did Mojtabah
say I shouldn't talk to him?"

"Leila, your Uncle Morad and I love each other very much, but on
some things we don't see eye to eye. He and his family follow a stricter
interpretation of Islam. Part of their belief is that women aren't the
equal of men, that men and women who are *na-mahram* should never
touch or speak directly unless absolutely necessary. According to the
Koran, once you turn nine, you're no longer a little girl but a young
woman, and you should have your hair and body covered like your
aunts and cousins. This is why Mojtabah believes it's improper for you
to talk with him."

"But what do you believe, Baba?"

"I believe that Allah created all men and women as equals and loves
each the same. I believe you and Amir should both have a good education and make your own way in the world. So while your cousins
Khorsheed and Noor will probably never go to school past six years, I
want you to go to college just like I wish it for Amir."

"Does Islam say this is true, Baba? Is Leila less than me in the eyes
of Allah?" Amir asked, only partly teasing.

"Amir, the love of Allah is for all, not for one less than another.
Some men choose to interpret the Koran to fit their small minds, but
the mind of God is not so easily contained. In the eyes of Allah, Leila
is your sister, your equal, and His love is not swayed by whether she

covers her hair but by the kindness in her heart. That's why you must always be kind and respectful to everyone. We are all Allah's children."

"Does that mean I have to respect Mojtabah too?" I asked. "I don't like him anymore."

"Yes, you must even respect those who don't think as you do. But you don't have to like it," Baba added with a grin.

EIGHT

In stark contrast to his small-town upbringing, where most never finished eighth grade, my father moved to the capital after finishing high school and got a teaching degree from Tehran University. While he loved teaching, it was soon apparent his teacher's salary would not afford the lifestyle he'd hoped for his family. He left teaching to devote his time to trading Persian art, his real passion.

One hot summer morning, I left the house holding Baba's hand as he searched the bazaar for antiquities and works of art. It was a happy time for me, basking in Baba's undivided attention. The bazaar was a place of wonderment. Stores of all kinds lined the narrow corridors. There were spice merchants with burlap-lined barrels heaped with fragrant cumin, cardamom, and allspice. The smells of grilling meats and spices mingled with the dusty air in a cacophony of aromas. Gnarled old men sat at stiff wooden benches pounding shining copper and silver into bowls and pitchers with ball-peen hammers. Beside them, fabric sellers of brightly colored cloths and tie-dyed treasures hawked their wares, and Persian rug dealers tugged at Baba's sleeve as he hurried past their open stalls. "Mr. Moradi, how nice to see you! Please, come look at this treasure I have in the back room." "Mr. Moradi, your clients would love this old tea service. Solid silver, I swear."

So many sights, sounds, and smells, it overwhelmed the senses. I was so proud to be with Baba, as it seemed everyone in the bazaar knew him and sought his attention. But no time to dawdle. Briskly stalking the narrow pathways, Baba occasionally stopped to greet a friend or merchant, a chance for me to catch my breath.

"Baba, what are we looking for?" I asked, as much in exasperation as curiosity. We'd hiked the dusty halls for hours, peering into shadowed stalls adorned with regal colored drapes.

"I'm looking for only the most special items, *azizam*, things from ancient Persia—vases, platters, etched crystal lamps, tear catchers . . . like that one," he said, pointing out a polished glass vase sitting on a battered wooden desk. Its round base was intricately etched with a garden full of lilies of the valley, my favorite flower. The long narrow neck curved up to support a broad teardrop-shaped rim.

"Baba, why's the top look funny?"

"It's shaped to fit your eye, *azizam*, to catch tears. In ancient Persia, when a sultan returned from battle, he checked his wives' tear catchers to see who among them had wept in his absence and missed him the most."

As we entered the store, a man appeared from the back. "Ali, how good to see you. And who is this delicate flower?"

"*Salam*, old friend," Baba replied, greeting this strange-looking man with a kiss on each cheek. Turning to me, he said, "Leila, this is Mr. Nourbakhsh. And this is my daughter, Leila. Mr. Nourbakhsh went to Tehran University with me, but of course he's much older," his face breaking into a smile.

At that, Mr. Nourbakhsh burst into laughter, his great round belly shaking as he clapped my father on the shoulder. "Don't you believe a word of that, Leila *khanoom*. Your father spends so much time in constant motion, he can't enjoy the pleasures of life, which I, a more sedentary creature, have come to appreciate."

I leaned timidly against Baba's leg as I studied this man. The top of his head was bald, except for the few straggles of thin brown hair he pulled over from one side in an attempt to disguise the shining crown. Thick, round, gold-rimmed glasses made his eyes appear to bulge from his head, particularly when he smiled, which seemed incessantly. A paisley tie hung loose around the collar of a white-on-white dress shirt, covered by a slightly worn seersucker jacket that would never again be buttoned. He was a striking contrast to Baba's lean, almost patrician frame and conservative brown suit. But he seemed a jolly man and clearly Baba's friend, so I deemed him safe.

"To what do I owe this pleasure, Ali?" he asked as they stepped deeper into the shop.

"To that," Baba replied, pointing to the ruby-colored tear catcher.

"What an eye you have, my friend. Isn't it exquisite?"

I stood aside as the haggling began. Baba was an unmatched negotiator. I hopped up to sit on the tall pile of Persian rugs until finally agreement was reached. Baba pulled out a wad of money and counted off the Tomans while Mr. Nourbakhsh carefully packaged the fragile vase in tissue. The expedition was a success.

When we got home, I held the tear catcher under one eye, pretending my tears were flowing through its neck to the base. "Baba, can I keep it in my room?"

"No," he said, "but one day I'll buy you one of your very own."

As Baba uncovered a global market for Persian art, he began trading antique treasures. He traveled for weeks at a time, returning with a suitcase full of souvenirs, evidence we were on his mind. Business prospered, and he opened a retail store. My father's passion for Persian art seemed contagious. His enthusiasm and depth of knowledge attracted more and more clients, each more important, more wealthy, or more famous than the last. But these clients were overshadowed by the one who became his biggest patron and friend. Two years into his business, Baba came to the attention of the Shah of Iran. Shah Mohammad Reza Pahlavi became an exclusive client, ushering in a whole new life for us. Amir and I quickly became pompous, bragging to friends that we knew the Shah personally, though we'd never met him.

The Shah and my father discovered their shared passion during their first meeting. Mutual admiration of Persian art led to hours discussing the rich history of artifacts and the monarchy itself.

"Your Majesty, this vase is from the Sassanian dynasty, over a thousand years old," Baba said, referring to a lone vase perched on a glass shelf behind the emperor's chair.

"You have an incredible eye, Mr. Moradi. Tell me how you know this." His eyes beamed with pleasure that someone else shared his love for Persian antiquities.

"If Your Majesty would examine the metalwork inlaid in the ceramic, it's evident this is the work of that period. It was during those years that artists introduced precious and semi-precious metals into their work. There's no mistaking it," Baba said confidently.

"And there's no mistaking you know of what you speak. It's so difficult to find the real treasures of our past, so few who know the genuine work when they see it. Mr. Moradi, can you procure some pieces for me? I am an avid fan of miniatures. I'd like you to find me an exquisite antique miniature painting, the older the better."

"I'm certain His Majesty is aware that miniatures were introduced in Persia in the fourteenth century. So what I find will not be thousands of years old like some of the pieces that surround His Majesty today."

The Shah smiled, running his fingers through his salt-and-pepper hair and leaning back in his ornate chair. The mahogany-backed arm-chair was inlaid with gold leaves accenting carved flowers, a gift from the King of France to a Persian ruler centuries ago. The upholstery was a tightly knit tapestry, so intricate it was akin to a photograph. "I admire a man whose work is his passion, Mr. Moradi. You and I must discuss this more over tea another time."

"It would be an honor, Your Majesty." So began what would be one of my father's most profitable relationships.

As his business prospered and he entertained customers at home, my parents decided on a more extravagant setting. Our new house was beautiful and huge. On the main floor, antique silk and wool Persian rugs lay gracefully atop pale green- and beige-specked Italian marble floors. Along the north wall, at an angle, sat a pearl-black Steinway baby grand. A spiral stairway led to the second floor, where a less formal sitting area with a bay window overlooked manicured beds of roses and lilies, blossoming in colors of yellow, red, white, and pink. A large swimming pool glistened in the sunlight, its deck furnished with lounge chairs and umbrellas. Swallows skimmed the sparkling surface as they dipped in flight for a drink.

Amir and I secretly congratulated each other that we lived in a man-sion. To our dismay, neither of our bedrooms overlooked the pool, but Amir's room was twice as large as mine and faced the rose garden. I was upset by this blatant favoritism, but I was afraid to object. I suspected Maman had picked the better room for Amir in line with our position in society. He was a boy, the first-born son, while I was the daughter. But why must she treat us differently? Baba didn't.

Since Maman didn't drive and Baba was often away for business, he hired Mahmood to be our chauffeur. Amir and I truly felt like royalty.

One night, my parents made an announcement.

"Children, we have wonderful news. We've decided to send you to boarding school in London. You'll master the English language and get a great education there," Baba said excitedly.

This couldn't be happening. My own father was going to send us away.

"I don't want to go. I love our new house and my school. I won't be able to see the rest of the family or my friends. No way! I'm NOT going!" I screamed in a petulant voice and stormed out of the room. I didn't wait for Amir's opinion, nor did I see the disappointment in my father's eyes. I ran to my room, shut the door, and burst into tears. Neda would understand my feelings and empathize, so I called her.

"She hates me. It's all *her* doing. She wants me gone so she doesn't have to take care of me," I said madly, referring to my mother. "And I'm so sick of her putting Amir on a pedestal all the time."

"Leila, he's a boy, and that's the way things are. But you weren't singled out in this case."

Her logic defied my emotions. "I must be adopted," I said as a final effort to explain this horrid turn of events. As I reached for a tissue, I saw my face in the mirror and realized how I was clearly a composite of my parents. Blessed with dark curly hair (impossible to avoid when both parents are so graced), I had my mother's receding chin and my father's brown eyes and curling black eyelashes. To complete the genetic signature was Grandmother's birthmark on my neck, passed on by my mother. So how could they do this to us?

I stopped sniffling to listen to voices from the first floor. Moving closer to the door, I overheard Maman and Baba in heated discussion.

"I have no problem with Amir going, but you want to ship your only daughter off to a foreign country? It's a terrible idea. She'll pick up bad habits from Western girls. Before you know it, she'll be fantasizing about boys and thinking she can grow up and marry anyone she chooses, like those English girls," protested Maman.

"Soraya, be reasonable. She's young, but she's as bright and capable as Amir. I have great dreams for my daughter . . ."

"Stop this nonsense," Maman interrupted. "She's an Iranian girl. She should be raised here and learn how to be an Iranian wife. I know your grand dreams. You want her to go to college like Amir. Well, I don't. They're different."

"How could you not want the best for your daughter, Soraya?"

"Are you implying somehow I am not good enough because I didn't go to college? What's wrong with me? I left school at sixteen to marry you. Haven't I been a good wife and mother? I cook, sew, and run the household. I arrange grand parties and stand beside you in society with my head held high. That isn't good enough for Leila?"

"She should have every opportunity Amir has. I won't treat them differently."

Quietly, I closed the door and sank in my bed. If I stayed in Iran, which was what I wanted, I'd be raised like my cousins. Was that so bad? There was a nagging in the pit of my stomach. Something hungered for more. Who was right—Maman or Baba? The following day, we were given a reprieve.

"Amir, Leila," Baba began. "Your mother's convinced me boarding school is not a good idea. We'll enroll you in Miss Mary's school here in Tehran, which is just as good as those English schools."

Perhaps it was the best of both worlds. Baba was pleased that, like Amir, I'd get a good education, and Maman could raise me as a proper Iranian woman.

NINE

That spring, my father bought the farm in Sohanak where I was born. He planned to build a house so we could spend the summer months away from the city. Maman spent less and less time with me, devoting herself to Amir. The more I sought to gain her attention, the more she grew disinterested and aloof. I couldn't understand what I'd done to offend her or why she withheld affection from me while lavishing it on Amir. My feelings danced between anger and anguish with each new rejection, real or imagined. I only knew there was a hollow ache in my heart, an unnamed torment that, from time to time, threatened to reduce me to tears. I wanted more than anything to bring back the days when I, too, enjoyed the warmth of her love, but her reluctance to grant it left me perplexed and hurt. If I could regain her affection, perhaps then life would be complete.

Following graduation from Miss Mary's school, we enrolled at Iranzamin, an international high school in Tehran. We read great works of literature, held dances and bake sales, and put together plays. We even celebrated Christmas, complete with a trimmed tree and Santa Claus. In this microcosmic existence, we learned and lived Western culture. I tried hard to fit in to this mixing pot of Eastern and Western culture. I wanted to be a good girl, which of course meant no boyfriends. But many girls secretly had a boyfriend, and my desires, no matter how I tried to suppress them, were real. My first crush was on Amir's friend Homayoon.

"You like him, don't you?" Amir asked teasingly after I suggested he invite Homayoon to my birthday party.

"What makes you say that?"

"Because you want me to invite him to *your* birthday party. I don't want to invite him. You do. And you hang around us whenever he's here, being annoying."

"Oh, *pa-leeeease*. I was just being nice, thinking you'd like your friend at my party so you're not bored. Guess it doesn't pay to be nice around here."

"So it wouldn't bother you to know he has a girlfriend, right?"

"Why would it bother me?" I asked, blood draining from my face. I'd not considered that possibility, but quickly added, "Speaking of girlfriends, who's that cute sophomore you're hanging around with? Is she your girlfriend?"

"So what if she is? Are you gonna tell Maman and Baba or something?" he shot back. He looked back as he left my room, "Forget I even said anything."

I had been trying to shift attention but apparently hit the nail on the head. He had a secret girlfriend; how interesting. Good, I'd keep this to myself, a card I might need to play someday. I immediately felt guilty at my thought of betrayal; Amir would never tell on me.

During high school years, the time when an Iranian girl is considered ripe for marriage, I was focused on school, or so my parents thought. They didn't accept invitations from suitors as my cousins' parents did. Baba was my reminder that education was important. Maman was my reminder of what life would be as an Iranian woman. She taught me womanly tasks and enrolled me in a sewing class, despite my objections. To help me master the skill, she gave me projects, like sewing a blazer for Amir. At first I resented it, but when Amir tried on the tan blazer with its stamped brass buttons, his appreciation melted my resentment.

"I really like this, Leila," he said stretching his long arms into the sleeves. After that, each time he wore the blazer, I flushed with pride. I might not have liked how society treated men as more important than women, but I loved my big brother.

Once, Maman came down with the flu and asked me to make dinner. "It's good practice," she said, as though perfecting rice or stew should be the goal of my life. That night, I made *abgoosht* lamb stew. We were seated at the dining room table, and I served *abgoosht* into each china bowl, making certain not to spill on the white tablecloth. Maman smiled and lifted the first spoonful to her lips.

"You didn't add enough salt," she began, her smile fading.

"I'm sorry, Maman. I was afraid of using too much salt."

"Also, the beans need to cook longer. Just for next time, dear," she added with a frown. "And you should have used tomato paste, not sauce."

"But I thought for sure you always used sauce."

"No, I always use paste. Next time, maybe you can consult me while you're putting the dish together. I can teach you the right way."

"Well, I think it's delicious," said Baba with a wink, rising to my defense as he ate another big spoonful.

"Me too," added Amir. "It's not like Maman's, but it's still good."

"Well, if you two want to tell her what she wants to hear, that's fine. I'm trying to teach her to do it correctly. Someday, she'll have to do this for her husband. It will be a poor reflection on me if her *abgoosht* is tasteless and watery. Her mother-in-law will think I didn't do my job," concluded Maman, resentment clear in her tone. This was her territory, and she didn't much appreciate male interference.

"No, Maman, you're right. It does need more salt, and the beans are a little tough. I'm sorry, I should have asked you." And with that, she displayed a smile of victory.

"For a first attempt you did fine. We just need to improve next time, yes?"

"Yes, Maman." I just didn't want an argument.

I sat quietly through the rest of dinner, deflated despite Amir and Baba's support, and sought solace in my room when dinner was over. Was this about me or her? Was she concerned that I become a proper Iranian wife or about protecting her reputation? Regardless, I didn't want to be her. I didn't want to be a hostess, throwing lavish parties to entertain a future husband's business friends. I wanted my own business friends. I didn't dream of marriage and children. I wanted a career. The thought of raising children and driving them to swim or piano lessons held little appeal. I loved my mother, but I couldn't be her. In my heart, I wanted to be like Baba.

During this time, my grandfather passed away. Maman Rouhi's colorful silk head scarves and clothing gave way to nondescript black. In mourning, she wore nothing but black for one year and no jewelry but her wedding band.

The burial service was my first encounter with death. Grandfather's body had been washed and wrapped in a white shroud in accordance with Islam. He was carried on a pallet to the grave site, where he would be placed in the grave on his right side, facing Mecca. I walked with my father behind the bier, trying to picture Grandfather lying in the tightly wrapped shroud, as unbidden tears stung my eyes. It hurt my heart to think I'd never see him again, never sit on his lap, never feel his rough beard against my cheek or savor the lingering aroma of tobacco that seemed to cling to him.

I found myself engulfed in the crowd of mourners, all dressed in black, wailing cries of grief. As for my mother, she trailed behind in a long black dress and silk shawl wrapped around her shoulders. Leaning on Amir for support as they walked to the grave, she continually wiped her face and half-closed eyes with a black organza handkerchief, which did little to absorb tears, making it convenient for her to wipe her face many more times. To her other side, my cousin Neda waved a wooden Chinese fan in front of Maman's face. Standing at the grave site, Maman cried louder than anyone else, muttering unintelligibly. Her entourage doted over her and offered a chair when she felt faint. Her melodramatic display was puzzling. When he was alive, Maman had shown no deep attachment to her father. In fact, she often complained that her siblings were his darlings and she the neglected one. Were her pronounced wailings an expression of remorse for her prior lack of affection, or just another plea for attention? I stood next to Amir, stealing an occasional glance, wondering if he was as embarrassed as I by her exhibition, but he revealed no emotion.

Maman repeated the same dramatic behavior three days later at the *khatm* memorial service and then again at the haftom seventh-day ritual. She wailed so loudly, we could hardly hear the Mullah recite the verses of the Koran. Several days later, as we sat at dinner, Maman told us that she'd asked Grandmother to move in with us. "She can't take care of that big house by herself."

"That's great news," I replied. "I was worried about her being alone."

"When will she move in?" Amir asked.

"She insists on having the *chehelom* fortieth-day ceremony at her house, so it'll be sometime after that."

With her arrival, my deepening relationship with Grandmother began. Maman Rouhi became the surrogate, providing attention I desperately sought from my mother. Despite the loss that would grow more profound in the weeks following this experience of death, there was comfort knowing my grandmother was near.

Secretly, I wondered if Maman also longed for her mother's increased attention. After Grandfather's death, my mother's feigned and real afflictions soared to new heights. She developed migraine headaches, which put her in bed for days. She complained of a rash, an allergy to garlic she'd recently contracted. She found a cyst in her right breast, and while we anxiously awaited test results, she sulked in her room in a stupor of self-pity, stating she was as good as dead. It was benign. She was never well except when Amir was around, always managing to find the energy to fix a snack or serve him tea, things she never did for me.

As summer came to a close, Amir, who had graduated high school, was heading to college in the U.S. He was accepted at a top university. We hadn't heard of Lehigh University, but in the brochures, it looked lush and green, with majestic old buildings and cheerful-looking students. Though we'd prepared for this day, it was emotional nonetheless. My big brother was leaving. That day, after we dropped off Amir at the airport, Maman took a sleeping pill and slept all day. The house seemed quiet and empty. Feeling lonely, I took refuge under the pomegranate tree and allowed my thoughts to wander, looking out occasionally at the rose garden with blossoms of every color, the pool glistening as swallows swept its surface for a drink. Only when I felt hungry did I realize how much time had passed.

The following weeks were difficult for Maman. When I came home from school, I'd go to her room, carrying a cup of hot tea with sugar cubes, the way she liked it.

"Hi, Maman, would you like some tea?"

"*Merci*, Leila. Just set it down," she said, pointing to the nightstand next to her.

I pushed back the framed picture of Amir to make room for the small tray. His skin was tan, his black hair highlighted with streaks of light brown, having just returned from a trip at the Caspian Sea. He wore a navy suit and maroon striped tie, with dark sunglasses that made him look like a movie star. The picture was taken at a wedding. It was Maman's favorite picture of him. When she looked at the couple's wedding album, she asked for a copy of this one. Not to be rude, she ordered one of the bride and groom, which she then threw out.

Maman sat resting in bed, the pillows behind her head and a blanket over her legs as she stared blankly out the window. I handed her the cup and she gave a small smile, never looking in my direction. I wasn't sure if she wanted me to stay or leave but decided to test the waters.

"School was really tough today," I said, trying to start conversation. "We had a math test. I think I did okay, but I've got so much homework tonight."

"Well, you'd better start on it then." Was she dismissing me?

I could see she'd been crying, her eyes puffy and moist. She tried to be pleasant and listen, but I could tell her mind was on Amir. No story of mine, no matter how amusing, no matter how wild, could draw her from her self-absorbed state of loss. So I left and buried myself in my books.

It was some consolation for Maman when my cousin Mojtabah moved in with us while he searched for an apartment before starting studies at Tehran University. Baba encouraged Mojtabah to attend university and paid his expenses since his brother couldn't afford it. Mojtabah's presence was a welcome distraction for Maman. She doted on him at dinner and even brought him tea afterwards.

For my part, I had little desire to be nice to my cousin, given his indifference over the last years. Each time I ran into him, he'd greet me politely, but always with downcast eyes. His strict Islamic mindset and dress made me uncomfortable in my own home. He was so stoic in his loose white tunic, gray dress pants, black beard and mustache. I'm sure he didn't approve of me either, since I dressed in Western clothes and didn't wear a head scarf. Eventually, Mojtabah moved to his own place, and we only saw him occasionally for dinner, which was fine by me.

TEN

Tehran Prison, 1988

Screaming . . . I awoke to screaming. Was it a dream? No, I'd been dreaming of Amir leaving for college and my sanctimonious cousin, Mojtabah. Did he know I'd been arrested?

There it was again: A piercing scream echoed down the prison walls, resounding off the cold concrete. I couldn't tell if it was a man or a woman; the pitch seemed inhuman. Now moans, pleading, a whimpering voice begging for mercy as the guards laughed. The sound of nightsticks striking flesh, a dull thwack followed by screams, then silence.

I rolled over and pulled the blanket to my face. Tears washed my cheeks, and I wasn't even aware I'd been crying. They beat me like that a few days ago. The memory still gripped me. What kind of human beings were these? They may have looked like my fellow countrymen, but what demon possessed their souls that they could so easily and gleefully torture another? I shivered with fear. Were they coming for me again? Why? Always in my mind, the question, why?

I slept a short while; I don't know how long. I awoke when the damp cold permeated my bones and a pulse of pain rose again. Silence hung in the air like a noose. No moans or screams, just silence. A tomb; yes, I thought, silent like a tomb. On the floor by the door was a plate with a crust of hard bread and a lump of feta, moldy, but still . . . A few weeks—or was it months?—ago, I would have turned away from what now seemed a delicacy. I spread the crumbling cheese on the hard bread with my finger and licked the taste off my finger, knowing it might be weeks till I'd taste it again. I took my time with each bite, savoring the taste but also passing time. I'd barely finished when the footsteps came down the hallway, marching, the cadence of booted men coming toward the cell. The key turned in the lock, and the door swung open. Not again.

"Out! Get out now!" Lt. Mehraban shouted down the hall.

"Come on, move," the short, stout guard demanded. "Don't make me drag you. You have to walk. Come on." He came inside, quickly glanced behind him, took my hand and helped me to my feet. "Don't give him a reason," he whispered.

A reason for what, I wondered. More shouts echoed down the hallway. The soldier led me down the hallway to the left following the Lieutenant. I was surprised this time that they didn't cover my head. Was I to be killed? Were these my last moments? We walked through a barred metal door and out into a large open field, flat and dusty with struggling tufts of grass. It was big enough for a soccer field, though why that came to mind I don't know. Surely no one played soccer here, so close to . . . The sky was gray and overcast, with thick threatening clouds disguising the time of day. I'd been so long in my cell I stared at the sky in wonder. The air was still and parched, the only sound the scrambling of prisoners inside.

Lieutenant Mehraban signaled the guard, who shoved me up against a dull red brick wall. I stood in silence facing a line of guards holding rifles. This was it. I would be executed. My heart sank, and I tried to steel myself for the end. With a dull clang, the metal door swung open, and two guards dragged another prisoner into the yard. The man's face was badly bruised, his eyes sunken and vacant. The front of his shirt was torn in several places and splattered with blood. His legs dragged behind as they carried him, twisted at an unnatural angle, and one arm dangled lifeless. With eyes closed, he sobbed quietly, mumbling words I couldn't comprehend. They dragged him a few feet from me and dropped him to the ground. His head struck the hard ground with a thud. Nothing but a groan escaped his lips.

"Knees. Put him on his knees." Lt. Mehraban marched the makeshift corridor separating us from the line of guards as the two soldiers positioned the prisoner on his knees facing me. So I would be executed along with this man. Who was he, I wondered. Perhaps a politician from the Shah's régime, one of few who hadn't yet been executed? He turned to look at me but seemed to see nothing. Brown eyes darted here and there without focus, his trembling lips moving as though in prayer. I was surprised he could stay upright; his grasp on consciousness seemed tenuous at best.

"This man was given the opportunity to confess his crimes and receive the mercy of Allah and the Iranian people. He refused. Let this be a warning. The will of the Islamic Republic cannot be thwarted. The word of the Supreme Leader will not be disobeyed."

Lt. Mehraban stood behind the kneeling man, who continued to mumble incoherently. Removing his pistol from its holster, he held it inches from the man's head and pulled the trigger. The sound seemed to pound me to the wall. The front of his head was blown away, and he collapsed like a puppet shorn of its strings. I was deafened by the explosion, so much I couldn't hear my own sobbing as I closed my eyes, waiting my turn. A hand grabbed my arm. The stout soldier pulled me away from the corpse toward the metal door. He walked me back to my cell without a word and left. With my ears still ringing, I stared at the blank wall where a vision of murder and a blood-splattered corpse seemed all too real. I closed my eyes and tried to escape to dreams, to memories of friends and family and life before this hate-filled revolution.

ELEVEN

Tehran, 1975

With Baba traveling and Amir off to university, Maman became a recluse. Perhaps in self-protection, I buried myself in school and focused on learning, but my burgeoning sexuality and social interactions put my desire to "be good" to the test. Although my first crush had dissolved before Amir left for college, it wasn't long before I replaced him with another.

An American family moved in across the street. Their son, Mark, was a senior at the American high school in Tehran. At first sight I was smitten. Straight blond hair fell seductively across his forehead, shading sapphire blue eyes. He was tall, over six feet, and deliciously handsome. I tried to get his attention, but to no avail. As we passed each other in the street, he'd wave and say hello, then duck inside, leaving me disappointed. I was so infatuated that one night, while babysitting his little sister, I "borrowed" a picture. Standing with two other boys in his football uniform, he looked totally dreamy. A football player boyfriend was very cool.

Over the next months, my fantasies of Mark intensified. In real life, we rarely saw each other. But at night, alone in bed, I'd imagine him running to me down a hillside blanketed in bluebells, the flowers rippling like the sea around him, his eyes reflecting the colors surrounding his tall, slender body. Smiling with arms outstretched, he'd scoop me up, twirl me around, my hair swaying in the breeze. Then gently he'd lay me down amid the flowers, caressing my cheek while gazing in my eyes. In slow motion he'd bend, touching my lips with his, and my heart would almost stop. I'd wake up from this dream breathless.

This imaginary connection grew so real that one day I decided to tell close friends I had a boyfriend. While it was a stretch, Mark was real, and I could portray him in detail.

"He's so handsome," I bragged.

"Has he kissed you?" asked Bita, a girl I'd known since kindergarten.

"Oh, yes, and he's a great kisser."

"You're not going to have sex, are you?" asked Bita.

"Of course not. I'm not that type."

"But does he want to?"

"It doesn't matter. I'd never do that," I said, as though my interactions with Mark were real.

Having a boyfriend, especially an American football player, made me cool in the eyes of friends. I showed them his picture and said I'd taken it at a game. Having been to an American football game to watch my boyfriend play made all the girls envious. In reality, all I had was that picture, tucked safely under my pillow. I studied it nightly in the quiet of my room, my fantasies carrying me to a world otherwise forbidden. Just innocent teenage longings.

After his freshman college year, Amir returned home for the summer. Maman was overjoyed, bouncing around the house with energy we hadn't seen in months. Though she'd spent the previous day in bed complaining of not feeling well, the day of his arrival she went to the salon, had her nails manicured a coral red, her hair colored honey brown, and even makeup applied, the type of makeover she generally reserved for weddings. Baba was in Shiraz, so Mahmood drove us to the airport. I'm not sure which of us had missed Amir more.

The first week Amir was home, we spent a lot of time together, but we could never be alone. Maman was always on the prowl, seeking him out from the time she woke till she retired for the evening. I wanted Amir to myself but could rarely manage more than five or ten minutes. As his welcome-back visitors dwindled, he became more absent, going out with old friends. I was left to find other distractions.

One cool summer evening, Neda and I decided to go to the movies. They were showing Zeffirelli's *Romeo and Juliet*. Neda's father drove us to the cinema and arranged to pick us up when the movie was over. Before we crossed the street to the theater, we passed Whimpy's, a teen hot spot, and noticed it was packed. I saw several boys from Iranzamin School, seated at a corner table, in rapt conversation.

"Neda, see that guy on the right? Isn't he cute?"

48Nahid Sewell

"You know them? Let's go in," she suggested, not waiting for my answer.

"But what if your father sees us?"

"We've got plenty of time. Besides, he's meeting us by the theater, so he'll never catch us."

Inside Whimpy's, we nonchalantly sauntered toward the boys, purposely avoiding eye contact. In a moment of embarrassment, I tripped over a cracked tile and my purse slipped off my shoulder right in front of their table, spilling its contents across the black and white tiled floor. Lipstick, mascara, and eyeliner scattered under chairs and tables, some disappearing altogether. The cute boy rushed to my rescue, displaying a dazzling white smile that made my chest tighten as I struggled for air.

"Can I help?" he asked, looking at me as I began my search and rescue on the floor.

"Thank you," I said, feeling the blood rush to my face. "I'm so embarrassed."

"It could happen to anyone. My name is Kamyar, by the way. I've seen you at school."

His arm brushed mine as we both reached for the renegade mascara under a chair. Kamyar was a few inches taller than I; his long dark hair was brushed straight back. His eyes held playful intelligence, and his smile gave me goose bumps. He was wearing khaki pants and a black fitted knit shirt that accentuated his well-muscled chest. I sensed him looking at me from the corner of my eye, and I melted like butter on a hot day. The smell of his cologne was intoxicating. Whether my blushing was evident I don't know, but the next seconds seemed like hours as my mind wandered into a fantasy.

In a dreamy haze, I hear Kamyar whisper, "Let's step outside."

I nod yes, and ignoring the others, drift from the restaurant holding his hand.

"What a beautiful night," I say.

"Not as beautiful as you."

His lips press mine in a fervent kiss as he holds me tightly in the alley behind the restaurant. My right hand touches his face as we kiss, the other caressing the small of his back, pulling him closer, feeling his muscular body, hard against me. Lost in reverie, I am so alive, so hungry for his touch and . . .

Suddenly the reverie is broken, and I'm tumbling on my backside after reaching for the renegade mascara, to the amusement of the group. The fantasy is shattered. But Kamyar is still smiling as he offers his hand to help me up.

"Why don't you and your friend join us?" he said.

Before I had a chance to speak, Neda accepted on our behalf, immediately taking the chair next to his. Just as well. Perhaps separation could dispel the arousal gripping me. A part of me wanted to leave, but Neda was engaged in conversation, and I didn't want to spoil her fun. I joined the chatter, stealing glances at Kamyar, wishing I were beside him, feeling his arm brush mine again as flashes of the alley dream replayed in my mind with rising intensity. The rapid interplay of conversation continued about school, the firmness of our headmistress, and the gentle smile of the principal.

Across from us, I noticed a neighbor's son with another boy, sipping orange soda. Dara was a shy, reserved boy about my age who barely managed a "*salam*" if we saw each other on the street. His family was devoutly religious. I thought about saying hello, but each time I glanced in his direction, he turned away. His discovering Neda and me with these boys made me uncomfortable, but I ignored it. Later, I noticed he'd left.

Busy with the chatter and excitement, we lost track of time, forgetting that my uncle was waiting for us at the cinema. When Kamyar and the others decided to leave, we realized we'd missed our ride. In mild panic, we hailed a cab and dropped off Neda first. I entered our house through the kitchen, hoping not to be discovered. Mahmood was seated at the counter, slicing an apple with a sharp kitchen knife. He offered me a slice as I passed by, which I politely declined. I just wanted to disappear.

"Leila *khanoom*, your father wants to see you—in the library." He carefully slipped the apple slice resting on the tip of the knife to his mouth. Never looking up, he continued, "I would have picked you up."

"I know . . ." The knot in my stomach tightened. Even Mahmood knew I was in trouble.

I made my way through the kitchen, anxiety rising with each step. The library was a grand vaulted room, highlighted by rich built-in mahogany shelves from floor to ceiling with rows of neatly arranged leather-bound volumes. French classical figures holding open books stood like sentries along the walls. Matching regal lion-head bookends on the desk added a classic feel. They were solid ivory, a gift from the Shah to my father following a state visit to India. The musky smell and high ceiling were intimidating, with my current circumstances adding fear to the mix. As I walked in, Baba sat up in his black leather chair, running his hand across the top of his balding head as he glanced up.

"Come in, Leila," he said gently, motioning toward a seat.

I tiptoed to his desk and sat facing him. Moments plodded by as I stared at my feet, sensing my father's cold gaze. I had never before been frightened of Baba like this. I sat on my trembling hands so he wouldn't notice. That would be tantamount to an admission of guilt.

"Leila," he finally said, in a quiet tone. I looked up, fear etched on my face. "You know I'm proud of you, of what you've accomplished was in school, the young lady you've become, the respect you show for others." There was a pause as his tone lost its tenderness. "But, I have to question the company you're keeping," he said, frowning. "Do you want to tell me about it?" He crossed his arms and leaned back, looking me straight in the eye.

"Baba, I'm sorry I'm late. Neda and I just lost track of time and . . ."

"Leila," he interrupted sternly. "I don't want excuses. I want an explanation."

"And while you're at it, explain this," added Maman, storming into the library. With the pounding of my heart, I hadn't heard her approach. Now, as I turned around, she stood behind me, holding up a Polaroid. My body went rigid like a tightly coiled spring.

"It's not what you think. It's just a picture. I . . . I . . . ," I stuttered.

"Under your pillow?" she asked, not really asking. Why couldn't she take my side for once? I was already in trouble. Did she have to bring more? She'd never do this to Amir. She'd protect him. But for me, she just made things worse.

"I found this picture of boys under her pillow." Maman walked over, handing Baba the photo. "I told you this Western education was bad for her. I knew she'd start chasing boys and ruin her reputation." As I protested, Baba examined the photo carefully.

"Maman, I haven't done anything. How could I ruin my reputation?"

"Ask Dara and his family. Ask them what they think of you, of our family. You were out with boys, probably these same boys. And you do this openly, as though it's nothing. You've disgraced us." Maman's voice shook with emotion.

"Well, Amir had a girlfriend in high school. How come you didn't yell at him?"

The moment the words escaped my lips, regret rushed in. Amir had never exposed me, not even when I broke Baba's tear catcher, the one he'd bought at the bazaar from Mr. Nourbakhsh when I was a little girl. One day, Amir and I were arguing because he grabbed the phone while I was talking to Neda, saying I'd been on too long. I lunged to take it back and knocked the fragile antique off Baba's desk. It shattered into a million pieces. We both stood in shock, knowing the immensity of this crime, how my father loved that beautiful tear catcher.

Amir never revealed it was I who broke it. He made up a story about a stray cat running through the house, jumping on the desk, knocking off Baba's prized tear catcher. It crashed to the floor before he could catch it, he told Baba, weaving a believable tale. Baba was angry at him for chasing a stray animal through the house and grounded him for a week. But Amir never betrayed me. Now I bit my tongue, wishing to draw blood. But it was too late. Spoken words could not be undone. Quickly, I changed the subject, hoping to mask my betrayal.

"I can't believe you searched my room, under my pillow. Don't I have any privacy?" I demanded, anger rising over my mother's intrusion.

"Silence, Leila!" commanded Baba, setting down the photo on his desk. "You will not speak to your mother this way."

I wanted to tell him the picture was nothing. There were no boys. It was just fantasy, my imagination. But it didn't matter. In their minds, even fantasies were improper. I remembered Baba describing temptation when I was little. "Temptation is a giant beast," he said. "His body, arms, and legs are covered with dark hairs, thousands of them. Each hair plays a different tune, calling out to you, tempting you. Always walk away, Leila. Never look back."

I had let the beast tempt me. Worse, I had betrayed my brother. Best I quietly endure my pending punishment. An eternity of silence passed as I held my breath, fearing any noise might draw further rebuke.

"Go to your room," Baba said, dismissing me. His voice had grown gentle again. I looked up at him in confusion. Maman stood staring at Baba, equally confused. Was he going to spare me punishment? I tiptoed out without another word.

The next day, I tried to be inconspicuous, heading for a far part of the house when Baba came downstairs, hoping out of sight meant out of mind. At dinner, Baba made an announcement that shook me to the core, what I dreaded most.

"I've arranged a dinner with a suitor. The Motamedis are a fine family from Esfahan, and they're looking for a bride for their son. He's a few years older than you, Leila. Although they've approached me in the past, I've now decided to accept their request to meet."

Baba's words pounded on my head as though I were trapped at the bottom of a well. A lump shot to my throat. I looked at Amir in sheer horror. His own eyes were wide in disbelief, as though he'd just witnessed a head-on collision. He shot back a look of surprise, shrugging his shoulders. He knew nothing of this.

Later I learned that when he arrived home, Dara told his father he'd seen me flirting with boys at Whimpy's. Of course, righteously indignant, he wouldn't miss an opportunity to point out the faults of others. Dara's father felt it his duty before Allah, as a concerned parent and follower of Islam, to deliver this troubling news to my father. This one event, so seemingly inconsequential, would lead to Maman's victory that I marry before I was damaged goods and the family reputation destroyed. Baba felt he had no choice but to heed Maman's insistent advice.

"But, Baba, I can't get married," I implored once I caught my breath. "I want to go to university, like Amir."

"And bring more disgrace on your family? How can we allow that?" demanded my mother, wringing her hands in anguish.

"Maman, that's not fair. I've done nothing to disgrace you. You want to ruin my life because I talked to some boys?"

"Ruin your life? Was my life ruined when I married your father? Are you so special that this life isn't good enough for you?"

"Enough!" Baba interrupted. "Leila, the Motamedi family will be here for dinner on Thursday. You'll meet the young man and act with dignity as befits your family. We'll discuss this no further."

There would be no reprieve, no compromise. The matter was sealed. I spent the rest of the night alone in my room, images of a family from Esfahan dragging me away. Would they enshroud me in black, force me into a chador, and demand I recite *namaz* prayers five times daily?

The evening the suitor and his family came, I was relieved they weren't dressed in Islamic *hijab*. I did my best to act the dutiful Iranian daughter but couldn't hide the dread that gripped my soul. I hardly spoke during their visit, allowing my thoughts to carry me away to another place. I couldn't believe Baba would go through with this, but my actions and Maman's insistence left him little choice. He had to restore the family honor. Sitting across from me, Baba noticed the tears I struggled to hold back; Maman was oblivious to my sorrow. To her, this wasn't a punishment but cause for celebration.

That night, after our guests left, I cried on Amir's shoulder. I cried for myself and my lost future, but also tears of regret that I'd betrayed him. Did he know? Had Baba confronted him? If Amir knew, he said nothing.

"Leila, I wish you'd stop crying."

"I can't go through with this, Amir. What about my life? I don't want to marry anyone."

"It's not the end of the world. Who knows? Maybe you'll be happy. You'll have someone to take care of you." I guess he shared those ingrained roles like other men in Iran. His attempts to console me only left me more distressed.

"I'd rather kill myself," I said, holding my head down in my lap and crying. "Can't you talk to Maman? She'll listen to you, Amir. Please."

"I'm not sure it'll do any good, but I'll try."

I threw my arms around him and cried for a long time. Little did he know how ashamed I was that I'd betrayed him. Part of me wished he'd walk away and not care. That would have made me feel better. But once again, he stood by, loyally supporting his little sister. And so his rescue

mission began, to wear down my parents' resolve, commiserating with
me nightly while Maman discussed wedding details with the proposed
groom's family.

Over the next days, I stayed in my room, waves of depression over
lost potential threatening to drown me in sorrow. I called Neda to
share my anguish.

"Leila, even if you get married, we can still hang out and go shopping," she offered, as though that was my big worry. While sympathetic,
she'd never dreamed of college or any life other than being a wife and
mother. She was of no help.

One night, long after everyone had gone to sleep, I was in bed, with
the covers over my head, weeping into my pillow so no one could hear.

"*Azizam*, why are you crying?" asked Maman Rouhi, appearing
from nowhere. She gently pulled down the cover, exposing my face. I
just shook my head and continued sobbing. Maman Rouhi slid in the
bed next to me and held me. I grew calmer as she gently touched the
curls in my hair, kissing my forehead with her chapped lips.

"Leila, it's not so bad being married to a nice man. You're seventeen
and a beautiful young lady. Men have sought your hand in marriage for
years, and your father turned them away. He's only looking out for you."
She slipped into a reverie, recalling her own youth. "Times have changed
so much since I married your grandfather. Girls were betrothed much
earlier then, as young as ten or eleven. I myself was married at fifteen
and truthfully didn't know anything about marriage, men, or sex."

This was the first time I had heard the word sex from anyone other
than friends. I pulled away slightly, feeling the discomfort one feels
when confronted with a subject so taboo. Was she going to discuss the
birds and the bees? The last thing I needed was for my grandmother to
broach the subject, so I quickly found my voice.

"Maman Rouhi, your day was different. These days, girls don't get
married so early, and some girls go to college and have jobs."

"I know, *azizam*, but they work because they have no husband to
support them. That's what happens if you turn down suitors when
you're of age and pass your prime. If you've graduated high school and
still haven't found a suitor, you're a pickle."

"A pickle?" I giggled amidst tears.

Grandmother brushed back a strand of curls, "An unwed girl is a pickle because she's sour and no one wants her."

"That's silly, Maman Rouhi. Anyway, I'm not like other girls. I want to make my own choices in life, and I choose to go to college, not get married."

"My dear, you can get married and still go to college. It's not one or the other."

Realizing her old-world perspective was not about to change, I told her I was tired, successfully sending her off.

A week later, Amir proved my salvation. The wedding was off! When he couldn't charm Maman into seeing things differently, he worked instead on Baba.

"Amir, you're my hero. How'd you do it?" I exclaimed with relief.

"Don't give me all the credit. Baba didn't want to just toss aside your future because of neighborhood rumors."

"Thank you. You saved my life."

"Don't worry, Sis. Someday you can return the favor."

Amir's intervention spared me an early marriage. Though I wanted to jump for joy, a dark shadow of guilt weighed me down. What a hypocrite I was, while Amir acted with such integrity. Meanwhile, Baba was left to deal with my mother's disappointment that she couldn't plan her daughter's wedding. She pouted for a week.

This brush with tradition taught me several lessons. I lived in a country where, despite my family's indifference toward religion, Islam was part of the culture and dominated our lives. Appearances can be damning, founded in truth or not. And I had to be wary of narrow-minded religious perspectives that see only what they choose to see.

The summer came to a close, and once again my brother, my staunchest ally, left for college. This time, I felt the loss perhaps even more deeply than Maman.

TWELVE

During senior year, I began to lay out my future. I wanted to attend university in America like Amir. Although my mother was not in favor, Baba was an active participant and support. Even for him, though, the desire to keep his daughter at home occasionally came to the fore.

"You know, Leila, Tehran University, my alma mater, is a very good school."

"Baba, I really want to go to America. It's always been my dream."

"It's your choice, Leila. I want you to get a solid education so you can stand on your own feet." Baba's insightful words would carry a profound influence for years to come. The girls I knew were raised to marry, bear children, and run the household. That was Maman's dream for me too. She saw no need for college and resented Baba's support. Not surprisingly, the cold separation between us grew.

Amir returned home a few days before my graduation party. Although Uncle Morad and his family didn't make the journey from Esfahan, my cousin Mojtabah showed up, much to my chagrin. He'd just finished his sophomore year at Tehran University, studying political science and religion. "I'm fortunate to be taught by one of the most revered Ayatollahs, well-versed in both our traditions and the Koran," he told my father.

"Mojtabah, I'm glad you're happy," my father replied as I approached. Mojtabah, his back to me, was unaware of my presence.

"Thank you, Uncle Ali, for everything. Without your help I wouldn't be here, and it means a lot to my father." He paused and seemed to straighten himself. "You know I have the deepest admiration for you, but, respectfully, I must tell you I'm surprised you'd let Leila go to America. How can anything good come from that godless place?"

"*Salam*, Mojtabah," I said, stepping from behind him. If I expected any discomfort on his part, he certainly hid it well.

"*Salam alaykum*, cousin," he replied, his eyes on his shoes. "We were just talking about you." I hated his condescending, demeaning attitude with a passion. He hadn't looked me in the eyes since that fateful day in Esfahan when he declared me *na-mahram* at age nine.

"So I heard." He stood beside my father now, looking down at his hands folded in front of him. Baba shot me his warning look, his thick brows knotted in a small frown, knowing my blood was ready to boil.

"You'd do far better coming to Tehran University where you'd get a good education but, more importantly, be among the faithful."

The nerve of this guy. He had the gall to stand next to my father, in my own home, and preach to me. "Mojtabah, you're entitled to your opinion, but I'm going to America regardless." I suppose I should be grateful that he suggested I was worthy of going to university at all.

"But it's a nation of heathens, corrupted with drugs and pornography. It's hardly a suitable place for a Muslim woman." He looked up, stealing a quick glance at me as his passion rose, but quickly realized the inappropriateness of his act and returned to gazing at his hands.

"Cousin, clearly we don't share the same perspective of America. I don't see heathens and corruption. I see opportunity for freedom of thought, something apparently you find offensive."

"Uncle Ali, it's your decision where to send your daughter. I meant no offense." He bowed slightly in deference to my father.

"Actually this is Leila's decision. I respect her character enough to know she will bring honor to our family. But I appreciate your concern for your cousin, even if I don't share your point of view."

Mojtabah nodded and left to join Amir and the others.

"Baba, how could you let that arrogant ass talk that way?" The words rushed out before I could clamp a hand on my mouth. "I'm sorry, Baba. It's just he makes me furious."

"Leila, please, he's still your cousin. Because he doesn't see the world as you or I doesn't make him any less family. Is this the way I've taught you to treat others?"

"But who does he think he is, preaching and talking about the 'faithful'?"

"He's a devout Muslim. Remember, under Islamic law, you don't have the same rights as a man. Your father or husband makes choices for you. That's exactly why I told him it was *your* decision. I want Mojtabah to know, in no uncertain terms, that you have a mind of your own, as well as my blessing. Remember, Daughter, you don't open a mind by beating it down; you must raise it to the light." He held his hands up toward the ceiling.

"I love you, Baba," I said, my heart filled with admiration. He was so wise, delicately casting a soft radiance on otherwise unbearable feelings.

"I love you too, Leila. Now, go help your mother."

We rejoined family and friends for a wonderful evening. Maman glowed with pride as once again, she successfully choreographed a grand party. "If only it were your wedding," she sighed at evening's end. I smiled, knowing how desperately she wanted her daughter a bride. In bed that night, I marveled at Baba's faith in me. I was ready to meet the challenge and make him proud. I couldn't wait for college to begin.

*   *   *

I arrived at JFK airport in New York, nervously navigating through immigration and customs. Stepping into the arrival terminal, I searched for my big brother. Amir was just beyond the swaying metal doors, separating passengers from visitors, waving to draw my attention. His tanned face gave his olive skin a glow in this sea of foreign-looking people. He was so handsome and sophisticated in a neatly pressed blue pinstripe shirt with those inverted V-shaped eyebrows I so envied. I rushed over to greet him with three kisses, and we headed to his car.

"My friends are excited you're here," he said. "Tomorrow they're all coming over to meet my baby sister. Later maybe I'll take you to the Jersey Shore. But first, we're going to get a Big Mac."

I glowed at being called his baby sister. Although longing for independence, deep down I still wanted a protector, a white knight, a shoulder I could lean on. I wanted to know he'd still rescue me as he'd done many times before.

"What in the world's a Big Mac?"

"The best cheeseburger ever! You'll love it."

As the car sped away, I gazed in awe at the city skyline: The twin towers of the World Trade Center and the magnificent Empire State Building glistened like silver beacons of promise in the setting sun. It was incredible to see in person what I'd only seen in pictures.

"When can we visit New York?" I asked, looking through the back window as he exited the highway.

"We can go this week. I'll take you shopping at Saks Fifth Avenue and Bloomingdale's so you can pick up some clothes. First, let's get that Big Mac."

He drove through a lane marked "Drive-Thru" and ordered our food over an intercom, then pulled up farther to pick it up, all in minutes. This novel experience added to the exotic sense America held for me. The Big Mac was everything Amir claimed, but experiencing my first American burger from a drive-through made it even more novel.

During the ride, I marveled at the lush green land compared to Iran's arid, dry roadside. We approached the small town of Bethlehem, home to Bethlehem Steel and Lehigh University. Amir gave me a quick campus tour. We drove the wooded hills of Lehigh, taking in its impressive old-world charm and natural beauty. Some buildings, of Gothic stone with ornate carvings, reminded me of old European architecture. In contrast, there were modern brick buildings and all-glass structures scattered about. As we drove, peripheral movement caught my attention— furry little animals scurrying about the grounds, effortlessly charging up and down the trees.

"Are those rats?" I asked squeamishly.

"The little ones are chipmunks, and the ones with furry tails are squirrels," laughed Amir. "They eat mostly nuts . . . oh, and sometimes Iranian girls," he said with a smile. "Don't worry, they don't bite," Amir added, noting my apprehensive look.

The tour concluded with a drive up frat row. "This is where parties happen on weekends. Lehigh was an all-male school until 1971. Now, the men-to-women ratio is 10 to 1." My odds of finding a boyfriend were good, I thought, smiling inside. And this time, a real one.

Amir spent the next week introducing me to everything American. He took me on an architectural tour of New York City, pointing out places I'd seen only in pictures and movies. Times Square looked exactly as on TV, lights flashing brightly, even during the day. I craned my neck at the base of the Twin Towers, straining to see the very top until I got dizzy. The view from atop Lady Liberty overlooking New York harbor was breathtaking, sailboats sliding gracefully by like a ballet. From the distance, the Verrazano Bridge was magical at night, glamorously shining, bejeweled in light. I had never seen a bridge so expansive and beautiful.

In my first few weeks at Lehigh, I made a lot of friends. As the only foreign student in my dorm, the girls enjoyed the variation I brought. And I, in turn, relished their attention. When asked where I was from, I'd reply "Iran."

"Where's that?" was inevitably the follow-up.

"Persia." They knew of Persia, perhaps because they'd read about it in history books. But Iran was an unknown.

One day, the phone rang, interrupting my studying.

"Hello," the voice said. "Is this Miss Leila Moradi?"

"Yes, and who is this?"

"My name is Ali Farmani. I'm a junior at Lehigh, also from Iran. I'm calling to welcome you and invite you to join the Islamic Association of Lehigh. We mostly meet for friendship and prayer."

The friendship part was enticing, but I was apprehensive about prayer. Religious fundamentalists always worried me, and the prospect of meeting a bunch of zealots held no real draw. But maybe they were just students with something in common, a sense of belonging in a foreign land. No harm in checking it out. Besides, one could never have enough friends, so I agreed to go to a meeting.

Ali Farmani greeted me at the door. "You must be Leila. Salam." His accent betrayed his Iranian descent. Black khakis hung low on his narrow hips. His upper lip sported a sparse dusting of a mustache, and his big hook nose overwhelmed his face, a definite Iranian trait.

In the sparsely decorated room, folding chairs were arranged in a circle. Some milled about in quiet conversation, while a few sat alone. Ali and I took seats next to each other, and within minutes, a male student announced the start of the meeting. He was a heavy young man with a shaved head and a full black beard and mustache surrounding his mouth. I could barely see his lips as he spoke.

"*Besmellahe Rahmane Rahim*, in the name of God, the compassionate, the merciful," he began as he raised his arms toward heaven. "My brothers and sisters, welcome. My name is Ibrahim Al-Faid. I'm a Muslim from Saudi Arabia and a graduate student. Tonight is our first meeting of the year, so we'll decide on prayer groups and assign passages for reading."

My eyes shifted from his face, less attentive to his words and focused on the faces around me. The men wore normal attire, long-sleeved shirts, khakis, or other casual pants, no jeans. The women were in Islamic dress—a head scarf and loose-fitting clothes. In my short-sleeved blouse and blue jeans, I was the only woman not dressed according to *Shari'a*. I was suddenly uncomfortable. Jeans, being Western, are not worn by strict Muslims, and short sleeves are forbidden. But my most obvious offense was my uncovered hair. I was squirming in my seat, though no one seemed bothered by my improper Muslim attire. I sat up sharply when I heard my name. Were they going to reprimand me? Throw me out?

"This is Leila Moradi. She's a freshman and a Muslim from Iran. Please welcome her," Ali announced.

The comment "Muslim from Iran" irked me. I hated being pigeonholed, but I smiled, as all eyes were on me. To my relief, attention shifted as other new members were introduced.

When the meeting adjourned, Ibrahim walked over. Mostly he looked at the floor, with occasional glimpses at me. "We're pleased you're here and hope to see you at our next meeting." By saying we rather than I, he took me back to Iran, where acknowledging a one-on-one relationship between a man and a woman was deemed inappropriate. Several other group members came by to greet me. A woman who introduced herself as Elham was also Iranian and new to Lehigh. It was evident her English was weak, as she stumbled over her words before finally switching to Farsi.

"I cook Persian dinner for you sometime," she said.

"Oh, that would be nice," I said, realizing I missed Persian cuisine. The flavors of saffron, barberries, or herbs mingled with the sweet taste of lamb had no rival in the bland cafeteria food. Even American burgers had lost their initial thrill.

"I live in an apartment off-campus. You come next week for dinner."

She was friendly, even if she was conservatively dressed like my aunts from Esfahan. We exchanged phone numbers, and I headed back to my dorm and immediately dialed Amir.

"They freaked me out a little with how serious they are about religion," I shared.

"Leila, why'd you even go?"

"I don't know. I guess I can't say no."

"I said no."

"That's because you're a man. When you say no, it makes you decisive. A woman saying no is just plain rude. You know that," I said, mild resentment creeping up in me.

"That's in Iran, not here. If you're going to survive here, Leila, you need to be tougher," he advised.

"I suppose. But it's not easy to switch gears like that. These things are ingrained in me."

In my first months at school, I got weekly letters from Neda. In her letters, she unveiled secrets she'd once whispered in a bedroom or back-yard. She told of her clandestine boyfriend. He'd made sexual advances, which she promptly rejected. Perhaps I didn't write back as often because I had no boyfriend to write about. It was disappointing that despite the odds with so many men at Lehigh, not one asked me out. I was a bit jealous of Neda. As the year went on, her letters dwindled down to one every couple of months, if I was lucky.

Freshman year was drawing to a close. Much to Maman's dismay, Amir decided to stay and take summer classes. On the other hand, I was ready for home. School ended mid-May, a great time of year in Tehran. The climate would be perfect for weeks before the heat rolled in, fresh fruit and herbs abundant. I couldn't wait to see everyone. It had been almost a year.

THIRTEEN

It was 2 A.M. by the time I cleared customs and immigration in Tehran. Outside the secured area, I scanned the colorful sea of faces, and in the midst of hundreds of people, Baba's balding head, reflecting the glow of moonlight, was easy to spot. Then I saw the others. Maman was waving her arms over her head; Maman Rouhi was next to Uncle Mohsen and his wife and kids. I spotted other cousins, smiling and waving bouquets of flowers. Making my way through the jostling crowd, porter in tow, I could hardly contain my excitement. I hadn't expected so many greeters at this early hour. There were kisses and embraces amidst excited questions about life in America. My attention was torn in the crowd until Neda interrupted the din.

"I have big news. I'm getting married!"

"What!" I screamed. "When?"

"July 19th. I am sooooo excited you'll be here."

"Why didn't you tell me, Neda?"

"I wanted to surprise you."

How far we'd come. Neda, co-delinquent in our Whimpy's fiasco, was getting married. I wondered if Parviz was the one, the boy she'd been secretly seeing for a year. There'd be time to ask later.

The ride home was more subdued as excitement gave way to drowsiness. Maman Rouhi held my hand in her lap, her head bobbling as she dozed. I gazed out the window, taking in familiar sights of buildings and people roaming the streets. So many still bustled about at this early hour. Tehran, I remembered fondly, like New York, never slept. When we arrived home, I grabbed the bouquets and ran in, hearing the excited barks of my long-lost friend. I didn't stand a chance against big furry Rostam as he rushed to greet me. I stroked the line of white fur that started at the top of his head and meandered down his back like the stripe on a skunk. When he finally calmed down, I stood and took my mother's arm. "Make sure you wash your hands now," she reminded me. Dogs are not considered clean.

"It's nice to be home, Maman."

"You should be always home. Mothers need their daughters, especially as they get older. But I blame your father for this." This wasn't the greeting I sought. Guess some things never change.

It took me several days to get over jet lag and the nine-and-a-half-hour time difference, all the while receiving "welcome home" visits from relatives and friends. After a year's absence, they wanted news of me and my brother. If I had to answer "Why didn't Amir come?" one more time, I'd scream.

The house overflowed with flowers—deep red and peach-colored roses, mixed bouquets of daisies and mums, purple and yellow violets, pots of azaleas, and hydrangeas. Maman Rouhi scurried about, adjusting flowers in vases of all shapes and colors. Fatemeh complained there was no room for more gift cakes in the refrigerator. At least two were my favorite—the green ones from Shirni Danmarki, the famous Danish pastry shop.

My first weekend home, we went to Sohanak, our farmhouse in the hills north of Tehran. We always sacrificed a sheep there when anyone returned safely from a trip. Sohanak was special to me with fond memories of youth. I'd penned deeply moving poems of love and despair under the shade of huge pines dotting the grounds. I missed the two guard dogs that protected the sheep, the property, and its fruit trees. I even missed the tinkling sound of water trickling into the reservoir.

The day dawned scattered with clouds. As we left the city, sunshine infused the clear mountain air. A few billowy white clouds were pushed like tall ships across the sky by southerly winds. For summer in Tehran, it was a spring-like day, a perfect time to relax in the country. As we approached, I saw the familiar rooster that had once spun atop the weather vane, now dethroned and rusty with age. The farmer's youngest son ran up excitedly to open the wide wooden gates. The caretaker and his family were always happy to see us; their help for the day always resulted in a big tip from Baba.

Ahmad lived in a one-bedroom straw and mud shack near the

entrance gates with his wife and four kids. Their home sat within yards of the sheep's pen, and I wondered how they tolerated the hearty odor and the constant "baa, baa" of the sheep and lambs. While Ahmad went to choose the *ghorbani* lamb, I took a tour to reacquaint myself with the farm. The trees had grown taller, offering more shade than I recalled. The bushes were well-trimmed around the stream. Wandering the grounds, I noticed green peaches hanging in abundance, slowly ripening in the morning sun. I took in the scent of roses, tasted a spearmint leaf, plucked red raspberries, and let the flavor burst in my mouth. I made my way atop the hill to the reservoir.

Built to retain the irrigation water, it once also served as our swimming pool. I stared now at the sullied water, its thin film speckled with small insects that had plunged to their death. Years ago, it overflowed with clear, bone-chilling mountain water. I recalled times cousins and friends made bets on who'd take the first icy plunge. I'd jump in to show off, swim swiftly to get over the cold and then float on my back, letting the hot sun bake my body, tempering the icy cold waters beneath me. That sun had burned memories into my skin. Shedding my light linen jacket, I embraced the fullness of my childhood again. I looked down the hill and studied the heavily laden fruit trees, fondly recalling the sound of crickets swelling like a crescendo at night.

I turned to face Tehran in the valley below, its majestic buildings shrouded in a haze of thick pollution. I didn't remember this much smog over the city. But with increased traffic, the pollution levels had risen, obscuring the landscape's beauty. Even today's breezes couldn't disperse the blanket of brown and gray. To my right, a tufted line of trees kissed the horizon in the distance, the milky blue sky reaching down in an embrace. A sudden shiver stirred the cherry trees, filling the air with white and pink blossoms, slices of the orange sun peeking through their branches.

A voice drew me from my thoughts. "Leila, Leila . . ." I turned and saw Grandmother at the bottom of the hill, yelling something about the lamb. I ran down the slope, sliding with the cascading pebbles as I skidded downward. How I used to love that as a kid, testing how far I could ride the avalanche of stones without falling.

Everyone had gathered under the mulberry tree. The sacrificial lamb lay on her side, kicking and bleating, but I tuned her out as I had learned to do many times before. Ahmad tied her feet with a rope. She must have known what was coming and wriggled in fear. He checked her eyes and ears one last time to ensure she was healthy and then offered water, which she refused. When he popped the sugar cube in her mouth, she grew quiet, her dark eyes resolved to her fate. Though I had watched this a hundred times, it still tugged at my heart.

"The sugar sweetens her last moments," Ahmad justified, noting I'd turned my head. "I don't torture the poor things," he said consolingly as he pulled a long sharp knife from its black leather case. I looked at the lamb, now struggling for freedom as she sensed imminent danger.

Muttering *"Besmellahe Rahmane Rahim*, in the name of God, the compassionate, the merciful," left to right, with one quick slit, Ahmad finished the deed. Slaughtered in *zabiha* tradition to minimize pain and drain the blood, Ahmad believed this act was blessed by Allah. The lamb twitched in seizures of death, blood from its neck soaking the ground by the mulberry tree. In moments, she'll be at peace, I thought, watching her lie motionless under the tree where others had gone before her.

On the terrace, we sat on two large wooden benches, enjoying the afternoon breeze. Maman Rouhi served tea she'd made on the samovar. Popping a piece of saffron *nabat* in my mouth, I savored the hot liquid. I loved Grandmother doting over me. As my mother's affection seemed to have been withdrawn over the years, I drew on Grandmother's that much more.

The wind carried the aroma of burning charcoal to the terrace. Ahmad's wife was making *lavash* bread inside the tanoor, the clay-lined oven in the ground. While I was lost in daydreams, enjoying the scents and sounds, my father had set up the backgammon set.

"Time for *takhte nard*. Come, let me give you a thrashing."

"Not a chance. I'll beat *you*," I said, knowing full well it was an idle threat. "I'm a college kid now," I boasted, as though a year in college might have made me better at backgammon.

"But I'm the undefeated *takhte nard* champion of the world," he bragged loudly. And in truth, I had never beaten my father.

"Okay, what color do you want: brown or white?"

"I'll take white. Did you know Lehigh's colors are brown and white?" I added, making the connection.

"And how is school?" He rolled the dice. Six and four: a good combination to start.

"I like it a lot. I enjoy the business classes and would like to take more." Five and three: not a bad combination for me. I moved my checkers.

"You should." Double fours. Damn; he always rolled great numbers. He was positioning his backgammon checkers closer to home, building a strong base. Meanwhile, I managed only blots or single checkers.

I rolled a one and a two. Then he rolled a five and a three, took out two of my checkers, and looked up beaming. I had four hits sitting at the bar, waiting to be saved and be back on the board.

"Surrender?"

"No way. I can still win," I said adamantly, knowing full well my cause was lost. "Baba, I went to an Islamic Association meeting."

"Well, Daughter, it's good to be open-minded. Just be careful with religious groups. Religion is a good thing in moderation. It can be a comfort in times of need. It can guide us to be better, gentler people. But taken to extreme, it becomes destructive. By the way," he said, changing the subject, "did I tell you that the Dean at Tehran University asked me to teach a class?" He sat up straight, beaming. "They want me to teach Persian art history."

"Are you going to do it?"

"I think so. It'll be fun to teach young people about something I love, and it's a diversion from my normal routine."

I watched as, one by one, he moved his checkers closer to the home board and took out mine. The end of the game was near when he brought up the changes in Iran.

"There is a lot of unrest here in Iran. It's in the outer cities now and hasn't yet affected Tehran."

"What's it about?"

"A group of ayatollahs and mullahs wants to return Iran to an Islamic state. They've picked up quite a bit of support, especially from impoverished areas and villages."

"Well, the Shah has a loyal army. He'll fight it off."

"There are rumors his forces are brutally suppressing the rebels. I don't know what to believe. How can a man with such deep love for art condone violence and killing?"

"I hope it doesn't affect my return to school." I was eighteen and preoccupied with how events affected *my* life. Politics held little interest.

"You'll be fine." And, with that, he threw his last roll of the dice for the win. "Ready for game two or give up?"

"I surrender, Baba," I said, holding up my hands.

We enjoyed the *abghoost* Maman prepared with the fresh lamb, its aroma tantalizing us for the last hour. We dined on fresh-cut herb salad and homemade *lavash*. The only thing missing was Amir. As we ate, conversation centered on family and friends and Neda's wedding.

The day ended with the beauty of a spectacular sunset. I looked one last time at the sky awash with streaks of orange, gold, and purple. Relaxed, well-fed, and safe from evil, I was ready to go home.

FOURTEEN

Throbbing pain threatened to numb my shoulder and woke me from dreams as I lay pressed against the bed. It had been several days since my last interrogation, something I could judge based only on the number of times they'd given me food. Keeping prisoners well-nourished wasn't really part of the Pasdaran's strategy, so we were fed once a day, twice at most. It seemed I was always hungry, and the rough sackcloth robe now hung baggy because of the weight I'd lost. Memories of Maman's wonderful lamb *abghoost* on the terrace of Sohanak stayed with me, so real I could taste it. From beneath the thin mattress, I pulled a crust of bread saved from my last meal and nibbled it as I sat.

"I'm trying to be strong, just like you'd want me to, Baba, but it's so hard." Baba never answered me when I spoke to him like this. I worried about the day he would, when I could be certain my sanity was gone. I touched my face, gently probing for particularly tender spots that might mean broken bones. The swelling had gone down some, but I could only imagine how I looked. Touching my cheek, I felt the wetness of tears. Sometimes the tears came unbidden, almost unnoticed when I'd think about my parents, my brother—all those taken from me. I had to steel myself, call on inner strength. Others before me had endured far worse.

The outer hallway door swung open with a clang against the concrete wall. Footsteps drew near. Be strong. A key unlocked my cell door, and it swung inward as Lieutenant Mehraban entered. He never came to the cell himself. What was this about? I stood up and faced him, the crust of bread clenched hidden behind my back.

"We just received this letter from your husband. He's spoken with the prosecutor concerning your father. Here, I'll let you read for yourself. I'll speak with you after you're done." He handed me a slip of paper and left, locking the door behind him.

I couldn't believe it; finally some word from Farhad. Was it possible he'd found me? Now surely he'd get me out. I unfolded the paper, feeling faint from excitement.

My Dearest Leila,

I can only imagine the horrors you've endured and, as it turns out, for nothing. My father has spoken with the prosecutors, and they've clarified their position. They no longer seek to arrest your father, as they understand he's a loyal supporter of the régime, Alhamdolillah, praise be to Allah. They only want to question him about the student radicals. They are the real targets, not your father. So you see, you suffer for nothing. If you tell them where he is, you will be released.

I long for your embrace and have missed you so. My parents weep for your return, and even your grandmother is begging that you speak so you are returned to us. I remain your ever-faithful and loving husband,

Farhad

Holding the note at arm's length, I stumbled backward toward the bed as I read it again, my hands trembling. I might be freed? My father was only wanted for questioning? Tears of joy flowed. Farhad had come to save me after all. I read the letter again through tears streaming down my face, stinging open wounds.

My Dearest Leila,

Could these be Farhad's words? Was this his handwriting?

They no longer seek to imprison your father, as they understand he's a loyal supporter of the régime, Alhamdolillah.

My father was anything but a loyal supporter of the régime, and Farhad knew that. Plus, Farhad didn't have a religious bone in his body. He'd never write "praise be to Allah." I don't even think he knew how to recite *namaz* prayers.

My parents weep for your return, and even your grandmother is begging that you speak so you are returned to us. I remain your ever-faithful and loving husband.

I never saw his mother, much less his father, shed a tear for anyone or anything. My grandmother would never suggest I betray my parents. And *faithful and loving husband?* I'd confronted him with his infidelity right before my arrest. He was brazen, but he'd never write something so obviously untrue. He would never humble himself to his wife. This was all a cruel hoax, a trap, an attempt to trick me, to weaken my resolve. Relief turned to anger, and I wanted to scream. I ripped the paper to shreds and shoved the scraps through the cut under the door.

"Liars! It's all lies, isn't it, you bastards. Liars . . ." My voice trailed off with my whimpering and echoed unanswered down the empty hallway. I sank to my knees, holding my head as any glimmer of hope left me.

FIFTEEN

Unrest continued spreading in the countryside. News of protests and arrests were on TV, on the radio, and in the papers nonstop. I was getting nervous and even thought of skipping Neda's wedding to go back to the U.S. While I hated to miss the wedding, I didn't want to be stuck or even delayed in Tehran due to civil unrest. But the wedding day was around the corner, so I pushed worries aside and became occupied with wedding plans.

As the date drew closer, I spent the days with Neda, helping run errands and gossiping about her soon-to-be in-laws. Furniture was rearranged at Aunt Firouzeh's house for the ceremony. Caterers, florists, and tailors made last-minute preparations. Neda's fiancé, Parviz, was not permitted in my aunt's house until the wedding day, though he'd been often enough before. Now it was all about appearances.

When the big day arrived, Aunt Firouzeh's dining room was transformed into a magical place. Walls were covered with flowing white lace, affixed with bouquets of fresh white roses, their fragrance intoxicating the senses. The older folks sat gabbing over tea and cake as my cousins and I huddled in Neda's room. The wedding dress hung in her closet like a queen's gown awaiting the coronation. Carefully, she took it out to show us. Made of silk taffeta, the bodice was decorated with shiny beads in an intricate pattern that Neda's sister, Tara, our family artist, had designed. There were sequin bouquets of calla lilies wrapped in thin satin ribbon. Clustered lilies of the valley with tiny pearl heads were choreographed together like a well-manicured garden. Additional white and silver sequins were sewn together to form surrounding foliage. The beads, sequins, and pearls trailed into the skirt in beautiful splashes down the length of the chapel train. It was the most beautiful wedding gown I'd ever seen. We took turns holding it in front of us in the mirror.

On my turn, I took a quick glimpse and passed the gown to Tara, Neda's older sister. It brought back unpleasant memories of the arranged marriage I'd barely dodged.

"Tell us about tonight, Neda. What will you and Parviz do after the party?" quizzed Golnaz teasingly. She was always the teasing cousin.

"Have you guys done anything, you know, hanky-panky?" asked Tara.

"No, we've kissed and . . . I'm not telling." Neda blushed and looked away. Slowly, she faced us again, as though we were experts in the matter and asked the question she'd obviously been brooding over. "You think he'll want sex tonight?"

"Oh, *yeah*," said Golnaz, with an air of authority, despite the fact that at twenty-five she remained unmarried. "He'll be all over you like bees on honey the moment everybody leaves."

"Are you nervous?" I asked.

"A little. It's not like we talk about these things."

Girl-talk went on into the afternoon as guests began to arrive. We helped Neda into her gown. She looked truly beautiful. The flowing mermaid shape highlighted her long legs; the bodice accentuated her bosom ever so discreetly, while ringlets of jet black hair fell gently on her shoulders. With a veil that reached her knees, she looked every part the bride. The excitement of the day reflected in her glowing skin, eyes moist with anticipation, hands trembling slightly—the virginal bride.

The doorbell rang. The groom and his family had arrived. While the men were led to the living room, the women proceeded to the wedding room. Everyone waited in hushed expectancy. The *aghd* ceremony was about to begin. All that was missing was the *akhoond* clergy. Within minutes, he joined the groom's family in the living room. Wearing a white turban, he was dressed in a white collarless shirt and traditional brown cloak. He had a full mustache and beard speckled with gray as befit a cleric and wore thick, old-fashioned, wire-rimmed glasses. Aunt Firouzeh came for Neda.

"Are you ready, Daughter?" she asked, pausing to gaze on her second child in full wedding regalia. "Ahhh," she breathed, hand on her chest. "You look stunning." She was beaming with pride as she fussed with her daughter's veil.

"I'm ready," Neda said, as Tara helped lift the train of her dress. We led her to the wedding room, where she sat on a bench. On the floor, before the bride, was the *sofreh aghd*, wedding tablecloth, facing east. The white damask *sofreh* held traditional items. A leather-bound Koran lay open on an antique *khatam* book-holder. A single goldfish swam lazily in a fishbowl, symbolizing life. White candles in tall, ornate, silver candlesticks burned brightly on each side of a mirror, for luster in their life. A special loaf of *sangak* bread, sprinkled with colorful seeds, was displayed for prosperity and feasting. A bowl of honey symbolized sweetness. White gauze packages wrapped in ribbon contained *noghl*, a white wedding candy. These, along with small golden coins, would later be thrown over the bride and groom's heads to symbolize sweetness and prosperity. There was a small prayer rug, reminding the couple of the importance of *namaz* prayers. And finally, the brazier of smoking *esfand*, or wild rue, warded off the evil spirits.

The bridegroom, dressed in a navy pin-striped suit, took the seat to Neda's right, symbolic of the respect he'll receive from his bride. The older women, including the groom's family, were standing in the room. The men huddled in the living room, the French doors draped to isolate them from the wedding room. They could hear but not watch. Here, women were in charge. Aunt Soheila and Aunt Firouzeh stood on Neda's sides, holding a canopy of white silk over her head, a job designated for happily married women. My mother stood behind Neda, showering her with crystals as she rubbed cone-shaped blocks of sugar together throughout the ceremony to symbolize sweetness of life. Did she wish it were me beneath that canopy? Would this serve as a reminder that I, too, was of marrying age? Would Maman yet again raise her desire for me to be the bride? And how long before her influence would overcome Baba's hopes that I finish college?

"The bride is ready," announced Aunt Firouzeh, pulling me from my reverie.

Silence fell on the room. "*Besmellahe Rahmaneh Rahim*, in the name of God, the compassionate, the merciful," began the *akhoond*.

For nearly fifteen minutes, in a monotonous voice, he read aloud the *aghd nameh* wedding contract. The bride's dowry was detailed: bedroom and living room furniture, rugs, dressers, dishes, and appliances.

Then the *mehrieh* was disclosed—twenty gold coins. This money, defined in *rials*, or gold coins, is bestowed upon the bride by the groom in case of divorce. Oddly, during the most romantic event of a couple's life, the terms of divorce, negotiated by parents or elders, are announced to the world. Family elders brag about their *mehrieh* negotiation skills and are proud to have it broadcast to wedding guests, seeking nods of approval as it's announced. Neda had her share of nods and murmured approval.

I noticed Grandmother sewing at one end of the veil canopy, while Neda sat beneath.

"What's Maman Rouhi doing?" I whispered to Golnaz, keeping my eyes on the ritual.

"Stitching the veil symbolizes closing the mother-in-law's lips, so she says nothing to meddle in their life."

When he finished, the *akhoond* asked the bridegroom for his consent, to which Parviz replied yes. Then he asked the bride, and everyone listened for Neda's affirmation, knowing full well it wouldn't come. She stared ahead. Female relatives of the groom scurried to approach Neda, ceremoniously offering gifts of jewelry. Parviz's aunt placed a gold bracelet on her wrist. The bride was to consider her gifts while pondering her response.

For several minutes, Neda contemplated in front of the *sofreh*. She cast a shy, furtive glance around the room but held her tongue. Her long pause was the *akhoond's* signal to read through the vows and contract again. We stood in silence as he repeated a full rendition of the marital vows, terms, and conditions. Once again, he asked, "Do you agree?" More women scurried about the room. Parviz's other aunt and sister approached Neda, one placing a second matching gold bracelet on her wrist while the other clipped pearl earrings to her ears. We watched in anticipation as the bride continued to quietly consider her new gifts but spoke no word. Neda played her role beautifully. Anticipation built. The crowd breathed silently.

With no affirmative, the *akhoond* patiently read the *aghd nameh* a third time, as lengthy and detailed as the prior two. When finished, he asked the inevitable question again. This time, the groom's grandmother approached Neda, seated like a regal queen, and placed a triple-stranded pearl bracelet on her other wrist. She stood by while Parviz's mother adorned the bride with the grandest gift of all—a double strand of pearls around her neck. She kissed Neda on both cheeks, whispered something in her ear, and stepped back to await the elusive yes. The bride finally looked down at the beautiful *sofreh* and ever so demurely whispered a yes. The *akhoond* in the adjoining room couldn't hear but was slyly given the signal.

"I can't hear you," he announced in a loud voice.

"Yes," whispered Neda, audible only to us in the room.

"I can't hear you," yelled the *akhoond* one last time, suggesting she, too, must raise her voice. There was hushed silence in the room as everyone held their breath.

"Yes," she repeated with more force.

Neda disappeared in the swarm of women surrounding her, showering her with kisses and clapping joyously while the *akhoond* struggled to be heard as he read a passage from the Koran. When the rings were exchanged, everyone began to applaud while I covered my ears to muffle the loud *li li li li li li* ululating noise of the women.

In turns, Neda and Parviz dipped their fingers in the bowl of honey and placed them in each other's mouths to symbolize the sweetness they'd give each other. As they left, everyone threw the *noghl* and gold coin packages over their heads. There were hurried kisses and hugs in departure to the banquet hall for the party.

Once the room cleared, I stood taking in the beauty. I could hear excited voices outside as guests arranged rides. My mind wandered to the day when I was ten and imagined myself a bride. Maman had pulled out her own wedding gown to show me, and I begged her to let me try it on. She smiled and helped me into the long milky gown covered in Chantilly lace, pulling back my black curls and pinning them for an elegant up-do. From her closet, she produced a strand of pearls so beautiful it took my breath away. She closed the clasp around my neck and stood back watching. I stared at myself in the mirror, the hundreds of sequins and beads a dazzling reflection in my dark eyes. My cheeks glowed, and I smiled as I saw the look on my mother's face in the mirror. She was proud of me; I could see it in her eyes and the dimples on her cheek. I ran to her, dragging the gown along the floor. She held me in her arms and kissed me and said, "Someday, *azizam*, someday."

"It's time to go, Leila." It was Maman's voice, pulling me from the flashback.

"I'm coming, Maman," I replied, a single tear rolling down my cheek.

"What are you doing?" she asked.

"I was just looking at all this. It's so beautiful."

"Someday, *azizam*, someday."

SIXTEEN

The horn-blowing procession of vehicles followed the newlyweds in their white Mercedes draped in white roses and daisies. Maman was particularly jovial and talkative. She so enjoyed weddings. She clasped my hand as we walked into the banquet hall, re-introducing me to friends and relatives I hadn't seen in ages. She was practically bragging about me. I almost fell over when she introduced me as "my beautiful daughter." Her unexpected enthusiasm made me blush.

I was kind of glad Amir wasn't there; he would have stolen her attention. I remembered the time I was five and Maman was playing with me in the yard. She chased me around the *hose*, lifting and whirling me about as she turned in circles. With each whirl, I burst into giggles. As she picked up speed, my pink plastic sandals flew off my feet, shooting to opposite corners of the yard. Hearing my giggling, Amir came out, stood in the middle of the yard, and announced he wanted a snack. Maman immediately set me down to follow him into the house. She left me standing on the hot stone pavement, lifting one foot then another as I eyed my plastic sandals. No, it was a good thing he wasn't here today to steal her attention.

We spotted friends and acquaintances exchanging greetings and idle chit-chat. I noticed old family friends, the Ghorbanis and their children, Javad and Negar. They rushed to greet us with hugs and kisses.

"Neda *khanoom* is a beautiful bride, but Leila *khanoom* will be even lovelier," said Mrs. Ghorbani, laying a gentle hand on my shoulder. But she wasn't looking at me; she was looking at my mother, as though sharing a secret message.

"Yes, yes," chimed in Mr. Ghorbani in his soft-spoken voice. "You're of age, you know. Time to consider a husband."

I hated it when conversations turned to husbands and marriage.

That's all parents seemed to think about.

"Well, Leila's in college now. There's time for marriage," my father said. He'd read my mind. I could've kissed him.

"Ah, but Ali, you don't want your daughter to pass her prime," Mr. Ghorbani reasoned in a more serious tone.

Mr. Ghorbani was a quiet man, dressed in a navy suit with gray pinstripes and a blue-green paisley tie too wide for the current style. His bald crown sported tufts of unruly hair on the sides, with a long strand drawn across the top and seemingly pasted in place to hide the barren expanse. Thick curling lashes framed his dark brown eyes. He stood a few inches shorter than his wife, something rarely seen in Iran. Once, at their house, I thought it odd that he looked taller than his wife in a framed picture.

"They stood him on a pedestal to make him taller," my cousin Tara snickered. "A man isn't supposed to be shorter than his wife; it means he's inferior."

"Leila's only eighteen," my father said, justifying my single state. "There's time."

"Practically nineteen," corrected my mother, siding with the Ghorbanis.

"Leila, let's get something to drink," Golnaz and Tara said, appearing from nowhere to the rescue. They dragged me away from this most annoying conversation. We spent the next hour wandering the room, meeting friends, commenting on the bride and her gown, her hairdo, and other trivialities. My parents were in a permanent state of huddle with the Ghorbanis.

Chimes drew us back to our table for dinner. It was quite a feast.

"I can't eat another bite." I'd had seconds of roast lamb and *shirin polo*, the sweet rice with pistachios, almonds, and saffron traditionally served at weddings.

"And the cake is yet to come," reminded Maman.

"Come on, we'll dance it off," said Golnaz, always the energetic one. "The party's just getting started." Persian dance music filled the room. A five-piece band played songs that drew first women, then men, onto the dance floor. Dancers cared nothing for gender or age but moved together in rhythm to the music. I was observing dancers while in my seat when Mrs. Ghorbani grabbed my arm and dragged me to the dance floor. There was no opportunity to decline. As the song neared its end, it was my chance to flee, but before I could take two steps, Javad appeared from nowhere, blocking my exit. Mrs. Ghorbani stealthily vanished as Javad took her place. Well-choreographed, I thought suspiciously.

"Let's dance, Leila," he said. "I like this song."

Reluctantly, I danced to a popular song, *How Beautiful You Look Tonight*. His dancing was miserably off-rhythm, and he moved with all the grace of an ox. I was uncomfortable and prayed for an escape. I needed to get my mind off dancing.

"So how's your work?" I asked with feigned interest, eyes on other dancers.

"It's going very well. I have my own practice and more patients than I can handle."

"That's great, great." Silence. I wished he'd say something. I didn't know what else to ask. One glance confirmed that, like his father, his hairline was rapidly fleeing. Soon he'd no doubt resort to a similar sparse comb-over to deny its regression. Though still a young man, he looked older and was devoid of physical appeal. Short like his father, dark like his mother, he'd missed out on his father's long eyelashes and his mother's full lips. He'd managed to inherit his parents' least desirable features: narrow beady eyes and an absent chin that fell away from a too-thin mouth. I was 5'5" and in slight heels, but the top of Javad's head barely reached my eyebrows. As a doctor with a prestigious degree from George Washington University, his parents bragged he topped Tehran's most-wanted bachelor list. He stared up at me as we danced, his eyes boring into my soul. I looked away, occasionally confirming he was still staring. It was unnerving.

"Like the song says, you look beautiful tonight," he said, finally breaking the silence.

"Thank you," I replied, blushing.

"Someone as young and pretty as you must have a boyfriend, no?"

I ignored the question and kept moving to the music, wishing it would end.

"Do you have a boyfriend in the U.S.?"

"No."

"What about suitors?" It was starting to feel like an inquisition.

"I'm not interested in getting married right now."

"Really? Doesn't every girl dream of marriage? And there aren't a lot of good husbands to choose from," he said with a pause, "once you're past your prime." Was he implying I was a pickle? With each passing second, every word, I felt more annoyed but was trapped for the duration of the song.

Javad was about twenty-nine. Perhaps he was hoping to marry one of these days, but I found his questions personal and intrusive. It was none of his business whether I found a husband. Why was he asking if I had a boyfriend? I just wished the song would end and he'd go away. I was trapped, and walking away would have been rude, an affront to his family.

"Leila, I like you, and I hope it pleases you to know that my parents are discussing us getting married."

The music ceased in my head, and I stopped in my tracks in shock, too stunned to reply. A sense of indignation rose, as though he had offended with a caustic remark. The earlier conversation with his parents flashed in my mind. Suddenly, it was apparent why Maman was so happy all night and why the Ghorbanis were in perpetual conclave with my parents.

I tried to retain my composure, "Javad, I'm flattered by your interest, but I really want to finish my education. I've no desire to get married." I could end this politely, I thought.

Unwilling to hear my answer, he continued, "But why do you want this education? I can care for you quite adequately, you know. I come from wealth. Besides, it's not necessary for a young woman to have so much education."

I stared down at him, startled by his chauvinistic remarks. He'd responded like most Iranian men, assuming education was wasted on a woman. Sadly for him, that wasn't the way I'd been raised. I tried to keep cool and be respectful to a family friend, but inside I was seething. Taking two steps back, I said, "Perhaps I was unclear. Let me say it again. I'm not interested in marrying you." Then, thinking I'd been rude and would anger my parents, I added, "I'm sorry, but I need to find my cousin," and walked away before he could respond.

I was flushed, my heart pounding. I ran to the bathroom, locked myself in a stall, and began sobbing. I was infuriated, my tears filled with angry defiance. I felt threatened by his proposal, not flattered. Mostly, I felt betrayed. My mother had been part of the scheme. Just as I basked in her newfound affection, she turned on me again. Someone entered the bathroom, interrupting my thoughts. I fought back tears.

"Leila, are you in here?" asked Aunt Firouzeh.

"I'll be out in a minute," I responded, trying to conceal my crying voice.

"They're going to cut the cake. I didn't want you to miss it."

"I'll be right there."

I waited for the door to close before stepping out and washing my face in front of the large mirror. I touched up my makeup and lipstick to mask signs of tears. As I entered the main hall, everyone was gathered around the wedding cake. I searched for my cousins but could only see my parents, so I stood by them.

"The Ghorbanis were just talking to your father. They suggested a marriage between you and Javad," Maman whispered victoriously in my ear, one hand covering her mouth to ensure only I would hear.

"*Beekhod*, to no point," I barked.

"Now, *azizam*, don't say that. He's a nice, well-educated man and wealthy. You should be flattered he's interested." This was the first time Maman had used the endearing term to address me since I was ten. She was really trying to butter me up.

"Well, I'm going to school, and I'm not getting married."

"You don't have to get married immediately. You can be betrothed and then get married when you finish school. He's a good catch, you know."

"I don't want to talk about it, Maman." Maman noticed my voice getting louder as Baba glanced at us with a questioning frown.

"Okay, okay. They're cutting the cake. We'll talk about it later."

"No, we won't." I pouted. My mother approved of this? How could she? Given her own life, I guess she just couldn't understand my dreams. But why couldn't she let me live my life? Wedding cake suddenly seemed unappealing. I was shaking and felt sick to my stomach.

"Can we go home?" I asked Baba, intentionally bypassing Maman.

"We can leave whenever you want if it's okay with your mother."

"We need to say goodbye to everyone first so we're not rude. Then we can leave," said my mother, noting my sour mood.

Farewells took an hour, as no one could say good-bye without interjecting a story or two. It was an excruciating time as I sought desperately to avoid the Ghorbanis. I was in no mood to face them. I told Baba I'd wait in the car and left the banquet hall, nervously scanning the room for the Ghorbanis. Making a circuitous exit, I avoided contact and found Mahmood by the car.

"Where are your parents, your grandmother?"

"They'll be right out. Can I wait here?"

"Of course, Miss Leila," he said, holding open the car door. I hopped in the back and slid across the leather seat to the far corner. I was so angry over Maman's plot to get me married, the clandestine arrangements with the Ghorbanis, and her now-suspect newfound affection. Mahmood, who'd slipped in the driver's seat, heard my sniffling.

"Are you alright, Leila *khanoom*?" Opening the glove compartment, he handed me the travel-size Kleenex box. I wiped my tears in somber silence. Disjointed thoughts rushed through my mind. I was only eighteen, with three more years of college ahead of me. I wasn't sure I wanted to marry even then. Was my father in on this too? Maman had to know this proposal was coming. Over and over, I replayed the night's events till my parents approached. Baba took the front seat as Mahmood held the back door open for Maman.

"My mother wants to stay a while longer. Would you mind coming back for her, Mahmood?" asked my mother.

"With pleasure, Mrs. Moradi."

I quietly stared out the window during the ride home while my parents recounted the party in vivid details for Mahmood. I felt tension in Maman's presence. "Are you catching a cold?" Baba questioned, hearing me sniffle more than once. I simply said no. They left me alone the remainder of the ride. Probably wise.

I said a curt good night at the house and ran up to my room. I would give them no chance to bring up the M topic.

The phone rang shortly after we arrived, but I wasn't about to answer it. While I lay pouting in my room, I heard my father take the call and listen intently to the voice on the other end. Returning the receiver to its cradle, he turned to my mother. "Mojtabah's been arrested. He was participating in a demonstration at the university and was taken to the *kalantari*, the police station."

"Oh no, what are you going to do?"

"I'll arrange his release. A former student of mine is police captain. If I have to, I'll petition the Shah himself."

"Don't put yourself at risk, Ali."

"He's my nephew, my brother's son, my flesh and blood. I'll do whatever's necessary." And with that he left the house.

SEVENTEEN

I tossed and turned in bed, the evening's events disrupting attempts to sleep. Each time that I beat my pillow into submission, I fought back tears, desperately trying to stop the images and words that haunted my mind. I heard Maman Rouhi's gentle steps and the creak of her bedroom door. After what seemed hours, sleep came. The light of dawn on my face woke me; I'd forgotten to draw the curtains. I found my way to the kitchen, where morning tea was brewing. Fatemeh was always up before sunrise, planning the day's meals, and always pleasant. Today I was in no mood for her cheerfulness.

I carried the cup of tea she poured me to the terrace. She remembered to put the *nabat* on the saucer. Sitting, I gazed into the still waters of the pool and struggled with the marriage proposal. I wasn't sure what bothered me more: the idea of marrying Javad, a man with no redeeming qualities, or that my mother was the agent of this clandestine agreement. Did she care so little for my happiness, or did she really believe I could be happy with a man they chose for me? Was it just about money, seeing my future secured? Why didn't she care about what I wanted, my hopes and dreams? My thoughts rambled in the dark cavern that was our relationship, without a glimmer of light.

I heard footsteps quietly approaching. It was Baba. I looked up and smiled. Then I saw Maman, trailing behind, enough to restore my somber mood.

"Beautiful morning, isn't it?" he asked. No one replied.

He took the chair next to mine, put one hand behind his head, the other shading his eyes.

"It sure is bright this time of day," he commented.

"Well, we're facing east, Baba," I remarked. "By the way, what was the commotion last night? What happened to Mojtabah?"

"I want to know too. You got home so late, I didn't want to ask too many questions," added Maman, taking the chair to Baba's right. "Here's your tea, Ali." She handed him a cup. Baba shook his head at the sugar cubes she offered; he never took sugar, but it was always offered.

"It's a long story," Baba began.

It was almost 2:00 A.M. before Baba discovered where Mojtabah was being held and hours later before he was able to use his contacts to attain his freedom. The police were opposed to releasing those arrested, but Baba's connections and heavy bribes proved persuasive. A uniformed guard led a reluctant Mojtabah out of the closed area while he protested to remain with his fellow students.

Baba grabbed him by his shirt collar and pulled him along. "You'll come with me now." Outside the prison, as they walked to the car, a dejected Mojtabah again raised a protest, but Baba silenced him with an upraised hand. As the elder, he was to be obeyed.

"I know you feel loyalty demands this, that you should remain with your friends. But you must understand. Many of these friends of yours will be dead before the day is out, shot as traitors or beaten beyond recognition. You're my brother's son. I can't allow you to suffer that fate."

"But, Uncle Ali, we did nothing wrong. We stood for what we believed."

"Mojtabah, right or wrong matters little to a dead man. And since when do you think you are free to stand for what you believe in this country?" With that, they climbed in the car.

Then Baba related the events that had led to the arrest. "Mojtabah was very close-mouthed at first, but I insisted he tell me."

It began quietly without fanfare, a few students gathering after class to discuss events of the day. Most were drawn by their love for Islam or hatred of the Shah and his dreaded secret police. More than one had a relative or friend who had suffered at the hands of the SAVAK; everyone knew at least one person affected. All were intelligent, the best of the brightest with visions of a new world order, where their families would no longer be poor and the oil wealth now in the hands of the few would spread to the masses. Some believed the *toodeh* communist manifesto and were party members. Others were driven by religious fervor and desire to see Islamic law rule the land.

In this fertile ground, Mojtabah found new friends and purpose. The teachings and writings of the Ayatollah Khomeini were increasingly available from Iraq, where he lived in exile, and in them Mojtabah found his path to righteousness. Exceptionally bright and by now a gifted speaker, he began to play a prominent role in these impromptu gatherings. Soon the meetings took on a regular schedule. While at first thoughts of strikes and a revolution were not mentioned, with time, their growing strength of numbers and emerging popular discontent fueled those very concepts.

"Timing is an incredible thing. A few years ago, Mojtabah was working for his father in Esfahan, selling office supplies at the bazaar, wondering how he'd eke out a living. Then, with my help, he finds himself transported to a world of knowledge and new ideas. This education challenged his mind and his faith in ways he couldn't imagine. Now, at twenty-one, convinced he has all the answers, he holds a position of leadership with a growing number of students and workers who will no longer tolerate the status quo." Baba sighed as he sat up to take a sip of tea. He couldn't understand why Mojtabah, with such a bright future ahead, would take such risks. Setting his teacup on the saucer, he continued.

Mojtabah's teacher, Hussein Ali Montazeri, had made a lasting impression with his intense faith and fiery dialectic, a source of rhetoric Mojtabah often drew upon. Further, the man's conviction and humility were an example Mojtabah sought to emulate. Khomeini might be the leader in exile, but Montazeri was here and present, reaching the students and lifting the veil of Western corruption from their eyes, exposing the godless actions of the Shah, the suffering of the people.

All this Mojtabah took to heart, a burning fire that sparked anger and desire for change. Young enough to dare the risk, but not yet wise enough to grasp potential consequences, he was the right person at the right time. Those students pure in heart, the ones who could clearly see the crimes of their government, would lead the revolution that would bring down the pawn of the Great Satan and restore the Ayatollah Khomeini to his rightful place as spiritual leader of Iran. Soon they had the numbers needed. Mojtabah started gathering strength in the countryside, among the poor, among the people of his home in

Esfahan. While it had to start in Tehran, the impoverished and down-trodden would quake the earth and bring down the monarchy.

For weeks, they'd planned the demonstration. It would begin at Tehran University, where Hussein Ali Montazeri would rally the students. From there, they'd march down Takhteh Jamshid Street, ending in front of the American Embassy. Their anger with the United States was not based on first-hand knowledge, but America supported the Shah, and his régime had to go.

Mojtabah fully expected thousands of students and blue-collar workers to join their cause. While this demonstration might not deliver the ultimate goal—the return of the Ayatollah Khomeini to Iran—it would give notice they could not be ignored.

"How many students will join us?" Montazeri asked his young disciple.

"Hundreds. The question is whether the workers will march at our side."

"These are great days that will shape our nation, Mojtabah. It's good we're here to be part of it."

"Will they call out the army, do you think?"

"If Allah so wishes. We can only make our voices heard. A few martyrs might even help our righteous cause. But let's hope there is no violence."

"Well, we'll be ready. Hamid and Bijan have made preparations and have told everyone to bring a mask or cloth to cover their faces if they use tear gas. We don't want anyone carrying weapons. That'll just lead to deaths, but we won't be lambs either."

"You have done well in this effort, my son. It will be remembered and rewarded by Allah himself, my son." Montazeri patted him on the back, proud of his disciple.

Mojtabah, glowing at these words, nodded silently and moved to the window to gaze at the streets below. Everything seemed so normal, traffic moving as usual, the flower peddler on the corner, the spice vendor by his shop. But the world as they knew it was about to change, and he would be an agent of this change, *Allah O Akbar!*

The students and their fanatical leaders were so naïve. Did they really imagine the Shah would sit by idly while they plotted treason

and spouted religious drivel? They were so blind, they never even suspected Hamid. They accepted him as one of their own, as he shouted the
same trite phrases with equal enthusiasm. What nonsense, what idiocy.
Hamid couldn't imagine how they thought that old fool Khomeini
would even live to see Iran again. No, this would never be a country of
these radicals if he could help it. Long live the Shahanshah!

Hamid left Mojtabah and the Mullah after learning the details he
needed. They were so trusting, it made his job child's play. He walked
down the street toward the tea house for his message drop. In his late
twenties, Hamid easily passed for a student and was enrolled in a theol-
ogy course at the university. But his purpose was to watch, to listen, to
spy on those elements that sought to overthrow his government.
While there was little reason to suspect these amateurs might mount
any surveillance, his contact would never meet him in the open. Their
meetings were pre-arranged at a specific time and location, places
Hamid regularly frequented so no suspicions were raised.

Hamid walked into the tea house, brushing aside the hanging
beads at the entrance, and sat at a table along the back wall. The dreary
interior was a dull yellow and probably hadn't seen a fresh coat of paint
since the Shah took the throne from his father thirty-six years ago. It
was a small, poorly lit place, often clouded by a haze of smoke from the
hookahs, the rich smell of strong tobacco sweetening the air. Music
played from a small radio tucked behind the counter, with an occasional crackling noise from poor reception. Today there was only one
other customer, sitting at the counter enjoying his tea with a Winston
cigarette, a pleasure proffered thanks to America.

Hamid ordered a cup of tea and waited patiently. Occasionally, he
stroked the black stubble on his face as he looked around nonchalantly.
When his contact walked through the door, he took no action. The
man was dressed nicely, looking rather like a successful merchant. He
asked the owner about the bathroom and was pointed to the back. If
he didn't return immediately, it meant the coast was clear and Hamid
should make the drop. If he returned in under a minute, there was
reason to suspect they were being watched. These rules and mind games
seemed over-zealous to Hamid, but a careless man didn't survive long
in the service of the SAVAK. No sign of him. It was safe for the drop.

Hamid took a final sip of his tea, then set the newspaper he'd been carrying with its message tucked inside on the table. He calmly stood, paid the proprietor, and left. Once outside, Hamid returned the way he'd come, confident the message was delivered. Even if it fell in the wrong hands, it would convey little meaning. But to his contact, an agent of the SAVAK, the meaning would be clear. The student demonstration was tomorrow at the university, 2:00 P.M. sharp. The right people would be in the right place to crush this once and for all.

The well-dressed man left, carrying the newspaper he'd retrieved from the empty table. Classic dead-drop maneuver as taught by instructors from the American CIA. Now they'd give these silly fools a lesson in power.

"So, as you might imagine, the planned demonstration was less than a block from the university before the police swept in and began making arrests. A lot of the kids scattered at the first sign of trouble, but the police ignored them and targeted the leaders. Mojtabah was stunned when his so-called friend Hamid pointed him out in the crowd. He and twenty more were arrested. Fortunately, I was able to get him released, or he'd be dead by now," Baba concluded.

"What will happen to him now?" asked Maman.

"If he keeps his nose clean, he should be alright. I convinced them to drop his name from the arrest list so there's no record. I had to offer substantial bribes. I tried to help Mojtabah understand the risks of repeating these actions. But frankly, I didn't get the impression he was listening. He's as stubborn as his father was at that age. I suspect he'll dive right back into this chaos."

"Well, there's nothing more you can do, Ali. He's in control of his own destiny," added Maman, "and we have to get ready and go to Neda's for the *pa takhti*."

EIGHTEEN

Family and friends gathered at the newlyweds' home for the *pa takhti* bedside ceremony bearing gifts for the bride. I asked my grandmother the nature of this custom. The bride and groom had already received their wedding presents; why more gifts the next day, and why just for the bride? Grandmother replied, "For her trouble." I didn't understand and was too shy to ask.

Neda glowed with happiness. She was just as beautiful as the prior day, with wedding day curls still streaming over her shoulders. She wore the gifted jewelry as expected. I partook in the polite greetings, then dashed off in pursuit of my cousins. I was safe from the Ghorbanis here; they were not close enough to be invited. I found the girls upstairs.

"*Salam, azizam,*" said Golnaz. "Did you sleep well? You left early last night."

"I'm sorry. I was very tired, maybe not quite used to the time change." I didn't want to share the thoughts rummaging through my head. They wouldn't understand. After all, neither of my cousins had gone to college. Golnaz took an office job with a construction company after high school, and Tara taught sewing classes and tutored young children in painting. They'd think I was crazy to be offended over a marriage proposal, so I kept it to myself.

"Neda lost her virginity last night," said Golnaz with impish delight.

"How do you know?" I asked, wide-eyed.

"Oh come on, Leila. Why do you think everyone's bringing her gifts?"

"Maman Rouhi said it's for her trouble."

"And what do you think that means?" She burst out laughing, with Tara joining in. I looked at my cousins, blushing, as the puzzle fell into place.

That evening, in the quiet of our home, with my parents and grand-mother gathered in the family room, Baba turned to me.

"Leila, I know you were upset last night. I want you to know I'd never force you to marry. When you finish college, we'll find a suitable husband, someone you'll like. I told the Ghorbanis you're going back to college and wouldn't be marrying their son."

I looked at Maman's expressionless face. Her eyes wandered the room as though we weren't present. Maman Rouhi sat crouched on the couch next to her, listening.

"Merci, Baba. I don't want to get married right now." I dared not say "and I'd rather meet someone, fall in love like in the movies, then *maybe* get married."

"Besides, you're still young. I told them we're not interested."

"What'd they say?"

"Not much," he said, keeping details to himself.

I was elated, a sense of relief replaced by respect for my father, even if his decision upset Maman. She was clearly deflated, since, as I suspected, she'd been the primary architect of the plan.

Years later, I discovered how my refusal affected Javad and his family. When he left the dance floor, Javad rushed to tell his parents of my rejection.

"She just ran off the floor and left me standing."

"What? Why, that's awful. What horrid manners," Mrs. Ghorbani said to her son, anxiously rolling her gold bracelets up and down her tanned, wrinkled arm. "What did she say?"

"She said she's not getting married, especially not to *me*." Javad fumed.

"How very rude. I can't believe they raised a daughter this way. The nerve of her, talking to you like that," Mrs. Ghorbani said, visibly upset at her son's dejection. "She's lucky we even considered her."

"When we talked to her parents, they seemed completely receptive. Maybe she was just surprised. Ali will talk sense to her," reasoned Mr. Ghorbani, trying to restore calm, which was quickly fading.

"I don't even want her. She probably has a boyfriend in the U.S. I don't want to marry that kind of girl." Javad, now the scorned suitor, rejected *me*.

The next day, the Ghorbanis awoke, anticipating my father's apology. But when the call came, it was not what they'd expected.

"Hello, my friend," my father said cheerfully.

"*Salam*, Ali. Wasn't that a beautiful wedding?"

"It certainly was, but you left early. We didn't get a chance to say good-bye."

"Yes, my wife had a terrible headache," he lied. "I'm sure you understand."

"Of course. Is she feeling better?"

"Yes, thank you."

"Well, I talked to Leila, her mother, and grandmother," my father said, finally raising the subject. "I'm afraid we must decline your proposal. We want Leila to finish college, and then, if she's ready to marry, we'll find someone suitable."

"So, my son is not suitable, Ali?"

"No, no. That's not what I meant at all. Your son's a fine young man and will make a marvelous husband. Unfortunately, I don't think Leila likes him, and I won't force my daughter to marry someone she doesn't want."

"Ali, I can't believe my ears. You're telling me you approve of your daughter rejecting Javad? You allow *her* to make a decision in such an important matter? Our families have been close for generations. This is an opportunity to cement our relationship."

"I understand how you feel, but I won't force Leila into marriage for the sake of friendship. As much as I value our relationship, my daughter has the right to make her own choices."

"The right! What is this nonsense? She's a foolish young girl who should do what her father tells her." Mr. Ghorbani became more upset with each word, veins standing out on his face. His comb-over strand slipped off his head as he shook in anger and fell dangling down the wrong side. "Instead, you fill her mind with nonsense and send her away to a country filled with filth, prostitution, and alcohol."

"Mr. Ghorbani," interrupted my father. The formal address signified discussions had taken an ominous turn. Baba was clearly upset with Mr. Ghorbani's narrow-minded comments. "You're entitled to your opinion, but it changes nothing. My daughter won't marry your son. That's final."

There was a bang as Mr. Ghorbani slammed the phone in shock and anger. Dragging the renegade strand of hair back in place, he related the conversation to his wife. Both were enraged, vowing the old family friendship was over for good.

"But when I talked it over with Soraya, she was thrilled," exclaimed Mrs. Ghorbani, with a confused tone.

"I will never again associate with that family," protested Mr. Ghorbani to his wife. "They've raised a spoiled, arrogant child, just like Ali himself. I put up with him and his superior attitude all these years, and now his daughter. I will *not* tolerate it. He can come begging, and I won't allow Javad to marry her."

"Calm down, dear. There are dozens of families who'd give anything to have Javad as a son-in-law. He's the lot in the lottery. It's their loss," his wife consoled, feeling deflated herself.

Javad overheard the exchange from his bedroom. As his parents' conversation ended, he turned and, with as much strength as he could muster, drove his fist through the wall.

For me, Baba's words purged unpleasant memories. I was three weeks from returning to school as political unrest grew. With my pending departure, the fires of insurrection seemed to be further fueled. The turmoil intensified and gained momentum like an avalanche.

NINETEEN

Tehran Prison, 1988

I awoke with a start, vivid memories of Neda's wedding in my mind, of Mojtabah's fire-brand radicalism and arrest, of Javad's proposal and what followed its rejection. In my tiny cell, I was recovering from yet another senseless beating and interrogation. The walls had become familiar, their gray peeling surface almost a comfort in the monotony of days. With imaginary strokes of color, I envisioned Monet's water lilies as shadows cast by the bare bulb washed across the walls. I'd been here over a month now, my second menstrual cycle marking time. The anger and confusion of earlier days had given way to pondering my fate. Would I ever get out? Would I see my family again? I'd made paltry attempts to cleanse myself with the cold water hose, but by now the stench of my body and filthy garments were almost as bad as the squat latrine.

I heard the click of boot heels down the hall. Not again. Wasn't it just yesterday they'd taken me? How much more could I stand? I sat up in the bed as the guard turned the key and swung open the door. It was the short swarthy man who kept watch during second shift, accompanied by a female guard.

"Get up," he said with almost an air of gentleness. "You get to take a shower."

"Really? *Merci, merci.*"

"Don't thank me—rules. Follow her." I could have been wrong, but sometimes I'd catch him actually looking me in the eyes, almost with sympathy. No, it was wishful thinking. He was like the others, just carrying out orders.

The woman took my arm and led me down the corridor. No cuffs this time. No hooded mask. He followed behind, rifle dangling on his shoulder. The adjacent cells were empty, but down the corner of a large corridor, I heard men's voices. She pushed open a shiny steel door covered in smudged fingerprints, leading to a small courtyard. I was relieved it was not the same courtyard where I'd witnessed that poor man's execution. I closed my eyes to the assault of the bright sunlight. Slowly, I focused to see an open area surrounded by faded red bricks topped with razor wire three meters high. The courtyard was five-by-five meters, its rough dirt ground dotted with patches of grass struggling to hold fast in the face of Tehran's summer drought. After so long enclosed by concrete walls, the smell of fresh air was a welcome reminder of life. I took several deep breaths. A vine of wisteria grew in one corner against the wall, a blanket of mauve drooping in lament from its vines. The grapelike flowers hung pendulous, almost funereal in color. Newer violet flowers at the base struggled toward the light beneath the older ones. Several outdoor showers stood against one wall. There were no windows, so it offered privacy. The female guard tossed a ragged towel on a tangle of weeds near the first shower and said, "Be quick about it. You're allowed five minutes." She left, closing the heavy door behind her.

I untied the scarf from my head and pulled off the rough tunic. Turning the single knob, I closed my eyes and let the cool water caress my body like silk, gently streaming down, soothing my senses. It smelled rusty and fetid as though it, too, had been imprisoned for months. I opened my eyes and stared in wonder at the blue patch overhead. I picked up a cracked sliver of soap from the ground and rubbed its rough surface against my skin. It felt wonderful to scrub weeks of sweat, blood, and grime from my aching body. As my hands moved over my body it felt foreign; I could feel my bones. It's silly, I know, but standing naked amidst the water, I realized my breasts had shriveled. Would Farhad still want me? The sun was hot, almost directly overhead, sometime around noon. I watched with fascination as my shadow moved in silhouette against the hard ground, a sight I'd not seen in months. A pair of mourning doves fluttered by, settling on a corner of the courtyard wall, gently cooing.

Suddenly the door flew open, striking the brick wall with a bang, startling the doves into flight. I jolted back to reality and covered my body with my hands, not knowing who the intruder was.

"Time's up. Turn it off and get dressed." It was the female guard.

Hurriedly, I dried myself with the rough towel, pulled on my tunic and head scarf, and walked to where she stood waiting. She led me inside but, to my consternation, didn't lead me back in the direction we had come.

"Where are we going?" I asked, fearfully. Had they let me shower before they put a bullet in my head, like a last meal before a prisoner's execution?

"Be quiet and keep moving."

I stumbled along the hallway to an open doorway covered by a white curtain. Pulling it aside, she motioned me into what looked like a doctor's office.

"Wait here," she said, then turned and left. A gurney stood vacant against a whitewashed wall. A stethoscope and blood pressure cuff lay on a metal table. I walked over to a small mirror hanging on the wall. The woman staring back was thin and pale, her eyes sunken in shadows with purple and yellow bruises covering her face. I reached up and touched my cheek, watching as she winced with me in pain.

I heard a toilet flush and turned to see a small elderly man walk through a door I hadn't noticed, struggling with his zipper as he entered the room. He wore an open, once-white physician's coat, now a dingy gray, over ragged black pants and a yellowed white shirt. He shuffled toward me in battered brown shoes as old as he was. His face was wrinkled and tanned, his hands drawn up like claws. He stared at me with black beady eyes behind thick black-rimmed glasses.

"Sit," he said gently, motioning to the gurney. Picking up the stethoscope and blood pressure cuff, he came closer. I grimaced in pain from the squeezing cuff. Using short, stubby fingers, he applied pressure in different spots on my face, asking if it hurt.

"A little."

"Good, good. How about the ribs? Take a deep breath."

I inhaled and exhaled as he pressed the stethoscope to my chest, repeating the routine several times.

"Blood pressure is low, but given the food, that's not unusual. Your heart rate is slightly elevated, but you don't have any broken bones. Good news—you'll live, at least a while longer," he said with no emotion.

The female guard stepped in through the curtain as she heard these words.

"Give her some lamb tonight—she needs the protein."

"Yes, doctor," the guard said, motioning me to follow her.

"And you just ask for me if you need anything, dear," said the doctor. I looked back at him to make sure he meant me. He winked as I walked out the door.

I never thought I'd be so relieved to be returned to my cell. I didn't realize how fast my heart had been beating the whole time. As she opened the door, I mustered the courage to ask, "Please, may I have some books?" With the humanity I'd just experienced, there was hope they'd softened.

"What do you think this is? Summer camp? Get inside, whore!" She screamed and shoved me into the cell. Wrong again.

The unexpected compassion of a shower and medical attention was a respite in the midst of suffering. It wasn't the rusty smell of the water I recalled but the cool, refreshing feel it left on my skin, reviving my senses. The blue sky and cooing doves remained, if only in my mind. I thought of the care the doctor had shown in contrast to the rough treatment of the guards. Suddenly, I felt exhausted and dragged the weight of my body to the bed. I wanted to dream again, to remember my family and times of beauty and kindness. I wanted to remember Jack.

TWENTY

A few weeks after Neda's wedding, I returned to Lehigh, relieved there'd been no issues with my departure. I delighted again in the furry animals scurrying up and down the stately old oaks. As a sophomore, I was allowed a car on campus, so Amir helped me buy my first, a ten-year-old faded blue Volvo. He sat patiently in the passenger seat while I refined my driving skills. We narrowly escaped several near collisions and celebrated each successful driving lesson at McDonald's. During one of our burger-and-fries sessions, I mentioned the Ghorbanis' marriage proposal. To my surprise, rather than offer sympathy, Amir laughed out loud.

"What's so funny?"

"Relax, Leila. It *is* funny," he replied with a smirk.

"Oh, yeah? How'd you like to be facing an arranged marriage? Would it be funny then?"

"Okay, I'm sorry. It's just imagining you with Javad—he's got to be four inches shorter than you. If you'd married him, he and his dad would both be on platforms for family pictures." He burst out laughing again.

"Stop it, Amir," but I had to admit, the visual imagery made me smile.

Classes started, and my routine began. It was in philosophy class, while struggling through Kant and Sartre, that I met Jack. He was almost six feet tall, with blond hair reaching his shoulders. But it was the magic in his steel blue eyes that caught my attention. There was something about him. At first I didn't know what, but I eventually made the connection. He reminded me of Mark, my cute American neighbor from Tehran whose picture under my pillow almost led to an arranged marriage. That explained the attraction. I glanced in his direction from time to time in class, and he'd return my look with a smile. I fought the urge to smile back, yet something about him drew me. We shared small talk at first after class. He asked where I was from, and when I replied "Iran," I was surprised I didn't have to add "Persia."

"I love Persian literature. My favorite's Ferdowsi's *Shahnameh*, the Epic of Kings."

"How do you know Ferdowsi?" I asked, recalling how Baba read to me from the *Shahnameh*. The tales of Rostam and his son Sohrab, whom he killed in battle while unaware of his true identity, were permanently etched in my memory. Baba would read as I sat in his lap, my head nestled on his shoulder.

"Guess I'm just an avid reader. Did you read the *Shahnameh* in school?"

"No, my father read it to me."

"I read it in high school. It's a great story of the ancient Persian kings and heroes, a total classic. And Ferdowsi's such a poet; his words just kind of carry you to ancient Persia."

"What else do you know about my country that I don't?" I asked teasingly.

"Meet me for dinner tonight and I'll tell you," he chuckled.

"Deal," I said, suddenly realizing I'd accepted a date. I panicked, wondering what he might think of me. Had I been too quick to accept? Was he joking, or did he really mean to ask me to dinner? It really wasn't a date, was it? Just dinner with a classmate who happened to be a handsome guy. Then again, I'd been dying to be asked out. I decided this was a date. It gave me something to brag to Neda about if I could bring myself to write her a letter.

Slightly nervous, I went to the dining hall to meet Jack. Never having been alone with a man like this, I didn't know what to expect. Cultural traditions against casual interaction with the opposite sex loomed despite my more Western upbringing. I spotted Jack waving across the crowded room and made my way to him. Dressed in a pale blue polo shirt that further intensified his eyes, he wore his hair in a ponytail. He stood up smiling, and for an instant, my heart stopped. I froze in my tracks.

"Hey, it's okay," he said, calmly reaching out to me. I let him take my hand as we sat down together as he added, "I promise I won't bite."

"I'm sorry. It's just in my country this would never happen. We don't date."

"Really? Well then it's a good thing we're here and not there," he smiled.

As we chatted over bland turkey and gravy, my nerves relaxed. Jack listened intently as I told him of my summer, omitting the marriage proposal. He shared his interest in Persian art and literature, topics dear to Baba. Despite the obvious physical differences, much of his unfolding character reminded me of my father, though I must say that at that moment Baba was far from my mind.

I enjoyed his voice as much as his words and the way his eyes flashed when he smiled. While a novice at courtship, I think Jack enjoyed our time too. After dinner we said good night and headed to our dorms. I almost wanted to shake hands with him. What does one do?

That night, I tossed and turned, even after the dorm grew quiet, thinking about Jack. Did he like me, or given his interest in Iran, was I just interesting conversation? Would he ask me out again? Was this even a date? In truth, it was the first time a man had shown interest in me, outside of my unwanted suitors. It made me giddy to think Jack might like me. Finally, sleep came.

When the next day came and went with no word, I wondered if I'd hear from Jack. All day long, in classes, at the library, the football game, he occupied my thoughts. Exhausted after a sleepless night and the flux of emotions, I fell asleep by 8:00 P.M. I awoke at the crack of dawn and slowly dragged myself from the comfort of bed to the bathroom. I brushed my teeth, got dressed, and went for a walk. It was a glorious fall morning, with crisp air chilling my face, bright sun warming my body as the scent of fallen leaves filled the air and painted campus pathways in colors of red and gold. I walked past the library and science buildings, then past Drown Hall, where philosophy class was held. As Jack's image flashed in my mind, I noticed a lone jogger in the distance. He looked familiar. It was Jack! My heart beat faster, and I turned to walk away, pretending I hadn't seen him, but it was too late.

"Hey, good morning, beautiful," he yelled from the distance.

I waved and smiled as he approached, tickled that he'd called me beautiful.

"You're out early," he said, a little out of breath.

"I woke up early, so I decided to take a walk."

"Me too. Figured a jog would do me good. Okay if I walk with you?"

We walked up and down the hills of Lehigh. Other than the squirrels rummaging for breakfast, the campus slept. We talked about our past, our families, likes and dislikes. We sat on a bench under a gorgeous big tree, the surrounding ground covered in its bright red leaves. Jack told me of his mother's death two years earlier.

"We were real close. She was totally devoted to my brother, Greg, and me. We'd stay up late Friday nights eating popcorn, watching old movies, you know, like black-and-white ones. My Dad didn't have the stamina for late nights, but we three did. It was our thing."

"How did she die?"

"Cerebral hemorrhage. I'll never forget it. I was home for a long weekend. Nobody else was around. Mom was in the kitchen cooking while I was watching TV. I heard a thump and said, 'Hey, everything okay?' There was no answer. I went to the kitchen and found her sprawled on the floor. I called 9-1-1, then just sat on the floor, holding her head in my lap. I watched the life flow from her. It was, like, totally surreal. One minute she's warm, present, and the next she's gone. The paramedics couldn't revive her."

"I'm sorry."

He paused, glancing at the fallen leaves on the ground, "I was, like, crushed. There was this huge void. At first I was kind of broken up and stuff, but then I got pissed, you know? I guess I felt abandoned."

"I can't even imagine what it's like to lose a parent. How did you cope?"

"I came back to school, thinking maybe classes would be a distraction, but after weeks of wandering in a fog, I quit. Her dying made me realize how fragile life is. That's when I started to find comfort in church. I'd spend hours just sitting alone. Sometimes, I swear I could feel her presence. I even thought about being a priest, but I like girls way too much. My desire for the priesthood lasted all of about thirty minutes," he said with a smile. Despite his little joke, I could feel the tension enveloping him.

"A rather short-lived vocation," I said, teasing, trying to ease his stress.

"Anyhow, the next semester I came back. How about you? Did you go to a mosque in Iran?" Jack asked.

"Oh, no, my family's not very religious."

"I wasn't either, but it's helped some since my mom's death. In fact, there's this Catholic group around here I visit sometimes."

"There's a Muslim group at Lehigh too. I went to one of their meetings last year, and now they won't leave me alone. They keep inviting me back."

"This Catholic group's not part of Lehigh."

"So, you're really into it?"

"Nah, I wouldn't say that. I went to a couple of meetings, so I'm, like, 'on their list.' They invite me to things. I go once in a while, but I've got way too much schoolwork to do."

"And I've got too much partying to do," I said jokingly. "Speaking of partying and studying, I haven't done much of the latter, and our philosophy test is Tuesday."

"We can study together if you'd like. Want to get together Monday night? My roommate isn't usually around."

"Sure, sounds good," I said, as Jack jogged off. Was this another date?

A tempest was brewing in my heart. The feelings bubbling inside were completely foreign. I tried to dismiss the attraction as I had many times before. But one thing was sure: Jack stirred new feelings I found unsettling.

On Monday evening, I went to Jack's room. I'd taken care to freshen up and spray on a dash of perfume. I knocked three times with a shaky hand.

"Come on in, it's open."

"Hi, Jack."

"Hi, Leila. How's it going?"

"Okay, but to be honest, I don't feel much like studying tonight, particularly not about the impact of feminist philosophy on religion. What a bore," I said with a feigned yawn.

I sat in the chair at Jack's desk as he pulled his roommate's chair over next to me.

"I didn't know you played football," I commented, noticing the framed picture on the desk. It was Jack and two others in football uniform, LU helmets under their arms. I touched the frame with my finger and smiled, remembering the picture of Mark that got me in trouble.

"I don't anymore. I quit when my mom died," Jack sighed, as he stared at the photograph. I could see the pain in his eyes, the spark now a dull smoky hue. His shoulders dropped, and I sensed his distress. I couldn't help it. I put my arm around his shoulder and gave a quick squeeze. "I'm sorry" was all I could mutter.

"It's cool. Let's study," Jack said, and his demeanor changed, as though he'd shrugged off a battered old soul and returned a fun young man. Before long, we were enrapt in a speculative discussion.

"But the image of women in ancient religions is distorted," I protested.

"That's true. The problem is all the critiques and challenges we've discussed focus on Christianity and don't really consider alternative religions, like a more cross-cultural view."

"You know, even though there've been women philosophers and theologians, their inherent suspicions of religion's tolerance of gender inequality has made them weaker and slow to gain acceptance."

"Totally. Okay, back to the test . . . what character in which book said, *'When I say religion, I mean the Christian religion, and when I say the Christian religion, I mean the Protestant religion, and when I say the Protestant religion, I mean the Church of England!'*?"

The Adventures of Huckleberry Finn, I answered, an attempt at humor.

"Nope. Try again."

"How about *Of Mice and Men*," I said, still not serious. "Just tell me; I don't have a clue," I said in a flustered tone.

"It was *Tom Jones*. Remember Reverend Thwackum? You really aren't in a studying mood, are you?"

"I feel like talking about anything but philosophy." I was not focused, partly because the butterflies in my stomach threatened to take flight. Every time Jack's arm brushed mine or when I listened to the pitch of his voice as he read a passage, my heart skipped a beat. I'd never felt this way and was uncertain how to react. I had to distract myself.

"Why is religion so important to you, Jack?"

"That's kind of boring. You sure you wouldn't rather stick with philosophy?"

"I'm really interested. Were your parents religious as you grew up?"

"Yeah, I guess it was sort of ingrained in my Dad. He suggested I go to this retreat in high school. The message was you're loved by God and you've got something special to offer the world."

"Is it what you'd call evangelical?"

"Nah, not really. Evangelical usually refers to a Protestant version of Christianity. That's the confusing thing about Christianity—all the segments and sects. You know, there are Protestant groups who are dead certain the Catholics are all going to hell and Catholics who are just as sure the other guys will suffer eternal damnation."

"Kind of like the Sunni and Shiite Muslim sects. At least your variations aren't killing each other."

"Not today maybe, but over the centuries, they've fought over who God loves more, whose is the true faith. Pascal once said, 'Men never do evil so completely and cheerfully as when they do it from religious conviction.' Seems crazy, doesn't it?"

It *was* crazy. Jack talked about the Romans and early Christian believers who were martyred for their faith. Then, when the Christians came to power, they persecuted the Jews. Later, they crusaded against the Muslims who invaded Jerusalem. Throughout history, it seemed religion was more about power and destruction and gaining wealth and property in the name of God, Allah, Mohammed, Jesus, whomever.

"But, Jack, if it's so crazy, why do you believe?"

"I was raised Catholic, and even with its flaws, I get something out of it. That's why I got involved with this Christian community years ago."

"How'd that start?"

"My senior-year high school teacher introduced me, and the people were really sincere and had this, like, intimate way they talked about God. Plus they were really supportive when my mom died."

He stopped for a second. I could sense the grief still clutching his soul and took his hand. He smiled gently and continued.

"After her death, the community kind of became family and helped me see that God had a plan for my life."

I understood Jack's attraction to this community, but his story raised many questions, enough to have my head spinning for one night.

"So much for studying tonight," I finally sighed.

"Maybe we should get a good night's sleep and get up early to study," Jack suggested, gazing into my eyes. My heart was rushing. Was I feeling the heat of his body, or was I flushed with excitement being near him? I felt the warmth of his leg against mine as we'd pulled our chairs closer during the hours. He was looking deeply at me, our eyes locked for what seemed an eternity. He caressed my cheek, drew closer, and gently pressed his lips to mine. It was my first real kiss.

"I have to go," I whispered, my lips so close they still burned with his heat. I pulled away gently and stood up, feeling weak in the knees.

"Did I upset you?"

"No. I just have to go. It's late"

"Can I walk you back?"

"I'll be fine. Good night, Jack."

I walked back to my dorm awash in mixed emotions. Had I done the right thing, letting him kiss me? How could I face him again without blood draining from my face? I tried to deny the sexual energy that had me flush with arousal, but it was impossible. I wanted more. That night, I lay awake for hours and relived his kiss, the warmth of his body, the emotions it stirred. I tossed and turned, fluffing my pillow as though it were the culprit depriving me of sleep. But no matter what its shape, the pillow didn't lead me to sleep. Morning came too soon.

I was nervous about seeing Jack the next day and equally unprepared for the test. In the rush of novel feelings, I'd forgotten all about the exam. In class, Jack was in his usual chair. Anxiety made me want to walk right out, but I took the seat next to him.

"Morning, Jack."

"Hi, Leila. How are you?"

"Terrible, I didn't sleep a wink."

"Me neither."

Our eyes spoke unspoken words. I looked away, struggling to control the renewed rush of emotion. I had to focus on the test, I told myself. It was the longest hour, but when class was over, Jack and I left together.

"Will you meet me for dinner tonight?" he asked.

The conflict he stirred in me was profound, yet I stunned myself by immediately accepting. It left little doubt how I felt about him. These sensations were so new, so different. While I'd had crushes on boys in Tehran, this was the first time I'd embraced the feelings. Over the next few weeks, we spent more time together and grew more comfortable with one another. When I was with Jack, I felt happy. When we were apart, time passed in slow motion until we were together again. In the mornings when I woke, those blue eyes were in the front of my mind. Despite the happiness, my emotions ebbed and flowed. Guilt brought thoughts that my parents might someday discover this relationship and worries that I'd never be able to marry an Iranian man if knowledge of a boyfriend reached my home community.

TWENTY-ONE

Religious radicals were gaining momentum in Iran. Word of demonstrations and uprisings spread, but for the most part, Lehigh was isolated from such news. Students at Tehran University gathered in anti-Shah rallies, my cousin Mojtabah leading the pack, much to my father's dismay. His arrest, which he chose to publicize despite Baba's efforts to erase it, and friendship with Ayatollah Montazeri brought him celebrity status. A second arrest would have dire consequences, so Mojtabah wisely played a more strategic role and left the front lines to others. He now had disciples of his own.

The long-exiled Shiite leader, Ayatollah Khomeini, was spearheading the religious movement from Iraq. His followers declared the Shah was "in bed with the great Satan," exploiting Iran and its people while pocketing oil money and leaving the majority in direst poverty. Iran had to be returned to its pristine state as an Islamic Nation, and the current régime had to go. This news was confusing; I didn't understand what had become of my country.

While these conflicts raged at home, Amir and I met one afternoon for tea.

"It looks like the Shah's really in trouble," Amir began. "Have you been able to reach Maman and Baba by phone?"

"Only once in the last few weeks. How about you?"

"I talked to Baba last month, and they're closing Tehran University every other day because of demonstrations, but he sounded okay and said Maman was fine. I sure hope the religious fanatics don't get complete control."

We sat in silence, alone with our thoughts, sipping tea. I wanted desperately to confide in Amir about Jack, but I was worried about his reaction. Finally, I took the plunge. "Amir, I have something to tell you, but you can't tell Maman or Baba."

He looked at me quizzically and asked, "What, are you going to be a Christian or something?"

"No, silly, I'm not going to be anything. But I've met someone, and I think . . . I think I'm in love," I replied, my face flushed.

"Oh, is that all? I've seen you around campus with some guy, so it's not a big surprise."

"You knew? You saw us?"

"Come on, Leila, the campus isn't that big. I figured you'd tell me when you were ready. What's his name? Where's he from?"

"His name is Jack, and he's from Washington, D.C. He's so smart and so nice, Amir. And he knows things about Iran even I didn't know. We've been seeing each other for a while, and I really like him. I'm not sure I know what love is, but this could be it."

"Wow, that's kind of big, Leila."

"I just know he's special, and I'm happy when I'm with him. I know Maman and Baba wouldn't approve since he's not Iranian, but . . ."

"Don't be so quick to assume what Baba would think. He might be more open than you expect."

"Well, Maman certainly wouldn't be. You know she never wanted me to come here in the first place. If it were up to her, I'd already be married to some fat old man with money who'd beat me regularly just to keep me in my place," I laughed.

"Yeah, she's a little more traditional, but she loves you too, Leila. I suspect you're right, though, that she'd have a harder time with you marrying an American. Just take it slow, okay?"

"I will, but I'd like you to meet Jack. I think you'll really like him." I curled my arm through his as we left the cafeteria.

"I look forward to it, little sister. Now I've got to get back to studying if I'm going to pass accounting this year."

What a relief; the secret was out. It was almost too easy. Amir acted like it was nothing. His acceptance and approval meant a lot. I knew he'd like Jack, so I started planning a get-together.

The day arrived, and I found it impossible to focus on classes. I'd made reservations at Giovanni's, just off campus. It was a popular pizza place frequented by students, with checkered tablecloths and candles melting over wicker-wrapped Chianti bottles decorating tables and waiters who occasionally picked up a battered guitar and broke into song. It was a great spot for a fun evening.

When I arrived, Amir was already seated, rapt in conversation with a very attractive girl.

"Hi, little sister," he said with his usual charm, and kissed me on both cheeks.

"I guess I'm not the only one with a surprise tonight," I whispered in his ear.

"She's just a friend; figured it might be more comfortable for Jack," he whispered back.

The girl flashed a warm smile as she stood up. She was tall with shoulder-length auburn hair splashed with honey highlights, walnut-brown eyes, and a striking complexion of subtle freckles scattered across flawless ivory skin.

"You must be Leila. Amir has told me so much about you. I'm Jessica. I'm in your handsome brother's accounting class."

"It's nice to meet you, Jessica." Leaning over to Amir, I whispered, "Just a friend, huh?"

Amir and Jessica took a sip of their beer. Not yet twenty-one, I settled for Tab. We'd just started small talk when Jack arrived. He was handsomely dressed in khakis and a royal blue dress shirt. He kissed me on the cheek, then shook hands with Amir and Jessica.

"Amir, Leila tells me you'll be a senior next year," Jack began.

"I sure hope so, but if I can't do better in accounting, that's questionable."

"You'll do fine, and you know it," Jessica chimed in. "He's the best student in class. He's just fishing for compliments."

"Not true. I never fish for compliments," he chuckled.

"Amir, be careful, or the length of your nose will make you spill your beer," I laughed.

"Well, congrats. I've got another year to look forward to," Jack added.

"Thanks. It's good to have the end in sight. But exciting as that topic is, enough about me. Tell me, Jack, how'd you and Leila meet?"

Jack related the story of our meeting in philosophy class and mutual interest in things Persian. I sat quietly as he spoke with Amir.

Occasionally, he glanced at me with such warmth in his eyes, it made me melt. At one point, I noticed Jessica's hand slip across the table to take Amir's. Yeah, just friends. But she gave me the courage to take Jack's hand, something I would never have done in front of my brother in Iran.

Amir and Jack hit it off, talking about school and even politics. Then Jack asked to be excused. I looked at Amir and he smiled back. "I like him a lot," he said, his eyes dancing. A weight shifted off my shoulders.

Suddenly, a voice filled the room to the sound of a guitar.

"Here, there, making each day of the year . . . changing my life with the wave of her hand . . . nobody can deny that there's something there."

Jack stood on the small make-shift stage, potted silk plants behind him, guitar in hand, crooning away. I didn't even know he could sing. His eyes captured mine as his rich tenor voice filled the space and drew fellow diners from conversation. Amir and Jessica smiled, but my gaze was locked on Jack as he strummed the guitar and sang the tender Beatles ballad. When the song ended, Jack walked over, eyes never leaving mine, and wrapped his arms around me tenderly as the room erupted in applause.

"That was beautiful," Jessica exclaimed.

"Leila didn't tell me you're a man of so many talents. What else have you been hiding?"

"Thanks, I've always loved to sing. Nice to have someone to sing for," Jack replied, his arms still wrapped around me.

The evening had gone better than I could have imagined, and my boyfriend even serenaded me. No night could ever be this wonderful again. Then it struck me, after all those years of imagined longing: I finally had a boyfriend.

TWENTY-TWO

After Giovanni's, Jack and I wandered across campus hand in hand. I was aglow. My big brother approved of my love interest and seemed to have one of his own. Jack had been attentive and thoughtful the whole evening. Everything felt so right. I don't know the precise instant I decided to make love with him. Perhaps the thought had lingered in the shadows of my imagination for weeks since our first kiss. My Middle Eastern sensitivity had been screaming in protest, and my mother's sharp tongue echoed often in my mind, bemoaning the ruin I'd heap on my family. But that night, after a perfect evening, those voices were silent.

"I had a wonderful time, Jack." I rested my head gently on his shoulder as we walked. I could feel the heat of his body, and my whole being seemed to respond to its summons.

"Me too, Leila, and I really like Amir. I'm sorry I didn't meet him sooner."

"Well, we can get together with him again now that the news is out."

Jack smiled. He understood the cultural proprieties.

We walked in silence, enjoying the warm breeze rustling through the trees. Flickering street lamps joined the occasional lit window to cast dancing shadows across our path as stars shone overhead in a moonless sky. I tasted the fragrance of hyacinth in the air as I stopped near a gnarled oak. Turning toward Jack, I offered my lips in a kiss. He brushed his lips on mine while his arms enfolded me in warmth.

Gently, he broke our embrace. "Maybe we should stop."

"I don't want to stop, Jack."

"Are you sure?"

"I'm sure. Please, no more talking," I replied, touching a finger to his lips. Taking his hand, I led him to my dorm. I closed the door and pulled him to me once more, fervent longings rising like a volcano.

I fell asleep that night after Jack left, a dreamless sleep of satisfied fulfillment. Long before dawn I awoke, my mind awash in a tidal wave. The voices that had been silent were suddenly blaring at 4:00 A.M. A parade of accusers marched through my mind, aunts and uncles, and of course my mother with her "I told you so," all wringing incessantly in my ears. Each relished the chance to rebuke me for surrendering my virginity. All the years of good-girl indoctrination flooded back. I tossed and turned in bed, in the same spot that hours earlier had been heavenly, but sleep was impossible. Finally, the early morning song of a bright red cardinal outside my window stirred me from torment. I stretched and tried to push the rumbling voices aside, but they remained insistent. Sitting in bed, I held the pillow to my chest and imagined what would happen if my parents found out, or even my brother. He might like Jack, but this? And suppose Jack wasn't the man I'd marry? What would another man think of me? In Iran, they stoned women for this less than a century ago. Tears began to well as I struggled with a rush of regrets.

I decided I couldn't meet Jack for breakfast. I simply couldn't, not feeling this guilt, not with the clamoring voices so present. I would just not show up, and of course he'd be upset, but he'd just have to deal. That was it, I'd stay here and . . . and what? Feel sorry for myself? Let the cacophony of cultural traditions continue to beat me into submission?

"Stop it," I told myself. "Stop right now. You love him and he loves you." I remembered how it felt to hold him, to feel his hands move over my body, the immense pleasure of being one with him. Yes, the nagging voices would return, and I'd never be completely free of them. But this morning, I couldn't let them destroy our moment of joyful unity and love.

I rushed to shower before hurrying to the dining hall. I was only ten minutes late. Jack was there, sipping orange juice. He gave me a soft kiss in greeting.

"Hi, how are you?" he asked.

"I'm fine. Sleep okay?"

"It was alright. How about you?"

"Until about four, then I woke up and couldn't go back to sleep."

"Sorry to hear that." He looked away. "Let's get breakfast."

The rattling of silverware, plates, and cups echoed in the dining hall as we ate in silence. Thoughts rampaged through my head. I wanted to tell him about the voices, the regrets, and guilt, but I was tongue-tied. No words could escape. After playing with my food a bit, I excused myself and said I needed to go study. As I was leaving the dining hall, I turned to look at Jack. He seemed so forlorn, staring out the window, not noticing my backwards glance.

Who was I kidding? I wasn't going to get any studying done. Between the morality play in my head, with my mother as prosecutor and my father as the robed judge, interspersed by replays of last night's love story with Jack, attempts at study were pointless. I hated leaving Jack sitting there, but what could he know of the guilt I was battling? After all, he was without the culturally imposed yoke I carried. And guys don't feel these things like women do, right?

As afternoon wore on, I began to win the battle. Yes, this was a big deal, but it wasn't the end of the world. Yes, my parents would be devastated if they knew, but they'd never know. I loved Jack and I believed he loved me. Was what we'd done really that wrong? It sure didn't feel wrong while it was happening.

Jack called and said he needed to see me, so I fixed my hair and put on a little makeup. Maybe I could look relaxed even if I didn't feel it. He stood at the bottom of the steps as I came out of the dorm. He took my hand as we wandered familiar paths across campus. There was the gnarled oak tree where I'd kissed him last night, its branches budding with new life, flushing green with pride. The scent of hyacinth still graced the spring breeze that wound through campus. Jack motioned toward a bench and we sat.

"Leila, sorry I was such a zombie this morning."

"No, no, it was me. I'm sorry."

"Please, let me say this. It's been bugging me all day."

Oh, God, what was he going to say? That he didn't love me, it was all a mistake? Having given myself to him, was he going to leave me?

"I wasn't being honest when I said I slept okay last night," he began. "Truth is, I hardly slept at all. I've never slept with anyone before, Leila, and the guilt was driving me crazy all night long."

"Oh, God, me too, Jack. But I didn't think you'd understand if I told you."

"Of course I understand—we're coming from similar places. Christianity is as strict as Islam about premarital sex, maybe even worse. All night, I battled inside my head, struggling to decide what was truth or lies. When I was a kid, this priest told me masturbation would lead me to hell. Needless to say, I've not exactly had a well-balanced understanding of sex. That's why I was quiet this morning."

"I had the same thoughts, Jack, only it was my parents in my head accusing me of bringing shame to the family. I'm not religious, and I'm still struggling."

"Well, the more I thought and prayed about it, the more at peace I was. I know maybe the opposite should be true, but I remembered what Jesus said about the woman caught in adultery. The crowd was about to stone her, and he said, 'Let him who is without sin among you cast the first stone.' I don't see him rising up to accuse us when we give ourselves to each other in love. Maybe I'm wrong, but I'm done feeling bad about it."

"Oh, Jack, I thought you'd laugh if I told you what I was feeling. It seems we struggled with the same things. I don't want to hurt my parents, but I can't stop loving you because of what they might think. I don't know that I've reached the same conclusions, but I'm trying. I really liked being with you."

"Last night was special, Leila. My regrets are gone as I look at you. I do love you."

"I love you too, Jack."

We spent the afternoon smiling, conversation interspersed with an occasional caress, a kiss. The demons would return, screaming petty decrees about what good girls do and don't do. Perhaps for Jack, angels would prod and poke his conscience for taking pleasure in our physical love. For both of us, a bridge had been crossed, and we'd found a Promised Land intended for lovers in springtime. If there was a God, how could he not be smiling with us?

TWENTY-THREE

As the semester wore on, I did my best to focus on schoolwork. Classes were intense, but Jack provided a much appreciated distraction. We met at the cafeteria for breakfast or dinner and sometimes for lunch, if our schedules permitted. We no longer shared a class but spent our spare time together. After dinner one night, he came to my dorm.

"Things are, like, totally out of control in Iran, aren't they?"

"I think it'll all settle down," I said, denying my gnawing fear the opposite was true.

"You worried about your family?"

"Not really. My father did some business with the Shah, but he stayed out of politics. He doesn't think there's any risk. It's primarily a religious movement, and what are the odds of a bunch of fanatics getting control of the whole country?"

"Is this all about religion or politics?"

"Oh, it's about oil money."

"So money *and* politics. Why do people do these things in the name of religion?"

"I wish I knew. Maybe that's the reason religion gets a bad name."

"By the way, I didn't tell you what happened last time I went to that Catholic community meeting. Two of the leaders pulled me aside and said the community was concerned about my being involved with a Muslim girl."

"I knew this would happen. Muslim girl?" I asked defensively.

"It gets worse. They said a true believer in Christ can't have a good relationship with an unbeliever. There's even a term for it—unequally yoked."

"What's that mean?"

"It's like two oxen yoked to a plow. If one doesn't pull straight with the other, you get crooked rows. If two people don't share the same faith, they're gonna have trouble living a holy life together. In their words, 'the community strongly suggests' I stop seeing you."

"Oh? And what does that mean for us?"

"It means nothing, Leila. I love you. I don't care what anybody thinks."

I heard the words, but I also sensed his conflict. It was curious, I thought later after Jack left. Why would anyone care about the two of us? With religious radicalism gripping Iran and now this, I was beginning to appreciate that my parents had not forced religion on us. Islamic militants waging war to control a country; a Christian community deciding it had the right to denounce a relationship. It was bewildering.

The ringing phone interrupted my thoughts. It was Elham inviting me for a home-cooked Persian meal. I'd seen her on campus a few times, but other than that, we rarely talked. I intentionally remained aloof, feeling our worlds were really quite far apart.

The following evening, I drove to Elham's in my dusty blue Volvo. When she opened the door, I noticed a group of others milling about inside.

"Welcome," Elham smiled, leading me into the apartment, furry caterpillar-shaped eyebrows lifting on her forehead.

The apartment was plain, with a small tan couch and matching chair in the living room. A copy of the Koran rested on an old wooden coffee table for guests to peruse. The dining table was covered with a stamped tablecloth from Esfahan. In another corner, I noticed her prayer rug, carefully folded. I knew what it held inside. The clay *mohreh* was a most precious stone, touching Elham's forehead as she knelt on her prayer rug to recite the *namaz* verses and kiss the *mohreh*.

"I didn't know you were having a party." Ali Farmani was there, as was Ibrahim Al-Faid, the Islamic Association's leader, and several other faces I remembered from that one meeting. I waved hello, then cornered Elham in the kitchen. "Is this a meeting?" I whispered.

"No, no. Just dinner for friends," she whispered back, her gold bangle bracelets jingling around her delicate wrist as she stirred the rice.

"I thought it was just you and me."

She said nothing as she continued stirring. Feeling regret already, I walked into the living room and joined in conversation with the group. Talk focused on classes and professors. Then Ibrahim asked why I'd stopped attending their meetings.

"I'm taking some really tough classes and just don't have the time."

"I see, but perhaps you should reconsider. You must make time for faith."

"Maybe you're right. So who did you have for Finance 201?" I asked, attempting a change of subject. But before he could answer, Elham announced dinner. We enjoyed a dinner of lamb stew, no doubt *halal*, and rather clumpy Minute Rice. A good cook she was not. After dinner, as the others cleared the table, Ibrahim turned to me, "Leila, we are concerned about you. As your brothers and sisters, we want to help." He tugged at his beard while he spoke.

"Oh, I'm sure my family's safe," I replied, assuming he referred to my parents' safety.

"Well . . . actually, several of your brothers and sisters"—I hated his saying 'brothers and sisters'; I barely knew these people—"have seen you on campus with a man . . ." The blood drained from my face as I realized I'd been trapped. "We are concerned that a Muslim woman is spending time alone with a man, much less a Christian man."

I sat in shocked silence as Ibrahim spoke, others at the table offering their awed support. This was the same thing Jack had faced with his community. What business was it of theirs? Muslim, Christian, Jew—why did it matter?

Ibrahim wrapped up his declaration, "It is true that Allah accepts all people of the book, but theirs is not the true faith. You are a daughter of Islam, and we hope to protect you from evil as you'd protect us. If we surrender to temptation, we surely face hell. Being with that man is a sin. You must stop seeing him."

As he uttered these last words, I quietly stood up and turned to Elham. It took all my strength to control my outrage. "Elham, thanks for dinner, but I've got to go," and walked out, not looking back.

That night, I tossed and turned as Ibrahim's words spiraled in my mind like a blinding sandstorm. It wasn't that I gave his "protect from evil" any credence; I was angry anyone felt they had the right to intrude into my life. It suddenly occurred to me that the tension and indignation

I felt were nothing compared to what Jack must feel. For me, Islam was a cultural influence. Jack's belief and devotion to his faith ran far deeper.

The following day, I was prepared to relate the story to Jack.

"It's amazing how many people know what's best for us," he replied. "I mean, faith is important, but don't you have to follow your heart? If love is a gift from God, what's wrong with loving each other?"

"I feel the same way, Jack. I love you, and I don't care what these Islamic brothers and sisters think."

Jack walked over to me. He knelt down, took my hands in his, and gazed into my eyes.

"Leila," he said, tears welling in the blue of his eyes. "Your love gives me strength; it's my joy in the morning, and it carries me through each day. You're the most incredible thing that's ever happened to me, and I never want to lose you. I love you."

"And I love you, Jack."

With his head on my lap, I felt his sobs. I caressed him as tears of my own came. I had fallen in love, and it was glorious, but I was also confused. Was love meant to bring such turmoil? Was I even allowed to love Jack? Was there a God somewhere who played no favorites over race, religion, or culture? What would my father think of this man? Would my family accept me for loving someone the way I loved Jack? I whispered "I love you" again, and confusion lifted like fog. The cultural walls encircling my heart were gradually eroding each time I said the words, like waves crashing over sandcastles on a beach. Now they came out in a thunderous whisper whose echo filled the room. I was certain. This was love.

TWENTY-FOUR

As the insurgency unfolded in Iran, it became clear I couldn't go home for summer break. With the dorm closing, Baba wired money, suggesting we buy a house to live in. "It's a good investment." I never questioned his financial wizardry.

Amir screened at least a dozen houses before he found one he liked. We drove to see it together one evening. The sun was setting behind the two-story red brick and cedar home nestled in a clearing bordered by tall trees, shrubs, and bushes. In the back, a bubbling brook meandered through a forest preserve, a haven for whitetail deer. Carefully planted daisies, amaranths, and geraniums splashed bright colors against the russet and beige exterior. The house and lot were stunningly beautiful, exuding serenity. We made an offer on the spot. After my last exam, Amir and his friends helped me move. My friend Janet planned to move in with me since she was taking summer classes, and I was glad for the company.

Summer passed quickly, lazy days spent reading on the patio. At dusk, I'd make a cup of tea, set down my book, and watch the forest for signs of life. Inevitably, a family of deer wandered out to graze, providing moments of pleasure. After a while, I got to know the return visitors and gave them names. On weekends, I hung out with friends. I talked to Jack every day; he was doing a summer internship with a local newspaper in D.C. He came to visit several times, but after our experiences with religious "friends," we felt uneasy, wondering if we were being watched.

Meanwhile, back home, problems grew for the Pahlavi régime. Ayatollah Khomeini moved from Iraq to a Paris suburb; thousands of Muslim believers lined up to see him as though it were a pilgrimage. He challenged imperialism in one of the most powerful countries in the Middle East. Iran was constantly in the papers, and word was the Shah's grip was slipping. In November, students tore down his statue at Tehran University. His picture was published on the cover of *Newsweek*, where he was dubbed a fallen leader. This news made my heart heavy. Like water slipping through fingers, order in my country was disappearing.

Contact with my parents was sporadic, as calls to Iran were difficult. I wondered if the government controlled the number of calls to more effectively monitor them. The day I learned of an uproar at Tehran University, I spent hours dialing and redialing until I got through. I learned that Uncle Mohsen had moved his family to Paris and wished my parents had joined them.

It was a cold, snowy day in Bethlehem in January of 1979 when I read news that the Shah and his family had left Iran for a so-called vacation. Two weeks later, Khomeini arrived in Tehran, greeted with cries of *Allah o Akbar,* God is great. Within days, suspected SAVAK agents were rounded up. The Shah's generals, Chief General of SAVAK, and Prime Minister Hoveyda were arrested, put on trial, and executed days after the 2,500-year old monarchy crumbled. People whose faces I knew, leaders of my country, were gone in a flash. The Iran I knew was irrevocably changed.

Each passing week, with more articles and news of turmoil in Iran, I began to lose hope. I thought of my life in this beautiful land. I recalled the busy streets of Tehran, bustling with cheerful people day and night, children munching on roasted corn from street vendors in the park. I pictured the *chelo kababi* restaurant down the block, where friends and family met Fridays for dinner and conversation. And I recalled places I'd been with friends. What was life like now, with rioters roaming about, gun-toting military monitoring movement in streets? Did anyone linger at the French cafés over cappuccino, smoking ciga-rettes, or were they locked in their homes fearing the unknown? Was any place in Tehran safe? Was anyone immune?

The next school year passed with fundamentalists consolidating control in Iran. Again, a visit home that summer was impossible. Amir graduated and, to my dismay, decided to return to Iran. With the revo-lution and political unrest, he was concerned for our parents and felt he should return. He looked so handsome as I snapped his picture in his navy cap and gown.

"Amir, I can't believe you're leaving. I thought you liked it here and would stay."

"I do like it here, but I've got to go back. Maman and Baba are alone." Worry was etched in his face.

"What about Jessica? I thought you might marry her someday."

"Jessica was just a friend; I told you that. I'd never marry her. Someday I want to marry an Iranian girl." He stunned me; I thought Amir was more Western-minded.

"Didn't you fall in love with Jessica?"

"I'm not sure I believe in *falling* in love. Love is something that has to grow in your heart. It blossoms when two people commit to spending their lives and raising a family. I like American girls, but I'm not sure they'd be good wives and mothers. Iranian girls are raised differently. They're pure, and once they're married, they're committed for life. That's what I want."

I guessed he meant virginal when he said pure. What would he think if he knew I wasn't pure? The stigma of sex before marriage applied more rigidly to women than men in Iran. We'd never discussed it, but I'd assumed that, like me, he dreamed of finding a soulmate. When he said Jessica was a friend, he meant a "friend for now," not someone he'd give his heart to.

My surprise turned to disappointment. For the first time, I couldn't relate to my brother. This traditional perspective was a chasm between us, much like my cousin Mojtabah's strict Islamic views on life. How naïve I'd been. Amir was raised in Iran, deeply influenced by the male role models around him and by my mother, whose vision of a good Iranian man he fulfilled. She'd be delighted. He'd become just the son she wanted. Perhaps it would soothe her disappointment with me, as I clearly was not a daughter molded to her image.

Baba was thrilled to have Amir return and take over the business. Maman was beyond giddy in anticipation. A week after graduation, Amir left.

"Please write," I said tearfully. "These days I get so few letters from Iran."

I wrapped him in my arms. In that moment, I wanted to beg his forgiveness, to admit I'd told Maman and Baba about his high school girlfriend, to apologize for the punishments he'd endured for things I had done. I wanted to thank him for rescuing me so many times. Though I longed to speak, the words evaporated. Through childhood conspiracies, my first brush with an arranged wedding, and my relationship with Jack, Amir had been my confidante. In a flash, my constant moral support was gone. The loneliness of his departure gnawed at me for a long time. Without him, Lehigh felt empty. But his parting words echoed disturbingly in my mind.

TWENTY-FIVE

To keep busy that summer, I volunteered at the library, mending worn books. I wanted to see Jack in Washington, D.C., but he insisted on coming to Pennsylvania. During one of his visits, it became evident how entrenched he'd become in his Christian world when he told me he was living with a family in a Christian community.

"We can't stay there together since we're not married. The community doesn't like that kind of thing. Young people don't even date without approval, and if they do, it's always a double-date. As much as I'd love to have you visit, it's just not possible. Plus, they'd have a problem with your lack of religion."

"Lack of religion? Where did that come from?" I asked, a frown wrinkling my forehead.

"Leila, it's not what *I* believe. It's the way *they* think."

"So where does that leave us? You live in a Christian community. I'm not a believer—Christian or Muslim. What're we doing together?"

"Leila, I love you. You know that. I want to be with you. I want to have a life with you."

"How's that possible, Jack? You say the words, but you live a different life. How can we ever be together?"

"I don't know, but we'll find a way," he said as he held me. Despite my growing anxiety, his arms melted fear away. There was warmth and tenderness in his embrace. He was the first man I'd loved, the first to touch my heart so deeply. I couldn't abandon the naïve belief that somehow our love would find a way. The next morning, I kissed him good-bye, and he drove off, leaving the house empty and silent once again.

That very day, I received my first letter from Amir. Giddy with excitement, I poured a cup of tea and took the letter to my bedroom, propped up a pillow, and sat down to read.

Dear Sis,

Well, it's been an interesting journey. When I first arrived in Tehran, there was so much change. I can't begin to tell you the stories I've heard and things I've seen. But first things first, Maman and Baba are well. Maman Rouhi is as healthy as ever. It's hard to believe she's in her eighties; she's so vibrant. I catch her every so often looking through your photo album, reminiscing. Maybe you should send her new pictures. She misses you.

The streets of Tehran aren't as clean as they used to be. The curbs are covered with trash and weeds. Broken glass is scattered on sidewalks, along with scrap metal and car parts from explosions. Burnt-out cars line the streets, tires and even engines removed. You can see shells of abandoned buildings, scarred black with their windows boarded up. No one's bothering to restore the crumbling remains.

As for the streets, all the Western street names have been changed. People remember the old names and secretly still use them, but it could cost them if the wrong ears were to hear. The other day, I needed directions to the courthouse. If Baba hadn't translated it into the old street names, I'd never have found it. Pictures of Khomeini are everywhere, on walls of buildings, in newspapers, on TV, and in every store.

Everyday life is different than you'd remember. There are all kinds of shortages, especially of food: meat, chicken, dairy. Everything is rationed. You have to take the whole family's birth certificates to a government office to collect food coupons, rationed based on family size. The trick is finding a store that has what you want. You can't just go to a store and pick up a chicken. No, you wait and hope you find a store that has chickens before they run out. You can find the stuff in the black market, but you pay for it. Since we can afford it, Maman and Baba give their coupons to Mahmood or Fatemeh. It reminds me of Communist Russia—part of me wonders if these shortages aren't all made up. The average person is so preoccupied with ration coupons and standing in line to get food, they've no time to think about politics or the bloody mess these Ayatollahs have created.

I go to Baba's store every day. He went over the inventory with me, showing me the pieces and how they're tagged. Just learning to decode the tags took a week! But I have it figured out now. He introduced me to his business contacts. And, of course, he had the accountant go over the books with me. It was really funny when he proudly explained that I had just graduated with a business degree from the United States and knew balance sheets and income statements inside and out! The problem is those things look totally different in Iran. Just learning business words in Farsi has been tough. But I'm making progress. Baba wants to take me to Brazil to buy some antiques, but he's having a tough time getting us visas. Maybe it's a blessing in disguise. Business is down, with everybody worried about the economy and new government; even the rich are hanging on to their money—that is, those who haven't run.

A lot of our friends have left. Remember the Hakasians, the jeweler and his wife? They're in London. And the Manuchehris, neighbors to our right, are gone too, somewhere in Europe. Everyone who fled early took their money. Now, customs is so strict, you can't even take out jewelry, except for your wedding band. Here's a funny story. Tara was going to Frankfurt for her friend's wedding. At Mehrabad airport, the customs guy was giving her a hard time 'cause he figures it's wrong for a woman to travel alone. He picked out a pair of shoes from her suitcase and endlessly questioned her. He asked where she'd bought them, how long she'd had them, and why they were brand-new. She explained she bought the shoes to wear to this wedding, but he kept questioning her. Apparently, he didn't believe her. He lifted the shoes and banged the stiletto heels against the table, breaking them off to see if anything was hidden inside, then he hands her the pieces and says, "Okay, you can go." She was so angry! But what could she do?

And Mojtabah, your favorite cousin (just kidding), is now working in the Ministry of Intelligence and Security. Remember Baba got him out of jail after that demonstration at the university? It seems his association with Montazeri elevated him to a position of power. Remember pin the tail on the fly? Wonder whose tail he's pinning these days!

I have to go now. I'm going to Fariborz's house for dinner. You remember him? He's the kid from school with the freckles? He was going to college in Sweden 'til they arrested and executed his father. They accused his father of arranging demonstrations. No questions, no trial, nothing. One night, Pasdaran came to their house, pulled his father out of bed, and dragged him away in his pajamas, his wife screaming. The next day he was shot and killed. Just like that. His wife was devastated and tried to kill herself. So Fariborz quit school and came back to take care of his mom. Anyway,

write me soon, and make it long. TV and radio here suck. It's all religious programs and chanting. All the news is about the ugly economy, arrests, and the "Great Satan." I'm bored to tears. Waiting to hear from you,
    Your loving bro, Amir

I set my teacup on the nightstand. Absorbed in the letter, I'd not even tasted it. I replayed Amir's letter, trying to imagine the streets he'd described, to visualize long lines and ration coupons. I pictured Tara at the airport, angry over her Italian shoes, and a smile crept over my face. And Mojtabah was now part of the Ministry of Intelligence. I should have guessed his brand of Islam would fit right in with the new régime.

I picked up the letter and read it again—this time slowly, savoring each word, pondering each scene. The images flashed in my head. It was hard for me to comprehend all this, but it had to be true. Worry began to set in. What if a government censor had read this? My family would be in danger. Amir shouldn't have taken the chance he did. All I could do is pray his letter had slipped through unnoticed.

TWENTY-SIX

I was growing numb to the news from Iran. It was always the same: Shiite groups demonstrating; student uprisings at Tehran University; women forced to wear hijab or arrested for non-compliance; local restaurant closed and owner jailed for serving alcohol. By November, events in Iran reached a crisis point. Students stormed the American Embassy in Tehran and took sixty-eight Americans hostage. Iranian men and women marched in the streets, carrying messages of hatred and signs displaying "Death to America—the great Satan." The contrast to the Tehran of my memory was startling. I didn't recognize these people or these streets. I'd never seen so many people in Islamic attire, so many exuding such naked hostility. As I wandered the hallways or paths to class, I couldn't help wondering if people were staring at me, knowing I was Iranian. Was I guilty by association? No one said anything, at least not at first. But Iran was now on everyone's map.

Spring was around the corner. I welcomed warmer weather, as it had been a cold, snowy winter. By now, I'd enjoyed several business classes, so I decided to continue and get a Master's in Business. It made sense because I still couldn't return to Iran.

I was on my way to the dining hall after morning classes when three guys approached. I recognized Gordon, the tall, lanky student whose sexual advances I'd rejected at a party freshman year. The other two I didn't know. One of the boys was wearing a black T-shirt with the words "Nuke Iran" prominently printed in white.

"Hey, this one's from Iran," Gordon said. "Let's ask her."

"Yeah," echoed the second. "What's up with all this shit going on in Iran?"

It began to feel confrontational as they surrounded me.

"I don't like it any more than you do, but I have to get to class."

"Why the fuck do we let you people come here in the first place," said one as he blocked my way.

"Yeah. You hate America so damn much, maybe you should fucking go back to where you came from!"

"Please, I need to go, and I don't hate America." I was shaking, afraid they'd attack me.

"Leila, something wrong?" I heard Jack's voice from behind me. He touched my shoulder and stepped in front of me. He dropped his backpack on the ground and stood facing them, his arms loose at his sides, his broad shoulders a bulwark between me and my antagonists. He was shorter than Gordon by about four inches and smaller than the other two. But he stood up to them, clearly not intimidated.

"This is none of your business, buddy."

"Yeah, we're just telling the bitch to go back to where she came from!"

"Well, it *is* my business 'cause she's my girlfriend. So why don't you back off and leave her alone. She's done nothing to you."

Gordon took a step back, a chagrinned look on his face, as though he'd never intended this confrontation, but the other two, now filled with an adrenaline rush, were more than ready to push it. Jack stood between us, perfectly still in the face of their hostility.

"Whose side are you on, man?" the first asked.

The second didn't bother with words and lunged at Jack, taking a swing. It was a blur of motion as Jack stepped into the punch and blocked it. Moving under the blow, he grabbed the man by the front of his shirt and with a sweep of his leg, tossed him to the ground. The other one came at him, but again Jack ducked a wild punch and with a short kick to the knee crumpled his assailant like a stone. The man fell, holding his leg in agony. The first was still on the ground, the wind knocked out of him. As he moved to rise, Jack stood over him, fist poised to strike. The man held up his hands in surrender, and Jack stepped away.

His body was shaking as he put his arm around me. "You okay, Leila?" I nodded. "Let's get out of here," he said as he rushed me away. Looking back over my shoulder, I saw Gordon help one of the guys to his feet. He mouthed "sorry."

Jack was still trembling as we walked to the dining hall. "I'm sorry,

Leila, but they didn't leave me much choice."

"Jack, you just saved me, so please don't be sorry. Where'd you learn to do that?"

"I took karate when I was a kid, but we were taught to avoid a fight. But I just couldn't let those cretins treat you that way."

"I'm glad you were meeting me for lunch, because I don't know what might have happened. They were so angry."

"Me too, but believe it, I hate violence almost as much as I hate bigots and bullies."

We sat together as Jack's intensity dissipated and my fears passed. I may have lost my big brother as protector, but I'd found another in Jack.

*   *   *

Easter approached and Jack, Janet, and I planned our holiday weekend. The flower garden in the back was barren from the winter chill. In a few weeks, I'd plant colorful annuals to complement the perennials that would pop up, painting the yard with multihued vibrancy. I loved being surrounded by flowers. It reminded me of home. Friday evening, Jack cooked burgers on the grill on the second-floor deck while Janet and I enjoyed a beer and chatted about school.

"How did your psych test go?" I asked Janet, remembering her mid-term.

"It's really tough to define and clarify the differences between Skinner's behaviorist theories and Chomsky." Janet was a dichotomy, a brilliant psychology student who looked every bit the supermodel. Her pale, perfect complexion was offset by full lips evocative of pink roses. Her brows arched naturally, bridging intense blue-green eyes and perfectly straight teeth. At almost six feet tall, she had the long graceful legs of a dancer with a woman's curves. Long auburn hair masked her only physical flaw—the protrusion on her right shoulder blade, a birth defect. A twelve-inch scar along her spine was evidence of prior surgery, the one imperfection on an otherwise flawless woman.

"Yes, I have trouble with that myself," I said, teasingly. Janet looked at me for a moment to see if I was serious, while Jack burst out laughing.

"Alright, so I'm a bit consumed by my subject matter," she said, "but to answer your question, I did fine on the test."

We enjoyed dinner outside, the warmth of early spring tempering the cool evening air. I hoped we'd see the family of deer I'd gotten to know so well, but they remained reclusive. Later, Janet retired to her room to unwind before sleep. Jack and I stayed on the deck and watched the moon make its wandering journey across the night sky.

"Nights like this make me never want to leave," he said, wrapping his arms around me and pulling me closer.

"Good, I don't want you to ever leave."

That night, after Jack and I made love, I lay watching him sleep beside me. Despite the gnawing worry over the influence of religion, I was so in love with him. I'd started to imagine a life with him, coming home to a quaint little house in the hills, a chocolate Labrador barking, our children playing in the backyard, then running into the house to hug Daddy as he walked through the door. Funny how my longings for independence could surrender to visions of domestic tranquility with the man I loved. Holding that dream of a future, I drifted off to sleep.

"What's that?" Jack asked, leaping out of bed to check the noise from the lower level. We couldn't have been sleeping long.

"I smell smoke," I said, sitting up.

Jack ran down the hall while I got out of bed to turn on the lights. I rubbed my eyes to clear my vision through the haze and noticed Janet was by the door with a quizzical look. I slipped on my robe, and we made our way down the dark narrow stairs into the family room. We jumped back as flames burst from the kitchen.

"There's a fire. You guys get out!" Jack yelled from somewhere in the smoke.

"I'll call 9-1-1." I ran for the family room phone, but before I could reach it, I watched in horror as the floor collapsed in front of me, billowing flames from the basement shooting upwards into the room.

"Oh, my God," Janet screamed, grabbing me by the arm to pull me back. "Come on. Let's get the phone in my room."

"Hurry," I cried, filled with anxiety. "Jack, are you okay? Jack? Jack?" My heart pounded as I pictured him engulfed in flames. I thought to go downstairs to find him, but flames were consuming the floor, smoke had filled the room, and the stairs leading to the lower level were almost completely ablaze.

"Hurry, Janet. Oh, God, Jack isn't answering. Jack? Jack?"

"We've got to get out, Leila. Fire department's on its way."

"But I have to get to Jack . . . ," I said, tears filling my eyes.

"The smoke's too thick. We'll get to Jack from the patio door." Janet was amazingly logical in the chaos and helped me out through my bedroom window, then climbed out herself. We landed on the deck and ran down the wooden steps to the back patio door. We could hear the sirens closing in. I stared through the glass door and the smoke but didn't see Jack. The smoke alarm was deafening, increasing in volume as the fire grew more intense. Smoke seething like waves filled the main room, and still no sign of Jack. I was terrified, but I had to go in. I had to do it. I had to go in. No time to think, only to act. As I was about to go, I heard Jack's voice.

"I'm in the laundry room, throwing water on the flames."

"Jack, get out. This is too big. The firemen are here," Janet implored. We watched as the angry flames leapt off windows and doors, each more violent than the last.

Thankfully, the firemen took charge and pulled Jack out moments before a section of roof crashed before our eyes. He stumbled out, panting and coughing, covered in soot. We stood watching as the firemen did their work, splashing streams of water over the roof as smoke thickened, a sign the flames were being squelched. All around us, I noticed neighbors in robes and pajamas watching the spectacle in the early morning chill.

When the fire was out for good and it was deemed safe, the firemen escorted us in to collect a few essentials before the house was sealed for investigation. The family room floor had all but dissolved, its ceiling pocked with gaping holes. Black scorches on the kitchen walls stood as clear evidence of the horror that had consumed it minutes before. The white couch in the family room was mottled in shades of gray and black. The chief hurried us out, reassuring us we could come back in a few days. We spent the remainder of the morning theorizing, guessing, and second-guessing, without answers. A few days later, an article in *The Morning Call* covered the story. The incident was logged at 11:58 on Good Friday, April 4, 1980, as arson.

TWENTY-SEVEN

After the fire, Janet and I rented an apartment near campus while the insurance company completed its investigation before releasing funds to rebuild. My family was shocked to hear the news. Who would do such a thing? Arson? Why?

"Maybe it was just kids. I mean, you don't have enemies," Maman assured me.

"I guess it's possible, but kids in the house that late? It doesn't make sense."

"Drugs induce crazy behavior," Baba said. I imagine even Baba didn't believe this.

"I don't think it was kids. They wouldn't take a chance with people in the house. The fire was purposely set in three different spots. It almost looks planned."

"Leila, darling, it's just a house. The important thing is you and your roommate are safe. A house can be rebuilt," said my father. Of course, they had no knowledge of a boyfriend or that he was lying beside me that night. I felt a little ashamed.

"Baba, what's scary is that someone was inside and set the fires while we slept. The report says they used an incendiary device, so it was no accident. They're investigating me now, asking friends and teachers about any problems or disagreements I may have had recently."

During the call, Baba explained the Iranian government had frozen outbound transfers, and he wouldn't be able to wire money for a while. Not to worry, I was okay for the time being.

A few weeks later, I received Amir's second letter. I studied its Belgian postmark and wondered how it had made its way to me. Thank God he'd used better judgment and hadn't sent it through the Iranian post. I made a cup of tea and again settled on my bed to read.

Dear Leila,

I hope this letter finds you well. I've been worried sick about you since the fire. I wish I'd been there for you. How do you like your new place? Any idea when you can get back in the house? We're all doing fine here. I had a chance to send an unfiltered letter, so I decided to take advantage. You know how when someone leaves Iran, everyone asks them to take things to relatives abroad? Well, I'm following tradition. Fariborz's mother's friend was lucky enough to get a tourist visa to Belgium, so I figured why not? I knew you'd find this amusing. See, I'm picking up those old Iranian habits.

Life's not that bad for us, only because we have the means to buy what we need. But the impact of it all is like a domino effect. I told you about the food shortages. We send Mahmood to the black market, and they charge $20 for a scrawny chicken. Using ration coupons, the same chicken is 50 cents. It bothers me that our own people take advantage of us. C'est la guerre, I guess.

Iranzamin, our old high school, is gone. Gone! First, they separated boys from girls. Then they combined all thirteen Western schools in Tehran into one school for boys, one for girls. Obviously, they're trying to eliminate Western schools completely. Everything's taught in Farsi, and other languages are secondary. Even though the girls' school is only girls, they're forced to wear Islamic hijab. Fariborz's little sister told me that in first period every day, they do roll call. The girls have to put their hands on their desks, and the principal checks for nail polish. One day she forgot to take her nail polish off the night before. No big deal, right? Well . . . when the principal saw her pale pink polished nails, he took her to the office and hit her six times with a belt. They gave her polish remover and forced her to take it off while they stood over her. Then she had to return to class and cope with welts from the lashings and the humiliation of being caught in front of everyone.

I should have just left my blue jeans in Pennsylvania. No one wears jeans; they're considered Western. Men can't wear ties or suits. Women aren't allowed makeup or perfume. They must be totally covered. Boys and girls can't walk the streets together. If caught, they're in trouble. In fact, Neda and Parviz were driving to the supermarket in broad daylight. Guards stopped them at gunpoint and forced them out of the car and into the back of a government truck. The guards questioned them for an hour. Finally they convinced the guards they could produce their marriage certificate if they'd drive them home. Only then did they release them. Yesterday's newspaper reported a similar situation. A young man and woman were just walking down the sidewalk together. They were arrested, taken to the gendarmerie by force, and married on the spot by an official. Later, it was learned they were telling the truth; they really were brother and sister. It would be comical if it weren't so demented.

Sometimes I don't know whether to believe what I hear, but when it happens to someone close, you know it's true. You remember Sepordeh khanoom? She was home listening to the radio and heard that her son Kamyar was shot. On the radio! She listened in tears as the news reported that Kamyar was a traitor who'd led an anti-government demonstration and was shot on the spot. And that's not the worst of it. Two weeks later, she gets a letter from the government. It was an invoice for the bullet. It's all so crazy.

I'm sure you remember the Kalantaris. They threw a big bash for their daughter's engagement. Maman and Baba were in Esfahan visiting relatives, so they missed it. Thank God. Word got out that there was a party with men and women mixed. Who knows how Pasdaran found out; they have spies everywhere. In the middle of the party, agents stormed the house and arrested everyone and whipped them. Each man got eighty lashes and each woman forty, since they are weaker. Mrs. Kalantari showed us pictures of their bruises. It was awful.

Remember the Minister of Education? She was that high-ranking woman in government. Well, when the mullahs arrived, they shoved her alive in a burlap bag and publicly stoned her to death. The barbarianism of our so-called leaders is beyond belief. They've killed so many Jews and Baha'is, interestingly only the ones with money. They seize their estates, claiming they were illegally and immorally obtained. Funny how the poor are ignored, regardless of their religion.

I can't believe this is our Iran. You have no idea what it's like. I don't regret coming back; it's good for Maman and Baba that I'm here. But it pains me to see these bearded fanatics destroy our country and cripple people's spirit. I'm sorry to vent, but it's my only chance to express this without risking arrest. And I don't want you to worry. As I said, we're fine. I just wish we could return our country and our lives to the way they were.

I miss you, Leila. I miss being at Lehigh with all our friends. I miss your

excitement over the scampering chipmunks and our trips to McDonald's.
Summer is almost over, and I know you'll be busy once school starts, but
when you have time, please write soon,
    Amir

The tone of this letter was different from his first. It screamed the
naked truth, truth I'd not heard or had chosen to ignore. My country
had become a soul-wrenching machine, a totalitarian régime under
so-called Islamic rule.

I felt a sudden shiver. I picked up the letter and re-read it. Where
was it . . . that boy's name . . . Kamyar . . . Kamyar? Oh, my God, was
it the same boy I'd met at Whimpy's that fateful evening, who first
stirred such desire? I didn't know Sepordeh *khanoom* or her family all
that well. Could it have been him? I recalled his flashing smile, clear
eyes, and strong hands. Not one for prayer, I nonetheless murmured a
quiet appeal that my casual friend from that night of teenage mischief
was not this dead young man.

I did something I swore I'd never do again; I called Elham and Ali
Farmani and asked them to meet me for dinner. Despite their religious
leanings, I needed to talk with someone about the content of Amir's
letter. On this night, I got more than I bargained for, listening to stories
of events in Iran that surpassed my worst nightmares.

We met at Jimmy's Lebanon House. The owner stopped by our
table every few minutes to ask, "How is yourrrrrr Shawarrrrrrma?"
rolling the "r" with his thick Lebanese accent, not caring if we'd even
ordered Shawarma.

"Excellent as usual, Jimmy," we'd say simultaneously and return to
conversation.

Ali Farmani told about the confiscated alcohol dumped into sewers.
The Islamic council declared that alcohol was against Shar'ia and must
be destroyed. Government agents stormed every deli, supermarket,
restaurant, even private homes where they suspected liquor was present,
confiscating thousands of bottles. They further proclaimed that anyone with alcohol must come forward and rid themselves of this evil
Western poison. People could turn it in anonymously without fear of
reprisal until a deadline, after which anyone caught with it, no matter

the quantity, faced severe punishment. Anyone encouraging someone else to relinquish this Western poison was committing an act of *savab*— good religious karma. People urged neighbors to give up their alcohol. Families turned on families. Friends betrayed friends. Families and friendships were destroyed over bottles of booze.

Ali Farmani continued, "My cousin said for several weeks, the police were taking all the booze to a specific spot in each district. Thousands of people gathered, and government agents smashed bottle after bottle, letting it all drain into sewers. The people cheered with each shattered bottle, shouting *Allah o Akbar* until every last one was destroyed and the sewers flowed with alcohol."

"It must have stunk for days. Sounds like our fraternities with that permanent smell of stale beer." I tried to make light of the situation, but the joke flopped. Elham and Ali had probably never even been to a frat party.

Elham shared her own story. Her uncle, a professor at Tehran University, told her all Western and erotic books were banned. The Pasdaran went to bookstores and confiscated every banned book, took them to a public square, and burned them.

"What a shame. Some of these are great works of literature. The works of Hafez and Ferdowsi can be erotic. Where they burned too?"

"No, they're not in the category of Western." Judging from her sigh, I guess even Elham didn't approve.

The policy was clear. It wasn't the erotic nature of the books but the culture they represented. My country suddenly felt foreign.

TWENTY-EIGHT

The next day I was at the library attempting to study for finals, but I was still focused on the fire and Baba's comment: ". . . you don't have enemies." I thought about the confrontation at Elham's with the Islamic Association and Jack's Christian community condemning his desire to be with me. I called him to relate my theories.

"I never thought about it, Leila. Do you actually think these people would put our lives at risk?"

"I think it's quite possible our fundamentalist friends might've had something to do with this. Yes."

"But that's hard to imagine. Neither Christianity nor Islam would condone this."

With the rise in Iran of the Islamic Republic and articles on abortion clinic bombings in the U.S., it was clear religion often forced its narrow beliefs on others. It seemed so absurd. Religion had such potential to bring relief and comfort, acceptance and belonging. But when abused, it destroyed families, divided nations, and even advocated persecution or murder.

The police never identified the arsonists, but eventually they were satisfied I was a victim, not the criminal. The insurance company released the funds, and rebuilding began. School was still in session, so I went back to homework and tests. But I looked forward to graduation, a few short weeks away. Mr. McCormick, my advisor, called to congratulate me for being accepted to graduate school.

"There is a problem, Mr. McCormick," I said, trying to figure out how to broach the subject.

"What's that, Leila?"

"When the U.S. froze Iranian assets, the Iranian government banned money transfers out of the country. My parents can't send me money, and I don't have enough for tuition."

Within a week, Jim McCormick called to relay the news that the university had agreed to defer payment. When he hung up, I collapsed on my bed in relief and yelled "Yes!"

It was May, and wildflowers were in bloom, the grass was green, and trees flourished with new life. Much to my dismay, Jack had grown distant. He was less and less available, and when we were together, he was often withdrawn and pensive. Just before graduation, the issue came to a head.

"What's going on, Jack?"

"Nothing. Why?"

"I feel like there's a wall, a distance between us. You're not the same."

"You're right. I'm sorry." He sat, staring at his lap.

"Well, what's wrong?" I just wished he'd look at me.

"It's been hard for me, Leila. I never told you, but when I went back to D.C. after the fire, the community leaders told me I had to stop seeing you. They said it was against God's will, that the fire was clearly a sign."

"And you believe this?"

"No . . . not really. I just don't know what to believe."

"Why didn't you tell me before?"

"I didn't want to scare you, and I really didn't want to hear it. I want to be with you so much. But it's a lot of pressure, Leila." His eyes were focused on the desk, staring at a piece of paper. The paper was blank, an empty void, just the way I felt at that moment.

"It hurts that you didn't tell me this. When the Islamic Association ambushed me, I told you everything. I told you how I felt. It's none of their business, Jack."

"I know, and I'm sorry. I should have talked to you about it. It's just confusing. Sometimes I feel like if I don't do what they say, I'm turning against God. But I don't want to lose you either. I'm trying to find an answer. I don't get why it has to be one or the other."

"Jack, it's none of their business. Why do you even care what they think?"

"I've got a commitment, Leila. I'm trying to follow God's will, and sometimes that means sacrifice." His tone lost its anguish and became resolute, like someone with a mission, unflinching and grim.

"I thought you had a commitment to *me,* that we were committed to each other, that we loved each other. What about that? Each time you go back to this community, you return a different person, Jack. They're controlling your mind. Don't you see? They can't tolerate anyone who doesn't agree with them." I paused, hesitant to express what had been churning in my mind. "Could they have set the fire, Jack? We know they want me out of your life. Perhaps they'd even want me dead."

"How can you say that, Leila? Why blame my Christian friends for the fire? If they wanted to hurt you, why would they do it while *I* was there?"

"To scare you or punish you for getting involved with an unbeliever. In their eyes, by being with me, you betray your faith. They've wanted you to dump me so you would belong only to them. It seems they're winning."

"You know, it's a lot more likely the fire was set by your Muslim buddies. Which religion is showing how fast they are to use violence to defend their fundamentalist beliefs? Just look at your country."

I was shaking, struggling to hold back tears, clinging to what little strength I had now that hope was fleeing, and dark clouds of despair hung like ruin around me. "What's left for us, Jack?"

"I don't know, Leila. So many people are telling me this is wrong. I need time to find the right answer."

"What are you saying?"

"Well, maybe we should stop seeing each other for a while. Cool things off a bit."

His words pierced my heart like an ice-cold knife. I couldn't believe he was breaking up with me, over religion! My worst nightmare was coming true. The gnawing insecurity that had hovered in the dark recesses of my mind was suddenly real. The pain in my soul was overwhelming, but my anger was growing even more.

"I can't believe you're willing to let a bunch of religious loonies make your decisions, decisions about us. This affects my life, too, you know!" I lashed out.

"Leila, that's not fair," he said in almost a whimper of surrender.

Suddenly, the man I'd loved no longer stood there. I wasn't sure what hurt more—to have Jack leave me, or to stand by helpless as he surrendered his free will to this religious community.

"I think you should leave," I whispered, half meaning it.

I watched through tears as Jack walked out of my life. But tears did nothing to ease the pain. Less than a month earlier, I'd imagined a life with Jack, and now he was gone. For the next several weeks, I couldn't sleep and had no appetite. I spent time alone in my room, rejecting offers to hang out with friends. I even stopped going to the library for news about Iran. Life outside the tiny confine of my bedroom lost all allure. Several times, Jack tried contacting me, but I refused to take his calls.

Graduation day arrived. I decided to attend even though no family would be there for me. On a day of celebration, I wallowed in self-pity. During the ceremony, I spotted Jack in the crowd, and we exchanged brief glances. But it hurt my heart to see him. When I returned to the apartment that evening, a letter was waiting for me.

My dear Leila,

I can't express the agony I've felt since we last talked. I am sorry I made such insensitive comments. They were spoken in anger and in reaction to the possibility of losing you. I had no right. I hope you can forgive me.

I'm leaving tomorrow morning to live and work in the Christian community. I have an opportunity to teach at a private school, and the leaders feel that would be a good vocation for me. I wanted to try to make it as a writer at the paper, but for now that must wait. I know you'll find graduate school the kind of challenge you need to keep you occupied, and you'll do great. I'll be praying for your family and their safety.

For now, perhaps this is best thing for both of us. I need to follow the path God's chosen for me. In time, you'll find the road that's right for you. I wish you only peace and happiness,

Jack

With this simple note on cream-colored paper, in his own gentle hand, Jack said good-bye. My heart dropped, and I crumbled to my knees. I felt like I was drowning, sinking into the *kavir e namak,* the burden of grief dragging me under that sea of salt with the weight of an anvil. In seconds I was lost in its foul, fathomless depths.

TWENTY-NINE

After my breakup with Jack, I lost focus. At times I was in anguish, tears flowing in salty rivers as I poured out my sorrow. At other times I roiled with anger, wanting to strike out against the heartbreak I endured because of religious intolerance. How could he leave me? How could he just walk out? I couldn't believe he'd tossed us aside to follow these nuts. Seeing the destruction religious fervor wreaked in Iran was hard enough. Now it had touched me, personally. I desperately looked for things to occupy me during those summer months. The pain of losing Jack was intense, and I battled the lurking demons seeking to dominate my soul.

I went for long walks, fighting to banish Jack from my mind. Leisurely strolls often turned into jogs as anger alternated with anguish, tears splashing the black asphalt as I picked up speed, running faster and faster to leave the pain behind. In those meditative hours of exertion, I tried to lighten my soul, to remind myself of the beauty of love and the joys I had experienced, hoping to leave hurt and anger on the roadside. Heartache always seemed to catch up with me, but the hard runs left me exhausted, and I'd collapse in a deep, dreamless sleep. As summer came to a close, I was offered a research assistantship job, which relieved my concerns about tuition and living expenses.

The hostages in Tehran dominated the news, and Americans seemed incensed with Iran. I found it equally disturbing but wondered if national resentment might again become personal. Jack, my protector, was gone. After moving from country to country, the Shah finally took his last breath in July after a struggle with cancer. I'd been so confident he'd restore order in Iran, but the Shahanshah was gone. His loss depressed me further.

Sitting in bed, I picked up a notepad and pen. I'd been writing to Jack but never mailing the letters. Writing to him was like writing in a journal, a habit I'd abandoned after high school. Though it brought a rush of emotions, it was comforting. Unlike the letters before, I decided to mail this one. I wanted him to know.

> *Dear Jack,*
> *There's so much I want to say to you, but I don't know where to start. My life has not been the same since you left. I miss you so much. I miss the walks we took in the moonlight. I miss your gentle touch on my cheek as we kissed. I long for your warm embrace and the secure feeling I had when you held me. Sometimes at night when I'm alone in bed, I turn and almost feel you next to me.*

Tears flowed as sorrow and emptiness gripped me like a boat tossed in a monsoon. I tore the page, crumpled it, and tossed it in the corner. Wiping my tears, I started over, with a different tone.

> *Dear Jack,*
> *I hope you're doing well. I know it's been a long time since we've talked. But I wanted to see how you're doing. I'm doing fine, although I miss all my friends who've graduated and left, including you . . .*

I lifted the pen, ripped the paper, and again tossed it on the floor, watching it roll and stop next to the first. Frustrated, I slid down on my pillow, staring at the bare wall. I missed Jack and was upset he hadn't contacted me since he left. Not a day went by that I didn't think of him or want to pick up the phone and call, wondering where he was, who he was with, what he was wearing. Had he found a new girlfriend and forgotten me? Or was he too busy with his Christian community? Why didn't he call? Didn't he care how I was feeling? Tears came again as I pictured him in my favorite blue oxford shirt, the way it brought out the blue of his eyes. I pictured him walking down a street, holding an umbrella to fend off the rain, the way he had done when we were together. But there was no one under the umbrella with him. Was he as lonely as I? Did he want me back?

Setting down the pad and pen, I rolled over, sobbing into my pillow. I still couldn't understand how Jack could leave me. I had given myself to him entirely, heart and soul. I'd fallen deeply in love with him and only then chose to offer him the gift most valued to an unwed Iranian girl, something I could never recover. When I gave myself to him, I never imagined there'd ever be anyone else. Jack would be with me forever. Now, I could never marry an Iranian man. What if he learned I wasn't a virgin? Jack had taken that from me. No, someday I'd have to marry an American, if at all. While my love for Jack was real and I believed his love equally sincere, there was so much stripped from me when it ended, so much I'd lost. My hands shook as I struggled to regain composure. After all, I was my father's daughter and must be strong. As my sobbing subsided, I sat up once again and started to write, this time with more resolve.

Dear Jack,

I hope this letter finds you well. I'm sorry I haven't written sooner. I've been busy with school. I'm sure you've been reading the news about Iran. Things are unstable. I worry that my parents are in the heart of it. It must be hard for them, especially with me here.

I often wonder how you're doing, if you still stop to enjoy the colors of the sky at dusk, its orange and yellow fingers reaching across, casting purple hues against the midnight blue background. I wonder if you enjoy watching birds in flight, noting the hawks as they soar effortlessly below the clouds. I imagine you singing a Beatles song in a dimly lit pizza parlor somewhere, as you once sang to me. I remember you serenading me with "My Funny Valentine" as we held hands on a campus bench. Mid-song, you took my hand and danced with me under the stars. Passers-by stopped to watch, but you saw only me. I remember whispering, "I'm embarrassed," but I got lost in the dance, knowing there was no one else but you and me under the stars. Do you dance with another, or am I still in your heart? I wish I could express how much I miss you. I wish you knew. I am so lonely without you, so incomplete. My darling, I love you still. I'll never stop.

Leila

With tears lining my face, I carefully tore the paper from its pad and folded it. I set it on the nightstand to mail in the morning. But when morning came, I stared at the paper, painful memories resurfacing, and left it there as I headed to school.

THIRTY

In September of 1980, days after my twenty-second birthday, Saddam Hussein launched an attack on Iran over what he claimed was his territory. Of course, that's overly simplistic. There are age-old differences between the powerful Sunni Muslims of Iraq and the Shiite Muslims of Iran, and Arab-Persian disputes go back centuries. Perhaps Saddam feared Khomeini might seek revenge, as years earlier Saddam had tossed him out of Najaf, the holy Shiite city in Iraq. Whatever the reasons, he launched a bloody war. While I sat immersed in IPOs, bear and bull markets, and P/E ratios, my country was under attack. That same week, reconstruction on my house was completed, and I moved back in.

In January, two significant events took place. First, the American hostages in Tehran were finally released on the eve of Reagan's inauguration. The second concerned a call from Uncle Mohsen in Paris. He relayed news that my cousin Ali Reza from Esfahan had died while making a Molotov cocktail. Sadly, I discovered that wasn't a Russian drink.

"Uncle Mohsen, what's the draft situation?" He understood my concern was about Amir.

"They say it's voluntary, dear, but don't believe it. They draft for service by age. First, they took men over twenty-one, then anyone over nineteen. Now it's inching toward seventeen. Soon they'll take eleven- and twelve-year-old boys. If he can hold a gun and shoot, he's qualified."

"That's scary," I exclaimed, picturing a child thrust into war. "What about Amir?"

"College grads are second draft, so for now he's safe. But who knows, anything's possible."

Not long after that conversation, the nightmare became reality, and Amir was drafted.

"He had no choice. The war has already taken so many. Every able-bodied man is being called." I detected the strain in Baba's voice. "Don't worry, Leila. Allah will protect him." It wasn't often my father mentioned Allah in conversation. Perhaps he, too, was reaching for anything that offered hope.

What my parents spared me was how Amir had been drafted. Rumor was that young boys were snatched straight from school and sent to the front, with news of it never reaching their family. No one wanted to believe it or think it could happen to *their* son. But it was real for Ali Farmani's little brother. An honor student in his senior year of high school, he'd just passed the *Concoor* entrance exam to attend Tehran University. On a cool day in May, before graduation, Ali Farmani's mother frantically called her husband at work to say their son hadn't come home from school. She called the school and was told he'd been taken. The principal explained that Pasdaran had come and snatched several students, her son among them. She collapsed.

It was not the only time this had happened. The first time, the principal physically resisted the Pasdaran, trying to deny access to his school. He was beaten and jailed for a week and told to cooperate if he wanted to live. They ordered him to say nothing next time. Fearing for his life, he had little choice. For future drafts, he stood by, biting his tongue as soldiers dragged the boys away, inner conflict consuming him. The soldiers said government officials would contact the families, and he was ordered to do nothing. Again, he followed orders. He had a family of his own to look after. So when they took Ali's brother and five other boys that day, the principal stood by, frustrated in his impotence. The principal later committed suicide.

Ali Farmani's family suffered the ultimate consequences. Agonizing months after he vanished, they received a letter, informing them of their son's death. It stipulated a monthly stipend amount to compensate for their loss. Upon reading the letter, his mother collapsed again.

My brother was taken in much the same way. Amir was enrolled in a business Farsi course at Tehran University. After class, he left with his friend Mir Ali to get his car, parked off campus. Out of nowhere, a dark green Toyota SUV pulled in front of them and came to a screeching halt. Two men in army fatigues, weapons drawn, accosted Amir and said, "Get in the back. You're coming with us."

"Where am I going?"

"You'll know soon enough. Get in." With a shove, they forced Amir into the backseat and drove away, leaving a shaky, astonished Mir Ali behind. He stood in shock for several minutes, then ran to the nearest store and begged to use the phone.

"It's an emergency," he told the proprietor. Having observed the incident from behind his store window, he obliged. He, too, had lost a relative to the draft.

"Hello, can I speak to Mr. Moradi? It's urgent," Mir Ali said breathlessly.

"Who's calling?" Fatemeh asked.

"Please, *khanoom*. It's about Amir."

Fatemeh set aside formalities and dashed off to get Baba.

"Mr. Moradi. I'm Amir's classmate. We were just walking from class, and the Pasdaran pulled up and took him," the anguish in his voice evident.

"Did they say where they were taking him?"

"No, sir. Amir asked, and they said, 'You'll know soon enough.' I really thought they'd take me too, but they didn't. I'm sorry, sir. I didn't know what to do."

"There's nothing you could have done, son. Thank you for letting me know."

"I hope he's alright, Mr. Moradi. I'm sorry." And with that, Mir Ali hung up and hurried to the safety of his home, feeling lucky he hadn't suffered the same fate.

From his library, Baba called everyone he knew with government connections to determine Amir's whereabouts. It wasn't till the next morning, after a night of sleepless calling, that he learned the truth. It was suddenly clear: No one was immune.

THIRTY-ONE

Graduate school was drawing to a close, and my life was in turmoil. My first love had left me in the name of religion. My brother was dragged into the war with Iraq. My father's business had trickled to a halt. It was difficult, if not impossible, to transfer money in or out of Iran. Since much of his business was exporting to foreign art lovers, Baba accepted deferred payment from trusted clients. Maman suffered her usual ailments, amplified by Amir's absence, from aches and pains to colds and the flu, each worse than the one before. Grandmother needed a new hip. And Iran was constantly in the news.

Being in the house alone felt strangely isolating and threatening, like a storm on the horizon menacing a clear day. It held memories of Jack, memories I wanted to leave behind. It had been almost two years since we'd broken up, but anytime I saw a similar face in a crowd or caught the scent of his cologne, my heart broke in half.

I received another letter from Amir, his first since being drafted. I sat on the couch, opening it with trembling fingers, too anxious to prepare my traditional cup of tea.

My dear sister,

I'm so sorry I couldn't call or write before I left home. I'm sure you understand. I didn't even have time to pack clothes or grab cigarettes. Yep, I took up smoking. I know, I always told you not to smoke. But everybody smokes here, and before I knew it, there I was. Sometimes it feels good to just sit back and take a drag off a cigarette; it calms me down.

We barely have time to sleep, let alone write. There's always something going on near camp—a missile or bomb, shots in the dark. We have to be constantly alert. Sleep is such a gift when we can get it, two or three hours at a time. A lot of the soldiers are younger, so I'm the older brother who consoles them when they're homesick, sad, or worse, when we lose one of our own. The death and destruction wounds my soul, my whole being. But I'm not complaining. I'm treated well. We've plenty of food and water, and the officers are looking out for us.

The Iraqi soldiers are ruthless. They don't place any value on their own lives. It's like they want to be martyrs for their cause. I wonder if they're afraid, or if they've been brainwashed into believing Saddam's lies. They willingly sacrifice themselves for the chance to kill us. In one day, we lost over a thousand men. I heard they used chemical weapons. The corpses tell a horrific story. This is not Geneva Convention-style warfare, that much I know.

I've made new friends, and I truly believe in our cause. This is my country, and I will do what I must to defend it. I'm proud to be here.

Leila, I hope you're doing well in graduate school and are happy. God only knows when I'll get the chance to write again. I think of you, Maman, and Baba every day. I hope the war ends soon and I can come home. I miss you. Your loving brother,
Amir

His words left me breathless with worry. I imagined Amir sitting cross-legged in a tent near the front lines, pen in hand, composing this note. I pictured his clinched eyebrows as he struggled for the words to convey his feelings. My brother was not the type to be brainwashed. I didn't think for a moment that he believed in "the cause." What cause? This feeding frenzy of Iraqi Sunnis battling Iranian Shiites? No, Amir wouldn't believe in that.

Amir was a gentle soul. Once as children, we were playing outside when I spotted an army of ants marching in line. I grabbed the hose to drown them. Amir snatched it from me, too late to save the ants, and screamed, "You know what you just did? You just killed hundreds of families. How can you live with yourself? Would you like it if someone killed *your* family?" And while he watched, he never speared flies in Esfahan like Mojtabah and I. He put milk out for stray cats or asked Fatemeh for lamb bones and then carried them on his bike to the park and left them for stray dogs. Amir was first to approach a beggar and offer the change in his pocket. No, Amir was not a killer. He was in agony, being so close to death and destruction. He knew the army would read his letter and cloaked his true feelings. I knew my big brother.

*   *   *

That spring would shatter my heart in ways unimaginable. Daffodils bloomed. Yellow and purple crocuses pushed through the thawing ground after winter hibernation. The freshness of the evening air, alive with new growth, made me dizzy with joy. Even my longing for Jack had somewhat faded, and I was able to enjoy time alone without tears. I stood on the deck, scanning the back yard for the deer, spring air intoxicating my senses. Graduation was near. I had applied for a work visa, hoping to get hired and remain in America. Not an easy feat, but I was optimistic.

The day before graduation, I picked up my navy cap and gown at the bookstore, drove home, and tried them on in front of the tall mirror in my bedroom. I stood gazing at my reflection, contemplating what life might bring next. In my mind I saw Amir's reflection in the mirror, in the same cap and gown. I recalled his smiling, happy face on his graduation day. The ringing phone interrupted my thoughts.

"You remembered my graduation!" I said, excited to hear my parents' voices.

"*Azizam*, we have very bad news." Baba's voice was that of a man wrapped in distress as though trapped in a well.

"What? Is Maman Rouhi okay?" I asked, a logical assumption given her declining health.

"No, dear. She's fine. It's Amir," I heard him sob.

"What, Baba? What's happened to Amir?" Tears filled my eyes as I only half-dared ask the question I never wanted answered.

"He's, he's . . ." Baba groaned, struggling to continue. "He stepped on a land mine. He's gone," then he broke down completely. His sobbing became louder, more persistent. I heard my mother's cries over the other receiver. She couldn't speak.

The next minute lasted an eternity, punctuated by the anguished silence of breaking hearts. I stared at the blank wall, my head spinning, unable to grasp what I'd just heard. The screams inside my head drowned out my parents' sobbing. When capacity for thought returned, all I could mutter was, "It can't be true." My quiet weeping echoed theirs as nothing more was left to say.

I sat on my bed, still in cap and gown, longing to wail aloud, to rail at this injustice, but I was paralyzed, suspended in time, frozen in the pain of loss. I stared at the foot of the bed, at stains on the beige carpet, at anything and nothing. Webs of anguish enveloped me in their horrid embrace as I sat powerless to escape. I heard the phone ringing in the distance. Its clanging pierced my consciousness, and I searched for the source, only it was ringing in my lap.

"Hi, Leila. Want me to pick you up tonight?" It was Janet's cheerful voice.

"Uhhhh . . . I don't know . . . ," I mumbled, still in shock.

"What's wrong?"

"It's Amir . . . he's dead. He was killed by a land mine."

"Oh, my God, Leila, I'm coming over."

"I think I'd rather be alone, Janet."

"No way, I'm coming over. Or you come here."

"I'd rather be alone for now."

"Leila, either I'm coming over, or you get over here."

"Okay, okay, I'll come to you. I can't stay here anyway." She was insistent, and I was unable to think for myself. How could I?

"Sure, if that's what you want. Are you okay to drive?"

"Yeah. Give me half an hour."

"Okay. But call if you change your mind. I'll come get you."

I stared numbly at my reflection as I removed the cap and gown and tossed them on the floor. It was like watching an apparition. Graduation lost significance. In a catatonic state, I took my car keys and left.

I drove toward Bethlehem along the lush wooded Saucon Valley. The winding road bordered by deep forests had always soothed me, but not tonight. Even the moon was a dull lusterless color. My thoughts drifted to a war zone, land mines, gun-toting soldiers, bombs, bodies, my brother—my poor, sweet brother. The road curved down the mountain. It was dusk; the sun was setting. In the glare, I didn't notice the deer as it dashed across the road.

I awoke in austere white surroundings, Janet's soft hand on my arm. The forgotten war scene flashed again before my eyes. Tears flowed as reality returned, and my brother's face filled my mind. It was no dream.

"You were in an accident. You have a concussion, a broken ankle, and minor bruises. But you'll be fine," said Janet reassuringly.

"Did you call my parents?"

"No, I figured they had enough to deal with."

"No need to tell them," I muttered, the sedatives taking effect. They had their own share of grief, but I wanted someone to take pity on me. I was in agony, a pain I'd never felt before, a jagged-edged spear driven through my heart. Please, someone hold me and tell me it's a bad dream, that it will all go away.

I wished Amir were with me, standing among the bustle of families at graduation, telling everyone how proud he was of his baby sister. I wished I could see Maman fawning over him. I wouldn't mind. Why hadn't I told Baba the truth, that it was I who broke his tear catcher? When Baba punished Amir, I begged Mahmood to drive me to the bazaar, and I searched the shops till I found another one. It wasn't antique or nearly as beautiful as the one I'd broken. That night, I gave it to Baba when I found him alone in the library. "Baba, please don't punish Amir. He didn't mean to break it." My father wrapped me in his strong arms, holding me gently against his chest and said, "What a sweet sister you are." Then he handed me the tear catcher and told me I could keep it in my room. I should have told Baba then, but I didn't.

After my release from the hospital, I spent my days recovering at the house, with frequent visits from Janet. I telephoned Uncle Mohsen and shared what had happened but begged him not to tell Maman and Baba. For a change, I didn't want to steal their attention from Amir.

"What are you going to do now, Leila?"

"I don't know, Uncle Mohsen. I still don't have a job, and time's running out."

"Maybe you should return home, my dear. It's not good for you to be alone in a foreign land, and your parents could use your support. Besides, maybe it's time to consider marriage. Nothing would please your parents more and distract them from their grief."

"I know, Uncle Mohsen, I know." Getting married was the furthest thing from my mind, but being alone had given me time to think. Returning home might help me as much as my parents. I worried about them. My grandmother's health had seriously declined, and I missed her terribly. When she learned of Amir's death, she took to her prayer beads and remained a recluse. In a state of denial, Maman transformed Amir's room into a shrine. She spent hours sitting on his bed, touching and smelling his clothes, folding and unfolding them over and over until Baba coaxed her away. While America felt like home, Iran was my country. My soul was there. So was my family. Only in Iran could I say good-bye to my brother. There was nothing left here for me anymore. My decision was made. I made arrangements to leave. I contacted my friends to say good-bye. On my last day in Bethlehem, after painful consideration, I took pen in hand and wrote a letter.

Dear Jack,

I wanted you to know I'm returning to Iran. These past two years have been a long and difficult time. When you left, the pain was more than I thought I could bear. But I managed not to allow anger and resentment to consume me, holding on to the precious memories of loving you and being loved. Perhaps the strength I gained over these years sustains me now.

The day before graduation, I received terrible news. Amir, who had been drafted, was killed in the war. My family is devastated by his loss. I was so distraught when I learned of his death, I had an accident and was hospitalized. I'm fine. But I need to go home, for my parents' sake, for my grandmother. I need to be where my brother perished to say good-bye. I need to go for me.

You may not know how deeply you've touched my life. You'll always have a special place in my heart. I hope you're happy in the life you've chosen,

Yours,

Leila

P.S. Since I don't have your current address, I've asked Janet to find you and deliver this.

THIRTY-TWO

Tehran Prison, 1988

The clang of a cell door somewhere down the labyrinth of hallways startled me from my dreams. These were the worst times, waking from the recurring nightmare of Amir's death. It was always the same. I'd find myself wandering a barren field, pockmarked by shell-craters, strewn with broken bodies. The attar of carrion hung in the air, mingled with sulfuric smoke from burning corpses. I stumbled about this wasteland in a stupor, slipping occasionally on spilt blood, tripping over shattered limbs. Tears flowed as I searched vainly for my brother in the chaotic dreamscape of the battlefield. Then I found him, lying in the smoking remnants of a crater, his eyes staring unseeing into mine. He looked peaceful; no pain haunted his face. As I approached, I saw his legs were gone, his body ripped apart by the blast of the land mine. Then my screams began, echoing in the emptiness of war and destruction.

For so long my life consisted of this: waking, dreaming, nightmares interspersed with joyful memories, long hours of boredom punctuated by intense agony as the torture, the questioning, continued unabated. Interrogations accompanied by beatings and abuse that often left me unconscious had gone on for months. Every few weeks, I was allowed a shower—I guess even the guards who beat me couldn't stand the stench. I no longer dwelt on anger or fear. I'd resigned myself to this existence, my sole focus to endure the inflicted pain and survive. I'd given up hope of Farhad coming to my rescue and wondered if he was in prison himself for the crime of being my husband.

The absurdity of it all struck me occasionally, and I'd find myself laughing in mild hysteria, staring blankly at the concrete walls. How many times would they ask the same inane questions, and how many times would I answer, "I don't know. I can't tell you anything"?

To ward off boredom and encroaching despair, I'd begged for books, anything to read. The stout guard who'd helped with my period slipped a worn Koran under the door one day. While my vision blurred quickly in the sparse light, I read its passages from time to time. The irony of an Islamic state proclaiming the message of the prophet, while torturing its citizens in blind disregard for the words of peace and compassion, did little to ease my mind. But I continued to read, sometimes reciting passages aloud when I'd hear the guards marching the hallway, hoping a show of faith might suspend the beatings. It did not.

Then the abuse took a different turn. As usual, two of the guards returned me bound and hooded to my cell. This time, they didn't remove my shackles or hood before tossing me to the floor. One of them dragged me to the bed. At first, I thought his actions a kindness, an impression immediately dispelled when he shoved me down and pulled the rough robe above my shoulders.

"Make a sound, whore, and I'll cut your throat," he said in a gruff tone as I tried to pull away. He held me down, fumbling with his trousers, a calloused hand pinning my arms above my head as he forced himself on me. I tried to lift my head, to resist, but he punched my face and continued the rape. I tried to scream but could manage only a strangled croak. It was a blessing I was barely conscious as he finished. After him, his partner took a turn. I lay like a rag doll, blind and bound as rough hands groped my breasts, the putrid odor of their rancid sweat and the debasement of their assault making me nauseous. When finished, they spit on the floor as a gesture of disgust, slammed the door, and left me lying there.

I lay there shaking in tears, my mind screaming at the horror of the moment. My thoughts weren't on my assailants; they were animals, nameless, faceless perpetrators of a brutal invasion. Rather, I was gripped with fear—what will Farhad think? How could he accept a wife who'd been raped, brutalized? How could I live with the shame? Could I face my father after what these bastards had done to me? With the theory in Islam that a woman is the root of sexual temptation and sin, she inevitably bears the condemnation for men's brutal actions. Women didn't report rape. What would be the purpose? And in this hell-hole, no one cared.

In a fetal position, I sobbed until my tremors subsided. I pried myself

from the bed and pulled off my robe. Standing naked, I turned on the
hose, the cold water burning as I washed the blood and filth from my
skin. I scrubbed myself with the rough wet robe, purging the unseen
marks of abuse, knowing it would never go away, knowing I could never
tell a soul. I closed my eyes, silent screams echoing in my head.

Nausea gripped me as bitter bile rose in my throat. I fell to the floor
hunched over, holding my stomach as the retching began and brought
fresh tears to my eyes. I was blacking out and felt weak. I felt Amir's
gentle arm around my shoulder as he kissed my cheek and said it was
okay. It was okay I hadn't told Baba about the tear catcher. I reached for
Maman Rouhi's outstretched arm, prayer beads in hand, only to watch
her fall to the floor. I gathered the dozens of unmailed letters I'd written
Jack and tossed them in the air, watching them take wing and soar like
fledgling birds on virginal flights. Finally, the retching subsided as I
knelt, staring at the floor, the acrid smell of my own vomit filling my
nostrils. I was dizzy. The walls closed in, the room began spinning, and
then I found peace in the darkness of unconsciousness.

Cold water had pooled beneath my body, and I shivered uncontrol-
lably. Slowly, I lifted myself as tears again washed my face. How could
I live with this shame? How could I cleanse it from my soul? I turned
off the hose, dragged myself to the bed, wrapped the worn blanket
around me with shaking hands, and collapsed. I fought to rid my mind
of the images of the assault, the stench of the soldiers, their hot drops of
sweat searing my skin. I wanted someone to hold me, to console me. I
forced back the horrid images, looking for solace in a comforting vision,
something deep within my memory.

It was a sunny day. Jack and I drove to a secluded end of Lake
Noxamixon, an hour from campus. Finding an open glen near the
water, enclosed in a towering cathedral of pine and birch trees, we sat
on a blanket in the beauty of nature, sharing a picnic lunch and quiet
conversation. After lunch, Jack stood and said, "Come on—let's go for
a swim."

"But I don't have a suit."

"Who needs a suit?"

He stripped off his clothing before jumping into the water. I
watched him surface and stand, droplets of water shimmering on his

bare chest. I was still the young girl from Iran, far too shy for skinny-dipping. But I pulled off my shirt and jeans and walked to the water in my panties and bra. The soft mud squished between my toes as I gingerly entered the lake. The cold water made my skin tingle, its embrace refreshing. We swam side by side, laughing for precious moments, till I was too cold and climbed out. Jack followed. We lay together with the blanket wrapped about us like a cocoon, no sound but the occasional caw of the crows or cooing doves, the scent of pine needles and wild lavender caressing the air. Jack held me gently, and warmth enclosed me. There was a tenderness and quiet comfort in his arms following the illicit swim.

I felt Jack's soft breath like a gentle breeze caress my being, conveying whispered words of tenderness. I told him how I missed my family, my home. He wiped the tears from my cheek, his fingers moving slowly, carefully, along my face like a restoration artist, brushing away sadness. I drifted slowly to sleep, lost in the memory of that moment, the memory of his arms, feeling his chest rise and fall with each breath. How I longed for that comfort now.

THIRTY-THREE

Tehran, Summer of 1982

I returned to Iran five long years after my last visit. Grandmother had a new hip and walked with a limp. Emotional suffering crippled her more than her aging body, as it did my parents. My brother's death had unleashed a tempest of anguish, crushing my family. Maman's psychosomatic illnesses grew exponentially. She couldn't get through a day without needing rest from this ache or that pain.

Baba focused less and less on business, leaving day-to-day activities to his apprentice. The loss of his only son shattered something at his core. He stopped traveling after Amir's death, preferring to stay close to home. He still taught art classes at Tehran University, when student demonstrations or clashes with Pasdaran didn't shut down school. Passion for his students offered the only balm for the agony he endured.

I wondered how Neda was coping. Through her letters, I'd learned of the abuse she suffered at the hands of her husband, which she tolerated for the sake of their daughters. She suspected he had a *seegheh* arrangement. In a country waging a religious war and imposing strict Islamic law, practice of *seegheh* was condoned, allowing men to take a temporary bride for as little as twenty-four hours or as long as a year. Nothing like legalizing prostitution. I recalled the happy bride and groom on their wedding day a few years ago, and my heart sank at their crumbling relationship.

I pictured Fatemeh, our master chef and meticulous housekeeper, her scrawny legs miraculously supporting her body as she scurried about the kitchen, working her magic with food. In my mind, I began to compose a list of Persian dishes I missed most. I'd ask her to make *loobia polo*, followed by *shirin polo*, lamb's tongue, and her specialty, *tah-chin*. I couldn't wait to taste my favorites.

I thought about Mahmood, our loyal chauffeur, and his distinctive black mustache. My heart wept for him. A year earlier, his only daughter was diagnosed with cancer at the tender age of twenty-six. My father arranged and paid for the best surgeon and oncologist, sat with him at her bedside during chemotherapy, then held him in his arms as together they mourned her untimely death. So much sadness had touched our lives these past years.

The last segment of my journey on the Swissair Boeing 747, the part that worried me the most, arrived. The announcement came well into the flight from Zurich to Tehran, "Ladies and Gentlemen, this is the captain speaking. We are about to enter Iranian air space. All women must dress in accordance with the laws of Islam. Thank you."

Rustling noise filled the plane as husbands stood to retrieve their wives' head scarves and body covers, and women donned Muslim attire in preparation for arrival. I considered waiting till we exited the plane. Then it occurred to me there could be government spies on board to see who ignores the law and arrest her upon landing. Better not tempt fate. I pulled on my raincoat, which served as a *roopoosh*, and slipped on a head scarf. I hoped the floral design wouldn't draw attention or, worse, a reprimand. Like the other women, I sweltered in my raincoat for the remainder of the flight.

Our landing and exit through immigration went smoothly, though I felt uncomfortable with so many armed guards about. Tension hung like gallows over the room. I jostled my way through the crowd herding to the exit and their loved ones. Out of nowhere, a woman dressed head to toe in black, machine gun strapped across her chest, dragged me out of line.

"What are you doing?" she demanded.

"I'm sorry?"

"Your *roopoosh* must be buttoned completely. And look at your hair; your scarf doesn't cover it," she said, pushing renegade curls back under my scarf.

"I'm sorry. I meant no offense. I haven't been home in a long time, and . . ."

"If you go outside looking like this, you'll be arrested. I'm doing you a favor not arresting you right here. Remember, keep yourself covered. Now go." I buttoned my raincoat with trembling fingers and lowered the scarf to cover rebel hairs.

This was my initiation, jolted into the present state of life in Iran. What had I done coming here? I pulled myself together and focused on finding my family, anticipating the big group that had welcomed me on my prior trip.

Once outside, I stared into the new face of Iran, quite different from the scene I'd witnessed years earlier. The bright colors and crowds waving, cousins flashing bouquets of radiant flowers, and people stretched on tiptoes to spot friends or relatives were replaced by a sea of gray and black. Arms waved but were fully covered. No fashion fragrances perfumed the air; no makeup added life to drab faces. The monochrome scene was broken only by teeth flashing white in the dark morning hours as loved ones were spotted.

I spotted my parents. Even in the dim light, I noticed the lines of age and distress on my parents. They bore the pain of loss like a malignancy that withered their faces and broke their hearts. Our emotional embrace could have lasted a decade. But no aunts or cousins were there to greet me this time.

During the ride home, I sat in silence as my parents pointed out burned buildings, boarded windows, and homes that used to be.

"Look over there," Baba said, pointing to the barren divider in the highway. "Remember it used to be lined with red geraniums, how beautiful they were?"

"Where is everybody? The last time I came home, there were people everywhere, roaming the streets even at this late hour."

"Not anymore, unless they want to be arrested."

The sad shadows crushed images of my youthful days in a country full of color and life, now broken by war and oppression. I already missed America, but bleak and broken as it was, this was home. Here I would stay, at least for now.

Maman Rouhi was waiting up when we arrived. I ran to her bed as she struggled to sit. She held me for a long time, the sweet scent of rosewater she had dabbed behind her ears a welcome reminder of home.

"*Azizam*, it's good you're here. I'm an old woman, but your parents are still young and need you. Now they have only you."

I studied her ancient face. Her wrinkled creases were darker, standing in stark contrast to her ivory skin. The pain of loneliness and loss was reflected in her brown eyes, their shine given way to a dull glisten. She seemed exhausted. "I'll see you in the morning, Maman Rouhi. Get some sleep." I kissed her forehead, and taking her prayer beads, laid them on the nightstand beside her.

In my room, the ruby tear catcher sat on the dresser facing my bed, exactly where I'd left it five years ago. That night, thoughts of Amir haunted me, memories of days in this house, at school, with the rest of the family. Even faithful Rostam wasn't there to greet me; a failing heart had taken him a year earlier. Sadness lingered over the house like fog after a heavy rain.

I awoke to the smell of freshly brewed tea and a pleasant sunny morning. Everyone was gathered in the kitchen. I walked in rubbing my eyes and gave everyone a hug and kiss. I saved a special kiss on both cheeks for Fatemeh and shook hands with Mahmood. That was unusual, given our difference in societal rank, but I didn't care. I was so happy to see them.

There was excitement that morning, with no mention of revolution, war, or death. Only the pleasant exchange of good news: weddings, engagements, and babies. We sat for hours catching up while I enjoyed *barbari* bread with feta cheese. The phone started ringing as friends and relatives called to welcome me home and set dates for visits with cakes and flowers. Maman played social secretary, timing and coordinating appointments to avoid mismatched personalities or incompatible relatives. Sadly, none of my high school friends called. Those who were overseas when the revolution began never returned. Many who'd remained in Iran by now had fled or were killed. I felt isolated, but with guests to entertain, there was little time for the emptiness I feared would haunt me.

The comings and goings of visitors provided a pleasant diversion from reality. Air-raid sirens often broke the quiet of night. We'd wake and rush to the basement. By now this was so common that Baba had placed couches down there so we'd wait things out in comfort. I had the most difficulty adjusting to being fully covered before going out for even a brief shopping expedition, a new and exceedingly distasteful experience. It was amusing how my more Western cousins circumvented the restrictions of *hijab*. As they wandered from the car to the house, their faces were bowed under the mandatory head scarf, the *roopoosh* covering to their ankles. But once inside, off came the cloaks and scarves to reveal Armani, Gucci, and Yves St. Laurent. Of course, they couldn't wear blue jeans, but black designer jeans with sequined pockets, hidden under an outer cloak till the safety of a welcoming home, were prevalent. The outside world saw a submissive Muslim woman, but even the Islamic Republic couldn't stifle the women's spirit or their style. I fit right in with their little rebellion.

As the flood of visits declined, days grew tedious with lack of activity. "I need to do something besides wander from my room to the pool and back," I told Baba, asking him to find me work.

"I understand, Leila, but it's best that you stay home for a while."

"But Tara's working. Aunt Soheila's working. Why can't I?"

"They had their jobs before the revolution. If you look for work now, especially having just returned from America, you'll draw the wrong kind of attention."

"Can't I work for you?"

"Leila, trust me when I say now is not the time."

"Then what can I do?" I asked in frustration.

"Well, you know, several suitors have contacted me. Just yesterday, Mr. Arefi asked about you for their son, Farhad. Perhaps we can introduce you two and see how it goes. Only if you want . . ."

My father couldn't see my stomach churn at this suggestion of marriage, especially to someone the family would introduce. This was the only time I didn't like being with Baba, when he wanted to arrange my marriage. I'd imagined someday I'd fall in love and get married. That was the dream I thought I'd realized in Jack, now ashes. Perhaps I'd find it again, but not like this. Plus, I had a secret I couldn't share. How could I marry an Iranian man? I knew how tormented my father was over Amir's death, so I dragged my emotions under control and said only, "Well, we'll see"—my way of dismissing it.

In my father's mind, however, this registered as acceptance. That afternoon, Baba gleefully contacted Mr. Arefi and planned a dinner party to introduce the potential bride and groom. While he was busy arranging my betrothal, I decided to visit my cousin Neda, a visit with unanticipated consequences.

THIRTY-FOUR

Mahmood was vacationing with his family, so I decided to take the bus to Neda's rather than call for a private car. After all, it was a beautiful sunny day, no threat of rain, and I was ready for adventure. I put on my head scarf and Maman's *roopoosh*—I still hadn't come to grips with owning my own, perhaps an act of defiance. I nervously pushed my hair deeper under my scarf as I walked to the main street. Battling attempts at restraint, the curls rebelliously pushed out with complete disregard for Islamic law, daring a confrontation with the "Compliance Gestapo."

"Bus fifteen drops you right by her street," Maman Rouhi had said.

I walked toward the bus stop in the sweltering heat of mid-morning. I quickly found number fifteen among the row of parked buses. Some passengers were seated, while others boarded through the front and back doors. I walked to the shorter line in front, wondering why the man ahead stared at me like I had a third eye. I glared back. I'm in the Islamic Republic, and this guy is leering at me. Quickly, I learned he had no lustful intentions.

"*Khanoom*, you must go through the back door," he said, pointing to the rear. I looked at women and children slowly boarding the bus through the rear door. The front, where I'd mistakenly queued, was for men. I thanked him, feeling little gratitude, and hesitantly walked to the back of the bus. On the last step, I froze as I looked inside.

"*Khanoom, boro.* Miss, go," said a voice behind me as the women clamored to get onboard. With the gentle nudge from the woman behind me, I stepped into the bus and took a seat. Near the back of the bus, a metal rail separated front and rear. Women and children were confined to the back while men rode up front. A number of empty seats were available up front, while several women with small children remained standing in the cramped rear. I felt degraded and humiliated. As a woman in this country, I was left to feel inferior to men.

Faced with this forced segregation, I grew indignant. How dare they treat women this way? Are we less human, less important? If they want to keep men and women apart, why not have women up front? Fuming, I gathered my courage to climb the rail and defiantly sit in the front. I wouldn't stand for this. If Rosa Parks could launch the civil rights movement in America, I could launch women's rights here. Just then, the bus came to a screeching halt. It was my stop. My defiant act of civil disobedience would have to wait, perhaps a blessing in disguise. I couldn't get off fast enough, brimming with righteous indignation as I walked up to Neda's door.

"You won't believe what just happened," I said, practically out of breath.

"You look upset. Are you okay?" asked Neda.

"Did you know about the segregation on the bus? How dare they?"

"First, why didn't you take a private taxi? Second, welcome to the new Iran."

The words struck like a hammer on anvil. Yes, it was a new country. Rules were different. Laws had changed. And I had to adapt to stay out of jail, even to stay alive. I recalled my father's words: "You don't want to draw attention. As long as you do your own thing, head down, no one will bother you."

Neda's little girls, Taraneh and Mina, were overjoyed to see me. Born while I was away, I'd met them when they came to welcome me home, and they fell in love with Auntie Leila from America. The older, Taraneh, sat in my lap, her little arms wrapped around my neck, and looked at me with big brown eyes, "Are you going back to America, Auntie Leila?"

"No, darling, I'm staying right here."

"Can you come live with us?"

"I'd love to, Taraneh, but I live with Maman and Baba. You and Mina can come over anytime and go swimming."

"Girls, go play with your tea set so Auntie Leila and I can talk."

My heart wept for the girls as Neda began relating the abuse she endured at the hands of her husband. Although Parviz was good to the girls, they'd more than once seen him strike their mother.

"Why don't you leave him, Neda? Get a divorce?"

"Leila, what'll I do then? Even if he agrees, what good is a divorced woman with two kids in Iran?"

"Get your own place. He'll have to support you and the girls."

"He'd make our life miserable. He'd take the girls away from me, you know that. The father has all the rights here."

"But this isn't good either. Ultimately it hurts the girls as much as it hurts you."

"Welcome to the new Iran, Leila. It's the way life is."

For the second time I heard "welcome to the new Iran" in the context of intolerance and abuse. After the revolution, women lost most of the rights they'd gained under the Shah. Two weeks earlier, our neighbor had brought over a document requiring two signatures. After both my parents signed, the neighbor asked if my grandmother could sign as well.

"But I thought you just needed two signatures," I asked, puzzled.

"Your father's is fine, but I must have two women's signatures to equal a man's."

With my growing awareness of conditions in Iran, I understood Neda's plight. What could she do without a husband, without a means of support? Having more than one wife, beating her, or keeping a *seegheh* was common practice. Many men did so openly. Parviz, knowing my family would disapprove, kept his mistress a secret.

The day proved therapeutic for Neda as she unburdened herself. We talked about my parents' relentless suggestions that I get married. Her experiences as an Iranian wife made me cringe at the idea of marrying an Iranian man. It was my inauguration to cynicism.

For my return, a private taxi seemed best. From the back of the car, I studied the streets and people wandering about. It truly felt like an Islamic nation, but not in any good sense. Islam shares much with Judaism and Christianity. Muslims consider themselves children of Abraham, just like the Jews. But as with any religion, you can't control the masses through moderation and compromise. Only by taking religious tenets to extremes can ruling powers sustain the fervor and discipline needed to dominate a nation. This brand of Islam spouted intolerance and hatred, not the charity and love spoken by the prophet. Buildings bore paintings of Khomeini, bleeding soldiers, and "Death to America" slogans. The radio no longer included the music of Googoosh or Mahasti, popular stars of earlier years, but was dominated by chanting male voices. The whole atmosphere was gray and morose, like the never-ending funeral of a long-lost friend.

THIRTY-FIVE

"Leila, have you seen your father?" Maman Rouhi asked one afternoon.

"No, why?"

"I haven't seen him this happy in years."

"And why is he so happy?"

"He's excited about tomorrow's dinner with the Arefis."

"Wait a minute. Are those the people who want me to marry their son?"

"*Azizam*, why do you say it like that, like it's a bad thing? Besides, nobody said he wants to marry you. Get off your high horse." Maman Rouhi limped over, grinning like a co-conspirator and gave me a hug.

"Maman Rouhi, I don't want to marry anyone. You're all wasting your time."

"Don't go rushing to judgment. Maybe you'll like this young man. After all, he was educated in America like you. I hear he's quite handsome. Besides, he can give you a lifestyle to which you're accustomed. Not everyone can do that, you know."

"I have all the lifestyle I need."

"If you say this in front of your father, you'll break his heart. Just give this a chance. Meet the young man and see if you like him. If you don't, no one will force you to marry. Remember the Ghorbanis' proposal years ago?"

"How could I forget?"

"Your father isn't looking to just marry you off. He wants your happiness more than anything. But he also wants to be sure you're provided for once we're gone. It's a father's duty."

"By the way, whatever happened to the Ghorbanis?"

"The relationship ended. Sometimes we see them at a wedding or party. Each ignores the other and walks away."

"Did Javad ever find his bride?"

"Apparently he never married."

My rejection of that marriage proposal had angered parents and son alike. Now I was facing the situation again. After years in America and being in love with Jack, the thought of an arranged marriage made me sick to my stomach. I understood Grandmother's concern for my father's fragile feelings, so I decided to play along and save my parents some grief; they'd suffered enough. No harm in a dinner.

The big evening arrived. I wore a chic, sleeveless white dress with pale pink roses and matching pink flats. My hair fell around my face, ringlets hanging loose and bouncing at the slightest turn. My nails were in a French manicure, and I wore just enough makeup to appear natural. I touched the Le de Givenchy perfume to my throat and wrists. While I had no intention of being chosen a bride, I wanted to please my father.

Baba's glistening eyes betrayed his joy, and a look of pride swept his face. I mustered a thin smile at his "You look absolutely beautiful, darling." It was as though I'd given him a precious gift. Maman bustled about the kitchen with last-minute preparations. While she trusted Fatemeh, she was a perfectionist when it came to important guests. And to her, these guests were very important.

It was eight o'clock when, at the sound of the doorbell, my sub-dued anxiety took wing. My parents and grandmother were in the formal living room talking with Aunt Firouzeh and her husband, who'd arrived earlier to participate as family elders. The buyers had arrived to appraise the bride. Would they open my mouth to inspect my teeth or perhaps have me prance about the room like an Arabian?

Fatemeh escorted the Arefis into the living room.

"Welcome to our home," Baba said, greeting Mr. Arefi with a firm handshake.

"This is my son, Farhad," he replied, nodding to the younger man walking with his mother, "and my wife, Marieh."

"And this is my daughter, Leila, and my wife, Soraya."

An elderly couple accompanying them was introduced as the grandparents. As Mrs. Arefi shook my hand, she turned to her husband and said, "*Bah, Bah,*" an expression of approval. Oh good, I was up one point.

The would-be groom and I exchanged shy glances. He was handsome, of medium height like his father, with broad shoulders and a fit body. His lean, well-muscled arms showed he was no stranger to exercise. Prominent, dark-rimmed eyeglasses complemented straight black hair, meticulously parted to one side. As he approached, I caught a hint of his cologne. Something familiar, Calvin Klein or Ralph Lauren; I couldn't place it.

"Leila, it's a pleasure to meet you," he said as he took my hand.

"Thank you, Farhad. It's nice to meet you as well."

Everyone sat politely in the living room, Farhad and I on two straight-backed chairs across from one another, while parents and relatives camped on Louis IV-inspired Italian couches. Conversation focused on the war, shortages, Iraqi bombings of civilian areas. The Arefis asked me about my schooling and how I liked being home. They proudly proclaimed Brown University as their son's alma mater and explained that Farhad now worked in his father's real estate development business. All that was missing was a wife. Everyone smiled at the last comment, though mine was probably the least genuine.

The plot thickened as we headed to the dining room. By design, Farhad and I ended up next to each other, everyone playing musical chairs till two seats remained. As it turned out, Farhad and I had much to talk about—stories of college years, classes, and other topics. As we sat through this formal affair, I caught glimpses of satisfied parents and grandparents on both sides. To them, our quiet conversation was a good sign. We'd hit it off.

Kisses on cheeks replaced handshakes as the Arefis left, a sign of growing familiarity. When Farhad came to say good-bye, the scent of his cologne sent shivers down my spine. I didn't want to admit it, but I found him attractive. To avoid conversation on the topic, I quietly slipped away to my room when the guests left.

"What'd you think of Farhad?" was Maman's inevitable question at breakfast.

"He seems nice," I replied nonchalantly.

"Yes, and handsome, isn't he?"

"I suppose," I said, blushing. Damn. I hated to admit that. Now they'd assume I was ready to marry him. But I couldn't retract the words.

My parents went about their daily routine, leaving Grandmother and me poolside. It gave us a chance to talk, about Amir's death, the changes the revolution and war had wrought, and about Farhad and a possible marriage proposal.

"Leila, you know your father's going to ask how you feel about this," she warned.

"I know, Maman Rouhi. I wish I knew how I felt." I wanted to be honest with her. It had been two years since Jack and I had broken up; the pain had still not dissipated. Initial anger had given way to grief, then resignation. I'd never see him again, but I wasn't ready for another relationship. How could I explain that? A good Iranian girl doesn't have a boyfriend and certainly would never embrace the intimacy Jack and I shared. Cultural heritage crashed headlong into my American experience of love and passion, of giving my heart completely to a man neither Muslim nor Iranian.

"What's so confusing, *azizam*?"

"Honestly, I had no intention of considering marriage. I'm happy being single. Besides, I just got home. I want to spend time with you and my parents. You all need me right now more than anyone else."

"Nonsense. Your parents are fine now that you're here. And nothing would make us happier than for you to marry a fine man from a good family."

I sensed truth in her words, saw it in my father's eyes at the *khastegari* dinner. But the part of my heart that should embrace love was still fearful. As much as I might wish to make my parents happy, could I go forward with a lie?

"Would you consider Farhad for a husband?" she asked.

"I don't know. He seems like a nice guy, and we have some things in common. I just never thought I'd marry an Iranian man."

"Why do you say that? He's as Western as you are."

"Maybe, but he's still Iranian. I'm just not sure about all this."

"And what's wrong with an Iranian man? Wasn't your grandfather a dream? And your father? Is there a better man in the whole world? I know you adore him, Leila."

"I know, Maman Rouhi. It's just that . . ." How could I rationalize this? My head swam with visions of sexual intimacy with Jack, of Neda and the beatings from her husband, not to mention his infidelity.

As if she'd read my mind, Grandmother said, "Parviz has a problem. He smokes too much hashish, and it clouds his thinking." She was referring to his temper, not the *seegheh*. Neda hadn't confessed her suspicion of her husband's mistress to anyone but me and my other cousins.

"I didn't know about the drugs."

"I know, dear. She's ashamed. Can you blame her? You must keep this to yourself. I'm telling you so you'll understand and not judge all Iranian men by him."

Why hadn't Neda told me about the drugs, I wondered? Although my grandmother allayed some concerns, memories of my days with Jack were painfully persistent, the joys lingering just beyond reach, the wounds still a little tender.

In reality, Farhad was every parent's dream son-in-law, and he was charming. Yet with all we shared in common, there was no spark, no nascent flames of passion to warm my heart. But this was Iran, where such things bore little significance, and families setting terms of engagement was expected. Would I ever adapt to this new Iran?

Over the next months, there were more gatherings to give Farhad and me a chance to get better acquainted. Each time I was around him, my mind ran less and less to the past; my heart felt less the loss of my first love. Perhaps I'd healed enough to embrace this man. Perhaps I could accept my role of Iranian daughter and push into the background my hopes for success, dreams of achievement, longings for passionate love. Besides, I wasn't sure I could bear my father's disappointment if I declined this marriage proposal.

Farhad was a good catch by all accounts. Born to a wealthy family, educated and handsome, he'd someday inherit his father's business. Any Iranian girl would jump at the chance to marry him. Day and night, my thoughts wavered. Each meeting with Farhad and his family at dinner or the country club was a reminder a decision was imminent. But I had to be certain the enduring memories of Jack could be held at bay. If I didn't marry soon, people would start to call me a pickle behind my back, and I'd end up a spinster. I tried to reassure myself over and over that being Western-minded, Farhad wouldn't raise the issue of lost virginity. In the end, I forced myself to push doubts and worries aside. While not the way I'd planned, it would please my father. Perhaps for the first time, I'd make my mother proud. Who knows, maybe I could find happiness in my new life in Iran.

Nine months after our initial meeting, the marriage proposal was accepted. At times I felt anxious, wishing I could take it back; other times, excitement climbed as the wedding day approached. After all, isn't it every girl's dream to be the bride in a fairy-tale wedding?

On our wedding day, there was so much going on I didn't have time to think, but I managed to pull Neda aside. We walked the gardens at the Arefi house where the ceremony was about to take place. Sitting on a stone bench behind a well-manicured hedge, I confided my fears and apprehensions.

"I'm really nervous, Neda."

"I was, too, on my wedding day. But he seems like a nice man."

"It's not that, Neda." Perhaps she thought I was worried about sex.

"Then what?"

"I told you about Jack, that I dated him? It was more than that. I fell in love with him. It broke my heart when he left me."

"Leila, you've got to focus on now. That's the past. Let it go, let *him* go."

"It's not that easy, Neda. God knows, I've tried. I know Jack's not a reality. I'll never see him again. But even though it's hopeless, part of me still yearns for him."

"But you just said it. He's gone. He's not real. This is real. A wealthy man with an American education," she added, "and he's hot."

I saw the smile in Neda's eyes. She was excited for me and happy despite her own troubled marriage.

"You know, Amir once told me, 'love is something that grows in your heart. It stems from two people who commit to spend their lives together and raise a family.'"

"I believe that, Leila. Besides, once you have kids, there's so much joy. It's a love one can't describe." Then she put her arms around me and said, "I miss him too, Leila. He was like my big brother too." She held me tight for a few minutes while together we fought tears.

Neda walked me back to the bride's room to help me get ready. It was a fairy-tale wedding, complete with graceful swans floating serenely on the lake on the property and white doves released to a cloudless blue sky. The Iranian daughter became an Iranian wife.

In anticipation of our marriage, Farhad had bought a house in Tehran. On our wedding night, festivities over, Farhad held my hand as we sat in the back of my parents' white Mercedes, blanketed in white flowers. His touch felt warm and comforting as the procession of honking cars wound its way to Farhad's, and now my, new home. Everyone said good night at the front door and left.

Farhad gently led me to the bedroom. He began quickly, if somewhat clumsily, to remove my wedding gown, in eager anticipation. In the darkened bedroom, my gown and veil came off. He pulled down the covers and led me to our bed. I lay there feeling as anxious as if it were my first time. Then he removed his clothing, eyes fixed on my body. My heart pounded, and I could sense his excitement as he climbed into bed. We hadn't even kissed. I felt his skin against mine and wished he would kiss me, touch my face. But our lips never touched. With fumbling uncertainty, he probed his way, and with all the gentleness of a bull, began thrusting against me. In seconds, it was over, and he rolled off me, catching his breath, never having uttered a word. I stared at the ceiling and wondered, is that all there is? After a few minutes, I got up to wash off my makeup.

When I stepped out of the bathroom, Farhad stood transfixed beside the bed. The lights were glaring, and he was in pajama bottoms, arms crossed and a scowl on his face as he stared at the sheets. At first I had no clue what was going on. Was there a scorpion in the bed?

"Why is there no blood?" he demanded angrily, pointing at the sheets.

"What do you mean?" I asked, feigning confusion.

"There's no blood; it means you're not a virgin. Is this true? Tell me, I must know now." His voice grew louder, his olive complexion turning a bright red.

"Farhad, I don't understand. What are you talking about?" I said, again pretending I didn't know what he was saying.

"I want to know NOW. You're not a virgin. Admit it!" he barked.

Not exactly what I'd hoped for on my wedding night. What do I say? How do I answer his accusations? I couldn't admit the truth, that's for sure. In the new Iran, who knows what would become of me? I had no intention of being forthright about my previous sex life.

"Farhad, you lived in America how many years? Women use tampons, which sometimes rupture the hymen. Just because there's no blood doesn't mean I've slept with another man. Please, you're being medieval."

"LIAR!" he screamed. "I don't believe you. You've deceived me and my family."

"I'm sorry you feel this way. I don't know what to say."

"You're sorry? I don't want to hear you're sorry. What am I to do now? How do I explain this to my family?"

"You plan to tell your family?" If I were outside looking in, I wouldn't know whether to laugh or cry. As though I had any assurance he was a virgin, not that it mattered for a man. It only mattered that the wife is pure. Blood on the sheets must be a rite of passage to manhood.

"I can't say anything; it would be a disgrace," he said, resigned to conceal this dreadful secret. "For your family too," he added. I supposed he was right. If word got out I wasn't a virgin, it would disgrace both families.

"Farhad, you must believe me," I said, knowing the truth served no purpose. I stood by the bathroom door, shaken, as he stormed from our room to sleep in the extra bedroom, leaving me to spend my wedding night alone.

THIRTY-SIX

I awoke from a restless sleep. Despite the bedroom turn of events, I had to pull myself together for another day with family and friends. Rising from the empty bed, I pulled on a white lace robe, a gift from my in-laws, and wandered into my new family room to find Farhad seated on the couch reading the paper, smoking a cigarette.

"I didn't know you smoked."

"I do now," he said in a monotone voice, taking a drag.

I wasn't much good at small talk in the face of his sullen pouting. You could cut the tension with a knife, but within a few hours, guests would arrive for the *pa takhti* ceremony to celebrate the "happily wedded" couple's first day. I made tea and put bread and cheese on the table. We ate in silence. My eyes wandered from a crack in the wooden table to the tea leaves swimming lazily in my glass cup. I lifted the toast and wiped droplets of condensation on the plate with a finger, took a deep breath to say something, and decided against it. When we finished, I reminded him our guests would soon arrive.

"Yes, we must maintain appearances," he said.

Did that mean he wouldn't divulge his wedding night discovery to his family? Could we move on and have a life together? Or were we keeping up appearances for now?

The party went smoothly. Everyone was in a good mood, even Farhad, at least on the surface. His demeanor changed, presumably to maintain the charade. He was talkative, laughing and socializing. And the gifts "for my trouble" held special significance known only to me.

I pulled Neda aside and related the prior night's events. I'd not spoken with her about the physical side of my relationship with Jack, uncertain she'd approve. She never asked and I didn't offer. "Neda, I mean, come on, is this Neanderthal or what?"

"Leila, it's the way Iranian men think, what they expect of a bride."

"But Farhad lived in America. I'd hoped he'd have a more reasonable view of women."

"But he grew up here, in this culture. Did you really think four years in America would wipe away all the years before? My friend Goli told me when she got married she hid a razor under her pillow. When her husband went to the bathroom after sex, she cut herself down there just to make sure the sheets were bloodied."

"You're kidding!"

"No, I'm not. Frankly, you ought to be grateful he didn't drag you into the street and denounce you last night—he wouldn't be the first."

"It's not exactly what I'd hoped for on my wedding night."

Neda put an arm around my shoulder. "I know, Leila. But don't worry; he'll get over it."

In a way, I wished the guests wouldn't leave me to face Farhad alone. But all good things come to an end. Once everyone left, Farhad went to the patio with his cigarettes and left me to clean up the mess.

That night, he slept in our bed but may as well have been on another planet. He stayed as far from me as he could; another inch and he would have fallen off the bed. No words were spoken. His mood was just as dark and sullen as the night before. I could only imagine what our honeymoon would be like if this silence and tension continued. I had half a mind to suggest we don't go, but that would just alarm our families. Maybe time away would soften him, particularly since the weather held the promise of sunshine and warmth.

Our honeymoon was a gift from my grandmother, a luxury trip to the Caspian in a beautiful villa on the beach. The next morning, Farhad and I exchanged obligatory "good mornings" and a few brief but necessary words. Mahmood drove us to the airport for the short flight to the Caspian. When we arrived, a driver was waiting, his placard stating "Mr. Arefi," with no mention of "Mrs." A short drive brought us to the villa, where two giant stone lions menacingly guarded the black wrought-iron gates. Inside the grounds, a massive white building with Grecian columns was nestled among palm trees and lush tropical foliage. An arched marble doorway framed a mahogany door with a stained-glass circular window near the top and a ponderous brass knocker. The house stood majestically down the hill from the main road, isolated against a backdrop of blue-gray water capped by foaming crests that pounded the shoreline in rhythmic frequency. The scent of hibiscus and tuberoses filled the evening air as the sun set, offering a spectacular panorama of plum and orange as it sank into the sea, nature's spectacular evening performance.

Although September, it was hot and humid by the sea. The villa's caretaker and his family lived in a separate building on the property and greeted us cheerfully, offering their services at any hour. The grounds were manicured like a tropical paradise. No doubt a wealthy friend of my grandparents owned the property. Maman Rouhi had carefully arranged everything: a driver to take us sightseeing, a cook and housekeeper to care for domestic needs, floral arrangements gracing two hall tables, and much more. I looked at Farhad and saw, for a brief moment, a smile as he watched the beautiful blue waters crashing against the white sand.

"It's really beautiful, isn't it?" I asked, hoping to draw him from silence.

"Yes, it is. The house is gorgeous, and the location's perfect."

For the first time since our wedding night, I sensed him softening. If I took things slowly, perhaps it wouldn't disrupt his positive mood. I gently suggested dinner outside, which he accepted. The patio was inlaid stone with beautifully maintained tropical plants and miniature palm trees in huge clay pots surrounding the perimeter. The rattan furniture looked inviting, its large pillows covered in a red floral pattern. White candles burned on the glass table, and bouquets of local fresh flowers stood in ornate vases scattered about. Farhad sat in the single chair facing the sea, then said, "You know, it's too hot out here. Let's eat inside."

At least he was responsive.

As evening fell, the caretaker lit citronella candles, strategically placed throughout the maze of hedges and shrubs that defined the walkways in the gardens. The grounds glowed with an eldritch light; the air smelled of sea salt, and a gentle breeze caressed my face. It was a romantic setting, yet my heart felt none of the euphoria I should have on my honeymoon. On the contrary, I felt alone. Farhad remained aloof, the silence during dinner broken only by the screech of polished silver utensils against the Wedgwood china.

On my honeymoon, I was already growing cynical. Farhad was not the only one disappointed. He'd become a man I didn't know. Perhaps I was disappointed in myself, upset I'd succumbed to cultural pressures.

Throughout the week, the chauffeur drove us around the lush Alborz Mountains. He took us up and down winding roads, conducting a tour of the area, secluded national parks, and public beaches. We asked if he'd take us to the Ramsar beach for a swim.

"Ah, yes, it's the most popular beach in the area," he informed us.

"Wonderful. Can we go for a swim this afternoon?" I asked.

"Well, no, you cannot, but Mr. Arefi can. You, *khanoom*, can go tomorrow morning."

"We can't go together?"

"Beach access is allocated to men and women at different hours. Guards keep order. Women in the morning, men in the afternoon."

"So families and married couples have to separate to swim?"

"Yes, ma'am."

So much for a romantic dip with my husband.

As the days went by, Farhad grew more relaxed, even moving closer to me in bed at night. On our final night, he made love to me. His efforts, while fumbling and brief, were still a welcome change from his prior reticence. Perhaps the nightmare of our wedding night was behind us. I stared at the ceiling in the dark, wondering if I'd ever feel passion again the way I'd once known it.

We returned home to the sounds of heavy artillery. The intensity of the Iraq war had increased. Saddam Hussein, who'd not anticipated Iran's military strength and tenacity, was taken somewhat by surprise. To gain the upper hand, he'd ordered his troops to use poisonous gas on Iranian soldiers fighting in the Khuzestan region. Thousands were killed, leaving Iran to mourn the heavy death toll of its sons. International organizations denounced this use of chemical weapons but did nothing to stop it. In the city, people began to board up windows and hoard water and food in preparation for worse. At night, we often huddled in darkness with drawn curtains, anticipating the bomb that might find our house. We'd hear the sirens in the distance, sounds of shattering glass, and screaming. Daytime was generally quiet and safe, but at night, no one dared go out.

In spite of the war and the constant reminders of destruction around us, day-to-day life went on. During telephone calls and visits, Neda confided her growing despair in a hopeless marriage. "Leave," I'd urge, but even I knew she was trapped.

I couldn't bring myself to share with her the emptiness that had taken root in me. Farhad was now consumed by work. He took no notice of a new dress or hairstyle. In general, he was pleasant, but there was no closeness between us, no passion or physical desire. On the rare occasions we did make love, my mind would wander to Jack. The memories helped me tolerate the physical aspect of marriage. But even fantasies left me guilty and longing for more.

Farhad left early each morning and didn't come home until after eight, at which time he expected dinner to be ready. I enjoyed cooking, so I didn't mind these demands. One evening, he unexpectedly arrived home early at six o'clock.

"When will dinner be ready? I'm starved."

"It'll be awhile. I have to cook the rice and fry the eggplant for stew."

"Why isn't it ready now? What've you been doing all day?"

"Farhad, that's not fair. You're never home before eight. How was I supposed to know you'd be home early today and immediately want dinner?" I replied calmly.

"Don't talk back to me!" he shouted. Though his tone didn't frighten me, I was not accustomed to being spoken to like that. I wasn't about to let him intimidate me.

"Why don't you make dinner yourself from now on?" I said defiantly.

"How dare you? You can't speak to your husband this way."

"And you can't speak to me this way. I'm not some dumb, backwards country girl. I want you to treat me with the same respect you expect from me."

The argument ended as quickly as it began. I stormed to the bedroom and slammed the door shut. I'd set him straight. But emotions took over, and I started crying. It wasn't his disrespect or anger that upset me, rather the hollow emptiness inside. Again I flashed back to my days with Jack, how we'd talk for hours, sharing anger and joy, sadness and fear. We'd analyze how something made us feel and spend hours probing emotions and reactions. In the end, he'd hold me in his arms, melt me in warmth. With my face pressed to the pillow, my sobbing drowned out the opening bedroom door. It always creaked, yet I heard nothing as Farhad entered the room. I felt a gentle hand on my shoulder and opened my eyes to find him sitting on the side of the bed.

"I'm sorry, Leila."

I stopped crying and rolled over. He took my hand, brought it to his lips, and kissed it. "I'm sorry; you're right. How could you know I'd be home early tonight?"

"But that's not the point, Farhad."

"What is the point then?"

"It's the way you spoke to me. That's not what I want in our marriage. I won't take it."

"I have every right to speak to my wife that way, even beat her if she's defiant. The Koran says so."

"Since when do you quote the Koran? When was the last time you went to a mosque or said your *namaz* prayers?"

"You don't live in America anymore. This is Iran. Get used to it."

"So I should expect you to treat me with disrespect, because we live in Iran?"

"That's not what I said."

"That *is* what you said. All I'm asking is for your respect."

"Okay, I'm sorry. I'm sorry. I'll respect you. Now, can you please finish dinner? I'm starving."

"In a minute," I said, doubting his sincerity but feeling mildly victorious.

This became the complexion of life with Farhad. His expectations grew more traditional as my adaptation to the new Iran seemed more challenging.

One day after dinner, he was in a particularly good mood. That's when I broached the subject of finding a job. "It'd give me something to do. I'm so bored sometimes."

"You've got plenty to do here. If you need more, I'll fire the maid and you can clean the house yourself."

"I want a professional job. I didn't go to college to clean house."

"It's difficult for a woman to find a job in Iran. Things would be different if we lived in America. But here . . . perhaps you should focus on being a wife and a mother."

This was the first time he'd mentioned motherhood. We hadn't discussed a family, but I suppose it was taken for granted. I'd always been apprehensive about having children, yet I felt bound by tradition; a woman gets married and has children. That's the model I knew.

"In fact, maybe you should stop taking birth control so we can have a baby."

I said nothing, just stared at him for several moments. How did he even know I was on the Pill? I had taken painstaking measures to hide it. I didn't want to get pregnant after the difficulties of our first months of marriage but wasn't sure he'd let me take birth control. What he didn't know wouldn't hurt him. But all along, he'd known and said nothing. I was chagrined I hadn't trusted him to be part of this decision. And now there was no rebuke, just a suggestion. Farhad sometimes surprised me with unexpected gentleness and understanding.

Although his voice held no command, I took his "maybe" as the way things would be. I dreamt of children that night, a son and daughter running about the house, playing in the yard. A daughter playing piano, a son playing tennis. I imagined taking them to football practice, swim lessons, and the piano tutor. I envisioned my life with children, cooking dinner as I shared idle gossip with relatives, friends, and neighbors. I tossed and turned, wondering if I'd be happy in such a life. The next day, I stopped taking the Pill.

THIRTY-SEVEN

Tehran Prison, 1988

I awoke drenched in sweat and wracked with pain, wincing with assaults of cramps. I held my stomach with each onslaught, sighing in relief as it passed. I pulled my knees to my chest to lessen the pain. My sweating had soaked the tattered old mattress, yet the cramping wouldn't stop, gripping me like death and not letting go. In the solitude of my cell, no one heard my moans. No point in calling out; by now they were immune to cries for help, offering only insults in return. Only the one guard had been kind in interactions, and even he was recently brooding and surly.

A warm flow trickled down my thighs as the pain grew sharper. I wanted to scream but held back. Struggling to stand, I dragged myself to the latrine. This was a particularly brutal period. Another sharp cramp, and I doubled over. A floodgate burst and blood spurted out, streaming from my body. This went on for what seemed an eternity before the cramps lessened in intensity. Barely able to stand, I tried to drag myself to the bed but never made it.

Lying on the floor, I struggled toward consciousness as a voice asked, "Are you okay?" But it couldn't be real; no one cared if I was okay. It was just another dream, the deceitful kind that promised hope. I dismissed it as yet another fantasy. A face appeared, then disappeared, like fog on the Caspian. It was the kind soldier. I knew I was dreaming.

The odor of ammonia overpowered other stimuli assaulting my senses. I struggled to clear my vision but saw only blurred images moving in slow motion against the blank white walls. Through the haze of semi-consciousness, I heard a voice, "There was so much blood, I thought she was dying."

"Not dying, but hemorrhaging. Give her water, plenty of water."

The earlier image reappeared. The kind soldier is beside me, lifts my head with one arm, and holds a glass to my lips. Cool water streams down the sides of my face. I feel the cold sensation down my throat as it slowly courses through my body. Little by little, the images grow clearer, more real. This was no dream. The soldier was there, on a chair beside me as I lay on the hard gurney. I heard the voice of the doctor I'd seen weeks ago. I'd never forget that nasal tone. "She's had a miscarriage and has lost a lot of blood. The bleeding is stopped for now, and she'll be alright. But she needs water, lots of water."

I was awake now, aware of the words and their significance. As I lay in the sterile surroundings, tears filled my eyes. After the years Farhad and I had spent trying to conceive a child, after enduring his insults that I was barren, to have conceived by rape in this hell-hole was unthinkable. Then I lost this infant life as a result of the beating just endured. Perhaps it was God's mercy, the beginning of the end, and I could leave this place of torment, if only through the kindness of death. Return me to my cell. Let me drift back to sleep.

THIRTY-EIGHT

Tehran, 1987

While I wasn't one to obsess, Farhad seemed to be smoking constantly. I detested the lingering stale smell on him and in the house. If I said it bothered me, I got an "Oh, well" and a shrug of the shoulders through the haze of smoke. Every other Friday, his buddies came over for poker night, another outlawed activity. They played, smoked, and drank incessantly. I watched as they downed glass after glass of vodka, straight up. By the end of the night, they were wasted, barely able to stand up. They'd randomly break into song, off-tune of course. One would fumble drunkenly through an off-color joke, and they'd laugh like it was the funniest thing ever heard. At evening's end, they'd mutter slurred good-byes and stagger out. And that's when Farhad hoped to conceive a child. Stale tobacco aroma mingling with the cloying sweetness of alcohol was no aphrodisiac, but I dared not say a word. Often enough, he fell asleep before completing the act.

One Friday, just past midnight, the doorbell rang. I set down my book and cast an anxious glance at Farhad and his poker friends, wondering who it could be.

"I'll get it," he said, motioning me to relax.

"Who could it be at this hour?" I asked, puzzled.

"It's the mailman," he said, and they all burst out laughing. Things always seem more humorous when you're smashed.

Farhad opened the door and escorted two burly men carrying a carton to the dining room table. I followed Farhad into the bedroom.

"Who are they? What's in the box?"

"Liquor."

"Your secret suppliers?"

"That'd be them," he chuckled. "Have you seen my alcohol meter?"

"Alcohol meter?"

"Yes, to measure the alcohol content for purity. There's so much bootlegged booze out there."

I never knew how proficient my husband was at buying bootlegged alcohol. Returning to the dining room, Farhad dipped the alcohol meter in to sample each bottle. He inspected the results before saying "*Khoobeh*, it's good." At the conclusion of this ritual, the men left with their money. He bought the whole lot.

Farhad and his buddies celebrated their new purchase by sampling each bottle, raising glasses to toast "*Be salamati*—to your health," each cheer louder than the last. Growing up, I never knew anyone who drank. Now people drank to excess behind closed doors, risking arrest. Alcohol had become a national obsession.

"Can I take a sip?" I asked out of curiosity.

"Better not. After all, you're trying to have a child."

I was disappointed, not over the denial, but because my husband made the decision for me. I recalled Neda's words, "Welcome to the new Iran," but this was a battle not worth fighting. Later when everyone was gone, I reopened conversation with Farhad.

"So does this stuff come from Russia?"

"Some, yes. But much is made right here."

"You're kidding."

"No, seriously. Sometimes they pour domestic stuff into Russian or American bottles and sell counterfeit booze. It's a major enterprise. In fact, the empty bottles downstairs are worth a lot of money. They're refilled and sold as originals."

"I never thought of that. It must be quite an operation."

"It's a huge black market. But if they're caught, they're as good as dead. You have to be careful whom you buy from; some dealers are really undercover government agents. But I know these guys. If they get busted, they won't reveal their customers."

"Is it dangerous for us to have the empty bottles in our house?" I asked, realizing the risk Farhad was taking.

"I'll turn them in for money one of these days."

I went to bed, considering Prohibition and the rise of organized crime in America. Now it led to the same in my country. Bootlegged alcohol was imported or manufactured in Iran. The irony is that Islam doesn't forbid alcohol. The Koran states one must not appear before Allah in prayer under its influence. As is so often the case, fundamentalism took this to an extreme.

Another change was slowly taking root in Iran. While many feared the Pasdaran, women began their rebellion with a hint of makeup or by showing a bit of hair. My escaping curls no longer posed the threat they once had. On occasion, men wore red shirts or Western clothes, both forbidden. The unlucky were arrested, often for no other reason than to teach a lesson, but some got away with it. The spirit of the people was rising against religious oppression, having been imposed now for almost ten years.

THIRTY-NINE

It was a cool evening, despite the rising heat of summer. Farhad and I enjoyed a quiet dinner. He ate in silence, a glazed look on his face. That morning he'd received word his childhood friend had been killed. Kourosh was one of the most cheerful, easygoing people I'd ever met, always finding humor even in the most serious situations. He and Farhad had been best friends, separated only when Farhad left for college. Kourosh instead took a job at his father's battery factory in Tehran. His father had built the company from scratch into a profitable business. One day, Kourosh would run the family enterprise.

Because he didn't have a college education, Kourosh was first draft and was pulled, as Amir had been, into the Iran-Iraq war to fight a battle even he found senseless. Most people of wealth chose not to send their sons to war, leaving the task to those of lesser means. Kourosh's mother was angry that her husband didn't intervene and buy their son's way out. Apparently, patriotic feelings clouded his judgment, and he sent his only son to his death, a decision he deeply regretted when news his son's battalion had been decimated was delivered by phone.

After dinner, Farhad sat slouched on the couch, smoking and staring blankly at the newspaper for an hour. While I wasn't in love with him, I was sympathetic and wished I could ease his pain.

"Can I get you something?" I asked for the second or third time.

"No, I'm fine," he grumbled, staring at the paper glassy-eyed.

"Maybe you should go play poker with your friends. It might help take your mind off . . ." I stopped, thinking it best not to bring up Kourosh's death. Apparently, Farhad thought this a good idea, and after making arrangements by phone, said good night and left.

"Don't wait up; I'll be late," he added, the door slamming shut behind him.

Shortly after, I headed to bed and fell asleep. The phone woke me from a sleep so deep it took me several seconds to manage a weak *"Allo."*

"Mrs. Arefi?" asked the voice on the other end.

"Yes?"

"Mrs. Arefi, I'm sorry to call at such a late hour. This is Sergeant Shahroudi at the *kalantari.*"

My heart began pounding at the mention of the police, and I sat up in bed, awake and focused. "Mrs. Arefi, I'm calling because your husband was arrested. We're holding him at the *kalantari* until morning. We didn't want you to be worried."

"Why was he arrested, sir?" I asked, concern etching my face.

"He was pulled over for driving erratically on Vozara Street. We also found a bottle of alcohol in his car. When the officers confronted him, he became abusive and had to be restrained."

"Oh, my God, is he okay?" I asked, not knowing what else to say.

"He'll be fine by morning, though I suspect he'll have a headache. Please have someone here to pick him up."

I had the daunting task of calling Farhad's parents at this ungodly hour and delivering the embarrassing news. Never having been in a situation like this, I was clueless. Plus, as a woman, I wasn't able to do much for Farhad; he needed a man.

"I'll pick him up from the *kalantari.*" said a very upset Mr. Arefi. Given his prominence in the community, I'm sure he wanted this resolved before word got out.

When morning came, I was wired despite being up the rest of the night. I hadn't heard any news. At 10:30 A.M., a disheveled Farhad walked through the door. Without saying a word or looking at me, he went to our bedroom, closing the door behind him. I sat anxiously on the couch with the book I'd pointlessly been trying to read, listening for any clue to his activities. After thirty minutes, I quietly opened the bedroom door to find him snoring on top of the covers, still fully dressed. Quietly, I took a blanket from the linen closet, covered him, and closed the door. There'd be time to learn the details later.

I lay on the couch, but sleep wouldn't come. I couldn't focus on reading and was too tired to work in the kitchen. When I finally heard stirrings in the bedroom, I sat up and waited for Farhad to emerge. He looked like someone had just dragged him from a trash bin, his hair spiked in spots, eyes puffy and clothes disheveled. One side of his shirt was out of his pants, and the pocket on his green-and-white checkered dress shirt was flopped halfway down where it was torn. I'd been waiting to get a detailed accounting. But that's not what he had planned.

"Hi," I said in a gentle, but timid voice.

"Get me some tea with sugar," he said. It sounded like an order, something I didn't respond to well. But given the circumstances, I chose to disregard it. As I set the kettle on the stove to boil water, I gingerly broached the subject.

"What happened last night?"

"None of your business," he barked.

After pausing a moment, I used the most caring, understanding voice I could muster. "Farhad, I know this hasn't been a pleasant experience, but I'm your wife. I've been worried."

"Worried? The whole damn thing is all your fault." He glared at me with anger.

"How is this my fault?"

"You told me to go out with my friends. I was content to stay home, but no, you wanted me out. So out I went and got arrested. Now I have to live with the embarrassment of it all. I hope you're satisfied with the disgrace you've brought on our families."

"I know you're upset, but how can you blame me for what you did?" I replied, no longer fearful. "I suggested you play poker with your friends to take your mind off Kourosh. I didn't suggest you get drunk and drive around with a bottle of alcohol in the car. That was plain foolish, and you should have known better."

"Shut up, woman! How dare you speak to me this way? Get out of my sight before I do something you'll regret." Anger seethed in him like hot lava.

I stared in disbelief, but within seconds I went to the hallway, grabbed my purse, donned my *roopoosh* and head scarf, and stormed out of the house. I walked briskly down the street, no destination in mind. Memories of my bus ride to Neda's still vivid, I hailed a taxi and went straight to the Arefi house. My father-in-law, no doubt, would fill in the blanks. My in-laws graciously received me and recounted the story over tea.

After an evening of poker and heavy drinking, Farhad, distraught and drunk beyond reason, grabbed a half-empty bottle of whiskey and left his friends. They made futile attempts to detain him, but he would hear none of it. He sideswiped a tree as he drove down the wrong side of the street but continued his drunken trip until the police, lights flashing and siren blaring, pulled him over. Mouthing off, Farhad, who reeked of whiskey, challenged the cops for stopping him. Within seconds, they saw the bottle he had left sitting in plain sight. He hadn't even tried to conceal it. They tried to get him out of the car, but he resisted, taking a swing at one and cursing loudly. While his attempted blow missed its mark, they pinned him to the ground and beat him, tearing his shirt and leaving him with a bloody nose and bruised ego. Then, a defeated but still defiant drunk was thrown in the back of the police vehicle and taken to the *kalantari*.

FORTY

The color of the leaves changed to gold, interspersed with shades of red. Cooler fall temperatures were a welcome change. My grandmother's health declined, so I tried to see her as often as I could. I'd find her in her room, prayer beads in hand, counting time between her fingers.

Baba suffered no ill health, but I sensed a change. He was less focused on his business and more on teaching and his students. He spoke often of his art classes at Tehran University, describing his students and their families, their tribulations and trials. He became more disenchanted with the war and the government. To him, the clerics were conniving, money-hungry murderers in disguise. He was convinced his students shared these sentiments.

Following his arrest, Farhad grew more distant and cold. He picked on little things, like a stain in his shirt not coming clean or his food not being as hot or well-seasoned as he liked. He lashed out over minor offenses or for no reason at all. Initially, I was tolerant in the face of his cruelty. After losing my own brother in war, I understood the impact of his friend's death. But over time, his behavior grew insufferable. I began to resent him and talked back, sometimes engaging in heated arguments that inevitably ended with Farhad the winner, at least in his mind. Emotionally, I withdrew more each day and made plans to be elsewhere when he was around. If I could avoid his sour moods, at least I had peace.

One day, the phone rang while I was engrossed in reading. Golnaz breathlessly told me that Neda had been taken to the hospital. "They think she overdosed." Leaving a hurried note for Farhad, I dashed out.

The hospital lobby, adorned with a large picture of the Ayatollah on the building front, was virtually empty, not a soul in sight. Strangely, there was no reception area. A man, looking like a visitor, emerged from an open entryway. I asked for the emergency room and walked briskly through the metal swinging doors. I entered a brightly lit waiting room, abuzz with activity, doctors and nurses hurrying about in white uniforms. Rows of beige molded plastic chairs lined the walls, each pair attached. A large coffee table sat empty, devoid of reading material. The floor was marbled gray linoleum, scuffed and battered by constant traffic. The walls had no pictures, lending to the dreary antiseptic atmosphere. I found my aunt and her family at the far end of a row of chairs.

I embraced Aunt Firouzeh and Golnaz and waved at my uncle. Having spent years in America, I still had trouble remembering that men and women can't embrace in public.

"How is she?" I asked, catching my breath.

"The doctor's still with her. We don't know," replied Aunt Firouzeh.

"Is Parviz here?"

"He's on his way. He was in Qum on business."

"What about the girls? Where are they?"

"The next-door neighbor has them. Poor Taraneh. She woke up this morning and noticed her mother lying in bed. She called her name over and over and tried to shake her, but Neda didn't respond. So she called me. We rushed over right after we called an ambulance. The poor child was in a panic."

When my aunt and uncle arrived, Neda lay peacefully like Sleeping Beauty next to an empty bottle of sleeping pills on its side. She was breathing, but her pulse was weak and fluttering.

A bald, short Dr. Mirzahi, wearing a bright white lab coat, came out of Neda's hospital room. He confirmed the overdose and informed us that they'd pumped her stomach. Parviz arrived just as we were allowed into Neda's room. I looked at him with disdain as he sat on one side of the bed and held her hand. She lay in the narrow bed, her face mirroring the washed-out surroundings. Nurses had tucked her in, a top sheet perfectly overlapping the woven white blanket beneath. With her arms at her sides, she stared aimlessly into space. Parviz looked at us in reassurance that she'd be fine, for all I knew in blithe ignorance of what brought her here. My aunt walked to the other side of the bed, bent down, and gently kissed her daughter's forehead. I saw the tears welling in Neda's eyes as she blankly stared at the wall, not replying to questions. A cheerful Dr. Mirzahi came bouncing into the room. "Neda *khanoom* will be just fine. She can go home tomorrow. Lots of rest, perhaps a nice vacation will do her good."

Months later, Neda told me of the events that followed her release. After leaving the hospital, fearing his temper would further flare, desperate and forlorn, she begged Parviz for his forgiveness. Claiming she now clearly saw how she had failed, she promised to be a devoted spouse from that day on. She convinced everyone that the overdose incident had led to a new Neda. Parviz accepted her apology but showed little sympathy; she'd caused him embarrassment.

Had she resigned herself to her doom? She couldn't care for herself and her children, as no one would give her a job without her husband's consent. Her parents would never condone her leaving the marriage, and, in this total absence of support, she felt powerless. So she played the role of dutiful wife, her heart torn. Living the masquerade, she tried desperately to put aside her own desires, to follow her parents' direction, and to be a good mother and wife. While she cooked the meals and cared for their children, Neda clung to fantasies of a different world. Wearing the guise of submission, powerless to do otherwise, her dreams of a life away from Parviz seemed as shattered as her heart. He wouldn't divorce her, and her parents wouldn't stand up for her, leaving Neda to simply endure. Her situation was all too familiar—the abusive home, children forced to take sides, confusion and pain, creating a vicious cycle often repeated down generations. Abusive behavior like this was tolerated, even accepted, as cultural reality. With the rise of religious absolutism, women's rights were destroyed. Now, it was my own cousin and her children who were the victims, and I felt helpless. Neda wore her agony etched in lines on her face, her very posture like a crippled bird. While she continued to dream, hope of a better life sank like a ponderous weight in the sea.

FORTY-ONE

My life with Farhad, while not physically abusive, was far from happy. He was drinking and smoking from the moment he woke till his head hit the pillow. When he wasn't filling the house with stale tobacco and booze, he was away at work. We hardly talked. His demeanor tottered toward depression. On the outside, he defended the war and its mission, but the loss of his friend had infected his mind. His father, now on the city council, was part of the new government, and though Farhad tried to be supportive, he was obviously conflicted. He rarely went with me to visit my parents, making excuses to stay behind. Ignoring confrontation seemed his style as he became more withdrawn.

By now, I'd made a habit of visiting my grandmother daily, listening to her tell stories as she did when we were children on the rooftop. It was comforting for me and a diversion for her. My mother's mornings were spent gossiping on the phone or poolside with friends, her afternoons at rest or often in tears as she wept for her lost son. By evening, she'd recover and often go to the country club. The club pool, nightly bathed in silver moonlight, sat idle as men and women no longer could share a cool dip together. It remained a gathering place for those who could still afford the exorbitant fees. Conversations were guarded, spoken in low tones, not knowing if the wait staff or groundskeeper was a government spy listening for anti-régime comments. After class, my father sometimes escorted customers and their wives to the club, joining Maman and other friends. The club offered relief from the drabness of everyday life since there was no real entertainment in Iran. Radio stations broadcast religious chants or news (propaganda, as Baba would say) always delivered by men, presumably the very sound of a woman's voice being tantamount to sexual temptation. By now, most cinemas were shut, and those that remained open showed only religious films. There was little to do but gather and socialize. Fortunately, cigarettes weren't outlawed, and it seemed everyone had taken up the habit.

Farhad had to work late again, so I rang my parents and suggested dinner at the club. Mahmood pulled the Range Rover up to the arched white stucco entrance. The darkened brass letters "Caspian Club" that once sparkled with the glint of sun were barely visible. Like so much in Tehran, they were in desperate need of repair. The black wrought-iron gates swung open as the guard recognized Mahmood.

"Please pick us up at eleven, Mahmood."

"Yes, Mr. Moradi. Enjoy your dinner."

We walked the cobblestone path along the pool deck, spotlights casting dancing shadows on the ancient cypress trees that lined the path. Tables filled with guests dotted the pool perimeter. The Cape Cod wicker furniture shone with a pearl finish. Seat cushions in tropical fabrics of sand and blue added to the serenity of the evening. Guests at these tables were having dinner. Gray metal bistro sets with woven design and scrolled accents were interspersed among the dining tables for those simply there for tea or dessert. Occasional flickering flames could be seen as guests lit their Marlboros. The waiters, once uniformed in black tuxedos and white gloves, now wore long-sleeved white dress shirts buttoned to the collar and black pants, no tie or jacket as that was Western. Male guests were dressed similarly, while women wore the requisite head scarf and *roopoosh*, fanning themselves and wishing secretly for a reprieve from the compulsory uniform in the summer heat.

The evening breeze caressed the gleaming pool waters before brushing our faces. I enjoyed being alone with my parents this night. I couldn't remember when I last had dinner with them alone. My father, generally full of stories, was unusually quiet. We talked about Neda and her sad ordeal.

"I've done what I can to convince Parviz to find a better outlet for his anger than beating his wife," Baba said, "but who knows if any of it penetrated his thick skull. For all his wealth and business savvy, I swear sometimes the man's as dumb as an ox."

It was unusual to hear Baba criticize anyone, much less a family member. I giggled in perfect agreement, while Maman reminded him of better manners. I'm not sure when the discussion turned to politics. In his heart, Baba remained haunted by Amir's death, his feelings accentuated by the political leaders' recent changes to the laws.

"More and more, the fundamentalists take control. They're ruining this country, killing our people. Those less conservative are puppets, leading in name only. Like blind men, they follow these arrogant ayatollahs for fear of being murdered. Isn't it enough they murdered my son? How many sons, husbands, and fathers must they kill before they stop? When will the rest of us, who stand by like sheep, say 'That's enough!'?" His face tightened with anger as pent-up frustrations poured forth in a torrent.

"Ali, keep your voice down," warned Maman.

"I don't care anymore. It's time for change. Unless the moderates gain more power, this country is doomed. And I'm doing my part."

"What's your part?" Maman demanded, alarmed.

"I'm taking one step at a time. In my classes, I speak to the kids, one day at a time, one student at a time, and we discuss how the new régime's policies are destroying us."

"Baba," I said, "you know that's dangerous. The Pasdaran are all over the university. Their spies are everywhere, in every classroom. You know that. Remember, even Mojtabah was betrayed by someone he thought was an ally."

"I trust my students, and they respect me. They're young and idealistic with hope for the future. They want a life, not these lies of heaven and waiting virgins in return for martyrdom. Every one of my students has lost a relative or close friend, either in the revolution or the war with Iraq. They're all sympathetic."

"Ali, you've always stayed out of politics. What's gotten into you? What happened to keeping your head down and going about your business? Now's not the time."

"I know what I'm doing, Soraya. I'm careful, and you needn't worry. One thing's for certain. I can't just sit back and let this go on. I must do my part."

I sat back in the chair and stared at the wall in the distance. A tangle of withered vines had replaced the once succulent ivy. Like the people's spirit, it was merely dormant, not dead. In the shriveled vines clinging to the stone wall, I saw a simple life's lesson. Sometimes you must lie dormant to prepare for rebirth. While I admired my father's conviction, I knew how pervasive the influence of the religious right had become, how intently they listened for the slightest voice raised in protest. My mother's perspective was far more pragmatic, her fears justified.

"Leila, how's Farhad?" Maman asked, changing the subject. "Can we expect grandchildren anytime soon?"

"He's okay. And no. No grandchildren."

"Why not?" Baba chimed in, for the moment forgetting his political woes.

"I don't know. There's nothing there."

"Isn't Farhad good to you?" Baba asked with concern.

"He doesn't beat me like Parviz, if that's what you mean. But he's never around. He always works late. He smokes constantly and drinks way too much. I'm always alone. He does whatever he wants, while I'm expected to be obedient and attend to wifely duties. I'm so bored. It all seems so pointless."

"Maybe you should get a job."

"Oh, I tried that. He said no. He doesn't want his wife to work. I mean, I went to college and got an education so I can be a dowdy housewife? All I can tell you is I'm miserable. I'd be far better off single."

"You're starting to sound like your cousin. It can be lonely, yes. But Farhad's working hard so you can enjoy a good life together. He's building for your future. And you must work to keep your marriage together. It's like a garden, requiring constant attention, watering, and pruning. Farhad's a good man, from a good family. You just need to work at this. Take some yoga or art classes, for God's sake. And remember, children can fill your time and your heart."

"Baba, I don't love him. I never loved him. Why would I want to have his children?" I asked as a lump grew in my throat.

"What is love? Love is not a brick that hits you. Love grows in your heart. And that takes time. Stop talking like your crazy cousin." With that, I knew the matter was buried. Tears filled my eyes as I remembered similar words concerning love from my brother, the brother I'd never see again. Despite his wholly Iranian perspective on love and marriage, which I could never embrace, I missed him so.

Mahmood planned to drop off my parents before taking me home. It was 11:30 P.M. I remembered the time I was in the car with Aunt Soheila and Tara, returning home from a dinner party. The Pasdaran had set up a roadblock, as was customary during that time, and pulled us over at gunpoint, demanding to know where we'd been and why we were out so late. Aunt Soheila skillfully talked our way out of the situation, sparing us a lot of trouble. Tonight, we managed to avoid the gun-toting soldiers. As Mahmood pulled into my parents' cul-de-sac, we surprised two men, dressed in dark clothing, running from the house. Mahmood stopped the car abruptly and gave chase. By the time he reached the corner, the men had disappeared, and Mahmood returned out of breath.

Meanwhile, as my father examined the house exterior, I ran in to check on Grandmother and found her fast asleep in her room. We assumed the fugitives were burglars. But why were they lurking outside in the shadows? Why not climb the brick wall into the yard to enter the house? Inside, Maman came upon the answer. There was a single message on the answering machine. We gathered as she hit the replay button. An anxious voice said, "Mr. Moradi, you must flee! They're coming to arrest you. Please, you must believe me. I'm your student but can't say my name. You're a good man, a great teacher. They're coming for you, maybe as soon as tomorrow. I heard others talking about it. You must leave at once. May Allah bless you, Mr. Moradi."

Grandmother slept peacefully upstairs while we replayed the message twice more, making sure we caught every word, confusion and concern etched all our faces. For a few minutes, no one spoke as we stood like stone in the face of the situation. The lurking intruders, a warning from his student, and suddenly my father knew Maman's words at the club had been prophetic. Mahmood broke the silence.

"Mr. Moradi, this sounds real. You must leave right away. I'll drive you anywhere you want. But we'd better leave now."

"I'm afraid you're right, Mahmood. We can't stay here."

"You can hide somewhere for a while, with a relative or friend in Esfahan maybe, until this blows over," I added, offering a solution.

"No, Leila. Once you're on the list, you're on the list till they take you. We must leave the country tonight. It's the only way," replied Baba.

"How can we leave the country, Ali?" Maman asked, her voice shaking.

"I don't know yet. But go pack. We've very little time. I'll figure out a way to get us out tonight."

"Can't you go into hiding somewhere? Do you have to leave the country?" I could feel emptiness blossom inside as I imagined my parents gone.

"We have no choice, darling. If they're coming for me, it means prison and certain death. These men tolerate no dissent, no voice but their own. They've murdered many for far less than the words I've spoken."

"Mr. Moradi, I'll drive you to Turkey where you'll be safe."

"Mahmood, I can't let you take such risks. You have your own family to consider. I'm going to the library to make some calls. Soraya, go pack. Leila, help your mother. And Mahmood, wait here. We may need a ride to the airport." My father was in command, a strategy already in mind.

"I'll take Maman Rouhi home with me, but you can't just leave without saying good-bye to her," I said.

"First, help me pack some things," said Maman.

Baba slipped into the library to put his plan into action. As I helped Maman pack, a sudden rush of emotion overcame me. I walked over and held her, tears rolling down my face and onto her shoulder. We clung to each other as though it were our last embrace. It was the kind of tenderness I hadn't felt with my mother since I was a little girl. Less than an hour later, Baba came up with a plan. The son of a longtime customer who worked for Lufthansa had arranged two seats on a flight leaving in three hours. It was 12:30 A.M. They had to make this flight, or airport security would surely have their names by morning.

"It's possible they already have our names, but it's a risk we have to take. Let's go."

"I have to say good-bye to my mother," begged Maman.

"Of course, of course . . ."

Her farewell with Grandmother lasted but minutes, as bittersweet as a bird taking flight from its mother's nest. Maman woke her, held her in her arms, and related a synopsis of what had happened. My grandmother sat wide-eyed and silent, quite in shock. As Maman released her so my father could give her a kiss, she snatched her prayer beads off the nightstand and began murmuring in Arabic.

Downstairs, Mahmood had the engine running, the trunk open. I smelled the smoldering *esfand,* dried wild rue as we approached. Mahmood had awakened Fatemeh, who stood holding the urn and swinging it gently. The white smoke rising from the urn had a calming effect, a promised blessing of safety. Mahmood raised a copy of the Koran for my parents to walk beneath, one at a time, kissing the book before and after crossing. Tossing their bags in the trunk, they hopped in the car. I stood at the driver's side and watched through tear-filled eyes.

"They'll be fine, Miss Leila. Don't worry. I'll make sure of it." With that, the Range Rover peeled away in the dark early hours, and they were gone. Fatemeh held me for several minutes while I gained my composure and returned inside.

It was years later that we learned more details about what led to the events of this unforgettable night. At the Ghorbani house that evening, all slept peacefully. Javad, whose unrequited desire had burned for years, finally felt relieved of the long-harbored feelings of anger and resentment. Several days earlier, he'd approached the District head of Pasdaran for northern Tehran. There, he reported that his good friend attended art classes at Tehran University. His friend had told Javad that the teacher, Mr. Moradi—Ali Moradi—was spouting anti-government rhetoric. Mr. Moradi was attempting to rally the students and was planning a protest at the university to decry Islamic rule. He believed Mr. Moradi had even publicly denounced government officials. Javad told the Intelligence Director that it was his duty as a patriot and believer to report this treason, even though his family had been friends of the Moradi family for ages. He couldn't allow one arrogant man to commit despicable acts of treason against his beloved country.

The Intelligence Director was grateful to Javad, hailing him a hero. Javad left the Agency grinning and, for the first time in years, feeling triumphant. The Director reached for his phone and, within a few days, gathered all the data he needed about Ali Moradi and his family: names of children and relatives, addresses, professions, bank accounts, and more. Meanwhile, Javad bragged to friends of his patriotic actions. Friends told other friends until eventually the news was overheard by a student loyal to my father. At the risk of his own life, for by then the phones were surely tapped, he warned my father. We never learned his identity.

It was that kind of time in Iran. A time of deception and fear, when neighbors turned against neighbors, friends against friends, and children betrayed parents in the name of Allah. In some cases, pouting ex-suitors avenged their bruised egos, striking out in impotence with total disregard for friendship and lacking any human decency.

FORTY-TWO

The night of my parents' unexpected flight, I called Farhad, briefly explained what had happened, and asked him to pick us up. "Hurry, Farhad. I'm afraid."

"I'm on my way."

We got home without incident but were too anxious to sleep. Fatemeh made a pot of tea, and we sat up till the first rays of morning breached the windows, discussing the prior night's events and anticipating the police reaction when they discovered my parents' disappearance. It was nice to have Farhad involved rather than withdrawn for a change. We could only guess that my parents had made their escape. Mahmood hadn't called, and I was growing nervous. Had my parents made the flight? Had the plane taken off? Why hadn't Mahmood called? I prayed they hadn't all been arrested. Finally, the phone rang around eight.

"Leila *khanoom*, it's Mahmood," he said excitedly. "Thanks be to Allah you took your grandmother and Fatemeh. They've stormed the house. I went by this morning to check. When I saw the soldiers outside, I drove off. I didn't want to be subjected to questioning."

"Are you alright, Mahmood? What about my parents? Did they make it out?"

"I'm fine, I'm fine. And yes, they're gone. Your father bribed the gate agent so I could walk with them to the gate. I myself watched them board the plane. Then it just sat on the tarmac forever. I was worried they'd been alerted your parents were onboard. I finally asked the agent what was going on. He said they had a minor mechanical problem. Leila *khanoom*, I died a thousand deaths waiting for that plane to take off. Then I drove past the house to see what was going on. I'm so relieved your grandmother is with you. Allah only knows what would've happened if she'd stayed." I'd never heard Mahmood speak so quickly without taking a breath.

Just before dawn, a few short hours after Farhad retrieved us, four military vehicles and a dozen soldiers, guns drawn, stormed the mansion where I once lived. They searched the property and found no one, but they left two soldiers on guard. It was puzzling that no one came to my house. Farhad attributed our safety to his father's position on the city council. And for a while, that proved true.

Later that morning, the phone rang again. I answered with trepidation, wondering if yet another warning would be delivered.

"Mrs. Arefi?"

"Yes."

"Hold for the Ministry of Intelligence and Security," the voice commanded.

I sat down trembling, clinging to the receiver. Grandmother, who noticed my face flush, hobbled over and grasped my arm, staring at the phone as if it might help her hear what was being said. What could this mean? Had they arrested my parents after all? Were they coming for me? What would become of Grandmother?

"Leila? It's Mojtabah."

"*Salam*, Mojtabah." I answered nervously, remembering he worked at the Ministry of Intelligence.

"I just learned of the arrest warrant issued for Uncle Ali. I did what I could but was powerless to reverse the decision. Your father's words of sedition had reached too many ears."

I sat silently, trying to interpret the hidden meaning of his words, for surely it was there.

He continued, "Anyhow, I understand when the soldiers arrived at the house, they found it empty."

"Really?" I played dumb, suspecting he was fishing.

"Leila, I didn't call to spy. I just want you to know, and more importantly, for Uncle Ali to know, I would never allow this to happen if I had the power to stop it. I owe Uncle Ali more than I can ever repay." And with that, he hung up.

I sat in the armchair and stared out the window at the passing cars and people walking by, scurrying about as though nothing was changed.

Didn't they know my world had been turned upside down? Couldn't they sense my fears, my worries? I remained suspicious about Mojtabah's call. He was always the hard-liner, preaching strict adherence to Islam. I remembered him challenging my hopes for an education, wanting to force me into the mold of an Islamic woman. Perhaps he, too, had a conscience, a sense of family loyalty. It changed nothing, but for the moment at least, I could relax a bit. Still, I had a nagging feeling he couldn't be trusted.

My parents made their way safely to Paris after a brief stop in Frankfurt. Fortunately, their multiple-entry visa to France was still valid. The next day, they applied for political asylum. Weeks later, they moved into an apartment not far from Uncle Mohsen. While I missed them, I was relieved they were out of harm's way.

*   *   *

Months passed without incident. Though we learned my parents' phone number, we were afraid to call. The régime could trace the call and discover their whereabouts. We felt sure our conversations were recorded, and spies were everywhere.

Once over the shock of recent events, Maman Rouhi expressed a desire for a home of her own. Though Farhad and I begged her to stay with us, she wanted her independence. "Mahmood and Fatemeh will keep me company. And you can come see me whenever you like."

Through my uncle in Paris, I checked up on my parents, always in our own code. I felt it was best not to call them directly. They'd adjusted to their new home, spending their days wandering the neighborhoods and making new friends. I missed them terribly and longed to hear their voices.

Between the loss of my parents and the marital discord surrounding me, I began to lose hope. An air of melancholy crept over me. At least Farhad didn't beat me, I thought. Still, it felt wrong. I rarely saw him, and when he was around, he wasn't really present. I often fell asleep before he came home, then would see him briefly in the morning while he grabbed a quick breakfast and ran out the door. We barely talked, and physical intimacy was non-existent.

One morning, I awoke at 3:00 A.M. and realized my husband was not in our bed. In a panic, I searched the house, calling his name. I noticed his car missing from the garage. Reluctantly, given the hour, I called his parents. They didn't know where he was but said they would contact the police, just in case. These days, no one was immune from being drafted. I sat in anguish, staving off visions of him being arrested, in jail, perhaps in an accident, or bleeding to death somewhere. At 7:00 A.M., I heard the garage door open. Hugely relieved, I ran over to embrace him and asked where he'd been.

"Nowhere," he said, pushing away from me.

"Where's nowhere?"

"It's none of your business," he replied sharply.

"None of my business? I've been up half the night, worried to death, thinking you were hurt or arrested. Your parents are worried sick. You show up at seven o'clock and tell me it's none of my business?!" I shouted back.

"You heard what I said, and don't talk back to me!" With that, Farhad slapped me across the face so hard I lost my balance and fell to the ground. My cheek stinging from the blow, eyes watering with the pain, I sat where I'd fallen, in complete shock. I couldn't believe he hit me and just walked away.

Farhad called his parents from the bedroom to tell them he was fine. He said there was no cause for alarm; I'd just forgotten he was with his poker buddies. Then he showered, changed, and left the house without another word. Playing poker? What a lie. My face was burning, less from the blow than the shock of it. I went to the bathroom and stared in the mirror. There, like a harbinger of despair, a red, hand-shaped blotch distinctly marked my left cheek. Tears came as embarrassment and anger whirled inside. I'd be mortified if anyone saw me.

After that day, my life continued on this path of misery, with Farhad spending more nights away from home. While I wasn't a complainer, neither did I make a secret of my concerns. Two of my uncles took it upon themselves to play detective and followed Farhad to see where he spent his time. By the second evening, it was clear my husband was sleeping with another woman he kept in one of his apartment buildings. They broke the news to me at Grandmother's house one night.

"I knew but didn't want to know. Now it's certain," I said, tears forming in my eyes.

"We're truly sorry, Leila," said Uncle Mortezah.

"It explains a lot." I kissed Maman Rouhi good-bye and said I'd return the next day.

I was surprised to find Farhad at home. He was reclined on the couch, smoking and reading the newspaper.

"How was your evening?" he asked, not glancing up from his paper.

"Good. Why didn't you come?"

"I had work."

"Right . . . ," I said sarcastically.

Noting the sarcasm, he looked up from his paper. "What does that mean?"

"It means I know you weren't working. It means I know you have a mistress, a whore!" I spat.

Farhad shot from the couch, came at me, and slapped me again so hard I crumpled to the floor. "How dare you insult me? You were damaged goods when I married you. And you can't even give me a child!" he shouted, anger spewing out.

With that, he stormed from the house, leaving me once more on the floor, only this time I wasn't shocked. I went to bed, crying softly in my pillow, the pain of his blow nothing compared to the ache in my heart. Despite the emotions pillaging my mind, I forced myself to get up, wash my face, and return to bed. As I lay there seeking the release of sleep, I was haunted by visions of my parents in Paris, the broken body of Amir surrounded by bleeding soldiers, shrapnel shredding their chests. I cried for hours till sleep mercifully appeared. The next morning I awoke to the sound of keys in the door. My eyes were swollen from crying, my face throbbing and bruised. Farhad entered our bedroom, sat next to me, and took my hand in his.

"I'm sorry, Leila. I behaved badly. Please tell me you forgive me. Please . . ." I wanted to believe his contrition, to embrace the hope my life hadn't collapsed in the same well of despair my cousin endured. All I could do was nod my head. With that, Farhad kissed me on the forehead and told me to stay in bed. He would bring me tea today. I sat there, confused and still hurting. Could this really be a change of heart? Was there still hope for my marriage?

When he returned with tea, I asked, "I'll be late coming home to-day. I want to help Maman Rouhi hang her new drapes. Is that okay?" I thought it better to ask his permission than risk a change of temperament.

"Stay as long as you need. In fact, why don't we go out for dinner tonight so you don't have to worry about cooking?" he said in a jovial tone, as though a dinner out might close the chasm between us.

"That'll be nice," I said, surprised at his sudden change of mood.

FORTY-THREE

Evin Prison, 1988

My stoic resistance was wearing down. I'd remained silent in the face of torture and accusations because my parents' lives hung in the balance. But my own life was drawing to a close; I knew that now. This couldn't continue forever, and they'd never release me. Admitting this horror would be an embarrassment for the government. The day they'd kill me was drawing near. Thoughts of death no longer brought tremors of fear, and tears seemed to have dried up over the months of agony and loneliness. Perhaps this was despair, though it felt light. I was so tired, so very tired. I was ready to meet my destiny.

I had tried to get word to Farhad, thinking surely with his power and money he could change the course of events. Though I never learned his name, the stout guard who often patrolled the halls was less belligerent, more humane than the rest. During one of his rounds, as I sat in bed reading the Koran, despite blurred vision from beatings, he stopped and glanced through the barred window.

"Please, *agha*," I said, "you've been so kind, surely you are a man of faith and mercy. Please, can you get word to my husband that I'm here? His name is Farhad Arefi."

"I know who he is," he said, cutting me off in a harsh whisper. "I know who he is, and I sent him word weeks ago, a note delivered by my own son. I even told the boy to wait for a reply—there was none. He gave my son a lousy ten Tomans and told him to go."

"No, that can't be. Farhad would come immediately and get me released."

"*Khanoom*, you have no idea where you are, do you? You're in Evin, the worst prison there is. He cannot save you. No one leaves this place unless the Ministry of Intelligence says so. He may have money, though he's sure stingy with it, but no amount of money will buy your freedom from here."

So that was it. There would be no *deus ex machina* rescue, no bargain for freedom, no political favors to call in. Even my husband must have lost hope. I lay on the wooden pallet and turned to face the concrete wall. My sobbing echoed into empty space, though no one heard. As my spasms of grief gradually subsided, I grew calm. If this is where life would end, so be it. My father had given me the courage to endure things this far, and that courage would not fail me in the face of death. I could do nothing to hasten its approach, nothing to delay it. Let it come when it comes. I was no longer afraid.

The next day, the heavy outer door swung open, and uniformed men marched down the long hallway, their crashing boots inflaming my dread. They stood outside the cell in the semi-darkness while fear climbed like a lump in my throat. The cell door swung open.

"Get up, traitor," the first guard ordered, his foul breath wheezing from a mouth of rotting teeth. They dragged me again to the interrogation room. One guard pulled the sack from my head. I knew better than to look directly at them. If I stared or showed any hint of defiance, I'd feel the kick of a boot or the butt of a rifle. Worse, I was afraid they'd rape me again. Twice more I'd been ruthlessly crushed against that hard plank as soldiers forced themselves upon me. They kept me hooded for this degradation, so I never saw their faces, but I couldn't forget their smell, the overpowering putrid odor of corpulent bodies and unwashed sweat. Worse, I couldn't live with the idea of again being pregnant with a bastard child. These fears clawed and scratched at my senses. For all I knew, my rapists were standing in the room.

Lt. Mehraban, the Interrogator, stood aloof to one side. He seemed brooding and irritated. What had happened? Did he have news of my grandmother? Had they discovered my parents' location? Or was he about to order my death?

On the nod from Lt. Mehraban, one guard threw me to the floor, and they all began kicking. No questions, just a rain of blows. Mercifully, I lost consciousness in seconds. I awoke on the cold concrete floor back in my cell, weeping in agony, tormented with visions of rape and humiliation. No one heard my cries. It was as though the guards had vanished, abandoning me to the horror of my dreams. I sat hugging myself in the black silence till finally I drifted into darkness.

Footsteps in the hall startled me awake. My head was still pounding from the kicks and blows. My body ached. My lips were parched and dry. But at this moment in this dank, decrepit place, none of it mattered as the footsteps drew closer.

I tried to lift myself off the floor, my heart racing, and I felt the blood rush from my head, whirlwinds spinning in my mind. Was this it, the day they'd simply, without sentiment, put a bullet in my head? I would surrender to fate as it came. I was tired of battling to hold on to my sanity, tired of this desolate existence. Shadows of two men appeared at the cell door. Jangling keys released the lock. A commanding whisper, "*Pasho, zood bash*—get up, hurry."

I tried to stand, but my legs crumpled under the weight of my battered body. I struggled again, knowing better than to disobey orders. Not following orders meant more pain. At this point, death was preferable. I collapsed, and before I knew what was happening, two pairs of strong arms carried me from the cell. They dragged me down the narrow hallway in a rush. This time they didn't pull the burlap bag over my head. But I was so tired I couldn't open my eyes anyway, couldn't muster the strength to ask why I was being taken again, certain that death was imminent.

With eyes closed, I recalled my last moments with my grandmother, the soldiers striking her to the ground when she tried to intervene in my arrest. Was she still alive? I thought of my parents in exile among strangers in Paris, wishing they could return to their own home. Unbidden tears arose as other familiar faces flooded my memory: my brother, Amir; my cousin Neda; Jack. If these were my final moments, I had little time to cherish the images.

The sound of a car's engine shattered the stillness of night. The men dragged me toward the car. In the dim light, I saw a woman in Islamic *hijab*. She opened the back door as we approached and said, "Get in, *dokhtaram*, my daughter. It's going to be a long ride." My heart fluttered with joy at Fatemeh's sweet voice. Quickly, she drew a *chador* over my head, carefully arranging it to conceal my face.

"Watch your head," said another voice. As he gently helped me into the backseat, I beheld a vision, the face of Mahmood in the dim moonlight. This face I had known for so many years, his black button eyes and square jaw, his burly mustache and balding head now crowned with gray. I gingerly reached to touch him, to prove it was real, as he quietly closed the door. Tears flowed as I closed my eyes in quiet surrender and lost consciousness.

FORTY-FOUR

I awoke from dreams of imprisonment to radiant morning sunlight splashing my face. I struggled to focus, with no idea how long I'd been in the car. Having lived so long in semi-darkness, I was dazzled by the unblemished brightness.

"*Pasho*, Leila *khanoom*—get up, Miss Leila. We don't have much time." Mahmood's gentle voice was comforting beyond belief.

"Where am I? What's going on?"

"Miss Leila, you're safe. We're taking you to freedom," beamed Mahmood.

"How were you able to do this? Did Farhad get word to you where I was?"

But I could tell from the look on his face that was not the case. He recounted the story of my rescue.

*   *   *

A ringing telephone pierced the quiet of night, Mahmood began. While not unexpected, it still startled him as he wrestled with sleep. The last six months had been difficult for him and Fatemeh, following my arrest. Having worked for my family so many years, to be suddenly torn from our familiar faces was like losing part of himself. He'd lost his daughter to a horrible disease, and in that instance, Baba stood beside him. When his son got married, it was Baba who made the down payment on a house as a generous wedding gift. Over the years, my family had cared for him with respect and warmth, just as he cared for us. Yet he'd failed us when he was needed most.

He had flashbacks of the day I was taken by the Pasdaran as he stood facing the wrong end of a rifle. He could have done more. He should have disarmed the soldier. He should have fought, even if it meant death. But he froze in fear. He watched helplessly as Maman Rouhi fell to the floor, and they dragged me away, the little girl he'd watched grow into a woman. Guilt and regret had been constant companions for those six months. It was time to repay the many acts of kindness, to eradicate his shame. He lifted the receiver as the voice on the phone spoke a single word: "Tonight."

The plan had been set in motion weeks earlier: The guide to shepherd me across the border from Iran to Turkey, the driver to transport me to Istanbul airport, the process of procuring my passport, and even the Air France flight had all been arranged, awaiting this day. Now that it was here, the question of whether to trust the architect of the escape arose unbidden. Yes, the man was helping to set me free, but still, he worked for the government, hardly credentials to inspire trust.

Earlier, they'd tried desperately to learn where I'd been imprisoned. Farhad's father appealed to his contacts to no avail. Family members and friends exhausted sources of information and influence. Finally, bereft of options, Mahmood chose to take matters into his own hands and called this man, hoping he would help. Mahmood knew this request could result in his own arrest and execution, but his sense of loyalty overcame all fears, all risks. After first getting his wife's agreement, he'd made contact.

Even in his position of power, it had taken his contact time to locate me and make proper arrangements. It had to be accomplished without raising suspicion. It would be worth the months of anguished anticipation if the plan could succeed. Still, nagging fear whispered in Mahmood's mind. Perhaps the contact agreed only to arrest more of Baba's associates, to interrogate them as to his whereabouts. One thing was certain: The government used whatever means necessary to capture those accused of treason, those who dared speak against the régime. But fear did not deter him now, not when the moment was so near. He leaned over and gently kissed his sleeping wife on the cheek, trying not to wake her as he dressed. She stirred slightly as he pulled up his trousers. In a muffled voice, she said, "Be careful. *Khoda hafez*— may Allah protect you."

"I will, my darling. I'll be back before daylight, I promise."

He drove the quiet streets in the early-morning hours to pick up Fatemeh at Maman Rouhi's, where she remained as caretaker of the now-quiet house. Together, they'd rescue the one who had been like a daughter to them. They'd stood side by side helplessly when I was taken. Now, together, they'd see me freed. Fatemeh was waiting by the corner. The real danger lay in a random Pasdaran patrol. There could be no acceptable explanation for an old man and woman out at this early hour. Worse, they could be suspected of adultery, a crime punishable with death by stoning for her, lashes and imprisonment for him. One more stop a few kilometers away.

A man hovered in the shadows of the concrete building as the car stopped, and he then quickly climbed in the front seat. The dark turban and long brown robe of a mullah offered ample concealment at night, though that was hardly their purpose.

"Right at the next corner, then head north," the man commanded.

Mahmood did as instructed, taking several back streets to reach the right road. If this man planned to betray them, it would be over soon. If not, the chance he was taking was insane as well. The drive was uneventful as they prowled the dark, empty streets of Tehran. The prior day's rubbish overflowed silver receptacles, awaiting collection at dawn, its rotting aroma a reminder of the decay gripping the city. Streetlights cast shadows on the road, occasionally flickering as they limped toward their end of life. He stopped beside a nondescript three-story building, its gray walls accented by barred windows. The moment of truth.

"Come, let's get her out."

They walked through the large doorway, the robed man in the lead. A guard sat in the hallway, his rifle resting across the desk. In spite of the hour, he was alert, eyes clearly focused. He grabbed his rifle and stood as they entered. For a second, Mahmood felt trapped and almost reversed his path. The robed man whispered, "*Salam aleykum.*"

The guard returned the greeting and handed him a set of keys. "She's in the third cell down the hall, basement level. Hurry—my replacement will be here in less than an hour."

Somehow he'd arranged the escape with this guard, Mahmood thought. Taking the keys, the robed man led Mahmood down the narrow stairs into a darkened hallway.

"It took some time to discover where she was held," he said in a hushed tone. "Then more time to obtain a list of the guards and schedules. I had to be careful no one was alerted. Fortunately, my position allowed me to contact the guards without raising suspicion. I'd ask questions concerning several prisoners, casually dropping Leila's name. There was something different about this fellow. He was much more forthcoming, especially when I mentioned Leila. It turns out he's a former student of her father's. I'm grateful his sense of respect and loyalty outweighed the risk he's taking."

Mahmood understood; he knew how many lives Baba had touched. Yet until it was over, threat of betrayal remained high.

The stench of the place was overwhelming, and the damp air carried it like the plague. They came to the third cell, and as he swung the door open, the robed man stepped back and whispered, "Quick, we've got to get her and go."

Mahmood rushed forward at once, as did the robed man, and they took me outside. The guard was now at the doorway, scanning for activity as Mahmood and his accomplice helped carry me to the car, where Fatemeh held the door open in the dark. The robed man turned and tossed the keys to the guard by the doorway. He snatched them from the air and said, "My replacement's a useless fool who never leaves the desk, just sleeps his time away. He's been reprimanded more than once, so suspicion will fall on him, particularly as my report will state all prisoners were accounted for when I left."

"I'll remember this. *Kheili mamnoon*, thank you very much," the robed man replied.

Pasdaran would be an even greater threat now, as they were transporting a fugitive. To be caught was certain death. Mahmood gently closed the car door behind me, and before getting in the car, he turned to the robed man and said, "Thank you for your help."

"You must leave the city as quickly as possible. If you're not at the rendezvous before dawn, they'll be alerted and find you. Now, go quickly. And tell her father my debt is repaid," replied the man.

*   *   *

In the backseat, I shaded my eyes against the sunlight as I listened to the story, overcome with gratitude to Mahmood, Fatemeh, and my other liberator, whoever he was. Now I understood why the stout guard had shown moments of kindness. It always had to do with my father's influence, an act of kindness, or *savab*.

"Here we have to leave you with someone else," said Mahmood as he pulled the car over.

An old man and two donkeys stood by the side of the road, seemingly in the middle of nowhere. I took Mahmood's hand as he helped me out. As a daughter longs for her father's embrace, I wanted to wrap my arms around him in appreciation, but this wasn't permitted. "Please, put these on, Miss Leila. Over here, behind the car," Fatemeh said, handing me some clothes.

Mahmood turned away as Fatemeh's extended black *chador* served as a makeshift curtain. I stripped off the prison robe I'd worn so long and struggled to pull on the loose black pants and gray tunic. I could barely stand, still dizzy from the beating I'd endured only hours ago, and the effort was exhausting. Worn leather sandals and a long flowing head scarf completed my transformation from prisoner to peasant. Still squinting with the bright sunlight, I scanned my surroundings, dirt roads and arid countryside, barren except for a few withered trees and stunted shrubs. Fatemeh lifted a bundle from the back of the car and handed me a worn, tattered backpack. "Be careful, Leila *khanoom*. It's fragile." She threw an arm around my neck and kissed each cheek, the smell of rosewater behind her ears stirring memories.

"Leila *khanoom*, we're not that far from the Turkish border. This man with the donkeys is Samu. He'll take you to Turkey. There, you'll board a plane to Paris, where your family is waiting for you. After you cross the border, you're safe. *Khoda negahdar*, may God protect you."

In a rare move, as I was not his *mahram*, Mahmood bent and kissed my forehead. More eloquently than any words, this gentle kiss proclaimed his fatherly affection.

"Go now, my child," he said, and helped me limp over to one of the donkeys, as tears of gratitude streaked my face.

My Turkish guide was an ancient man, dressed in a tan-colored turban and loose-fitting local attire. His weathered face was sun-beaten

The Ruby Tear Catcher

and wrinkled like an old map, but his eyes twinkled with mirth, and his almost-toothless grin was reassuring. As he hobbled bow-legged between the donkeys, he appeared completely at ease, right where he belonged. We weren't safe by a long shot, and fear of being recaptured was real. Until I was out of Iran, danger was imminent. This seemed inconsequential to Samu, a simple man who took his time adjusting bundles on the donkey's back.

He signaled for me to climb on. "Brimbali," he said with a grin, slapping the donkey I would ride. Gently patting the other donkey, he introduced him as "Ali Baba." He took my backpack and attached it to his donkey's saddlebag. Gently, he hoisted me onto the rugged saddle. A bolt of agony screamed through my battered body as he lifted me. Sucking in a painful breath, I tried to gain my balance as Mahmood and Fatemeh hurried back to the car to leave. With an agility that belied his age, Samu sprang into his saddle, still holding the rope to Brimbali.

"*Y'allah*, to God, let's go," Samu said to Ali Baba, gently prodding the animal with his heels. As the donkeys plodded down the slope, my eyes followed the trail of dust as the old black Peykan sped off in the distance down the dirt road.

"*Khoda hafez*, may God keep you safe,'" I said, my lips moving soundlessly, as though Mahmood and Fatemeh could hear.

Leading Brimbali, the old man began a slow trot down the dirt road. There were no stirrups, and my legs dangled at the donkey's sides as we bounced along. How long could I tolerate the jostling ride? Samu spoke no Farsi, and I spoke no Turkish. I simply had to endure. Still, with months of torture, rape, and cruelty behind me, this was a ride into joy.

Dread of what might await kept me anxious. What if the Pasdaran were around the bend, guns drawn and incensed by my escape? They wanted me alive to learn of my father's whereabouts, yet I was shocked they hadn't killed me already. My execution would have been a brilliant strategy to lure back a mourning father. Had that manipulative thought crossed their minds? And in all of this, where was Farhad? Did he care anymore? We lumbered along, my donkey following stolidly down the path as I struggled to stay perched in its saddle. Only the crunch of hooves on dry gravel and the cry of an occasional bird marked our passing. Without a way of telling time, I had no concept of how long we'd been riding, though it felt like hours. I ached more with each jostling step.

As the sun climbed high in the clear blue sky, Samu stopped by a tree-lined pond. The green vegetation cloaking this haven stood in stark contrast to the brown and gray of the earth. The air was perfumed with the scent of hibiscus that graced the narrow isthmus separating the desert from the clear water of this oasis. Samu hopped down to help me off my donkey. Securing the animals to a nearby tree, he removed a sack from Ali Baba's saddle and motioned me to sit. From his sack he produced *lavash* bread, feta cheese, and a goatskin of water to share. Never had such simple food tasted so splendid. The animals contently grazed beneath the tree on their tethers, drinking water in the cool shade. When Samu finished his meal, he signaled it was time to go, muttering something in Turkish. What he said was inconsequential; his clear, sparkling eyes and gentle smile conveyed a peace and tranquility I could trust.

For the next several hours, the strenuous path continued unchanged. With no map, Samu traveled by memory and hard-earned knowledge of the back trails straddling the border between Iran and Turkey. Cresting a small hilltop through a dazzling row of cypress trees, I stared in awe at the setting sun. The view was breathtaking, a spectacular display of nature's glory. After months in my dark cell, I relished the lingering moments of sunset, its gold-and-purple-streaked robe a vision of serenity. Samu abruptly stopped and with arms uplifted, he yelled with joy, "*Turkieh!*" We had crossed into Turkey.

The remainder of the trek down the rocky dirt road moved quickly. Even the donkeys anticipated the journey's end and quickened their pace. In the distance, the shadowed outline of a village stood against the spectacular remnants of sunset, glowing with orange and yellow streaks against the darkening sky. It was a small village with short stout buildings of brick and mortar, hay, and clay. Entering the village, Samu navigated the dirt alleys till we came upon a man leaning against a dusty black Opel. He was a big man with a burly black mustache and somewhat fearful appearance, betrayed only by his gleaming smile.

Moving with speed that belied his size, he hustled me off the donkey and into the backseat of the car. Just before we sped away, Samu ran back to the car. I smiled and took the backpack from him, carefully setting it on the seat next to me. Before I could say good-bye, we were off, and my rescue team—Samu, Ali Baba, and Brimbali—were out of sight.

The driver spoke perfect English. "I am Massoud, a friend of your Uncle Mohsen. He sends his love and anxiously awaits you. The final stage of your journey is very close now."

"Thank you, Massoud. I wish I'd had time to thank Samu."

"He knows. Like the rest of us, he's been graced by your father's kindness and carries a debt of gratitude." I sat quietly, awed by the breadth of Baba's reach and the lives he had touched.

Massoud drove directly to the small local airport and explained.

"Here you'll board a small plane to Istanbul's Ataturk Airport. When you arrive, go to the Air France counter. You have a seat reserved on their flight to Paris this evening. It's best you go it alone from this point. And here's a change of clothes so you look more like a tourist."

Overwhelmed with the day's events, my head was spinning, fearful I'd forget his instructions. Massoud handed me the bag of clothes, a passport, and ticket before he closed the door to the small plane and it took off.

FORTY-FIVE

Paris, July 1988

I awoke as the plane touched down in Paris, having slept the entire flight. Unlike in the prison cell that had been my home, here I had no dreams, no nightmares. I was nervous. I'd checked no bags, had no purse, and traveled with just a passport and backpack. I stifled a murmur of pain as I reached to retrieve the backpack from the overhead compartment. Inside Charles de Gaulle airport, the familiar chimes that precede announcements echoed, bringing a smile. The tones, once annoying, now were a comfort.

The last beating had left me battered and bruised. As the rain of booted kicks had pummeled me, I'd curled into a ball to protect my head, exposing my ribs and thighs to the attack. Now, after the long flight, I was stiff and near collapse, favoring my right leg as I limped, approaching the Guichet de Passeports with pained effort. Lines were always long at Charles de Gaulle airport, and it was agony just to stand. But I could endure anything after what I'd been through.

Taking my place in one of three long queues, I felt conspicuous. Was everyone staring at this battered, emaciated woman? Did I appear a fugitive? I hadn't seen a mirror since my last infirmary visit and had no idea how I looked. I'd lost weight subsisting on bread and water and occasional lamb stew. My hair had grown long, and curls had given way to tangled frizzy strands falling below my shoulder. My nails, once in a French manicure, were broken, chipped, and uneven.

Why was this taking so long? Who was waiting in the terminal? Would my parents be there? Uncle Mohsen? Everything had happened so quickly, reality hadn't sunk in yet. I wanted to hold my father and draw on his strength, hug my mother, and let fear vanish in her embrace. Finally, it was my turn. I timidly stepped forward to the immigration agent. *"Bonjour, Monsieur,"* I said in my finest French accent, as though it were a requirement to being allowed in.

The man glanced up from my passport and gave me a strange look. I panicked, thinking he'd deny my entry. What if it was a fake passport? My heart began to thud, but then his eyes softened; he stamped my passport and handed it back. *"Bienvenue à Paris, Madame,"* he said. Welcome to Paris. Tension left me like flowing water.

"Merci, Monsieur," I managed with a weak smile, and I quickly made my way to the escalator before he had a chance to change his mind. I remembered the complex circular first floor as I stepped off the escalator. How would I find my parents? What if they didn't recognize me? What if they sent someone else? Could Muslim zealots in Paris have followed them? After all, Khomeini lived in Paris before returning to Iran. It was possible his followers were here searching for me.

I frantically stumbled through the terminal seeking a familiar face, passing conveyor belts brusquely dumping luggage in arrival bins. Then I saw Baba, hurrying towards me with open arms. I plowed into his chest and held on like a frightened child, crying for joy. I felt his shaking body and for the first time saw him sobbing, his tears mingling with mine. My mother took her turn holding me as Baba finally released me.

"It's a miracle," said Baba as his emotions calmed. "We never wavered in our belief we'd hold you again, my darling. Some days it seemed impossible, but we never gave up."

"Mahmood and Fatemeh put themselves in such danger to rescue me. I'm forever grateful. If the government finds out, they'll be executed. I don't even want to think about that. Right now, I just want to go home."

"Come, Uncle Mohsen is waiting in the car. He'll drive us home," said Baba.

Outside the terminal, my uncle climbed out of his silver Peugeot as we approached. He walked over and wrapped his arms around me. He'd never embraced me before.

"How are you, darling?" Then stepping back, he observed, "Look at you; you're hurt. We're taking you straight to the hospital."

"I want to go home, Uncle Mohsen," I pleaded. "Please."

"No, you clearly need immediate care," he said as he gently touched my battered face with a finger. "You're limping, and from the way you're breathing, I'm guessing you have broken ribs. Don't worry; we'll take care of you." Too exhausted to argue, I resigned myself to my fate.

Despite my weakness and obvious pain, the drive to Paris was full of chatter. Uncle Mohsen gave his family's news. His son, Farid, had taken a job in Bretagne and now owned a boat on the lake. Oh, and he was eager to take me for a boat ride. His daughter, Zari, was completing her final year at the Sorbonne and, with a pending degree in business law, was entertaining offers from prestigious law firms. She's eager to make my favorite Persian dishes. My parents took turns offering news of family members, how they were and what they were up to. I listened patiently, waiting for news of Maman Rouhi. When none came, my heart sank, fearing the worst. I finally gathered the courage to ask. For a few moments, they looked at each other, wondering who'd deliver the news. Finally, Baba turned and faced me. "She died two weeks after you were taken. They say she died of a broken heart. She kept calling for you. She wouldn't eat or sleep. The doctor put her on sleeping medication, but her health faded quickly. With your arrest, she lost her will to live. But thank God they couldn't torment her further. She died peacefully in her bed. Fatemeh found her one morning when she brought her tea. Farhad and your aunts made respectable funeral arrangements."

A fountain of tears rose unbidden. My grandmother, the woman who'd been more my mother, was gone. As I lay battered in prison, the country she had so loved finally crushed her. I couldn't imagine life without her joyful laugh, her calm wisdom and delightful stories, the scent of rosewater behind her ears. My tears flowed as I leaned against the car window, trying to control my sobbing. At least she was at peace.

Then I realized this was the first mention of my husband. "Where is Farhad?" I asked, with mixed emotions.

"I contacted him once we knew you were safely out of Iran. He'll arrange to come at once, though it may take him awhile to get a visa. But Farhad has connections; he'll find a way."

As I sat in the car, reflective in the moment's silence, I felt no sadness in his absence. Part of me hoped for his sympathy; another hoped he'd stay in Iran. I was baffled by my ambivalence. I should be angry and hurt, but I was too exhausted for anything but relief.

"Baba, how long was I in prison?"

"For almost six months. Believe me, I counted each painful day. At first, we didn't know who'd taken you or where. When they arrested you, Mahmood frantically called Farhad but couldn't reach him. He went to your house and waited till Farhad arrived. When he appeared and heard you were arrested, he got angry and started throwing things. He blamed Mahmood for letting them take you. But what could Mahmood do? The soldiers had guns. What could he do?"

"It doesn't surprise me Farhad would blame someone else. Poor Mahmood." What did he expect Mahmood to do?

"Anyway," Baba continued, "Farhad's father called everyone. It was weeks before they learned you were being held in Evin, but details remained buried. With all the influence and money that family has, they were powerless. Apparently the government really wants me."

"Why didn't Farhad come to see me?"

"You weren't allowed visitors, darling," said Uncle Mohsen.

"Who found me? Who arranged my escape?"

"We're at the hospital, Leila," Uncle Mohsen said as he pulled in front of the American Hospital of Paris. "Come, there'll be plenty of time to tell everything. Do you remember Dr. Farzani, the pediatrician from Iran? He's on staff here. He'll make sure you're treated well."

For now, details of my escape remained a mystery. I was dizzy and felt faint getting out of the car. As I took a step, I saw a vision of my grandmother. Holding out her arms, she reached for me. I reached for her hand, and everything went dark.

I awoke in a bed with white linens and a soft down pillow. Disoriented, panic rose as I thought I was back in jail. But my surroundings were sanitary and bright, not the dark grim cell I remembered. Was I awake or dreaming? Maybe I'd died and this was heaven. I struggled to open my eyes, fighting the urge for somnolent peace. I was about to give in when a jovial voice called, "*Salam, salam, azizam*—hello, hello, my dear."

As I clawed my way up from sleep, a familiar face materialized. I stared at Baba's haggard face, hoping he was real, that this was not a dream. Finally, I found my voice. "Where am I? What happened?"

"We're in Paris. You collapsed two days ago, and you're recovering at the hospital with the help of some strong medicine."

"Baba, you're really here? Is this real? Please hold me so I know it's real."

"Yes, darling, we're all here. You're safe. Allah has answered our prayers. Dr. Farzani says they need to keep you a couple of weeks." He leaned over and held me in his strong arms.

"A couple of . . ." I couldn't finish the sentence. "I just want to go home."

"*Azizam*, they must keep you for observation. You have internal injuries, a severe concussion, three broken ribs, and bruises everywhere. You'll need physical therapy too. It's a wonder you survived the journey. I promise we'll be here every day. And I have good news. Farhad is coming to Paris on the first possible flight."

Good news? My heart filled with dread at the thought of seeing Farhad. He'll have to know the truth. When he finds out, what will he think? What will he do?

"Baba, please . . . I don't want to see him. I can't face him yet."

"Why? He's your husband. He cares for you." Baba reached for me as I began sobbing. I could never tell my family the truth. I was so ashamed. How could I explain the rapes, the miscarriage? No, I'd rather die first.

"Baba, please, I'm so tired. I don't want to see him."

"My dear, you're angry he wasn't the one who rescued you. But he tried, *azizam*, he tried," he said as he took my hands in his.

"Baba, in jail they beat me. They tortured me in ways unimaginable," I said, playing the tune he'd laid out for me. "I kept wondering why my husband, with all his money and connections, couldn't save me. One of the guards even got word to Farhad. He told him where I was, but Farhad did nothing."

"My poor child." He stood, holding my face in his hands and ever so gently kissed my forehead. "I wish I'd been in jail instead of you. This is my fault. I'm so sorry, little one. Everything will be all right now, I promise."

A teardrop brushed my face, then another. This was the second time I had seen my father cry. I put my arms around him as we sobbed in the security of one another's embrace. I was sorry to upset him, but

I had to delay facing Farhad till my strength and resolve returned.

"Baba," I pleaded, "I can't see Farhad right now. I just can't face him. Please give me time. Please . . ."

All my energy was drained. I wanted sleep, to return to that drowsy state that bore no pain. Tears returned as I recalled the hard plank, the brutality I'd suffered at the hands of the soldiers who destroyed my innocence. That's when I'd prayed desperately that Farhad would save me. But he didn't.

"Hush, my dear. Rest now. I'll keep him away as long as I can. Just rest and get better," he said, his voice trailing into darkness as I drifted back to sleep.

FORTY-SIX

I dreamt of my last day with Farhad, my grandmother being struck by the soldier, her prayer beads bouncing across the floor. I saw my parents in the Range Rover in pre-dawn hours, veiled in the smoke of burning rue, tearfully saying good-bye. I stared at a scarred and broken landscape, the stench of burning flesh lingering over a cavernous hole, the place my brother died. I knew it was a dream but couldn't escape its clutches. I tried to open my eyes and look around. There he was again, my father, walking slowly with my mother toward me. In a semi-conscious state, I reached out to touch them. As my vision cleared, I clung to the sight of them and drifted out of the unpleasant dream. My eyes focused, and my mind became more lucid.

"Leila, we're in Paris, remember?" asked Baba, not waiting for my reply. "We remind her when she wakes," he explained to Uncle Mohsen, who was standing by my bedside. "The drugs put her in a hypnotic sleep. She can't always tell past from present. Each time she wakes up, I have to remind her she's safe."

My parents stayed in the hospital with me day after day. As I floated in and out of consciousness, they were there, one or the other helping me claw my way from nightmares to the present. The doctors slowly reduced the drugs, making me more lucid. Once a day, a nurse helped me walk slowly down the hospital corridor, but these trips were exhausting. Each step was jarring. Each turning in bed caused lightning bolts of pain.

I began to relate the events following my arrest to my parents. I told of the beatings and deprivation, but not the rapes. I couldn't do that. I spoke of my final moments of despair, willing to accept death if it ended the pain. "And then my saviors showed up," I said, referring to Mahmood and Fatemeh. "I don't know how much longer I could have taken the torture. How did they get me out?"

"Do you remember anything about that night?" my father asked. He sat on a wooden chair next to my bed, holding my hand. Maman was in a striped beige and white easy chair next to the window, listening.

"Just glimpses, Baba, bits and pieces. I remember the cell door opened and two men dragged me out. I remember the car, Mahmood and Fatemeh putting me in the backseat." I paused, allowing him to fill in the blanks.

"We tried for weeks to learn where you were held, Leila. I made discreet contacts with everyone. It was no use. Farhad tried through his father's acquaintances, but every avenue proved a dead end. We didn't know what else to do, and then Mahmood contacted Mojtabah. Together they devised the plot to save you."

"Mojtabah?" I was shocked. "But he works for the Ministry of Intelligence."

"Yes, and without his help, none of this would have been possible. It was Mojtabah who found out where you were held and helped get you out."

I tried to absorb this impossible reality. Suddenly it all made sense. The other man who'd carried me out was Mojtabah—my fundamentalist cousin and unexpected rescuer.

"But why? Why would he risk his life? He doesn't even like me."

"He's family, Leila, my brother's son. For some, the bond of blood is stronger than religion or government rules. If only more of our people felt the same."

Though my mind was still foggy, the depth of Mojtabah's actions gripped my soul. He'd surprised me with his call after my parents fled. Now I learned he was the agent of my release. Over the years, I'd rejected his religious pronouncements and narrow-minded perspective and, in doing so, rejected the man. But from within the depths of a theocracy that swallowed individual spirits like an all-consuming dragon, his family ties held true. His loyalty stood in striking contrast to the actions of my own husband.

"If Farhad had tried, he could've found a way to save me, particularly after he knew where I was held. Why didn't he do anything?" I asked, my mind returning to the sad reality of my marriage.

"Leila, his hands were tied," said my father, tears again filling his eyes. It was difficult for him to hear the vivid details of his daughter's suffering. "He tried, but he could do nothing." Baba was pleading my forgiveness, knowing I resented Farhad's lack of effort.

"Baba, he doesn't love me. He never has. He has a mistress, maybe more than one. He acts like he owns me, and he's hit me. I don't love him. There's no future with him. I want a divorce."

"Well, he'll be here today. He's coming straight from the airport," he said, perhaps thinking my comments on abuse and adultery were delusions of a drug-impaired mind. "Get some rest now. Your mother and I are going to the cafeteria to get something to eat." That was Baba's way of dismissing a difficult subject.

I was staring at the marbled tile floor as Baba stood to leave. It was then I caught sight of the old backpack Fatemeh had handed me. I had forgotten all about it.

"Baba, can you hand me that backpack before you go?"

"We won't be long," Baba assured me and handed me the bag. He kissed my forehead and they left.

The zipper slid easily, as though freshly oiled. I wondered what Fatemeh had put inside, perhaps a change of clothes. Then I remembered she'd said it was fragile. Curiosity piqued my interest as I lifted the flap. Carefully, I withdrew a bundle, wrapped in a tattered green-and-red striped towel. I lifted the corners to expose its contents. My heart stopped; my chest tightened till I felt it might explode. I must breathe, I told myself. There, in my lap, was the ruby red tear catcher I'd bought for Baba after I'd broken his and Amir had taken the blame. The day I had shattered the treasured antique, the flash of a skirt had scurried past the open doorway, the sleeveless red floral print dress Fatemeh wore on very hot days. She'd witnessed everything. She'd known all along and understood how precious this was to me, particularly after Amir's death. A whirlwind of emotions gripped me. As I stared at it through a mist of tears, Amir's face appeared reflected, smiling, the olive glow of his skin showing off his perfect white teeth. I smiled at him through my weeping. He gleamed with happiness. Then Baba appeared, frowning in anger, wagging a finger at Amir in reprimand. Amir kept smiling He looked in my eyes and opened his arms. I read his lips as he repeated, "It's okay, little sister. It's okay." Then his image vanished in the fog of shifting light.

"What is it, darling? Why are you crying?" It was Baba's anxious voice as he stood next to my bed.

It was minutes before I could speak. Baba noticed the tear catcher in my lap and smiled. He remembered. For the second time, I handed Baba the tear catcher. Amidst my tears, the words finally escaped. "It was me, Baba. I broke your tear catcher, not Amir. I'm so sorry. So sorry . . ." Baba placed the vase tenderly on the nightstand and held me tight against his chest. "What a sweet sister you are," he whispered and kissed my hair.

As my crying subsided, I began to slowly push memories aside. I had to steel myself to confront Farhad. While in prison, I'd had time to consider our relationship. When he didn't come for me, I was angry. Then I resigned myself to the fact that he'd never be my knight in shining armor. How could he? He didn't love me. Reaching that stark realization, I'd decided that if I ever got out, I would leave him. Hours in isolation and torment taught me that pain could reach deep into my soul, but those hours also instilled courage. If I could endure dehumanizing torture, mental and physical assaults, I could stand in the face of anything. I would claim my life, my rights, regardless of what any government, religion, or unloving spouse had to say.

That afternoon, Farhad arrived, looking drawn and tired. His usual clean-shaven face showed short black stubble, framing his square jaw. Dashes of gray now laced his hair. He stood next to my bedside as I spoke. He seemed only remotely interested in my recounting of what had happened and interrupted, "You don't know how my father and I tried. He called in every favor from government ministers, and I contacted everyone I knew. You can imagine how humiliating it was for us, having to tell people my wife was in jail."

"Yes, I can imagine."

"I didn't sleep well, either. I had nightmares thinking about it. I mean, how could I explain this to business associates? It's incredibly embarrassing, to say the least. My wife, a criminal?"

Admittedly, I was still under the influence of sedatives. But try as I might, I could muster little sympathy for his suffering. While he was embarrassed and humiliated, I was tortured, beaten, and raped. While he struggled to get sleep in our warm bed or another's, I slept on a cold wooden plank, sometimes doused in ice water, shivering for hours with nothing but a thin blanket. His narcissistic self-focus confirmed he didn't love me. It was all about his powerlessness, with little concern or sympathy for me. He was totally focused on how my imprisonment affected *him*, with little compassion for the real victim. If I asked for a divorce, he'd never agree unless he was the one in control. I searched his face for any sign of empathy and found nothing but a self-absorbed, hollow shell.

It took all my concentration to relate my story so as to realize my purpose. Drugs or no drugs, this was my one opportunity. I unfolded for Farhad the humiliating details of my time in prison, accentuating how the soldiers groped me, touched me, even the rapes. In a voice both controlled and calm, I spared no detail. Farhad sat wide-eyed, listening intently. He reached over and took my hand, though his touch was cold.

Oh no, had I miscalculated? Was he going to accept and forgive?

"Farhad, I hesitate to tell you the worst. Please, I beg you, try to stay calm."

"What? What could be worse?"

"After one of them raped me, I became pregnant. I miscarried weeks later when they beat me senseless again. I was hemorrhaging, blood everywhere."

It was the coup-de-grace, an unforgivable insult to his manhood. He drummed his fingers on the nightstand, a glazed look in his eyes. Any initial glimmer of concern quickly gave way to disgust, his reaction precisely what I'd anticipated. He began pacing the hospital room, glaring at me when he wasn't glaring at the blank walls. I sensed his anger building, but it was anger toward me, not my attackers.

"Farhad, I know this would be a disgrace to your family if word gets out. I only wish I could spare you the embarrassment and shame," I said, executing the plan I'd repeatedly rehearsed.

"Well, what're we going to do?" he demanded. Perhaps he thought I could turn back the clock and make the events disappear.

Taking advantage of his self-absorption, I weighed my words carefully and continued, "I'm willing to accept a divorce if it's what you want." I lowered my eyes in submission, hoping they wouldn't betray me, determined to appear self-sacrificing. "It may be the only fair course, if it's what you want, that is." My feigned sincerity had to work. It had to.

He stopped pacing and stared straight in my eyes. "Well, it's the only thing to do. It's a matter of family honor. But we must agree, not a word to anyone, ever."

With that, my victory was assured. For me, it was a proud moment, as a perfect plan met with perfect execution.

Farhad remained in Paris several more days, grateful for restored honor. While I felt a twinge of guilt in setting him up, I wondered if it wasn't the kindest thing I could've done for him. He seemed almost buoyant, more pleasant and amicable with everyone. I was relieved my parents didn't lecture me when I told them we were going to divorce. Their culturally driven reaction would have been to save the marriage. But now that it was reality, even my parents seemed accepting. I suspect deep in their hearts they understood my misery.

FORTY-SEVEN

I was free from religious and political repression, free from prison and torture, released from a desperately unhappy marriage. I had a second chance at life and would embrace it. And my country was finally free of the war with Iraq and its atrocities. Staying with my parents in Paris provided welcomed support as my recovery progressed. But after a couple of months in their cramped condo, it was time for a place of my own. I was near family, and besides, I loved Paris. Years earlier, we'd sold the house in Pennsylvania, and the proceeds remained in a bank in Bethlehem. Using that money, I could support myself till I found a job. I would start life anew.

I found a tiny furnished apartment near Place de la Sorbonne. Leaning my walking cane by the door, something I hoped to be done with soon, I removed the *à louer*—the "For Rent" sign—from the window. The living room had a tan fabric loveseat, casually adorned by eggplant-colored pillows with matching tassels dangling at the corners. Inside a small tiled fireplace sat an ornate silver candelabra holding burnt candles, wax drippings encasing the silver stems. The kitchen was barely large enough for me to move about, with a narrow white refrigerator and tiny stove. In the bedroom on the double bed lay a wine-red comforter, gold flowers splashed in a heart-shaped pattern, with matching curtains on the windows overlooking the cobblestone alley behind. The polished wood floor groaned and creaked like an ancient tree as I walked the hallway. But it was mine, and I loved everything about it.

I opened my bag, pulling out a few shirts, pants, a skirt, and a pair of sandals. I slid the pink silk pajamas, a gift from my aunt and uncle, under my pillow, hung the clothes, and carefully lifted the red and green towel to unveil the ruby red tear catcher. Its iridescent damask finish flickered as rays of sunlight streamed through the windows, casting wedged patterns of color on the bare white walls. Carefully, I placed it on the dresser. This was the first time on my own in so long, and it felt liberating yet a little unnerving.

Looking out the living room window, I saw l'Université Paris-Sorbonne only a few steps away. The small café by the corner was surrounded with outdoor bistro tables, bordered by flower boxes of red geraniums, gently swaying with each breeze. Called Le Café Bonheur—Happiness Café—it was aptly named for my new outlook on life, and it became my hangout. Each morning, I sat at the same table, savoring a double café noir and fresh baguette slathered in sweet French butter. I longed for the sour cherry jam my mother used to make, but her aches and pains, real or imagined, kept her from many kitchen tasks she used to enjoy. Besides, she complained she couldn't find good sour cherries in this foreign land.

For my parents, the fruit in Paris wasn't sweet enough, never perfectly ripe. The air seemed dense with moisture, too heavy to breathe after the arid climate of Tehran. They missed the bustling maze of the bazaar's tight, dusty alleys and haggling with bearded shopkeepers for tea sets with Nasser-o-Din Shah's picture, colorful rolls of fabric, and copper serving dishes. They missed the spice vendor on the corner, the pungent scents of cardamom, allspice, and dried wild orange peel filling the air. In Paris, bakeries sold baguettes and croissants. No bakery on each corner, specializing in the half-dozen varieties of bread found in Tehran. No longer were guests milling about at Maman's grand parties, every detail meticulously planned. There was no farm, no fruit trees in the backyard. No longer did the farmer shake the mulberry tree branches in Sohanak onto a white sheet beneath, pelting it with its white juicy fruits. For them as for me, there was so much to miss of Tehran. But now, Paris was home.

Each day at the café, I watched students come and go. Studying familiar faces, basking in newfound freedom, I began to recognize the regulars. There was the young couple, both with spiked hair, so clearly enamored, holding hands as they strolled past. An elderly pair of gentlemen always dressed in the same colored suit and tie passed each morning, pausing by the corner newsstand for a paper before continuing their walk. Brothers, maybe twins.

In the evening, after a day at the marché or musée, I sat at my café, sipped wine, and wrote in a journal. I began searching job ads in newspapers, looking for anything of interest. Several weeks went by with no suitable opportunities. I reconnected with old friends. My college roommate Janet came to visit once news of my whereabouts reached her. After so long away from America, it was healing to see her again. She was a licensed psychologist who'd married a psychiatrist, and they now had a joint private practice in New Jersey.

Janet brought news of Jack. Years ago, she'd run into him on a commuter train in D.C. while she was there on a business trip. Jack told her of his marriage to a woman in the Christian community where he lived. He'd asked about me but had to exit at the next stop, leaving her little time to share news. Janet didn't know where he was now, but her news brought back old memories. To cheer me, Janet brought pictures of our college days, some goofy, others happy, reliving great times we'd shared. We came across a picture of Jack. I paused, a rush of emotion gripping me. I could almost feel the curve of his cheek, the outline of his nose as we kissed, the brush of his lips on my ear as he whispered "I love you" so many times. The memories had faded, but the feelings resurfaced without warning. I blanched.

"Are you okay, Leila?"

"Janet, do you mind if I keep this?"

"Of course not." She carefully pulled the picture out of the album and handed it to me. Jack was leaning on the hood of my old Volvo, holding up his fingers in the peace sign. I recalled the day it was taken at the Jersey Shore. We'd walked along the beach, hands knotted together as the sun's last rays glistened on the deep blue Atlantic waters. Even with the coming of dusk, it was hot and humid. I remembered the beads of perspiration dotting his brow. I looked away for a moment as a rush of feelings took over and blotted my eyes with the tissue Janet offered.

Janet returned to the U.S. after a long weekend in Paris. I forgot to ask if she'd ever delivered my farewell letter to Jack those many years ago. It seemed trivial now, with so much time passed. We enjoyed a wonderful time laughing and reminiscing. I felt invigorated.

One evening, shortly after her departure, as the starry night enveloped Paris, I sat at my café with a snifter of l'eau de vie cognac the waiter had suggested. Even though I was reunited with what remained of my family, I felt a void, an empty place where longing found a home. Somehow, I still struggled to enjoy this beautiful city and my peaceful new life. The cognac warmed me to the core and helped ease the pain. That night, as I lay in bed, moonlight piercing the windows, I quietly turned Jack's picture in my hand. I remembered his touch, the way he used one arm to pull me close, the other gently caressing my face as we kissed. I began drifting to sleep with visions of Jack, the night we first made love, the angry look at our breakup, his sadness at graduation. That night I had a peaceful sleep.

Although I was determined to continue my job search, I was enjoying the leisurely life of an unemployed Parisian. One morning, I picked up the paper and sat down to read at my corner café. A headline caught my eye—Discourse on Fundamentalism. It piqued my curiosity, especially given my recent escape from the clutches of the same. I began to read.

Since the beginning of recorded time, man has sought to explain his existence, the complexities of life, and his place in the myriad of creatures in relation to a Supreme Being. Early man sought God in the wind or trees, the sun or moon. The Greeks, not being satisfied with a single deity to explain the nuances of man and creation, claimed multiple gods. Zeus, the father figure, was accompanied by Aphrodite, goddess of love, and Ares, god of war. When Rome came to power, these gods were Jupiter, Venus, and Mars, renamed but evoking the same qualities. And before Rome flourished, while the Egyptians worshipped Ra, a small band of nomadic people claimed direct connection to the "one" God who gave his name as "I am who I am."

Now, millennia later, the gods of Greece and Rome are mythology. They once served to explain human emotions or actions, the movement of events, and the relations of the stars in heaven to the fates of men. Now, they are legends with little or no meaning beyond an understanding of history.

Today, we deem ourselves far more enlightened, perhaps because major religions at least agree on the concept of one God, though He is named differently and places different demands on followers. This Supreme Being is asked by some to bless America, by others to destroy it. Some pray Muslims will convert to Christianity, while Muslims pray the infidels would follow the will of Allah. To some, Jesus is the son of God, divine and one with the Father and Holy Spirit. To others, He was a prophet who spoke the word of God, just as did Mohammed or Jeremiah centuries before Him.

For some, God dictates roles appropriate for men and women, the proper dress, what to eat, the appropriateness of alcohol or pork. From some, God demands sacrifice and tithing, ten percent of their earnings to support the church. From others, He demands their very lives, not to defend His truth or to proselytize unbelievers but to destroy those unbelievers and all that stands in the way of domination.

In every century, in every civilization, men have committed the most unspeakable crimes in the name of their God. Any student of history can rattle off the litany of inhumane and barbaric actions carried out in the name of religion. The French mathematician and philosopher Blaise Pascal said, "Men never do evil so completely and cheerfully as when they do it from religious conviction." Even today, some hear the voice of God speaking to them directly, demanding they take violent action to correct the sins of their fellow men. They bomb abortion clinics or murder the doctors in the name of Jesus. They set off car bombs or become walking tools of destruction in the name of Allah. They commit genocide, gleefully murdering and raping hundreds of thousands of their fellow men when the tribe across the river bows to a different deity.

I paused, struck by the writer's phrasing. There was something eerily reminiscent that sent shudders up my spine. It recalled conversations I'd had with Jack on just such topics. He'd once even quoted the same words of Pascal.

But is it really about God, religion, or even belief? How can religion continue and flourish if not through money and property, politics and power? Without man interpreting and proclaiming the word of God in all its variations, how would God speak to us today?

Religion exists for a very real reason—we seek explanations for existence, our purpose in life. It provides comfort in times of unbearable loss and gives hope beyond what Shakespeare called this "mortal coil." It lifts our thoughts to generosity and kindness: Do unto others as you would have them do unto you. But it can pervert and manipulate just as easily, morphing into evil so heinous no Supreme Being could tolerate it.

Within another millennium or two, will Christianity be a myth? Will Islam be a distant memory surpassed by some variation on the theme? Of course, those who proclaim Jesus Christ as Lord and Savior, or who prostrate themselves the requisite number of times a day facing Mecca, will denounce such thoughts as sacrilege or heresy. When Christianity was an upstart religion born in the distant Roman province of Israel, a true believer in Jupiter and Mars may have held the same opinion.

I am neither agnostic nor an atheist. I believe and take great comfort in the existence of God, a supreme and beneficent intelligence that transcends my own existence. I believe in the interconnected nature of all life, the spark of the divine in every person that requires I recognize their dignity, regardless of shape, color, or creed. What I don't accept and will vehemently oppose is that any man or men, no matter how profound or holy, has the right to dictate how I define my relationship to this Being or how I should dress, act, pray, make love, or treat my fellow man. I will not grant another person or group control over my choices nor allow them to make up my mind. To tolerate this surrender of self is to accept the "I was just following orders" defense for the Holocaust.

Some religious leaders guide and direct with the most pure and self-sacrificing of intentions, setting incredible examples that affirm the existence of God as His love shines through them. Far too many manipulate and control for ever-increasing power and wealth, demanding strict adherence to their singular interpretation of God's will and purpose. When this occurs, when political structures, threats, intimidation, or actual violence enforce religious conformity, then the myth has gone too far. Karl Marx called religion the opiate of the masses. For some, this may be true, as it lulls them with promised release from burdens and glory to come while their leaders grow rich in grand houses, watching the impoverished starve. For others, religion is the flaming brand raised in defiance and destruction, while again their leaders grow rich in grand houses, watching the impoverished starve.

My call is not to abandon God, or even religion. If you find in religion a comfort and communion with the divine to enrich the soul, then by all means cherish it. But let no religion deprive you of the right to disagree or walk a different path. Let no man dictate where or when you pray, how you should think, which books you should or shouldn't read, what clothes you can wear. Let no man or men control and manipulate you or, worse, an entire society, in the name of religion.

Legend has it that at the crucifixion of Jesus, Mary Magdalene wept, her tears captured in a roman vase to lay in the tomb with His broken body. Today, all the tear catchers in the world could not hold the anguish of God as He mourns our inhumanity and perversion of His truths. To denounce intolerance, hatred, and narrow-minded fundamentalism is not to deny God. Rather, it affirms a loving and benevolent deity who sees the people of every country and culture as His children and weeps over our propensity to kill and destroy in His name.

I was moved by the intense and perceptive analysis. It had to be Jack, I thought to myself as I scanned for the author's byline, my heart skipping a beat: by John Michaels, senior correspondent.

It wasn't Jack Saunders but someone else entirely. I sighed in disappointment. And yet I couldn't deny it—the writing touched me, intellectually and emotionally. There was conviction, words that cut like a dagger. It rang so true to the myriad discussions on religion Jack and I had shared over tea, what seemed a hundred years ago. The author's byline stated he was on special assignment to explore the impact of religious fundamentalism. I'd have to look for his follow-up articles.

It was odd to read words written by another while remembering the man who had walked away from our love for his faith. I couldn't hate Jack for the choice he'd made, no matter how it hurt me. I knew how incredibly difficult leaving was for him, the pressure of trying to reconcile our love with his belief in God. But why were these memories rekindled now? I didn't want to think of the past, only focus on the future.

FORTY-EIGHT

Once or twice a week I had dinner with my parents or my uncle's family, cherishing restored familial ties. I enjoyed several Persian dishes prepared by my cousin and went for the promised boat ride in Bretagne. My father took a part-time job at a small gallery and surreptitiously renewed contacts with former suppliers in Tehran. Discreetly, he started to import beautiful pieces of Persian art to Paris. Even Maman seemed to overcome her melancholy and was enjoying life, having met other Iranian expatriates. There were moments when living by myself felt lonely, haunted by memories of torment, but slowly those began to heal.

I kept the article on fundamentalism and re-read it from time to time, why I'm not sure. Each time, the words stirred something inside, like a leviathan rising from the depths of my soul to break the calm surface of my being. I mulled the words over at night, when dark clouds of prison closed around me. Memories rose uninvited and left me quaking in panic. Sometimes I awoke screaming. A faceless fetus hung by a noose, its lifeless body swaying pendulum-like in the dim light cast by the single bare bulb. I'd lie in a cold sweat, feeling the rough hands of my rapists pinning me against the hard plank. As I lay trembling, safely ensconced in my flat, I'd remind myself these were but dreams. It was then phrases from that article would penetrate the shadows of my fear. It seemed silly, somehow absurd that words could be such a balm. But I couldn't dismiss the soothing assurance they brought.

I believe in the interconnected nature of all life, the spark of the divine in every person that requires I recognize their dignity, regardless of shape, color, or creed. . . . To denounce intolerance, hatred, and narrow-minded fundamentalism is not to deny God. Rather, it affirms a loving

*and benevolent deity who sees the people of every country and culture as
His children. . . .*

Like a shining ray of light piercing the darkness of besieged memories, the words laid waste to my fear and gave comfort. With time, the
nightmares receded, replaced by more pleasant dreams. My nights were
no longer interrupted with cold sweats and anguished awakenings.

Weeks went by as I continued my job search. Admittedly, I was in
no rush, as I savored my liberty. One morning over coffee, I saw an ad
for a job to teach English to children in a small private school. Wasting
no time, I returned to my flat, called the school, and was promptly
invited for an interview.

The next day, I threw a wrap around my shoulders to ward off the
morning chill and headed off to meet the headmaster. Monsieur Forté
sat in a wide, cracked brown leather chair in his office. His salt-and-
pepper hair was cropped so short I could see the contours of his scalp.
His neatly trimmed black beard and mustache stood in stark contrast to
his hair color. Dressed in a fitted gray suit like a uniform, he reminded
me of Georg Von Trapp from *The Sound of Music*, a favorite childhood
movie. On the desk, there was an open pack of Gitanes Bleues and a
glass ashtray filled with a half-dozen butts. Though he flashed a brief
smile when he greeted me with a firm handshake, he remained austere
throughout the interview.

It was a part-time role teaching students aged six through ten. The
pay wasn't much, but the work sounded interesting. After our discussion and having passed Principal Forté's unofficial multilingual test, he
gave me a tour of the school. He walked beside me as we wandered the
dimly lit, narrow hallway with classrooms on either side. The metal
doors, painted battleship gray, had a small square window at eye level.
He stopped before one, peeked inside, and motioned me to do the
same. Boys and girls, dressed in navy blue uniforms and white shirts,
sat quietly in small wooden chairs. Each had a book open. I watched as
their little heads glanced back and forth from book to notebook as they
wrote. We continued down the hallway, the click of his boot against
the hard floor becoming louder and more noticeable with each step.
My left eye began twitching, the kind of anxious twitch you feel but no

one can see. A veiled sense of dread was hiding like a coiled serpent in my mind, waiting to strike. I had no idea why it was there or why I was feeling unnerved.

"What do you think, Madame?" he asked when we returned to his office. Behind him on a shelf was a picture of two soldiers in a metal frame engraved with the words *Liberté, égalité, fraternité*, the motto of the French Republic. The young men stood smiling in front of a green and tan tank. Next to that was a picture of a pretty young woman with wavy blond hair. It seemed older, its edges somewhat faded. The bookshelf held numerous photos of the same boy, from boyhood soccer pictures to one in cap and gown. I was reminded of Amir's graduation picture. "What do you think, Madame?" he asked again, drawing me from my reverie.

"It's a very nice school, Monsieur Forté. You must be very proud. And the job sounds great." Did he notice my eye twitching in the light from the bay window behind him?

To my surprise, he rose from his chair and said the job was mine if I wanted it. It all happened so fast, and though I was tempted to accept on the spot, the new cautious me thanked him and said I'd like to think about it and get back to him the next day.

I was excited but something made me uneasy. While I knew this job held challenges, I was eager to stretch my intellect. In the new Iran, there had been few opportunities for women to hold meaningful jobs. And when opportunities were there, women were guarded, as one word out of context or a slip of the veil could result in termination or far worse. With this job, I could finally get to put my education to good use. I called to discuss this with the one person whose advice and approval I depended on.

"Baba, you'll be so proud—I've been offered a teaching job."

"That's wonderful news, darling! What will you be teaching?" I could hear Baba pacing in excitement.

"I'll be teaching English to French students at a small private school. That is, if I take the job. I told the headmaster I had to sleep on it."

"I'm very proud of you, Leila, and so happy. Go get some sleep now so you can accept."

That was all the approval I needed. With that, the serpent uncoiled

and slithered away through the cracks of my mind. I smiled, basking in
Baba's affection, something I could sense even through the phone. It
was nice to be in a free world again, to enjoy life and family, to take a
job without fear. The streetlights outside my window cast dimly lit
shadows on the wall as the night sounds of Paris filtered through my
bedroom curtains. I loved my old apartment despite its drafty doors
and thin-paned windows. The sounds lulled me to sleep as I pulled the
comforter up over my shoulders.

While there were many nights when I fled from horrid dreams,
these days my dreams were more often pleasant, filled with tenderness. This night's dream began with my youth in Tehran, childhood
memories of popcorn in the park, picking red plums from the neighbor's
tree that hung over our wall, and Rostam following me around the
yard, stopping when I stopped and looking up, hoping for a treat. Amir
swam laps in the pool as Maman Rouhi cheered him on.

Like a curtain of falling mist, the scene dissolved, and I was encased
by rough gray walls, again seated before the Interrogator, my hands tied
behind me, blindfold over my eyes. I heard the whip of his riding crop
as his boots clicked against the hard floor. In the darkness he spouted
the same nagging questions. "Where are they? Tell me or I'll kill your
grandmother." "Tell me where they are, you piece of filth." "Your father
is a traitor." "Tell me or I'll kill you with my bare hands." Beneath the
blindfold, my eye was twitching. The blindfold was lifted, and as the
Interrogator turned to face me, I began screaming. It was Principal
Forté, and I was seated in a small chair in a classroom. He slapped the
whip across my face, and blood trickled down my cheek, mixing with
tears. I screamed till my throat hurt. I was tired, so very tired.

Monsieur Forté clenched an unlit cigarette between his thin lips, a
glint of madness in his eyes. A short, stout soldier in a jester's costume,
his face painted like a demon, ran up and lit the cigarette with a wooden
match. He inhaled deeply, then came closer. "Tell me where they are,
whore!" he commanded. I shut my eyes to avoid his angry glare. I felt
the flesh burning on my neck, its terrible stench filling my nostrils. I
screamed as he inflicted the pain again. This time I nearly passed out.
"Okay, okay. I'll tell. Just stop, please stop. I'll tell."

I awoke in sheer terror, a scream trapped in my throat, drenched in sweat from head to toe. I stared in panic about the dark room. A streak of light from a streetlamp cast shadows on the wall. I shot from bed and paced the wood floor, each creak echoing louder. Stopping before the mirror, I scanned my neck for burn marks. All I could see was my hereditary birthmark. I stumbled to bed and pulled my knees to my chest. Tears came as I picked up the phone with shaking hands and dialed.

"Baba, Baba, where are you?" I couldn't control the panic in my voice. "Is Maman with you?"

"Darling, what is it? Are you alright?" Baba was alarmed. It was 1:00 A.M. "Are you okay, Leila? What's the matter?"

"I told them where you are, Baba. I told them. I broke down and told them. I'm so sorry, Baba . . ." my voice drowned in tears, and I started the hiccups.

"Breathe, *azizam*, it was only a dream. You told no one. We're fine. And we'll be right over."

The next minutes felt like an eternity as my parents drove frantically to my apartment. By now, they'd grown accustomed to my nightmares and early-morning calls. The dreams were so real, there was no escaping their clutches. Maman gave me a sleeping pill, and I fell asleep on the couch, my head in Baba's lap, the way I used to lay when he read me tales from the *Shahnameh*. I awoke sometime mid-morning, my head heavy from the painful thoughts and sleeping pill. My parents again offered reassurance it had all been just a dream.

I'd told the principal I'd give my answer that day. Dreaming of Monsieur Forté as my torturer was symptomatic, heightened anxiety leading to reliving my captivity. And now I'd live with the realization that, at least in dreams, I'd reached the breaking point. I needed to face this demon head-on; it was the only way to defeat it. With my parents' encouragement, I made the call. Monsieur Forté, his voice as monotone as before, said he was pleased and asked if I could start immediately. Feeling reassured and calm, I sent Maman and Baba on their way.

As it turned out, Monsieur Forté did know how to smile, helping to calm my nerves. He was warm and gracious as he introduced me to the other teachers and personally took me to my first class. I spent my first day memorizing faces and names, asking my young students to tell me about themselves. I almost regretted when the closing bell rang and they left in a disheveled dash for home. Knowing I'd have to be prepared for the next day, I returned to my apartment to work on lesson plans. There was a bounce in my step and joy in my heart.

FORTY-NINE

The next day, once school was finished, I strolled back to my apartment. By now my walking cane was a relic gathering dust in the closet. It was a warm sunny day, and I wanted to savor it before the fall chill filled the air. As I took my usual spot at the café, casually writing in my journal, I lifted my head to a voice I hadn't heard in over a decade.

"*Bonjour, Madame,*" he said in a pronounced American accent. I removed my sunglasses to be sure my eyes weren't deceiving me. Despite the cropped silver hair and character lines on his face, there was no mistaking Jack's eyes.

"My God, is it really you?" I felt blood rush from my face.

"Who else could have such a bad French accent?" he said with a laugh.

"What are the odds?"

"The odds are good if you're looking for someone. I came here to find you, Leila."

"To find *me*?"

"I know it sounds crazy, but a few weeks ago I called Janet, and she told me about your ordeal and that you were living now in Paris. She remembered a street name but not your address. She gave me your phone number, but I didn't want to call. I wanted to surprise you. I knew you'd be in the Quartier Latin. We used to talk so much about it, remember?

"I do remember."

"So I decided to come and look for you. I've taken a small flat not too far from here, and when I wasn't working, I wandered the neighborhood, hoping to run into you."

I got up and embraced him. Jack held me closely, bringing back the sense of security and warmth I used to know.

"I can't believe you're here. It's been so long."

"Before you say anything more, I have to tell you how truly sorry I am about Amir. I know it's been years, but I want to offer my condolences. Also, Janet said you wrote me a letter, but I never got it. She found my address and came by the house, but Peggy, who was then my fiancée, took the letter and never gave it to me." Jack sighed. "We've got a lot of catching up to do, Leila."

Indeed we did. The waiter approached. "*Une bouteille de vin rouge, s'il vous plaît. Peut-être une Chateauneuf du Pape,*" Jack said. The waiter nodded and left to get the Rhone wine. It was a bright clear day in Paris, the sunlight glinting off the wavy, aged glass windows on nearby gray stone buildings. It seemed surreal, as though the passing years since we'd parted were inconsequential. It felt so natural to sit across from him, watching as he poured the wine, his eyes never leaving mine. Smiling, Jack handed me a glass, just like I'd imagined so often in my dreams in prison. He began his story.

Three years ago, he ran into Janet on the Washington, D.C., Metro. That's when Jack learned his wife had kept something from him—my letter. Janet told him of Amir's death and my return to Iran.

"Why do you think she didn't give you the letter?"

"I don't know. But when I learned that, I felt deceived, like the years of our marriage had been a lie. That may have been the straw that broke the camel's back to end our relationship. It forced me to question my life, the community, everything I was doing."

Jack went on to tell me of his path after our parting. Once he ended our relationship at the urging of the leaders, he immersed himself in the Christian community. Within a year, he married Peggy, the young woman the community paired him with. While part of him accepted the concept of elders directing these decisions, in the back of his mind, he felt conflict. But believing this was God's will, he suppressed those thoughts. After they married, Jack and Peggy moved into a household with another married couple and several single people. In their community, sharing the same living space was mutual support in growing toward God.

"Wasn't that hard on your marriage?"

"It sure didn't help foster intimacy. We were never alone. We were encouraged to treat all the 'brothers and sisters' in the same way, showing no special attention to our spouse. In theory, living together helped foster understanding, generosity, brotherhood, all within the context of daily prayer and scripture study."

"That's similar to the culture in Iran. Marriages are more or less arranged, with parents matching up their children. Usually newlyweds live with their parents for a while before moving to their own home. Everyone is in everyone's business. Individualism is discouraged."

"Did the revolution change things even more?"

"Completely. Now the government dictates how people dress, what they should or shouldn't say, how they live, practically how to breathe."

"At their core, all monotheistic religions are similar; they just hold a different source for the word of God. We were trying for a closer union with God. Part of that growth required self-denial. Christianity has always had an element of self-denial, but we took it to extremes. At times I fasted on nothing but water for days to do penance or discipline my body."

"That's like Ramadan. For one month, you fast from dawn to dusk to atone for sins. In my family, we were told Ramadan helped us be sympathetic to the poor."

"Same idea. We had other ways of punishing the flesh. For a time before I got married, I slept on a hard wooden plank rather than a bed, disciplining my body against lustful thoughts. Of course, these were perfectly normal thoughts for a young man, but sinful from the community's perspective. I lost too much sleep, so I eventually stopped. These things served as a reminder that the body was to be denied and desires of the flesh were sinful. I never took it as far as the penitents in Europe who walk the streets during holy week, beating themselves with whips till they bleed, but it was close."

"I had no idea that was also a Christian tradition. In Islam, during *Ashura*, men march the streets, beating their shoulders and back with metal rods and whips, mourning Imam Hossein's death. They bleed in obvious pain but keep walking and chanting," I said, recalling observations of the ceremony in Tehran.

"It's ironic that followers of Islam would take up a practice dating back to the early Christian church and the fall of Rome. To some degree, most religions embrace the idea that the flesh hinders the spirit; sex is a necessary evil, and the path to holiness lies in self-denial. It's as though the focus is to reject being human. When this is cloaked in the will of God and you're surrounded by people who embrace it, it's not always easy to see behind the curtain."

"What about work? You must've worked?"

The community found Jack a job as a teacher, and though he enjoyed it, it wasn't his dream. So he began writing in his free time. When his first articles appeared in a local paper, the community urged Jack to give it up and focus on work that drew him closer to God.

"Was your marriage happy?"

"I thought so. Peggy and I tried but couldn't have children. She wanted so much to be a mother. Maybe that disappointment brought to light other things that were wrong with us. I sought fulfillment in work; she threw herself more into the community. We drifted apart. Years later, in the back of my mind, the nagging question of why she didn't tell me about your letter remained. I guess she was trying to protect me, but it seemed cold and heartless. Our distance was only accentuated by the fact that I couldn't give her children."

"That was an issue with my husband too, that I couldn't give him children."

"You're married?"

"I was, for several years. It ended shortly after I escaped Iran. My marriage was not a happy one. But let's talk about that another time. I want to hear what happened to you."

As Jack questioned his marriage, he also questioned his involvement in the community. He struggled with the intolerance and double standards surrounding him. How could a Christian community counsel parents to reject their children if they marry outside the faith, yet emphasize bonds of brotherhood? How could they look the other way at an abortion clinic bombing, yet preach nonviolence?

"It made me look at my life and the way the community dominated everything. We lived in isolation, supposedly to sustain our life with God. But looking back, it was a lot easier to control people that way. Everything was black or white. Finally I couldn't live like that anymore.

I told Peggy I was leaving and asked her to come with me. She refused. She was angry and hurt when I asked for a divorce, telling me in God's eyes we were married until one of us dies."

Jack proceeded with his divorce. In a rare move, the marriage was annulled by the church. He moved into a small apartment and began his freelance writing career. That was over a year ago. "Then I heard you were in Paris and decided to come find you."

"But why?"

"When I chose to leave the community and my marriage, I was deserted by everyone. No logical reasoning could offset the sin of divorce in their mind. My time alone was in many ways a blessing. It was like emerging from a cocoon or stepping into Oz, where instead of a world of black, white, and gray, there were astonishing colors. It forced me to re-examine the decisions I'd made, the people I'd abandoned or hurt in the name of religion. I went back to many of them to ask forgiveness for the pain my intolerance or narrow-mindedness caused them. All along I was moving toward you. I'm hoping you can forgive me."

He paused for a moment and let out a heavy sigh. Looking down, he ran his finger along the rim of the wine glass. "There's so much I want to say. I'm really sorry for the way I hurt you. Sorry for listening to others instead of listening to my heart. I don't deserve a second chance, but I've never stopped loving you, Leila."

I'd never seen Jack as nervous as he looked now. His hands trembled as he picked up his glass and then set it down without taking a sip. For the first time since I'd known him, he wouldn't maintain eye contact, his blue eyes darting from my face to the ground. He reached across the table to take my hand. I accepted his touch as his eyes brimmed with emotion. All the sensitivity and passion I'd found so long ago were still there, his touch a solace to my wounds of neglect. But the walls I'd built around my heart remained steadfast.

Sensing my conflict, Jack added, "I know this is sudden, but until you tell me there's no hope and I should leave, I'll be here waiting for you, every day."

My throat tightened. It took all my strength to fight back the flood of feelings that came rushing to the surface. Quickly, I changed the subject. "What about your job? Don't you have to get back to the U.S.?"

"I'm here working on a series of articles on religious fundamental-ism in Europe—who better than a former fundamentalist? I have to make some side trips, but I'll be in Paris for a while."

Suddenly I made the connection. "Wait," I said reaching into my purse. "I found this in a newspaper weeks ago. Is this you? Are you John Michaels?" I asked, pointing to the byline.

"Yep, that's me. My editor thought it better to use a pseudonym. Did you like the piece?"

"I've read it so many times. I carry this around with me. The words were oddly familiar and comforting, but I didn't understand why. Now I know."

I lifted the wine to my lips and savored the moment. The skies over Paris had never seemed so blue, the air never so crisp. Having left behind so much anguish and sorrow, I never hoped for more than a chance to live my life. Now Jack was sitting beside me. While part of me wanted nothing but to bask in the comfort of his presence, the other part was confused, bewildered, and scarred by the past. The intelligent, almost middle-aged woman wanted to pull back, like a skittish horse chafing at the bit, while the free-spirited college girl longed to toss caution to the wind and once more embrace love.

FIFTY

We left the café and walked down Boulevard St. Michel toward my apartment. I enjoyed his quiet presence, taking serene pleasure in just holding his hand. For years, I'd been deprived this simple gesture of affection, considered anathema in Iran. We chatted nonchalantly about window displays, the elderly couple sipping cognac at a corner table in the cool fall air, the fading blue of the evening sky, all the while letting renewed familiarity engulf us. When we reached my place, I turned the key to unlock the door and invited Jack in. "Would you like to come up for tea?" I asked. Jack perhaps sensed my uncertainty.

"Not today. It's great seeing you, but I don't want to rush things."

"Tomorrow then. Let's meet back at the café at 6:30," I said. He kissed me on the cheek, his scent triggering a thousand images in my mind. I had to lean against the door to steady myself.

"I'm really glad you found me," I said, locking him in my embrace. "Me too."

Inside, I called Janet to deliver a teasing reprimand for her part in helping Jack find me.

"So, how does it feel seeing him after all these years?" She'd always been the touchy-feely one to my inner pragmatist.

"I know I shouldn't let school-girl emotions overwhelm me, but it felt wonderful to see him again. Everything about it was right."

"And what'd he say? Will he be in Paris awhile?"

"Yes, and he said he's never stopped loving me, Janet. But we've both been through so much; I just don't know if I can trust it this time."

"Leila, I know how hard it is for you to hear this, but having followed your head all these years, maybe it's time to follow your heart."

Her words struck the core of my being. All the choices of my life had been thought out, analyzed, and determined by logic. Janet challenged me to give my heart equal voice.

"He came to Paris to find you, Leila. A man doesn't make that kind of decision on a whim."

"I know, but it's only been a few months since my escape. My divorce was final only three weeks ago. I've had so much suffering, so much pain in the last years, I'm not sure I can survive another broken heart."

"So better to never love again and play it safe? Why not just cut your throat and get it over with!"

"But you know what it's like, Janet, to go through the agony of losing your love." Janet's fiancé from our college days had been killed in a motorcycle accident.

"Yeah, I know what it's like. But do you think for an instant I regretted falling in love after I lost David? In all the tearful, sleepless nights you and I shared, did I ever say I was sorry I loved him?" She paused but didn't wait for my reply. "Angry? Yes, I wanted to kill the damn drunk who caused the accident. Hurt? Yes, till I thought my soul was being ripped from my body. But I never regretted loving him. You don't get many chances at love, Leila. Don't let fear keep you from this one. For once, listen to your heart."

Despite the day's events, I slept a long dreamless sleep, uninterrupted by the night sounds of Paris. I awoke the next morning, excited about the day and what it might bring. After years in a loveless, abusive marriage and months in prison, to have Jack reappear in my life felt like a comfortable old coat in the dead of winter.

I was wrapping up my first week of teaching and looked around the small room at my students, all sitting quietly at their desks. These were well-disciplined young scholars, hungry to learn. The walls were bare, though a bright and cheery yellow. I resolved to add some art to the walls and books to the shelves for my pupils. But I felt at home in this room with the desks and blackboard, the smell of chalk and the solitary apple perched on my desk from an anonymous donor. After school I headed back to my apartment to work on the next day's lessons, my routine now becoming second nature.

At 6:00 P.M., I shoved books and binders back in my bag and washed my face to get ready to meet Jack. After a busy day filled with a glowing sense of purpose, I was more than ready to share my joys. I left the apartment and savored the smell of a wood fire from a nearby chimney. Like incense, the fragrance bore memories of my childhood in the mountains of Tehran, winter days gone by and all life had brought in those passing years. The streets were gay with lovers and children passing by, scarves splashing colors 'round ladies' necks, and the sound of hurried heels clicking against ancient cobblestone. I sat at my corner table and watched the parade as people hustled home from work, baguettes in hand or off to dinner.

As the crowds passed by, I reminisced about my first days in Paris. It had all seemed so novel and unrestrained, ardent and licentious by comparison to Tehran. I loved my country, its splendor awe-inspiring. The imposing Alborz Mountains climbing along the Caspian, the barren desolation of the road to Esfahan, even the hills of Tehran when on rare days the smog lifts, all were places of incredible beauty. It pained me to recall the wonderful childhood days at my grandmother's house, shared moments with family and friends, destroyed at a whim. Religion may be a boon to men's souls, but it had proven the antithesis to me. So many lives crushed as men used religion to force their will upon a nation.

I turned up the collar of my jacket to ward off the early-evening chill and pulled my wrap closer around my shoulders. Thierry, my usual waiter, waved and came to take my order, returning promptly with a bottle of wine and glasses.

"*Et le bon monsieur? Il arrive tout de suite?*"

"*Oui,*" I replied, he'll be here any moment.

He uncorked the bottle with flourish and offered me a taste, knowing I'd approve, and poured both glasses. I waited in the quiet calm of my own space while Paris bustled around me. Had I ever before been so surrounded by activity yet felt so at ease? Only my anticipation of Jack's arrival tugged at my awareness, a tender, gentle longing that in no way intruded on my comfortable sense of happiness.

The wine was delicious with flavors of licorice and berries and hints of oak from its long encasement. It warmed my mouth like the promise of a kiss. I pulled my wool wrap tighter against the slight breeze in the night air, carrying wafts of a Gauloise cigarette from the old man two tables down. Tonight, I took surrogate pleasure in the strong tobacco aroma. It made me wonder why I'd always found it so offensive with Farhad.

As I sat basking in the aura of Paris, Jack rounded the corner toward the café. In the moments before he saw me, I noticed his face was drawn. When he caught sight of me, the look of stress dissolved, replaced by a smile. He bent down to kiss my cheek as he approached the table. But something wasn't right.

"What's wrong?"

"It was a late night and a bit trying."

"Can you be a little more specific?" I quipped.

"Sure, but it would go better with wine," he said, lifting the glass to his lips. His smile was there, but so was the underlying concern in his eyes as he reached for my hand across the small table. In those few silent moments, fear rose up in my throat. He was going to tell me this was a mistake, that he was leaving me again.

"Are you going to keep me in suspense?" I asked. "Is it about me, about us?"

Suddenly he understood my panic. I watched him across the table as his blue eyes filled with tears and the strain washed from his face.

"God, no, Leila. I'm letting my work intrude. It's not about us. I'm so happy to have found you and to be right here, right now."

With that, he stood and walked around the table to embrace me. I floated into his arms and felt warmth and safety sweep over me. It was all I could do not to let my pent-up emotions erupt in a flood of tears. He pulled back a little and looked deep in my eyes. Leaning forward, his lips brushed mine in a gentle kiss. Thierry returned and nonchalantly refilled our glasses. His eyes sparkled as he poured, taking vicarious pleasure in our lovers' kiss.

Once we sat, Jack's glance conveyed a mountain of emotions. He held my hands and brought them tenderly to his lips. Reaching out, he gently caressed my cheek, brushing back my hair.

"Can I make you dinner tonight?" he asked.

"Oh, yes, I'm starving. Let's go to my apartment. We can whip something up."

Jack left some francs for *l'addition,* corked the remaining wine, and we walked the short distance to my apartment. All thoughts of religious zealots gave way to the pleasure of feeling him next to me. At the apartment, I gave Jack the quick tour.

"Is that a tear catcher?" he asked, seeing the ruby-colored treasure on my dresser.

"Yes, it's the only thing I was able to bring out of Tehran. It holds a lot of memories."

"It's beautiful and seems like it belongs here with you." He walked to the fresh-cut roses in a crystal vase on my nightstand and inhaled their fragrance. Their aromatic scent grew with sunset as though they took one last moment to give something back to the earth.

"When you've spent so many years in a black-and-white world, it's nice to feed the soul with color and beauty," he remarked, adding, "You know, I had a tear catcher once."

"Really?"

"I left it behind when I left the community. In early Christianity, a tear catcher symbolized hope after sorrow, resurrection after death. While I was hopeful about what life might bring, Peggy really wanted to keep it."

"Jack Saunders, we really do have a lot in common," I said, and gave him a kiss on the cheek.

In the kitchen, I stood aside as he moved with ease about the small space, choosing a small skillet, chopping ingredients. Dinner was simple, an omelet with shallots and shaved truffles, Comté cheese, chopped jambon, and remains of a breakfast baguette.

As we ate in the tiny dining room, conversation was minimal, bites and sips of wine interspersed with touches and glances. Evening comes early to Paris in the fall, rush-hour traffic sounds giving way to the echoes of diners seeking out restaurants, young people exiting cafés in a raucous exultation of life. Though the night air can be brisk and sometimes breezy, Paris embraces all with an affection that even looming winter's chill cannot erase.

After dinner, we sat on the couch in the cool evening with the windows slightly ajar, savoring the sounds of the city and sipping Armagnac, the rich warmth of the golden liquid reaching down to my soul. There was no talk of work or religion or even the past. There was just the two of us, lost in moments of intimacy once relinquished, now regained.

The restoration of my soul and spirit would not occur in a miraculous flash, and entrusting my heart to Jack's loving embrace would take time. But with this simple shared meal and quiet time in his presence, the healing had begun. I didn't know what tomorrow would bring or what further terrors might rise to confront us. For the moment, all that was banished. We were together, and for whatever time, I'd put aside other worries. A new chapter was beginning, and I looked forward to the future, knowing full well life holds no certainties. Yet if nothing else, I'd learned that in spite of all the hatred and intolerance, all the violence and fear in the world, there is also love.